Crisis of the House Never United

Crisis of the House Never United

A NOVEL OF EARLY AMERICA

Chuck DeVore

ISBN: 979-8355017712

Dedication

To my wife, Diane, who has tarried in faith to care for her parents.

Table of Contents

PREFACE

There is increasing talk of a so-called "national divorce" as Americans grow weary of each other. On one side, the proclivity to use increasingly vast federal powers—whether through Congress acting as the people's elected representatives, or through unelected bureaucrats wielding regulatory powers—has made large segments of society wishing to be left alone. On the other side, the demand to conform, to trade some freedom for security or collective equality (real or perceived) has caused some to wonder if they'd be better off without the benighted populations of flyover country.

These complaints that threaten to escalate into unrest are a symptom of a deeper problem, namely, that our constitutional order appears to be breaking down. Rather than a federal system with strong checks and balances, both at the national level and checked by the states, power has been increasingly centralized in Washington, D.C. with much of that power held by the administrative state—a sprawling professional bureaucracy.

But divorces are often ugly. America tried one divorce. It formally started in 1860 with the election of Abraham Lincoln as president. But the irreconcilable differences were decades in the making, papered over when the practical reality of the founding failed to meet the founding's ideals—namely, what to do about slavery. Slavery was but one of many issues that almost scuttled the new Constitution in 1787 with fears of a powerful central government overriding individual rights and state powers being a larger concern. Even so, had abolitionists demanded a ban on slavery at the onset, the Constitution never would have reached the required nine states for ratification.

Often forgotten in today's world, with its fictional claim that America's founding was predicated on slavery as embodied by the New York Times' 1619 Project, is that the Founders mostly believed slavery would disappear on its own accord. That the Founders, both North and South, largely saw slavery as a national sin is a fact. That they were at a loss to end it immediately was bound by circumstance. Even so, in Article I, Section 9 of the Constitution written in 1787, provision was made to provide for the outlawing of the importation of new slaves by 1808. Some 20 years later, Britain outlawed the slave trade in 1807. Further, modern arguments have completely turned on its head the rationale for slaves being counted as three-fifths of a person. The three-fifths formula had nothing to do with an assessment of a slave's humanity; rather, it was to determine the number of seats in the U.S. House of Representatives that each state was to be apportioned. Slaveholding states wanted each slave to count as a full person—that way, they'd have more clout in the House. Non-slaveholding states wanted slaves to count not at all. Three-fifths was a compromise.

In any case, by 1860, due to the Dred Scott ruling in 1857, northern laws abolishing slavery were nullified by the southern right to keep another person as property. As Lincoln said in 1858:

> *"'A house divided against itself cannot stand.' I believe this government cannot endure, permanently, half slave and half free. I do not expect the Union to be dissolved; I do not expect the house to fall; but I do expect it will cease to be divided. It will become all one thing, or all the other. Either the opponents of slavery will arrest the further spread of it and place it where the public mind shall rest in the belief that it is in the course of ultimate extinction, or its advocates will push it forward till it shall become alike lawful in all the states, old as well as new, North as well as South."*

Seemingly irreconcilable political differences spiraled into a move to split the nation soon after Lincoln's election. Even before Lincoln was sworn in on March 4, 1861, seven southern states declared their secession from the Union. In the wake of the Civil War, only four years later, as many as 1 million Americas were killed by battle or disease, with another 420,000 wounded.

The enormity of the Civil War so dominates the past that most Americans don't know that the America we know today almost didn't make it.

While much has been written about the challenges faced by the colonists and the struggles of the War for Independence, little has been said about that dim time in the American experience between 1783 and 1789—after victory over the British and before the ratification of the Constitution. Yet, this was the time of maximum danger, of intrigue, and of heated passions when men were not yet sure as to whether ballots or bullets would decide the fates of governments. The infant America was governed under the Articles of Confederation, a weak system of national government in which the states reigned supreme.

In the six years that elapsed from the end of the Revolutionary War to the ratification of the Constitution, America and world were torn asunder by rebellion.

In 1786, farmers in western Massachusetts, led by a citizen-soldier captain, revolted. Desperate over their inability to pay taxes and angry about a system that favored wealthy Boston merchants, they burned courthouses to destroy tax and loan records, then marched on Boston. In nearby Poughkeepsie, New York, sympathy riots broke out. Captain Shays almost toppled the Commonwealth's government before his followers were defeated by the state militia funded by the Boston Brahmins they opposed. Shays' Rebellion so shocked the political leaders that it proved to be a major consideration in the minds of those who drafted and ratified the Constitution.

Rhode Island was also a hotbed of dissent. In May 1786, a worker's coup saw the complete takeover of the legislature, the ousting of judges, and the printing of paper money to pay debts. It was a foreshadowing of the French Revolution—sans Guillotine.

Also in 1786, frontiersmen in the Wyoming area of Pennsylvania were seething over payments demanded by Philadelphia for land most had already purchased from the Connecticut state government (claims to most western lands were in dispute among states at this time, land sales being a prime source of income due to a lack of ability to levy taxes). The farmers recruited Ethan Allen, the hero of Ft. Ticonderoga, to lead a fight to form a new state if Pennsylvania did not see things their way. As Allen said, "When the rich subvert government and law and attempt 'to dispossess and ruin a large settlement of industrious yeomanry' then the people are in a 'state of nature' and have the right to resist under the greatest of all laws, to wit, that of self-preservation."

North Carolina also saw unrest in 1786, successors to the Regulators of the late 1760s who resisted the taxes and fees imposed by the Crown's officials.

After Shays' Rebellion was put down, many of its leaders fled to Vermont, itself an area under revolt from the state of New York. To bring the rebels to justice, Alexander Hamilton convinced the New York state assembly to recognize Vermont's statehood in exchange for Vermont surrendering the leaders of the revolt. In July 1787, Ethan Allen, now back in Vermont, signaled his intentions to not harbor the Shays' rebels. They were expelled to face justice in Massachusetts. Vermont was admitted as the 14th state of the Union in 1791.

In the Massachusetts gubernatorial campaign of 1787, John Hancock ran and won on a platform of amnesty for Shays' rebellion leaders—so long as they henceforth resorted to ballots, not bullets.

In the face of this increasing post-Revolutionary turmoil, 55 of America's wealthiest and most powerful men gathered in Philadelphia for a highly secret meeting in May 1787 to plot the overthrow of the First Republic. Over the next five months, these delegates would argue and compromise until, on September 17, they would agree to present a constitution for ratification by state conventions.

From October 1787 to March 1788, Alexander Hamilton, James Madison, and John Jay, writing under the name "Publius" in New York City, produced the *Federalist Papers* to urge approval of the Constitution. The Federalists argued that the Articles of Confederation were too fragile and that nothing short of the Constitution would allow the people to preserve the liberty and independence they won in the Revolution.

New York Gov. George Clinton, and other "Antifederalists," responded. Great patriots, such as Virginia's Patrick Henry (Give Me Liberty or Give Me Death), denounced the proposed form of government as tending to tyranny, saying, "the preservation of our liberty depends on the single chance of men being virtuous enough to make laws to punish themselves." These men, including James Monroe, George Mason, Richard Henry Lee, John Hancock, Samuel Adams, and Elbridge Gerry, represented the American people's distrust of a robust central government. Their strongest argument against the Constitution was that it lacked a bill of rights.

The success of the Constitution was by no means assured. It almost failed in Philadelphia, and it almost failed when it was sent out for approval. The Constitution needed to be ratified by nine of the 13 states to go into effect. The first five ratifications were quickly accomplished: Delaware, December 7, 1787 (unanimous); Pennsylvania, December 12, 1787 (on a vote of 46 to 23); New Jersey, December 18, 1787 (unanimous); Georgia, January 2, 1788 (unanimous); and Connecticut, burdened by import fees collected by both New York and Massachusetts on its commerce, ratified on January 9, 1788 (on a vote of 128 to 40).

On February 6, 1788, the Commonwealth of Massachusetts' Constitutional convention ratified the new form of government on the narrow vote of 187 to 168, and only after two prominent Antifederalists, Governor John Hancock and Samuel Adams, negotiated a demand that the Constitution incorporate a bill of rights, should it pass. The no votes mostly came from the western part of the state where Shays' rebellion saw widespread support.

Then, on February 13, New Hampshire's ratifying convention met in Exeter, with the winter timing and location planned by Federalists to discourage attendance by Antifederalist farmers to the north and west. The maneuver wasn't enough, and, sensing defeat, Federalist delegates moved on February 22 to postpone the ratification vote until June, the motion passing 56 to 51 with almost half the delegates wanting to kill ratification outright.

When George Washington heard the news about New Hampshire, he was distressed.

A month later, Rhode Island's grassroots democracy submitted the Constitution to town meetings boycotted by most Federalists (who may have feared for their safety) and on March 24, 1788, the voters rejected it, 2,708 to 237, making two losses in a row.

After the Massachusetts convention recommended amendments to the Constitution, all subsequent state conventions, except Maryland's, agreed that a Bill of Rights was needed. Maryland ratified on April 28, 1788 (on a vote of 63 to 11); South Carolina, May 23, 1788 (on a vote of 149 to 73); New Hampshire, June 21, 1788 (on a vote of 57 to 47); Virginia, June 25, 1788 (on a vote of 89 to 79); and New York, July 26, 1788 (on a vote of 30 to 27). North Carolina's convention adjourned without voting on the Constitution on August 2, 1788, by a vote of 185 to 84). Four of the five most-populous states, New York, Virginia, Pennsylvania, and Massachusetts (North Carolina was the third most-populous state in the 1790 census) had now approved the Constitution, and, with the seven others, exceeded the nine needed for ratification.

In October 1788, after setting up the timetable for the new government to take over, the Congress of the Confederation achieved a quorum for the last time. On March 4, 1789, the Second Republic was born, and the *coup d'état* was complete.

June 17, 1789, marked the start of the French Revolution, as if History was confirming that one revolution was complete, and another one of a totally different nature, was being launched.

It all could have happened very differently.

The Constitutional convention in Philadelphia almost broke apart over the vexing issue of slavery that would tear at the nation a little more than threescore and ten years later. The delegates also wrangled with how to apportion representation in the new Congress. Under James Madison's Virginia Plan, both houses of Congress would have proportional representation. The small states would have none of it and rallied behind the New Jersey Plan, which would have preserved each state's equal vote in a one-house Congress. It took another month of discussions before the Great Compromise resulted in today's present system of House and Senate, with the House representing the people and the Senate representing the states.

Once the delegates approved the Constitution and sent it out for ratification, it passed from one danger to another. Rejected outright by two states, the Constitution was narrowly passed by another four: Massachusetts (a 19-vote margin out of 355), Virginia (a 10-vote majority out of 168), New Hampshire (another 10-vote majority out of 104), and New York (only three votes out of 57!).

This novel examines this overlooked period in American history and asks the question: What would have happened if the Constitution had not been ratified? John Jay, writing as *Publius* in Federalist Number 5, warned that America might split into North and South and that each would seek European alliances to protect itself from the other. Alexander Hamilton, in Federalist Numbers 6 and 7, argued that neighboring commercial states are natural enemies and that only a strong central government can safely bind them, while in Number 13, he hypothesized that America might break into three nations without an approved constitution to supersede the weak Articles of Confederation.

By 1789, many of the Revolution's prominent boosters were looking to France for inspiration to lift Man to the next level. Others recoiled at post-Revolutionary unrest and excess, and plotted a dictatorship based on a monarchical form. Meanwhile, Old World agents were all too happy to sow discord and rebellion to enfeeble the world's newest power.

Lastly, three notes for the reader. First, the author makes no consistent attempt at employing the language of the day, except in direct historical quotes and documents. Second, deviations from actual historical outcomes are summarized in a separate timeline at the end of the book, allowing the interested reader to see what really happened and judge for themselves how closely America avoided disaster. And third, the author made every attempt to use realistic metrological conditions, times for sunrise and sunset, and overland and sea travel times appropriate to the era and seasons.

This book wouldn't have happened without two catalysts.

Foremost, the scholars at the Claremont Institute's Lincoln Fellowship program. In 2004, on the verge of taking office in the California State Assembly, I was privileged to be one of a dozen selected to study the origins of the Constitution, its implementation, and its champions and opponents. The great Professor Harry V. Jaffa was there, then a spry 85. It was there I learned how hard fought the ratification effort was and it was there I first conceived of this project.

I did a significant amount of research in preparation to write the book in 2004, even outlining some chapters, but the demands of elected office intruded, and the project fell by the wayside.

It was only in 2019, during long journeys across Texas to see supporters of my employer, the Texas Public Policy Foundation, that the determination to complete the effort exceeded the inertia to just let it remain an idea. During these trips of three to six hours, I'd often converse with the Foundation's vice president of events, Clint Nesmith. Clint, whose ability to organize events was only exceeded by his skill at golf and his rendition of the National Anthem, was fascinated with the idea, prompting me a few times to talk about concept for the novel in a van full of think tank staff. About the third time this happened, I realized that there might very well be broader interest in this project than I surmised.

And lastly, a hearty thanks to my editor Roy Maynard. A veteran newspaperman with ink-stained fingers (or are those cigar stains?), Roy edits all my opinion pieces—a weekly chore that he happily takes on at all times of the day, night, or weekends as the mission requires.

Chuck DeVore
Dripping Springs, Texas

1

Chapter One – People's Justice

Early afternoon, July 12, 1804, Gansevoort Street, Manhattan, New York City

Tears stung Jeph's face for much of the sleepless night and into the morning. He struggled with telling Molly the full truth—confiding in her his fears—for him, for her, their six children. But Molly was still recovering from giving birth to their youngest child, dear, sweet Theodosia—named in honor of his former boss's only living child who was, in turn, named after her mother, his boss's late wife. So, much needed to remain unsaid. This, naturally, upset Molly greatly, but her remaining reserves of strength were soon focused entirely on their baby daughter and rest.

Head down, he made his way to Gansevoort Street and the Court of Justice. The street had been blocked off as had the street running along the east bank of the Hudson. Between the river and its docks and the street were three execution devices—new gifts from Emperor Napoleon on his assuming the title in France only two months before—guillotines they were called.

He found Gansevoort packed. So was the public viewing stand erected on the street about 30 yards from the execution machines. But the business and building owners along the street were selling perches on their roofs, second and third-floor windows, or balconies, if they had them, for a penny.

At only 5'4," Jeph had no choice but to pay if he was to see for himself what was scheduled to be happening today. He reluctantly took a penny from his coin purse and paid for a third-floor window view overlooking the southern corner of Gansevoort and 10th.

The three guillotines were mounted on a stage about 10 feet tall. The very top of each machine across 10th was just below Jeph's eye. The machines' slanting steel blades were thick and fierce—impersonal, in a way—something one might expect in a butcher shop rather than a gibbet.

Beyond the docks, the Hudson was packed with vessels: barges, brigs, rowboats. It looked as if you could walk to New Jersey and not get wet.

North, or upriver from the execution stage, stood another new import from Europe standing as tall as the guillotines, a semaphore tower, its black folding arms, four to a side, perpendicular to the river and looking like the legs of an immense lobster.

Directly below his window, Jeph saw what he guessed was the officials' viewing stand. It was empty. The one directly opposite was larger and already filled with a mix of soldiers, militia, and assorted other politicians and judges. About 100 people in all.

Jeph took in a trembling breath as the official party appeared and marched to its place. The three high judges from the Court of Justice, two of them uniformed generals, two additional generals, George Clinton, the governor of New York and his nephew, DeWitt Clinton, the mayor of New York. And, walking between the two Clintons was the Frenchman, Edmond-Charles Genêt. Genêt was France's envoy from 1793 to 1794. But, when the French revolution took a radical turn, he was recalled. Facing certain death back home, he asked for asylum, and ended up marrying Gov. Clinton's daughter, Cornelia. And finally, coming full circle with Napoleon's rise, Genêt was recalled to diplomatic duty and asked to represent France's interests in New York.

As the eight-member official party stood, the President's bodyguard marched off a dock behind the execution stage, their deep blue uniforms accented by blood red cuffs topped by large, shiny black leather shakos with visors. The military caps added at least a foot to the apparent height of the guard—all of whom were already at least six foot tall—giving them the appearance of giants.

Jeph could still see well at a distance—though all his clerical work for the past 22 years rendered his eyes needing of spectacles for reading and writing—and he noticed that the first dozen soldiers in the Presidential Guard were carrying standard Army muskets topped with 15-inch bayonets, sunlight glinting off their unsheathed blades. But the following dozen Guardsmen, carried something altogether different, something without a bayonet. He'd seen such a weapon only once—when his former boss, now the President, showed him one. They were Girardoni air rifles! He surmised these were gifts from the new French emperor as well.

As the guard approached the stands, Jeph's nausea was temporarily forgotten as he spied glimpses of the President behind the three ranks of imposing soldiers.

It was Burr. He was wearing a simple jacket with tails that almost extended to his black boots which almost reached his knees. His black breeches were tucked into the boots. And he wore no hat and no white powdered wig—just his natural graying and receding hair. Burr's dress was a public statement of the new against the old—the people against the powerful.

Burr sat in the middle of the lowest bench. The luminaries' stand was more empty than full.

Then, without music or fanfare, the condemned were marched out from a naval brig, down the docks and up to the base of the execution stage. The three judges of the People's Court rose from behind President Burr and made their way to the execution stage. Other than their deep blue capes, they too were plainly dressed in black. No one wore wigs.

The chief judge nodded to the condemned prisoners' guards and they solemnly led the Enemies of the People and the State up the stairs.

Jeph could clearly see the first three condemned: Alexander Hamilton, a frail-looking Philip Schuyler, 70, a Revolutionary War general, and Hamilton's father-in-law, former candidate for New York governor John Jay. Their hands were bound behind their backs. Hamilton looked defiant. Jay was downcast, eyes firmly fixed on his feet.

The condemned were forced, face down, on the last bench they'd know in this world. The execution crew then bound them to the bench with thick black leather straps with large brass buckles. Each man was also gagged, though before Hamilton could be rendered silent, he pulled his head to face the crowd and yelled out in a clear voice, "May God have mercy on your souls!" The first few rows of spectators heard, some hissing, many looking down.

Now bound, each of them faced a large brass basin, its mouth large enough to catch the severed head and the large amounts of blood that would no doubt effuse from the lifeless body.

The three men, having been prepared, awaited their fates.

The gathered crowd was mostly quiet. The air was almost like church, which Jeph thought odd. There was none of the carnival atmosphere that attended a public hanging of a thief or murderer.

Behind the condemned, he could see another group of three being lined up. He recognized one as Stephen van Rensselaer, formerly the general in command of New York's militia cavalry division. Rensselaer was also John Jay's candidate for lieutenant governor and the owner of a large estate up the Hudson River—a 1,200 square mile estate known as Rensselaerswyck that was now forfeit, with the land devolving to the more than 50,000 tenants who worked the soil who would now pay rent to the state, not Rensselaer.

The chief justice of the Court of Justice, flanked by his junior colleagues, unrolled a parchment and cleared his throat, saying in a high, raspy voice, "The Court of Justice, acting on behalf of the people, having found the accused, Citizen Hamilton, Citizen Schuyler, and Citizen Jay, guilty of treason, sedition, and other high crimes against the state, do hereby pronounce that the sentence, death, is to be carried out without hesitation or mercy. May it ever be so with all enemies of the People and of the State!"

The chief justice, standing to the left of the leftmost guillotine—the one that held Hamilton—rolled up the parchment, looking straight ahead.

All three executioners tugged at the ropes releasing the blades. The chief justice involuntarily jumped at the sound as the blades swiftly descended and met their marks.

In seconds, it was over.

The crowd erupted in boos. The whole process was too quick, too surgical. There was no entertainment value at all. No kicking of legs as a man slowly strangled to death at the end of a hangman's noose.

Hamilton's executioner, a veteran of traditional executions, reached down into the large brass bowl and pulled out Hamilton's head by the hair, hoisting it aloft for the crowd, blood streaming onto his black trousers.

Governor Clinton looked away and covered his mouth with a handkerchief.

Jeph couldn't see Burr's face, as he was looking towards the guillotines.

The boos turned to cheers, and then a roar as Jay's executioner did the same at the far right of the stand. Then, hesitantly, so did Schuyler's executioner. The sound was deafening.

Not to be out done, a brig anchored in the river fired a ceremonial cannon shot.

In a moment, a terrible resolved displaced Jephthah Clark's dread. To do what, he didn't yet know. But he had to act. He looked down at his left hand and its missing middle and ring fingers—removed by a British Brown Bess musket ball during the Battle of Monmouth 26 years earlier when he was a lad of 16.

Chapter Two – A New Army

June 28, 1778, Monmouth, New Jersey

Sweat rolled down the commander's face. The thick heat, the sun, and the mosquitoes rendered his cheeks puffy and raw. Even so, he had a handsome face with alert brown eyes, a thin nose, and a solid chin. With a boyish frame of only 5'6," the lieutenant colonel appeared no older than 16, although he was a half-dozen years older than that and already a battle-hardened veteran. Today, he was leading just over 120 men into a fight against the British army.

The officer rode at the front. Lieutenant Colonel Dummer close behind leading his detachment of Pennsylvanians, 30 strong, and his own regiment of 90 at their heels, marching southeast down the road from Englishtown to Monmouth Court House where, hours earlier, General Charles Lee engaged General Clinton's rear guard and was forced to retreat in the face of a sharp British counterattack. The sporadic thud of musket fire to his front was punctuated by outbound cannon fire from Perrine's Hill to his left.

The road followed the terrain to the right and into a wooded area, but he marched his column to the left in open fields of corn behind the forming lines of infantry and cannon about 300 yards ahead on a gentle hill. He saw a well-kept farmhouse about 100 yards to the left and hoped its occupants would be unharmed by the fight—assuming they weren't Loyalists.

General "Mad Anthony" Wayne was somewhere ahead fighting the British.

He was bitterly disappointed that his command wasn't among the handpicked force to engage the enemy's rear guard. Or, now that the English turned to fight, that he was still out of action.

His men, drilled through the bitter winter of 1777-78 at Valley Forge by the foul-mouthed Prussian von Steuben, marched lightly in two rows on either side of the road, their muskets on their left shoulders, their blanket slings over their right—these containing a meager luggage: two shirts, a pair of shoes and extra soles, a pair of stockings and socks, a shoe brush, pipeclay (to whiten leather), and sixty rounds of ammunition. Each soldier also carried a canteen, already half-empty, and a pouch full of cartridges. Other than some paper, quills, and ink, the commander carried no more personal effects than his men. He was disciplined, to the point of harsh, and they grudgingly loved him for it because he was also fair and seemed to genuinely care for them. Oddly, though, he strongly disfavored corporal punishment.

Now 200 yards from the crest of the hill, sloping up about 20 to 30 feet, he saw four horse teams pulling cannon through the fields to the left and then disappearing below the crest of the hill.

He closed on the top of the hill and the gun crews came back into view along with more than 1,000 infantry stretching out to his left and, partially obscured by woods to his right. He recognized a fellow officer from Pennsylvania's 4th Continental Artillery Regiment.

Colonel Spencer, the 3rd Pennsylvania Brigade commander, greeted the officer with a shout, his face drenched with sweat and his horse working up a good lather. "Burr! Take your men down the hill. I want you to cover the bridge over the creek—Middle Brook, I think it's called. Lee's forces are beyond the bridge, and they've been in action for five hours. Make sure they get back across."

"Yes, sir!" Lieutenant Colonel Aaron Burr grinned broadly, sweat stinging his eyes and dripping off his nose.

Burr surveyed the scene below. About three-quarters of a mile away with a drop of some 50 feet, Burr could barely make out the form of a causeway across a creek. A low-lying ridge overlooked the creek, rising about 40 feet in a quarter mile. There, on the ridge, were signs of battle—musket smoke and the grayed-out blue of Continental Army uniforms barely visible through the haze.

Burr twisted in his saddle and called out, "Halt!" The command was repeated by his regimental sergeant major. Several of the men quickly grabbed their canteens.

"Also, keep an eye on the wood to your right flank. I don't want the British to flank our artillery without a fight," Spencer instructed Burr.

"Understood, sir."

The 20 Pennsylvanian gunners had already set up their pieces just below the crest of the hill along a spine that stretched out to the British like an earthy finger. A few camp followers, most likely the gunners' wives, gathered 50 yards to the left of them. A buxom woman strode towards the guns with four sloshing buckets, likely porting them up from the well belonging to that farmhouse about a half-mile back. Ruddy and plain-faced, about 25, she wore a red and white striped petticoat. She approached the gun nearest Burr and glanced directly into his face without a trace of the deference his men gave and then turned back to the artillerymen and called out, "Mr. Hays, Adam's Ale for the boys!"

She passed in front of his mount and jerked her thumb over her shoulder at the youthful commander. "Mind you don't sweat away your manhood like this poor skip jack shaver."

Hearty guffaws erupted from the direction of the guns while a soldier, probably Mr. Hays, widened his eyes, then looked at the ground and spoke through clenched teeth, "Come along, Mary!"

Burr called out, "Madam, were my father here, he'd whip you properly for your intemperate tongue!" Most within earshot laughed. The woman looked back with a grin, nodded, and then attended to her now relieved husband and his shirtless laughing comrades.

Cannon balls screamed through the hot summer air. They thudded into the top of the hill, 40 yards behind him, ripping out twin channels of grass and corn just behind a field gun. He couldn't tell if the gun's crew noticed the close call as they calmly prepared to return fire.

Seconds later, as Mary briskly stepped out to take water to the second crew in the line, a third iron shot carried away the bottom half of her petticoat, but otherwise leaving her, and the crew, unharmed. She looked down at her now bare, brilliantly white legs, and quipped, "Any higher and it'd have carried away me ware!"

Several of the gun crew stared disbelieving at her for a moment before attending to their cannon.

Burr watched the Pennsylvanians work their guns. First the sponger cleaned out the barrel of the hot gun tube, quenching any sparks with a water-soaked lambskin on the end of a pole. The large man labored in the heat, twisting the sponge pole three times counterclockwise then twisting the pole in the opposite direction three times. He had stripped off his jacket and his shirt was soaked with sweat.

A second crew member rammed his corkscrew-tipped wormer pole down the tube to clear any remaining debris.

The powder monkey then set to his task, inserting a cartridge of black powder, then a six-pound iron ball and packing it tightly against the bottom of the barrel with the ram.

The gunner called out, "In Battery!" and the crew wrestled the field gun back to position from which it had just fired, its wheels touching a four-foot-long piece of wood.

The hill erupted in fire and smoke as the Pennsylvanian gunners responded. A flaming piece of wadding from the artillery behind him flipped through air and landed just to his right. His mount shied away from the smoldering rags but stopped as Burr gripped the reins and reassured the horse.

Then in a loud, clear voice he called, "To the front, march!" Drawing out the "to," hitting a higher note on "front," and letting loose "march" like a cannonball.

And, so it begins again, he thought.

The column dipped down and rejoined the road, here tree-lined, and crossed a low-lying muddy stretch, and then marched up a small rise until the causeway came into view. The noise grew to greet them as the fighting, now less than a mile away came into view—or, more accurately, the smoke from the fighting. A steady stream of men heading back up the road from the fight met his gaze. He frowned, knowing his men couldn't see his face.

Burr recognized the soldiers. They were Pennsylvanians from General Wayne's command, three battalions' worth, by the looks of them, slowly slogging up the road from the bridge. He saw two injured men among them, both with blood streaming from their arms.

Burr ordered his men to halt to the right side of the road to allow Wayne's men to pass. The men quietly sweated and swatted flies.

A few short minutes passed, and Burr saw General Wayne himself at the rear of the column. He was red-faced and drenched, his uniform showing salt stains under his arms.

"General!" Burr called out with a salute.

"Colonel Burr, good to see you!" Wayne returned as he straightened up in the saddle and smiled, wiping sweat from his eyes. "General Lee is still out front with his contingent. Mind you hold the bridge for him. The British are pressing him hard."

"Sir!"

Wayne's passed by for two minutes before Burr ordered his troops back on the road. They were now marching in a column of twos next to a corn field; the plants not quite knee high. The farmer likely planted this field late after the brutal winter. The sun stood high overhead, its heat pressing through his dark blue French-style cocked hat.

Burr heard a rider pounding up the road behind him. "Colonel Burr! Where's Colonel Burr? Orders from His Excellency, General Washington for Colonel Burr!"

Burr turned to answer the dispatch rider, "I'm Colonel Burr!"

Several of Burr's men started animatedly pointing up the hill to the gun crews, some 400 yards to the back, laughing. Both mounted officers forgot the moment and looked up hill as well. A man sat by a cannon; his shirt sleeve bloodied. At the muzzle of the cannon, the same young woman who was bearing buckets of water, now bare legged, was quickly ramming a charge down the barrel! Another crew member tamped the shot home and the gun hurdled another iron ball towards the British just beyond the bridge.

Burr smiled approvingly at the scene. Washington's officer frowned.

"Colonel Burr, his Excellency, General Washington, requests your assessment and intent," the rider, a captain scanned the hillside, his focus narrowing on the backs of Dummer's men in the trees at the edge of the ravine, the bridge just beyond.

"Tell General Washington that the Malcolm's are forming up to attack to secure the causeway to make safe Lee's retreat."

Just before the road dipped too low to see the contest playing out 300 yards ahead, Burr saw two British grenadiers cut down by the cannons on the hill behind him. The British pressing General Lee's left were aiming for the bridge, seeking to cut off Lee's quickest route of retreat. It was to be a race.

Another battle, another humiliation by the better trained and better equipped British, he thought. Burr recalled Lee's caution. Lee was right, seeking to go toe-to-toe against these professionals was murder. What was that Virginia *planter* thinking, anyway? He shook his head at the thought of General Washington. Next to the debacle in the snows of Quebec in 1775, his brief and unhappy assignment as an aide to that uncultured *slaveholder* ranked as his most unpleasant experience in the war to date.

He twisted around in his saddle to examine the faces of his regiment, the Malcolm's, so named after Colonel William Malcolm, the Scottish-born businessman who raised the regiment and paid for it himself in January 1777. But, with Malcolm detailed off as Deputy Adjutant General, Burr was left to lead the regiment and another detachment beside!

Originally almost 500-strong, marching, desertion, and the terrible winter at Valley Forge reduced Malcolm's Additional Continental Regiment to 90 men—none of them had died in battle, though Burr did kill a man who tried to spark a mutiny a few months back. The discipline of the remaining soldiers was now unquestioned.

"Colonel Dummer! Place your men across the bridge. Double time. I will follow and deploy to your left. We must safeguard that bridge and cover General Lee's retreat." Burr issued the order calmly, his voice loud enough to be heard above the battle din, but without a hint of fear. A close examination would show that his eyes betrayed but one emotion: exhilaration.

Burr faced again to the south. Some of General Lee's men made the crest of the hill ahead and were marching on the downslope heading for the bridge only 100 yards away. These retreating Continentals remained composed. They were becoming an army—but would it be enough today?

Dummer's men were already across the bridge and trotting uphill in two columns, hurrying to deploy to cover the rest of Wayne's retreating men.

Burr urged his horse across the bridge. He had to get the rest of his command across before Wayne's retreating masses clogged the causeway.

He made the top of the low-slung hill. Dummer had deployed his 30 men in a skirmish line to the right of the road with Lieutenant Colonel Dummer and his horse just off the road to Monmouth courthouse, anchoring his formation's left flank.

Burr rode up beside Dummer and took in the battleground, narrowing his brown eyes, trying to pierce through the gun smoke and heat waves dancing over the corn on either side of the road some 600 yards away. He saw a disordered mass of American soldiers surging up the road. A group of officers rode out to the rabble and urged the near rout into an orderly retreat.

Burr grimly smiled that they were able to do that. More evidence of the winter's constant drilling under that profane Prussian.

Lee's infantry on the far side of the marshy Middle Brook turned to fight, smoke billowing from their muskets. The lead rows of British thinned a bit, then halted. More Americans stood their ground. Burr dared not hope the stand would succeed—surely the British bayonets would sweep the opposite bank clear of Continentals and then test his waiting men.

More ominously, he saw bits of red only 200 yards away to his left in the trees on the south side of Middle Brook.

"Colonel! Colonel!" an adjutant from Lee's command rode up from the bridge on his heavily lathered mount, breathlessly shouting, "Grenadiers are forcing the ravine!" His face was swollen from heat and mosquito bites. He excitedly pointed at the same area of Burr's concern.

He squinted past the older junior officer, raising his small frame up on the stirrups and scanned the tree line below. "Yes, I see them."

Heat waves danced over the low field of young wheat. The Lobsterback red was thickening in the trees along the creek. Uneven fire from the Rebel skirmishers forced the Redcoats to stay in the trees—for now. The British must have seen the small causeway over the ravine.

The colonel made another scan of his surroundings. The creek bent east, towards the enemy, as did the low rise above it. There was only sound and smoke.

The 22-year-old brigade commander summed up the situation. General Wayne's soldiers had already pulled back from supporting Lee's rearguard and were joining the main body on Perrine's Hill. British General Clinton's assault was now almost two hours old, with General Lee's force taking the brunt of the action.

General's Lee's wilting soldiers, and, more importantly, the last of his cannon, were in danger of being overrun if the British renewed their attack or pressed up from the trees along the creek in force. But the British had to make it across the bridge to get at Lee with their bayonets. Burr intended to block that.

Sweat ran down Burr's face. General Lord Stirling, Burr's division commander, was likely helping General Wayne reform his line on Perrine's. He was alone.

Dummer allowed his 30 men to fire at will at the British in the trees, their .69-caliber Charleville muskets belching fire and smoke as fast as each soldier could manage.

Burr smiled at the sight of the new muskets. They fired a one-ounce lead ball and had slightly greater range and accuracy than the .75-caliber English Brown Bess—and, unlike the British, the Colonials knew how to extract the most from that accuracy. The first shipment arrived at Portsmouth, New Hampshire, in April 1777. The French then quickened the pace of assistance significantly after the Americans whipped the British at Saratoga in October 1777.

Burr's 90 men had now formed up to the left of the road, closest to the British in the trees. They were in two ranks of 45.

Burr called out to his senior noncommissioned officer, "Sergeant Harris, Commence volley!"

Harris shouted, "Make ready!" The soldiers took their muskets off their left shoulders, cocked them, and held them vertically in front of their chests, the tip of their bayonets some six feet above their black felt tricorns.

"Take aim!" The first row of 45 men leveled their muskets at the British.

"Fire!"

Up on the line, the ten-pound musket pushed hard into Private Jeph Clark's shoulder as smoke and sparks obscured his vision and stung at his eyes.

Several feet back, Burr inhaled the satisfying smell of burnt gunpowder as it lazily drifted over his face.

Harris's 45 men in the front rank countermarched three steps to the rear. "Prime and load!" he called out.

In Harris's firing line Private Jeph Clark encouragingly called out the musket drill's training commands to the rattled soldier standing next to him. Though he was four years senior to Jeph's 16, the din of combat set the man's hands to shaking. The prime and load command—or just load—was the toughest with nine steps: half-cock firelock; handle cartridge; prime; shut pan; charge with cartridge; draw rammer; ram down cartridge; return rammer; and shoulder firelock.

The entire loading sequence took some 16 seconds with some of the less experienced soldiers also struggling with the sequence while under fire. Though the concentration required to execute the nine loading steps served as a partial distraction from the deadly threat to the front. The soldiers first pulled their firelock to half-cock and then opened the frizzen—a single piece L-shaped steel tab with the base protecting the flash pan from the elements as well as from the powder falling out during subsequent steps with the shaft of the L providing the striker for the flint on the hammer. The second step was to slap the cartridge box to settle the powder in the cartridges, grab one, tear the cartridge open with one's teeth and then tuck it under chin to safeguard it from any rain. Step three was the priming of the weapon by placing a small amount of powder in the pan. Four was pulling the frizzen back to cover the pan and then turning the musket around to load it. Charging was the fifth step—dumping the rest of the powder from the cartridge down the barrel and then dropping the paper-wrapped musket ball in. Six was drawing the ramrod out. Seven was ramming it down the barrel to tamp the ball securely against the powder. Eight was replacing the rammer in its place beneath the barrel. And step nine—place the musket on the left shoulder.

"Make ready" was the simple—simply remove the musket from the shoulder and cock it which was only two training commands.

And the final two commands were the same in training as they were in combat. At "Take aim," the soldier would level the firearm and find a target—though the British just pointed. And at "Fire!" the soldier fired.

Sergeant Heinz's men in the second row marched up to take Harris's place and repeated the fire commands, the men working like some sort of hellish automated scythe.

Burr nudged his horse down the road to get a better look.

Lee's vanguard was now surging down the road. Hundreds of men, dozens of horses, and four gun crews with their ammunition wagons.

Burr's men kept up a steady volume of fire into the British in the woods 200 yards away. The tree line suddenly became red as hundreds of soldiers emerged.

It was Harris's turn, "Make ready!" A British return volley passed harmlessly by. "Take aim! Fire!"

Burr turned to his troops, "Buck and ball, boys! Give 'em buck and ball!"

His men found their buck and ball paper cartridges, biting the end off the cartridge and dropping a bit of powder into their flash pans and then dumping the rest—gunpowder, three buck shots, a .69 caliber shot and the paper cartridge—down their barrels and then ramming it home.

"Load! Then a few seconds later, "Make ready! Take aim! Fire!"

Burr saw British fall—three, maybe four.

Lee's ammo wagons trundled across the bridge.

"Load! Make ready! Take aim! Fire!"

Three of Lee's cannon crossed the causeway, each pulled by two terribly lathered horses.

"Load! Make ready! Take aim! Fire!"

The British were 100 yards away. They paused their march and readied to volley.

Burr turned his mount to rejoin his lines.

Two of his men cried out, one falling with blood covering his face and the other with a wound to his thigh.

"Keep it up! Make 'em pay, boys!"

The last of Lee's men marched by between Burr and Dummer, masking the fire from Dummer's men as they passed between his skirmishers and the British coming up the creek draw. The almost 100 soldiers, sweat streaming off their faces, marched by. If they were afraid, they didn't show it—they just looked exhausted.

General Charles Lee was the last of his command over the bridge, a trickle of blood languidly traced its way off the grey horse's croup.

Burr saluted Lee. The general merely nodded and made his way down to the bridge lost in thought.

The British volleyed.

One of Dummer's men went down. He didn't move. In his own ranks he saw the Clark boy cry out, blood gushing from his left hand. He moved to fall out, though he still firmly grasped his musket. Burr saw the boy was missing a finger while another finger dangled uselessly from ribbon of flesh.

Down at the bridge, Burr saw an officer speak with General Lee who pointed up at Burr.

Burr turned back to the battle and rode out again to better survey the situation.

The third rank of British grenadiers were set to volley.

Colonel Barber, one of General Washington's staff thundered down the road from behind Burr, calling out his name.

Burr looked back.

Barber came alongside Burr. "You are ordered to return to the other side of the bridge! Retreat immediately!"

Burr frowned, "Sir, my men are checking the redcoats. We must continue the volley."

Burr heard a musket ball crash into his horse. The horse called out in terror and fell over, pinning Burr's right leg to the ground. The horse struggled to get up, allowing Burr to free his boot from the stirrup. His knee was bloodied, but he could walk. His mount thrashed around. Burr drew one of his pistols and put the beast out of its misery with a shot to the head.

A mass of smoke rose from the British line. None of his men fell. But moments later, a breeze cleared the smoke away and Burr saw the grenadiers were now marching towards them, bayonets leveled.

"Colonel Burr, order your men back across the bridge!"

High on Perrine's Hill, the order went out to fire on the advancing grenadiers.

Dummer, looking back at Burr and then at the grenadiers, started to make his way towards Burr.

Outbound cannon balls flew over Burr's head.

Dummer was 30 paces away and appeared to be about to ask Burr a question when an American ball took off the top of his skull and sprayed blood and brains on the backs of two soldiers.

Barber narrowed his eyes. "Burr, you will retreat. You have exposed your men to our batteries on the hill."

"Prime and load! Make ready! Take aim! Fire!" It was Heinz.

Burr looked back on Dummer's half-headless corpse, "I never knew Dummer had so many brains."

Barber suppressed a chuckle and pressed, "Burr!"

Burr ordered Dummer's men to pull back. They needed no encouragement.

He limped ten paces down the road clear from his men's volley smoke.

Harris called out, "Prime and load! Make ready! Take aim! Fire!"

The British had closed to 50 yards.

Burr gave Sergeant Harris the order to pull back across the bridge and winced as he followed behind.

On Perrine's Hill, American gunners, now more confident in their aim as the last of their compatriots added distance between themselves and oncoming British, poured it on. The grenadiers wavered, then stopped, losing several more men.

Having crossed the bridge, Burr ordered his men back into line.

Burr saw the Clark boy, having wrapped his injured hand in a strip of cloth, rejoin the firing line.

"Private Clark!" Burr called.

"Sir?" the slight young man seemed worried, as if he did something wrong.

"Bravo, private! Are you good?"

"Kedge, sir!" Clark replied with a bright smile, his cheeks covered with dirt, blood, and sweat.

Harris called out, "Prime and load! Make ready! Take aim! Fire!"

The grenadiers suddenly halted and then countermarched. They were retreating! The British formed into two columns and edged to the right down the road to Monmouth courthouse.

Burr commanded, "Cease fire, cease fire!"

His men spontaneously cried out, "Huz-ZAY! Huz-ZAY!"

Burr put his back to a tree and took a long pull from his canteen.

"Sergeant Harris, have the men drink. Your company will fill their canteens and those of Heinz's men. Heinz!"

"Sir?"

"Have your men clean their pans and report to me how much ammunition remains."

The cannon fire from the hill continued at a brisk pace.

Half an hour passed, and General Wayne reappeared at the head of a column of 400 of the Third Pennsylvania Brigade as they quickstepped towards the British. Wayne saw Burr seated with his back to a tree and called out loud enough for all his men to hear, "You there, Burr! Damn fine job! Damn fine! Now, fall in behind our column. We're attacking the British!"

Burr struggled to his feet as his men called out another string of huzzas.

Burr gave the order to form up his 112 remaining soldiers. Colonel Spencer came into view at the end of a second column, 300-strong. "Burr! Fall in! Great to see you! Though you look as you could use a horse."

Burr led his men back across the bridge, this time, veering to the right, due south, heading for the top of the hill that, hours earlier, had been contested by Lee and the British.

The sounds of the battle grew closer again. Burr reckoned there was about two-and-a-half hours of sunlight remaining as the sticky hot day reluctantly began to cool.

About a half-mile away and to the south, a rise overlooking a tributary of Middle Brook erupted in smoke, the constant thud of cannon fire indicating gunners had found their mark. But whose?

A mounted officer made his way up from the main lines on Perrine's Hill. His breeches were soiled but his black boots shined, and his uniform was immaculate. He looked down on Burr with piercing violet blue eyes.

"Colonel Burr, have you lost your mount?"

Burr briefly met Lieutenant Colonel Alexander Hamilton's gaze and looked past him, pointing at the hill to the south.

"Alas, Hamilton, my horse was fated for an English ball. Say, who's on the hill yonder?"

Hamilton smiled widely, "That's General Greene and his artillery on Comb's Hill. He's enfilading the last of the grenadiers."

Burr heaved a sigh. "Well, then, have we won?"

"We possess the battlefield. As for victory, I suspect General Washington will order a general attack in the morning. Where's General Wayne?"

Burr motioned to the right down the lines.

Hamilton tipped his hat and galloped off to find Wayne.

Burr watched the other 22-year-old officer ride off, the golden sunset illuminating his right side and seethed quietly.

Burr set about making sure his men were fed, resupplied with ammunition, and rested. Limping about his lines anchored on the left by a parsonage. By almost midnight, he fell exhausted at the base of a tree by the clergyman's house.

He heard someone calling his name. "Sir, sir?" The voice belonged to a New Englander. Burr forced his eyes open. A black face looked down on him.

Burr rolled on his side and grabbed a pistol, "Colonel Tye! Damned devil…"

Alarmed at first for being confused for the Black loyalist raider, the private said, "No sir! I'm private Poor, Salem Poor's my name! I'm with Glover's Brigade, 13th Massachusetts."

"Ahh…"

Poor bent down and touched Burr's hot, dry cheek. "Sir, you fell asleep in the morning sun. You are afflicted with heat sickness." Poor offered his canteen to Burr but Burr stared blankly ahead. Poor knelt down, uncorked the canteen and gently put it to Burr's lips. Burr coughed and then, eyes wide, grabbed the canteen and drained it.

Burr struggled to his feet, his head pounding. "The attack? Are we attacking?" Burr looked beyond Poor and saw three mounted officers trotting down the road towards the bridge. He pushed past the private and limped over.

General Washington looked down. He started to frown and then, seeing Burr's condition and his bloody knee said, "Colonel Aaron Burr of the Malcolm's, I heard you put up a good fight yesterday. Well done!"

Burr slurred, "The attack, sir?"

Washington briefly thought Burr drunk on duty, then removed his glove and leaned over, touching Burr's face.

Burr blinked.

"Take this officer to a doctor. He's been overcome by the heat."

"The attack, sir?" Burr persisted. He looked at the two officers accompanying Washington, struggling to focus.

"No worries, my son. The British slipped away last night. The battlefield is ours." Washington gently looked at Burr. "You are to retire to Philadelphia with two weeks of leave. You are no use to us in your present state. I need you to recover and return to the fight."

Burr nodded slowly. He looked down and rubbed his eyes and then looked up at the three horsemen. *Hamilton.* It was an immaculately attired Hamilton astride a well-groomed white horse.

The last thing Burr recalled before passing out was Hamilton's deep-blue stare.

Chapter Three – A New Jersey Interlude

July 1778 through March 1779, Northern New Jersey and Westchester County, New York

Burr's head had been pounding for days when he heard of Washington's ridiculous charge against General Lee. Lee was no "poltroon" as Washington was rumored to have called him in the heat of battle. And, were it not for Lee's extraction of his vanguard as British General Clinton moved to turn his flanks, his 2,500 men would have been lost to the cause.

A "shameful" retreat? Burr saw with his eyes that General Lee was the last of his command to cross that bridge over Middle Brook. Certainly not a coward.

But here we were in Brunswick, New Jersey, after chasing the British all the way back to New York. With Lee on trial for disobedience of orders, misbehavior before the enemy, in making an unnecessary, disorderly, and "shameful" retreat, and disrespect to the commander in chief in the form of two letters written to defend himself.

Burr thought the whole matter distasteful—and unnecessary, given that the Americans drove the British from the battlefield at Monmouth.

In less than a week after the victory, Washington tasked Lord Stirling— the quasher of the trumped-up Conway Cabal—with presiding over Lee's court martial. Then, for the next five weeks as the army kept a wary watch on the British across the Hudson, Lee's reputation was taken apart bit by bit with Hamilton leading the charge by providing eyewitness testimony.

Hamilton. He was merely trying to please his master—a mere message runner looking for table scraps from the commander-in-chief while the men who actually fought and bled were ignored or had their courage questioned.

As Burr fumed over Lee's mistreatment, Lord Stirling grew concerned that the young officer would run afoul of Washington again (Burr had served briefly on Washington's staff in 1776 after distinguishing himself under Benedict Arnold's ill-starred expedition to Quebec in 1775) and suggested Burr be employed to gather intelligence on British movements in New Jersey along the lower Hudson.

To this task, Burr saw himself as eminently suited as he enjoyed making friends—especially of the female persuasion.

Burr was developing some fruitful sources in one of Elizabethtown's better "academies" with a fine covey of doxies—some of whom, most importantly, were providing comfort to the English geographical bachelors across the river. Officers who, in vulnerable moments, would speak too much.

In matters of the flesh, Burr thought himself too practical, too mercenary, to be vulnerable. That is until he linked back up with Washington's mobile field headquarters at Ho-Ho-Kus, at 30 miles, a day's ride north of Elizabeth.

It was there, at a social function held by the mistress of The Hermitage, that Burr met his equal—Theodosia Bartow Prevost. Almost 10 years his senior, she was not yet 32, and with five children by her husband of 15 years, a Swiss-born British officer, Jacques Prevost, who, conveniently, was campaigning in Georgia. Burr was smitten.

This wasn't all like his infatuation with pretty little Margaret Moncrieffe at Kingsbridge two years earlier, he, a mere 20 and she six years his junior and a daughter of a British officer posted on Staten Island.

Theodosia was a wonderful paradox. Thoroughly educated. Fluent in French even before her marriage to Prevost, the two would openly discuss the principles of the American war for independence, Wollstonecraft, and Rousseau before stealing away to indulge in other activities.

And then there was multilingual Mary, the junior but indispensable member of Theodosia's household staff. Mary, with her uncommon looks and dark skin, caused some, at first, to surmise her a native—imagine the surprise when they came to find out she was one of the Indians Columbus originally set out to find!

Not that Burr ceased his outings to Elizabethtown's finest—those liaisons were of a different, more transactional, nature. Besides, the release provided relief from the incessant headaches he suffered after Monmouth—and, a release both he and Theodosia decided to deny themselves until the war ended in victory and divorce or her husband fell in battle.

Sadly, after five blissful months, the call of war, even in his weakened state, came again in the dead of winter. Burr was reattached to the Malcolm's and assigned to General Alexander McDougall in Westchester County, New York. Here, the challenge was to keep an eye on the northern-most British post at Kingsbridge while trying to maintain order among marauding knights of the road and plundering redcoats and rebels. That the highwaymen would advantage themselves in conflict Burr could understand, but much of the troops' misbehavior Burr chalked up to boredom rather than the design of any ordered plan.

A season of winter campaigning took a dreadful toll, both on Burr and the Malcolm's. Constant British raids and Tory plots forced Burr to remain on the move. He slept out in the open almost as much as he did indoors, rarely spending more than one night in the same place.

By March, Burr was a spent force. Constantly plagued by headaches and body pains, he resigned his commission. At 23, he now resolved to study law, though Burr did manage to keep up with the spying—how could he say no? Besides, it was a welcome break from the books.

Burr's last taste of combat was a short, sharp fight. It began when General Tryon, the King's former governor of New York, showed up in New Haven, Connecticut the day after America's third Independence Day with almost 3,000 lobsterbacks. Burr quickly gathered 50 Yale students to reinforce the local militia. The Yale minutemen temporarily checked the British who ended up sacking the city anyway.

Chapter Four – Triumph and Tragedy

November 22, 1783, Manhattan

It was shaping up to be a partly cloudy morning. When he awoke, it was just cold enough to see his breath, but now had gotten a little warmer.

Jephtath Clark had become a man in the Continental Army. Now a sergeant after almost six years of service, he was part of the force that was marching into New York under Generals Washington and Knox as the British evacuated.

The men did what they could to spruce up their uniforms, taking care to wash them and mend them before entering New York. Jeph was particularly proud of his red sergeant's epaulettes, though they were visibly frayed.

He should have been thrilled—after all, they won the war. But instead, a gathering sense of dread filled his heart. He had only heard once from his mother after he ran away from British-occupied New York to join the army in December of 1777. He was unsure if she was even still alive. He figured she'd be about 39 now. But, informally attached as she was to an English-born Tory lawyer, he doubted that the man would be foolish enough to remain the in city, leaving his mother to fend for herself.

He put his mind to marching and pushed away thoughts of his mother. Crowds of people thronged the way, shouting encouragement and throwing wreaths before them. Though after the mounted officers at the head of the column rode over them, the wreaths were largely mangled by the time the soldiers marched by.

By the time they reached the southern tip of Manhattan, their boots and trousers were splattered with mud and horse droppings—only part of the route was cobbled, and the rainstorm of the prior day ensured plentiful mud, the bane of all soldiers.

With the officers set to join Gov. George Clinton for a public dinner at Fraunces Tavern that evening, the men were to be quartered at various establishments around the town—all of which hosted the British not a day before.

Jeph figured things were going to change quickly for the Army. With consistently irregular pay and poor food, he doubted Congress would sustain the Army for long. Yet, he couldn't just leave his station without permission. He approached his company commander, a captain, and asked for permission to try to find his mother. The officer smiled broadly and said, "Sergeant Clark, you're on your own. Dismissed. As I told the men, you're to report back to the Battery within the week to be mustered out. You'll get your final pay then. It's finished. We're done. We won. You may go home." Seeing a major from the division staff, the captain quickly turned away from Jeph.

Jeph looked down. Home. He had none. His mother was a mistress to a British lawyer. Certainly, that man fled along with the thousands who were evacuated, and that's assuming his mother kept his interest or he hadn't left years before. In any case, there would be no "home" to go to. There was only his mother. Thirza. Thirza Clark or Davies or Roberts…

With his leave from his commander, Jeph set out to find the Almshouse operated by the city's Overseers of the Poor. If his mother wasn't there, she would likely be dead—or, and he really didn't allow himself this hope— residing in a boardinghouse somewhere in the city.

Jeph set out for the Commons where the Almshouse was situated. Within a half hour, he came upon a grey building with two floors above ground and windows near the ground indicating a partially sunk basement. There was a chimney on either end of the building between which there were five tall, rectangular windows on the second floor above four windows on the first on either side of heavy wooden door at the top of seven steps.

Jeph had to first enter a gate under the watchful eye of a man near the steps. Stretching out to the left of the Almshouse was a wooden barracks, more than twice as long as the Almshouse itself, though only a single story.

Preparing to mount the steps, he took a deep breath, and then regretted it—there was a distinct odor of death and filth.

The door flung open and Jeph stood the bottom of the stairs watching. A somewhat portly man in his 40s was speaking quietly with a whitehaired man of about 50. He had dark eyebrows and was also well fed, though Jeph wouldn't think him fat.

Jeph heard the older man say, "Yes, I know times have been difficult for you. They have for all of us. I will do all I can. I promise you, you will have the money you need to feed and clothe your inmates."

The younger man, completely oblivious to Jeph's presence, responded, "Thank you, Mr. Duane. Thank you. May the Lord bless you, sir."

Jeph saw Duane pass a golden coin to the portly man. "Here is a guinea. It should buy enough food for a day. I'll try to bring more tomorrow after I speak with some of the merchants. I want to see your books, though." The whitehaired man looked intently at the portly man.

"Yes sir. Thank you, sir."

Both men saw Jeph at the same time. The portly man frowned for a moment, while the whitehaired man smiled broadly and said, "Sergeant of the victorious Continental Army! Please, don't let me stand in your way. It appears you are looking for someone. This gentleman should be able to assist."

The older man put his hat on and walked down the stairs, stopping to warmly shake Jeph's hand, "I'm James Duane, pleased to meet your acquaintance, Sergeant…"

Jeph, nearly dumbstruck by such an interaction with a civilian so obviously superior in class—the last time he wasn't in uniform he was almost 16—stammered, "Uhh, sir, yes, uhh, my name is Sergeant Clark, Jephtath Clark."

"Well, thank you, Sergeant Clark, for serving in a great cause. We still have much work to do though. Is New York your home?"

"Yes sir. I'm here looking for my mother."

The man's countenance at the top of the stairs softened.

"Well then, Mr. Greene here will be happy to help, if he may. Now, if you please, I have matters to which to attend."

Jeph tipped his cocked hat in a salute and continued up the stairs, each step growing heavier than the last.

Jeph could hear Duane walking quickly away. His focus on anything but the inevitability of his mother's condition was broken when Mr. Greene, speaking behind bad breath, said, "Now, Mister, uh, Sergeant Clark, whom are you looking for? Please, step inside, so we can review our ledgers."

Jeph took the last step into the darkened building, as his eyes adjusted, he could see a large common area where people ate. Mr. Greene opened the door to his office right off the hallway to the common area and gestured for Jeph to sit while moving behind his large, clean desk. "Now, what is your mother's name?"

"When I left home six years ago, she called herself by the name of Roberts."

"We have no Roberts here right now."

"Davies? Clark? Her Christian name was, is, Thirza."

Greene's eyes lit up for an instance at the recognition, then darkened, "Yes, we took in a Thirza Davies four months ago."

"Is she, is she…"

"Your mother is alive, just so. I fear she is not long for this world."

"Oh…" Jeph struggled to comport himself in front of this stranger.

"She has consumption. As well, I'm sorry to say, venereal distemper."

"May I see her?"

"Yes! Yes! She'd be delighted to see you. I must caution you though, she is not in her right mind. She may not recognize you."

Mr. Greene got up and led Jeph through the mostly-empty hall—there were some inmates scrubbing the floor and cleaning tables.

He walked out the back and down wooden steps. There were two brick buildings to the left and right and a large, now fallow garden beyond.

Taking the role of a tour guide, Greene pointed to the building on the left and said, "This is where we prepare the meals. And this," pointing to the right, "Is our storage house where we keep workhouse materials such as rope, donated clothing, fabric, and other supplies that the inmates who are able work into items of value that we sell to support our operations. Though, as I'm sure you gathered from my conversation with Mr. Duane, it's not nearly enough to cover our expenses."

As they walked into the garden area, Jeph noticed three people, all men, one of them black, slowly hoeing the ground. They all looked to be in their 60s with long, unkempt hair and beards. To the right and left of the garden were two long barracks, likely built by the British occupation force, with a third barracks stretching out of sight to the right and left behind the first two. The fourth barracks he had seen on walking up to the Almshouse was now behind him and to the left. In all, Jeph figured at a regiment of at least 500 redcoats could have been bunked there just a few days ago.

Greene had been talking but Jeph's mind was wandering to, as he remembered them, happier days, when his mother had befriended Mr. Davies, the dandy London lawyer who immediately took the 10-year-old Jeph under his wing at his law practice, teaching him to maintain his supplies and quizzing him on vocabulary words. Jeph thought the man odd, but his mother seemed to like him, so, he liked him as well.

Jeph noticed Greene was still talking, "…and so we moved her to the barracks two days ago, along with five other inmates afflicted with consumption."

They were at the entrance to the barracks on the right. Greene grabbed the door latch and pushed it open. It creaked loudly. The barracks was dark, lit by a solitary candle. It smelled musty with piss and vomit and feces thrown in as well. Greene grabbed a chamberstick and candle off a shelf and lit the candle from the burning candle on the shelf. The tallow candles smoked. Greene pushed forward as Jeph shrank back, fear building in his breast. He could see eight beds in an otherwise empty barracks stretching off into the darkness. Six of the beds were occupied.

"Thirza. Thirza. Are you awake? There's a young man here to see you."

As Jeph hung behind Greene, afraid to even look at his mother, he heard her distinct, though now raspy voice, "A… a young man come a calling? Tell him I'm indisposed."

Jeph could see the woman fumbling with her thinned hair. He could see open sores on her face, one on her forehead, one on her chin, and one on her right cheek. But, as he edged closer, he could see the familiar outlines of his mother's face. "Momma," he choked out, tears streaming down his face.

Thirza stared up to the darkened rafters, looking confused.

"Jeph? Is that you? Are you back? Where have you been?"

Jeph rushed forward and gathered his mother's trembling husk of a body into his arms, weeping into her tattered nightgown.

"It's me, Momma, it's Jeph, it's me."

Now Thirza started to cry, alternating between dry sobs and a wracking cough. "Oh Jeph, my Jeph. I love you Jeph. Are we going home? Are you taking me home?"

For six years in the Army, death was Jeph's constant companion. Occasionally violent death at the hands of the enemy, sometimes violent accidental deaths, but usually death by disease. Four times, Jeph himself held the hand of a fevered, dying comrade. His mother was soon to pass. He gathered himself, thanking God for a brief moment that he could be reunited with his mother, if only for a few moments that he might comfort her, "Yes, Momma, I'm here for you, we're home." Jeph pulled back and held her face in his hands, looking into her rheumy eyes.

She coughed violently, blood spattering her chin and bed linens as well as Jeph's uniform. She started gasping for breath and then choking.

Greene grabbed a pitcher of water and poured into a clay mug for Jeph to give to her. Jeph grabbed the mug and turned back to his mother, her eyes staring lifelessly heavenward.

Chapter Five – Farewell

December 4, 1783, Fraunces Tavern, New York

"An unexpected pleasure, Aaron!" Hamilton smiled at Burr as they approached the entrance to Fraunces Tavern where General George Washington was hosting a turtle feast.

Neither of the men wore their uniforms, Burr resigning his commission in the spring of 1779 due to poor health, Hamilton, three years later to the month.

A small cannon fired a salute as a young officer opened the door to them. Hamilton grinned broadly at the cannon. Burr looked at Hamilton. They had both been admitted to the New York bar the year before and occasionally saw each other at courthouses in American-controlled New York or in social settings in the Hudson River Valley. But this had been the first time since the war that Burr and Hamilton had been together as soldiers—and this for a reunion of Washington's officers only nine days after the last British soldier had evacuated New York City.

Burr had heard of a turtle feast but hadn't yet been invited to one—they were far more common in Rhode Island and in the port towns of the northeast that commonly traded with Barbados. Occasionally a ship would arrive from the Caribbean with rum, arrack, limes, and sea turtles—the former three being turned into a potent punch and the later into a savory dish—together, an excuse for a "turtle frolic," some of which would last 12 hours until the last guests staggered home a couple of hours after midnight.

"You're in for a treat, Aaron," Hamilton said as they entered a tavern already crowded with uniformed men. "I understand the turtle is being prepared by a chef brought in from Newport. His master was a loyalist. Likely displaying his newfound affection for the victors by lending us his cook, whom, I hear, was trained by Cuffy Cockroach himself."

Burr's eyes widened, "Cuffy…"

"Cockroach. Yes, I know, not a name to inspire an appetite. Nevertheless, he is the best. It augers well for tonight and, I hope, as does a former foe extending olive branch bodes well for our future."

"I'm not inclined to sell my birthright for a savory soup," Burr responded.

"You haven't had the soup, or the roast turtle!" Hamilton laughed. Then, turning serious, Hamilton slightly leaned towards Burr and said, "It's the right of all Americans, should they wish, to contribute to building a nation. Besides, we're on the victorious side, we can afford to be gracious."

Burr was about to respond when Washington filled their view, towering seven inches over his former officers. He looked down at them, pausing to say to Hamilton, "My Little Lion! I'm so glad you're here." Hamilton blushed enough that Burr could see it by the dim light of the tavern. Washington's lips curled upward, though not enough to show his false teeth.

"And Burr! St. Clair told me of your spying missions after you resigned. He said you were indispensable. If Hamilton was ever captured, he risked bad food on a prison ship—if the British ever caught you, it was noose!" Now it was Burr's turn to blush, his balding head radiating warmth. He never expected Washington to be so gracious towards him.

They'd been at it for three hours already. The grey light from a clouded early December sky was starting to fade from the tavern's west-facing third floor windows. Burr imagined that only a fortnight ago, His Majesty's officers were exchanging teary-eyed toasts and making last minute arrangements to return home. Burr carefully nursed the same cup of rum punch through countless toasts, many from officers he recognized. A handful of men were visibly fishy, many more only wobbly.

Close to midnight, General Knox gathered his 250-pound, just over six-foot frame and gestured with his right hand for the men to quiet. Burr saw that, as always, Knox kept his left hand wrapped in a white cloth. The British spread the rumor that it was because he was always at the ready for surrender. The real reason was simple vain embarrassment: he lost his third and fourth fingers to a hunting accident—Knox was shooting at a turkey when the barrel of his firearm burst. "Gentlemen, gentlemen…" Knox boomed.

The assembled gradually quieted with a few of the more sodden soldiers needing a jab in the ribs. "Gentlemen, I give you our Commander-in-Chief, General George Washington!"

Washington rose, slightly taller and, though large at about 175 pounds, next to Knox's oaken frame, looked like a slender pine. For a full minute, he was silent, taking the time to look at each of the men. Several faces burned with tears. But Burr was detached and more interested in taking in the countenances of his colleagues.

Finally, Washington began, "We have completed one solemn task and now embark upon another, though more difficult. We must all consider it our indispensable duty to commend the interests of our dearest country to the protection of Almighty God, and those who have the superintendence of them, to his holy keeping. We won our independence. Now we must prevail in a more terrible struggle—that against chaos, anarchy and rebellion…"

Burr's gaze found Hamilton. He was enraptured.

"...it is with a heart full of love and gratitude, I now take leave of you. I most devoutly wish that your latter days may be as prosperous and happy as your former ones have been glorious and honorable."

The men erupted, "Huz-ZAY! Huz-ZAY!" The tavern's windows rattled for a full minute before they settled back into the night's business, some excitedly talking, a few openly weeping, and some just too drunk to care. It was from one of these latter souls that Burr, seated at the end of an adjacent table of eight finally spied something he'd only heard tales of—a besotted man making himself a Vice Admiral of the Narrow Seas as he clumsily unbuttoned his breeches and relieved himself under the table onto Hamilton's boots.

Burr smiled broadly at Hamilton. Hamilton smiled back, his eyebrows betraying a hint of confusion.

Burr quickly turned and buried his laughter in his cupped hands. He excused himself a few minutes later and alternatively chuckled and guffawed his way back to the inn where he was spending the night before heading back home to Theodosia.

Chapter Six – Molly!

March 12, 1784, Manhattan

Jephtath Clark's stomach had been empty so long it no longer growled. That wouldn't be so bad, except that it was cold and damp too and his legs were shaky. After spending three nights outside, he was also stiff.

He'd been looking for work for a week after a few months of odd jobs but was met with indifference. Yes, he was veteran, but there were plenty of veterans, real and claimed in the city and, for the Loyalists who never left or who were coming back to try to reclaim their property, being a veteran of the Continental Army wasn't seen as a positive attribute.

His greatest liability, he felt, was his slight build—that, and the missing two fingers on his left-hand courtesy of a British musket ball six years ago at Monmouth. Potential employers saw him as too small to perform hard physical labor. And, in his current condition, they'd be right.

Not that he wanted to do physical work—he had apprenticed for a lawyer before the war—but the poor state of his attire embarrassed him. He was in no condition to seek work in an office.

Jeph walked back up the dock towards Water Street, the East River and its noisy gulls to his back when he saw a maid, probably a household servant by the looks of her clothing, walking quickly down the cobbled street, sometimes swerving to avoid the horse droppings, sometimes jumping over them. A simple white scarf covered most of her head, though a few strands of loose blond hair could be seen. She was wearing a pale blue round gown. With her left hand, she gathered some of the fabric in an attempt to keep it safe from the road hazards. In the crook of her right arm she was carrying an enormous basket with a white linen covering its contents.

Jeph's eye was drawn to a flapping patch of white to the left, fluttering down from a rooftop, passing in and out of view from behind the stern of a ship. It looked like a sheet.

As the sheet approached the street crowded with laborers loading cargo onto wagons and people going about their day, a horse spooked. The horse reared up. The cart it was harnessed to was carrying some barrels that shifted suddenly forward, with that, the horse bolted, scattering two barrels onto the street, one that burst into a heap of foam.

The horse and cart were about 40 yards down the street and picking up speed. Jeph was 10 yards from the street. The young woman who caught

Jeph's eye was another 10 yards beyond Jeph to the right, walking, unawares, with her back to the danger.

As Jeph ran into the street, he heard a cry of someone crushed by the horse and cart.

He looked right just in time to see the maid look over her shoulder, unmoving, in fright.

The horse was slowed just to the left of Jeph when one of the cart's wheels hit a large barrel and sheared off, dashing the last barrel on the cart to the stone street. The cart, now missing a wheel, but completely empty, threatened to become a careening scythe.

Jeph grabbed the horse's bridle and in one fluid motion, leapt up onto its back, pulling hard on the animal's bit and calling out "Whoa!" in a voice as authoritative as he could make it. Though, hours later, he realized it cracked a bit at the end, more due to his present condition, he consoled himself, than to any proximity to boyhood.

Jeph looked down from the mount to see the maiden standing directly in front of him. She cupped the horse's muzzle in her hand while offering it a very large carrot from the other.

Jeph heard a crowd gathering, calling approval with a few scattered "Huzzahs!" that Jeph worried might cause the horse to bolt again. He soothingly spoke to the horse and stroked its neck.

From behind, Jeph saw a rotund man running red faced down the street. He pulled up on the left of the horse, bent over and took a big breath, and then grabbed the reins from Jeph, "Thank you! Thank you, my boy! You saved the day! How may I ever repay…" he gasped for air, "you for your bravery?"

Turning his attention from the young woman to the fat man, Jeph said, "A job. I'd like to have a job, sir, if you'll have me."

A man from the street called out, "Careful there, boy, old Wallace looks bacon fed, but he didn't get that way by being lazy, he'll work you as hard as that horse!"

Another man called, "Give him work, Wallace, he just saved your horse and that girl!"

The fat, red faced man looked into the crowd and then back up at Jeph, "Well, sir, if I am to hire you, I ought to at least know your name."

Jeph started to slide off the horse as he said, "Jephtath Clark, but you may call me Jeph, Mr. Wallace." Jeph smiled as he looked up at the larger man and extended his hand.

Mr. Wallace grinned broadly, his face now a lighter shade of red, and said, "What are you waiting for? We have a mess to clean up back there and a cart to mend!"

Jeph turned to look for the woman. She was already making her way down the street.

"Pardon me! Pardon me, miss? I didn't get your name."

The woman took one more step and paused. She then slowly turned around. Jeph could see that her eyes were the darkest brown and she had a sprinkling of freckles across the bridge of her nose. She smiled. Her teeth were white and straight. "My name is Molly, and yours?"

"Jephtath Clark, miss."

Molly started to turn to go.

Jeph wanted so badly to know her family name and where she lived, but in his current state, he was too embarrassed to be so bold, so, as she smiled softly and turned to go he ventured one last word, "You were very brave this morning Miss Molly."

Molly looked one more time at Jeph, blushed a bit, and then walked out of sight.

Mr. Wallace's lardy voice shook Jeph from his revelry, "She's a beautiful lass, isn't she. I know the family she works for…"

Jeph looked at Wallace, his face wide-eyed and his jaw slack.

Wallace laughed, his gut bouncing up and down.

"Let's get to it, boy!"

Chapter Seven – Family

June 2, 1784, Manhattan

For the past two-and-a-half months, Jeph had been working for Mr. Wallace, a generally happy, though sloppy merchant of beer and cider, who drank much of his profits. Wallace had given him a place to sleep in his small storehouse by the docks—with the added task of guarding the barrels of beer and cider—and occasionally whisky—from thieves.

Jeph was fed, though still frequently went to sleep hungry. But he now had a change of clothes (that Mrs. Wallace washed and mended for him) and was cleaner than he'd been since he ran away from home at age 15 and joined the army.

He made excuses as he could to run into Molly as she went about her business in the employ of a wealthy merchant and his family. He learned that Molly too was an orphan—a daughter of a prostitute who died giving birth to Molly. No matter. Every time he saw Molly in the street, his resolution to marry her grew. He just needed to accumulate the money and the courage to ask her to marry him, with the first fortifying the second—or so at least he told himself.

It was early in the afternoon, after helping Mr. Wallace deliver barrels of cider to eight taverns and boardinghouses, that Jeph was eating bread and cheese and washing it down with warm cider, when a man who looked familiar from his Army days approached him. The man was followed by a skinny lad of about 13.

"Is this Mr. Wallace's establishment?" he asked. He was fairly tall and sturdy, with reddish brown hair and blue eyes. The boy was already as tall as he was, though that wasn't saying much at 5'4."

Jeph rose from his lunch, "It is. Shall I fetch the proprietor?"

"No, I'm not here to see Mr. Wallace, but one of his men. I'm looking for Mr. Clark, Jephtath Clark." The man looked uncomfortable in the saying of it, as if he was discharging an unpleasant duty.

"I am Jephtath Clark," Jeph said with suspicion, wondering if he was in trouble for something, though he couldn't think of anything—besides, why would someone bring a very young man with him if he was expecting trouble?

The man looked up and down the street and asked, "May we step inside and talk?"

"Certainly," Jeph replied, his suspicion being aroused by the man's discomfort. Though, oddly, the boy seemed delighted, though silent.

Jeph invited the two into the cramped storehouse, filled with full and empty barrels.

"Are we alone?" the man asked.

"We are, for now," Jeph replied.

"My name is Johnathan Clark, and I am your brother. This is William Clark, he's our brother as well."

Jeph was dumbstruck. He knew that he was a bastard child of someone named Clark, but other than to say that his father was a Virginian moved to Kentucky, his mother had always remained tight-lipped about her past.

Jonathan said, "I'm sorry that we meet like this. I wish it could be under different circumstances. I understand your mother passed. We just came from the Almshouse."

Jeph's emotions were alternating between anger, sorrow, and curiosity—even verging on joy. Did he dare believe he had a family? Why didn't his father help his mother? She didn't have to die. Why now?

Jonathan's words became softer, "I am truly sorry about your mother's death. There is no excuse for our father's lack of responsibility. But, as he has grown older and stronger in his faith, his conviction to reach out to you and her grew. We were hoping to provide a measure of assistance to her—and you."

Jeph glared at Jonathan, "I should ask you to leave. 'Assistance'? Now? After 22 years? I…"

Jonathan cut him off, "I understand your anger…" He looked at Jeph's wounded left hand. "Pardon me for asking, where did you receive your wound? You look familiar to me."

"I look familiar. Look in a mirror! We're brothers!"

"I fought at Monmouth. Under Sterling's wing. You were in the Malcolm's under Colonel Burr, weren't you?" Jonathan's face, reluctantly at first, transformed from discomfort to the happiness of meeting a comrade.

Jeph looked at Jonathan and shook his head, then smiled, "Damn you. Damn you, sir. Yes, yes, I was at Monmouth, and I stayed in the Army until we were all discharged a two months ago. And this," Jeph held up his left hand with its two missing fingers, "I got at Monmouth from a British ball."

Jonathan stuck his hand out, "Colonel Jonathan Clark, lately of the Continental Army, at your service."

Jeph sighed and smiled, taking Jonathan's hand, "Sergeant Jephtath Clark, also lately of the Continental Army, pleased to meet you, sir."

"Well, it's good to learn of your service and in upholding the traditions of the family name even though we weren't able to guide you ourselves. Our oldest brother is General George Rogers Clark, the Hannibal of the West!

Poor little William here, he hasn't done anything yet except shoot some squirrels."

William tentatively walked forward, "Pleased to meet you, sir."

"And you, young William."

"Do you still want to kick me out into the street?" Jonathan asked.

"I rather do, but I won't. You're a colonel and we shared too many battlefields for me to hold our father's indiscretion and sins against you," Jeph responded.

"Well, if I may, we'd like to have dinner with you and correspond. Father will be very proud to hear of your service. And, there's the small matter of why we came here. If I may, I'd like to give you the money we were directed to give to your mother. I'm sure it cannot compensate for your loss, but it is something, something of value that may help—especially because our Army pay certificates are still next to worthless!"

"So true," Jeph admitted.

Jonathan reached into a pocket in his vest and pulled out a small, though heavily laden leather satchel. "There's ten doubloons here."

One on hand, ten gold pieces worth three months good salary was hardly payment enough for his pain and his mother's latter years of distress and shame but on the other hand, this windfall was entirely unexpected and would greatly enhance his chances with Molly. Jeph swallowed his pride and accepted the leather pouch, "May I suggest we dine at the Fraunces Tavern?"

Chapter Eight – Office Work

June 10, 1784, Manhattan

Jeph now owned two sets of clothes; his tattered and patched work clothes, and a lightly used grey wool greatcoat, white breeches, long silk (!) stockings, and black shoes with pewter buckles. He still had his old army cocked hat. New hats were just too costly to justify the expense. Besides, a hat wouldn't be worn indoors where Jeph thought he'd meet with prospective employers.

Jeph had already met with one attorney. Randolph Jones was pushing 70 and had a modest business, mostly defending old Tories from the state of New York's efforts to confiscate and sell their property. The old man wasn't particularly interested and, when he heard Jeph fought in the Continental Army, he frowned and said he had no need for help. Just as he showed Jeph the door, he stopped, stroked his chin, and said, "There is one man I recommend you see, Colonel Burr. His practice is growing."

And with that, Jeph set out to find Burr, thinking the man was one in the same with his former commander.

It was two days since his meeting with Jones. Mr. Wallace had three dozen barrels of cider that came in on a flatboat from the apple orchards upriver. Jeph spent much of Wednesday delivering them to various taverns and inns around Manhattan. The day was damp and chilly for June. But he worked swiftly, wanting a few hours to track down Burr's place of business. He found it just as the sun was setting. While his back, arms, and feet ached, his pace back to Wallace's warehouse was faster than usual. Thursday would be the day.

Jeph slept well Wednesday night. He awoke, cleaned up as best he could, put on his new set of clothes for the second time, and then ate a large breakfast with coffee at the nearby tavern.

Colonel Burr's office was 11 blocks away. Jeph set out, walking deliberately to avoid mud and horse droppings made worse by last night's rainstorm. The temperature was far warmer than the day before and the sky was clearing. Jeph patted the sweat off his face and slowed his walk. He wanted to be fully collected when he met Burr.

Jeph strode up to Burr's office door and knocked. He heard a chair move back and footsteps. The door opened. Colonel Burr, the attorney, was indeed the same man as Colonel Burr, Jeph's former commander in the Malcolm's.

Burr looked him up and down and then said, "May I help you, sir?"

Jeph cleared his throat, "Yes sir, Colonel Burr, I'm Jephtath Clark. I served under your command at Monmouth."

Burr frowned, recalling the events of six years ago. There had been 500 of them at Valley Forge, reduced to 90 by the battle. This young man would have been a mere lad… "Of course!" Burr grinned, extending his hands, and grabbing Jeph's in an enveloping handshake, "Of course! Private Clark! You were magnificent! Please come in, how may I help you?"

Burr motioned for Jeph to sit and as he brought his own modest chair from out behind his desk to sit facing Jeph in front of a desk covered in papers and strewn about with envelopes.

"Thank you, sir." Jeph responded as he sat.

"How is that hand of yours?" Burr asked, reaching out for Jeph's left hand.

"Well enough. The fingers and thumb work fine," Jeph smiled.

"You're right-handed?"

"Thankfully, yes."

"How old are you now, Jeph?"

"Twenty-two, sir."

"Sixteen on the field of battle. You looked like a mere boy. But you fought better than most men that day. Did you stay in the army?"

"Until the end, sir. I stayed with the Malcolm's and made sergeant after you left. The unit was merged into Spencer's Regiment, so I lost my rank, but I made it back with the 2nd New York."

"Twice a sergeant, that's quite an achievement." Burr seemed genuinely interested, giving Jeph a rare boost. After the triumphant march into New York, he hadn't a thank you or a warm remark about his service since—it was as if the city yearned for the British occupation and the Redcoats' steady coin.

"Thank you, sir."

"So, to what do I owe the pleasure of a visit by an old comrade? You're not in need of a lawyer, are you?"

"No sir. I'm not in trouble. Sir, you may not recall, but before I enlisted, I apprenticed to a lawyer here in Manhattan. He was British and left when the British evacuated."

"Really?" Burr smiled, "So, you can both volley and write? Ha!" Burr laughed at his joke and Jeph chuckled along with his former commander.

"Do you have a clerk, sir?"

"Me, no, does it look like I need it?" Burr laughed again, sweeping a hand towards his cluttered desk. "You don't have to answer that, Sergeant Clark."

"I was thinking, sir, that I could be of assistance to you. I can organize your office, keep you in supplies, write letters…"

"How about collections? Are you able to help me with clients who owe me money? I'll give you five percent of fees you collect."

"Five percent?"

"Fine, 10 percent. Does that work for you, Mr. Clark? And, as for as help, I can't pay you much. My practice is just getting established. I can spare $5 a month." Burr's levity vanished.

"Yes sir," Jeph was calculating that he'd likely be earning a little less than he did in the back-breaking work he did for Mr. Wallace. It was a start.

"Well, do I have my first employee?" Burr asked.

"Yes sir, I'd be proud to serve Colonel Burr once again!"

"Say, Jephtath, you look as if you've done well for yourself, why work for me?"

Jeph blushed, "I thought the food in the Army was poor and paltry, but it got worse after I mustered out. There has been little work for former soldiers in the city—at least patriot soldiers. And the three months' pay I got in the form of promissory notes from Mr. Morris' are worthless. It's a minor miracle that I even acquired the funds to purchase these clothes."

Burr seemed interested in Jeph's story. "What have you done for work in the past half-year?"

"I've worked the docks for a few months and then I've worked delivering barrels of cider and beer."

"So, you know the docks? Interesting. What do the workers' think of our late revolution?"

Jeph sighed, "They think the food and coin was more plentiful under the British."

"Indeed. Jephtath, a word to the wise. Hold those notes from Robert Morris, if you can. Their value will increase in time. If you must, I'll loan you $10 in silver for those notes as collateral."

"Thank you, sir, that's very kind of you. I'll hold them for now, thank you."

"So, when can you start?"

"I need to tell Mr. Wallace and I can start on Monday, if that works for you, sir."

Burr rose and extended his right hand, "I'll see you then, Mr. Clark. Nine O'clock would be good. Please bring a pound of coffee beans, ink, and paper." Burr reached his left hand in his coat pocket, pulled out two Spanish silver dollars, and placed them in Jeph's left palm. "Bring me the change."

Jeph took the coins and saluted his once and future commander.

Burr grinned broadly and returned the salute.

Jeph walked out into the street, squinting in the bright mid-morning sun and barely missing a large pile of horseshit.

Chapter Nine – Complications

July 4, 1784, Manhattan

Ten gold doubloons could buy a lot in money-poor America. In only four weeks, Jeph bought two sets of new clothes, a pair of good shoes, and two hats. With his new attire, he looked for employment among the city's lawyers—seeking to pick up where his apprenticeship ended on his running away to join the Army—and quickly found it.

His work for Aaron Burr was a start, though he needed to support more attorneys if he was to make a proper living. At Burr's suggestion, he approached Alexander Hamilton and Henry Brockholst Livingston, both lawyers. Livingston owned a building with some office space and Jeph offered to tend to their professional supplies, write letters requesting payment and the like. The two men had agreed yesterday and, with Hamilton's junior partner, Richard Harison, that made four attorneys. Even better, Burr was inclined to rent from Livingston too. Helping four attorneys would pay the bills nicely, Jeph figured. Almost as important, the work was far more interesting—and less strenuous, than delivering barrels of beer and cider for old Mr. Wallace.

There was going to be an enormous Independence Day celebration—the first since the Treaty of Paris, formally ending the war with Britain, was signed and ratified—and Jeph planned on asking Molly to marry him. And, with July 4 falling on a Sunday, Molly would be free from her household servant duties.

Jeph walked up to the boardinghouse Molly called home and asked to see her. The clerk went back to let her know she had a visitor and came back flustered, "Miss Molly doesn't wish to see you, sir."

Jeph was puzzled, then afraid. Had he said something? Was Molly no longer interested in him? Jeph just stood in the hallway, not knowing what to do.

"Sir? Sir, you should be making your leave now," the clerk said as officiously as possible.

Slowly, Jeph turned to go when he heard Molly's voice from down the hall, "Wait!"

Jeph turned back to face her, relieved, but worried, "Molly…"

"We must speak. Walk with me," she said as she walked quickly out to the street. As she went by, Jeph could tell she'd been crying.

They started walking down the street, the hot late afternoon sun to their backs, with an occasional cool breeze coming off the ocean.

Jeph swallowed hard and said, "Molly, I asked you to join me for the Independence Day festivities because... because I... Molly, will you marry me? Will you be my wife?"

Molly broke down in tears.

"Molly?" Jeph asked with alarm. "Are you, are you..."

"Oh, Jeph, I cannot." Molly sobbed.

Jeph reached down and held Molly's hand. She squeezed his. Jeph waited silently as they walked towards the Hudson River.

"Jeph, I'm pregnant."

Jeph's heart sank, but he still clenched Molly's hand. There was something more to this.

"Oh Jeph." Molly strained to catch her breath.

They walked silently for a half a minute.

Molly lifted her head and stopped. She reached around and grabbed Jeph's right hand, facing him and then inhaled, "My master got drunk... He. He had me. He forced himself on me. He was drunk. Drunk and angry at his wife. He accused her of spending their household into bankruptcy. She spoke harshly to him and left to spend the night at her sister's house, but not before she threw dishes at him. It made a terrible mess. I was cleaning it up when... Oh Jeph, I'm so sorry!"

Jeph's anger at her employer was countered by his relief that Molly wasn't mad at him. They were both bastard children. But they didn't have to be captive to the circumstances of their birth. They could do better and Molly wasn't a willing participant. "Molly, will you marry me?"

Molly stopped and looked at Jeph, her dark brown eyes gazing directly into his (she was the same height). Molly grabbed Jeph's free left hand and squeezing both of his hands said, "Yes, yes, I will marry you Jephtath Clark, I will marry you."

They watched the fireworks together that night, got married the next week and rented a small house. Molly gave birth to their first child, a daughter, seven months later.

Chapter Ten – Pilgrimage of Paine

July 1785, Bordentown City, New Jersey

Burr had only met Thomas Paine only once. It was in New York City in 1776 during his brief posting to General Washington's staff. Paine's *Common Sense* was already spreading like wildfire among the colonies. But it was *The American Crisis* that sustained a 20-year-old Burr during that bitter, hungry winter in Valley Forge. Without *The American Crisis* there would have been no Monmouth. Without the meeting the British on their own terms at Monmouth, there would have been no Yorktown and the whole enterprise would have ended in tyranny and the hangman's noose.

Now Burr, 29, had fought a war, married, founded a bank (with his sometime rival, Hamilton), and had been elected the prior year to the New York State Assembly. Burr finally felt accomplished enough to make a pilgrimage to see the 48-year-old revolutionary.

Burr puzzled at Paine's almost supernatural ability to move men with the written word. He was even more interested to find out if the pamphleteer truly believed the words he poured forth.

Burr was almost to Paine's house. Only some 200 yards from the Delaware River separating New Jersey from Pennsylvania, Paine lived in the northern end of town in three story home—the top story featuring a steep gable with a narrow window.

Burr inhaled deeply. He had to admit he was a little nervous. And that feeling, being uncommon, intrigued him. He dug into a pocket for his handkerchief and mopped the sweat from his brow. Burr knocked at Paine's door.

Nothing.

Burr waited a minute and then knocked again, only louder.

Burr heard something fall inside the house. A book?

Footsteps.

Paine swung the door open in a cloud of whiskey. Paine steadied himself on the doorknob with his left hand, extending the right to Burr. "Ahh, Aaron Burr, if it isn't the young banker himself come to pay his respects. Please, come in."

Paine swallowed a burp. It was early afternoon on a Thursday. Paine wore ink-stained pants and a nightshirt, variously stained with ink and, by the looks of it, a couple of days of food. Burr took in the scene, the house was sparsely furnished, but paper was everywhere. Books too. And bottles. Many bottles. Some full. Most partially so. Some empties on the floor. A chamber pot, dangerously full, was near what appeared to be Paine's main writing desk. The place could use a good airing out.

Burr swallowed and followed a wobbly Paine inside.

"Please, sit, my boy." Paine swept a few papers and books off a wooden bench and sat himself in an overstuffed wingback chair. "What brings the bankers' catch fart out to see old Thomas?"

Burr laughed.

"Well?"

"May I join you in a drink?" Burr decided to be bold or go home.

"Harumpph. Oh, why not? Shall we toast?" Paine grabbed a glazed clay jug and poured some whiskey into two unmatched dirty glasses that that he snatched off the floor."

"To the revolution!" Burr toasted.

"Revolution, hell. That was no revolution." Paine frowned and then said solemnly, "To the people!"

"The people," Burr affirmed.

"You want to know what I think, boy? I'll tell you. Your 'revolution' was anything but. It might have been a good start. But it guttered out. The spirit of rebellion was spent in the war and in purging the Tories after leaving none left for the common people. Life, liberty, and happiness... Whose happiness? Whose liberty?"

Burr took a sip. It tasted like a potent moonshine from the hills of Western Pennsylvania.

"Burr. Aaron, right?"

"Sir."

"Aaron, how many people voted in New York's last election for governor? How many people put old Clinton back into office?

Burr paused, "In the 1783 gubernatorial election Clinton received about 3,600 votes."

"And his opponents?"

"There were two, Schuyler and Paine—I suppose no relation—together they took about 1,100 to 1,200 votes."

"Schuyler? General Schuyler? Owner of estates and men both? Who's Paine?"

"Ephraim Paine's a doctor. He was active in the provincial congress, a county court judge and a state senator."

"So, a man of substance."

"Yes, of means."

Burr sipped again. Paine took a long draught and refilled his glass.

"Tell me, how many people live in New York?"

"More than 300,000, I'd say."

"So, about 150,000 men." Paine was gathering to his point.

"Well, about 80,000 are men 16 and older."

"White men."

"Well, not Indians or slaves. There's about 20,000 slaves."

"So… and, I must admit, maths is not my strongest skill, less so with this." At which Paine gestured with his drink, took a gulp, and resumed, "So, 3,600 men—white men of property—voting to determine the fate of 300,000? Is that right? Do I have the numbers right?"

"More or less. Though if you include all the votes, close to 5,000."

"Fine then. Give it 5,000. You're the banker. What fraction is 5,000 of 300,000?"

"Well, that's 5 of 300… one in 60."

"Right, well, you have one in 60, all men of property, determining the lives of the other 59. Does that sound like a revolution to you, Aaron? What is it John Jay, our illustrious Secretary of Foreign Affairs, never tires of saying? 'Those who own the country ought to govern it.' Ehh? You own a bank. What do you think?"

It was a challenge. Burr sipped again, his tongue numbing a bit. "Well, I help run a bank. I don't own the Bank of New York."

"A distinction without a difference for our purposes, boy."

Burr chose his words carefully, "I believe our form of government is superior to monarchy. As you wrote yourself, monarchy is an institution of the devil, it has heathenish origins."

"True! I did write that. What else did I say about aristocracy along with monarchy?"

Burr felt he was back in Princeton—but with far more alcohol—and more filth.

"Twin tyrannies…"

"Close. Two ancient tyrannies."

"But we have neither monarchy nor aristocracy."

"Really? What do you call Washington, but a king in all but name? What of yourself? Hamilton? Jay? Hancock? The Adamses? Clinton? Morris? Deane? Even Jefferson! You're all aristocrats. Where is the common man or woman in your republic? And the slaves? Don't drive me to drink on the slaves! Your war for independence turned out to be nothing more than a scheme by the wealthy for the wealthy—just upset that old King George demanded a share. How much money do you suppose that bastard Silas Deane made on your war? And Morris! Robert Morris made a mint off the fighting. And John, 'those who own the country ought to govern it' Jay. How much did that merchant 'patriot' make? I hope he at least deposited some of that Spanish gold into your damn bank!"

"Political developments should be taken carefully, incrementally."

"Convenient."

"Not all the people are equipped to govern even themselves." Burr looked at the besotted democratic philosopher.

"Ah, so you're with Jay?"

"Let's just say that many believe that democracy leads to tyranny. That the passions of the masses govern widely and irresponsibly. Look at the Greeks. It's in the nature of men to be ruled by passion, not reason."

"But one of 60, Aaron? One of 60!" Paine's cloudy eyes started to smolder with righteous anger.

Burr noticed something that looked like a draftsmen's sketch on an adjacent table.

Paine smiled. "You like my bridge, boy? Perhaps your bank can build it."

Burr rose to look at it. Paine unsteadily joined him, the smell of whiskey likely covering other, less pleasant odors. "That's my iron bridge for Philadelphia over the Schuylkill River. A single-arch iron bridge of my own design." Paine's anger quickly ebbed.

Now Burr was truly impressed. Paine firmly believed the things he wrote during the war... *These are the times that try men's souls: The summer soldier and the sunshine patriot will, in this crisis, shrink from the service of his country*... and, *Tyranny, like hell, is not easily conquered; yet we have this consolation with us, that the harder the conflict, the more glorious the triumph.* But here was a practical side to the man he would have never imagined him having.

"So, do you have funding for your bridge?" Burr inquired.

"I do."

"From men of means? The city?" Burr pressed gently as they both stood looking at the design.

"Yes."

"So, wealth has its purpose?" Burr tried to make it not sound like a trap.

"Yes, but not to set itself above us as kings."

"Yet you own this house?"

"Yes."

"You can vote?"

"Yes."

"And you're a man of substance." It wasn't a question.

"I suppose I am now, though it weren't always so. I see where you're going, Burr. But know this. Your revolution has a distance yet to travel. You freed the merchants, the shippers, the bankers, the estate holders and you did so while making a bold claim, '...that all men are created equal, that they are endowed by their Creator with certain unalienable Rights, that among these are Life, Liberty and the pursuit of Happiness—That to secure these rights, Governments are instituted among Men, deriving their just powers from the consent of the governed—That whenever any Form of Government becomes destructive of these ends, it is the Right of the People to alter or to abolish it...' Impressed? Ha! I helped old Jefferson write it! Be mindful that the other 59 may take it upon themselves to think this promise applies to them as well. God help you when they do."

Burr lost himself in Paine's words the two days' ride back to New York City.

Chapter Eleven – Massachusetts Troubles

August 1786 through February 1787, Massachusetts

"The Hatfield Convention was a waste of parchment. The Boston merchants and lawyers won't listen to reason; they'll only listen to force!"

The speaker had a yeoman farmer's sinewy build, his face creased by years of toiling in the elements, his eyes, a sad intensity burned into them by the horrors of war. A militia veteran of Lexington, Bunker Hill, and the great victory over Gentleman Johnny Burgoyne in that fateful October of 1777 at Saratoga, Daniel Shays felt betrayed and desperate—he was angrier today than he ever was at King George and his agents. Promoted to captain before he was wounded in 1780, forcing his exit from service, Shays, and his fellow veterans had been sporadically paid for winning America's independence from Great Britain.

"What about Congress? If Congress pays us, we could pay our debts!" said Jimmy Wells, a militia soldier who saw action in Connecticut at 32, and now, 41, was facing foreclosure on his 60-acre farm in Hardwick. Like many other farmers in New England, he had borrowed hard cash to expand his operations late in the war when British General Cornwallis put the South to the torch in 1780. But when the war ended, farm commodity prices crashed, leaving him without cash to repay loans—or pay the higher taxes demanded by the Commonwealth of Massachusetts as they sought to repay their own wartime loans.

"The Con-tin-en-tal Congress!" Shays spat, "Do you think I'd've marched to Northampton under the red pine tree banner if I thought Congress would do right by us? Do you think Congress cares about its obligations? Hell, most of them dandy prats don't no bother to even attend their meetings. What good are they?"

Several farmer-militia pressed around Shays and Wells, nodding vigorously.

"It's twistical!" a large man from Barre said, "The Common Court already allowed them merchs to take my farm. No property, no vote. I got nowhere to go and nothing to lose!"

A militiaman from Shutesbury who was missing the last two fingers of his left hand chimed in. "You want twistical? I'll tell you twistical, ya' hear 'bout bloody Bowdoin's 'Slaves to the Commonwealth' scheme?"

Shays narrowed his eyes skeptically at the older man.

"T'ain't hookee walker, bloody end to me if I didn't hear it meself when last I was in Springfield. Governor Bowdoin figgers if'n we can't pay tax, we can sure as hell work. He's asked the legislature to ponder forcing us to leach potash in place of payment. Even the British wouldn't have dared enslaving us so!"

Shays drew a long breath, almost whistling it past his tobacco-stained teeth. He drew himself up and projected to the larger mass of minutemen, perhaps almost 1,000-strong, "Men, we can help our neighbors, our brothers and their families right here. We are in Hampshire County at the edge of Northampton to pay a visit to the Court of Common Pleas!"

The men roared their approval.

"Now, I want to make it plain clear, we have no quarrel with the town, nor anyone in it. But we cannot allow macaroni lawyers from Boston or judges who work for the merches to take our farms. To take our livelihood! That's not the freedom you and I fought for. So, we will march—march in good order down to the town square. Once there, we will mind our manners and be friendly. But, by Jove, we won't allow that court to convene. No judge, no attorney, will be allowed in the courthouse. Savvy?"

"Huzza! Huzza!"

The men were smiling broadly, some wearing threadbare Continental army uniforms, others turned out as local militia, and most adorning their tricorns with sprigs of hemlock, as was the custom in the late conflict with England.

No farms were foreclosed that day as no judge or lawyer could work. The Northampton Insurrection was about to burst into Shays' Rebellion.

"The commotions and temper of numerous bodies in the eastern country, present a state of things equally to be lamented and deprecated. They exhibit a melancholy verification of what our Transatlantic foes have predicted, and of another thing perhaps… that mankind when left to themselves, are unfit for their own government. I am mortified beyond expression… I am lost in amazement… that the great body of the people, though they will not act, can be so short-sighted, or enveloped in darkness, as not to see rays of a distant sun through all this mist of intoxication and folly.

"You talk, my good sir, of employing influence to appease the present tumults in Massachusetts. I know not where that influence is to be found, nor, if attainable, that it would be a proper remedy for these disorders. Influence is not government. Let us have a government by which our lives,

liberties, and properties, will be secured, or let us know the worst at once. Under these impressions, my humble opinion is, that there is a call for decision. Know precisely what the insurgents aim at. If they have real grievances, redress them if possible, or acknowledge the justice of them, and your inability to do it in the present moment. If they have not, employ the force of government against them at once. If this is inadequate, all will be convinced that the superstructure is bad, or wants support.

"These are my sentiments. Precedents are dangerous things. Let the reins of government, then, be braced and held with a steady hand, and every violation of the constitution be reprehended. If defective, let it be amended, but not suffered to be trampled upon while it has an existence."

Letter by George Washington to Henry Lee, October 31, 1786

"Rebellion against a king may be pardoned, or lightly punished, but the man who dares to rebel against the laws of a republic ought to suffer death."

Samuel Adams, Massachusetts, revolutionary orator, brewer

"A little rebellion now and then is a good thing. It is a medicine necessary for the sound health of government. God forbid that we should ever be twenty years without such a rebellion."

Letter by Thomas Jefferson from Paris to James Madison, January 30, 1787

"Our present federal government is a name, a shadow, without power or effect."

Henry Knox, Boston bookshop owner turned general of artillery

---

Shays' Rebellion gathered strength in fits and starts, starting in Western Massachusetts and rolling east towards Boston. They called themselves "Regulators" in honor of a popular movement by the same name that aimed to stamp out corruption among royal colonial officials in North Carolina nearly 20 years earlier. They demanded an end to the foreclosures and tax levies in hard currency—something only the Boston merchants had ready access to. They also wanted the issuance of easy paper money and its acceptance for mortgage and tax debt—something done in neighboring Rhode Island after that state's government was essentially seized by a mob.

When the Regulators took control of a town, they acted to stop the Commonwealth's courts, replacing their functions with local council—a people's court of sorts. All lawyers were, of course, expelled as agents of an oppressive system. Other Commonwealth officials were also exiled.

Once the common people had the courts in control and with the check of formal law and order exiled, the Regulators would set about methodically destroying all the court records: loan documents, tax records, and even records of birth and death. By this effort, they aimed to restore land to farmers whom they believed had been wrongfully dispossessed by the rich and powerful.

As the Regulator's rebellion grew, it represented a clear and present danger to the merchants of Boston. Not only was their wealth being destroyed by the dissolution of contracts, but law and order itself had rapidly disintegrated.

Governor John Hancock saw the coming trouble in 1785 and offered his resignation as governor, vainly hoping that the legislature would beg him to stay on and give him the power to address the growing crisis. They didn't. Instead, James Bowdoin, running on a platform of fiscal responsibility, won a bitter three-way contest for governor that was so close, the legislature—known as the General Court—had to decide it.

And now Governor Bowdoin, seeing the rebels gathering strength, burning court records, and closing in on Boston, acted. He and other wealthy merchants raised private funds to finance a 3,000-strong militia. They appointed Benjamin Lincoln to lead it. Lincoln was formidable, having been a Revolutionary War General and the young nation's first Secretary of War when the Battle of Yorktown was won in 1781. And now Lincoln was marching out with his private militia to meet Shays and thousands of armed and angry farmers.

Shays and his democratic militia were spread out over Massachusetts, focusing their efforts on stopping the courts to save their farms. If they had a plan to march on Boston and lay siege to it as the Patriots had done to the British only a decade before, Lincoln was about to spoil it, marching first to Worcester on January 19, 1787.

Daniel Shays was in a dilemma; his rebellion had grown more quickly and been more successful than he could have ever hoped for. But, by its nature, the rebellion was practical—self-serving, even. Farmers aimed to protect their land, no more, no less. As a result, Shays found it impossible to concentrate his forces. They also lacked an animating principle and now they were growing scared.

At Governor Bowdoin's urging, the General Court had prohibited speech critical of the government and suspended habeas corpus while offering two concessions to the farmers: that some prior tax liens could be paid with goods instead of coin while pardons would be granted upon taking an oath of allegiance to the Commonwealth.

Even so, warrants had been served on several of the protest leaders, with some already arrested. More of Shays men thought that the government in Boston was moving from merely avaricious to tyrannical.

Shays thought it wise to pull back from around Boston and reprovision his forces from the big armory at Springfield—an armory and arms factory run by the Confederation Congress.

Shays and his makeshift staff of four officers rode into Worcester from the west on a crisp winter midmorning. He was gut-foundered, having not eaten since breakfast yesterday. Up ahead, in the town square next to the courthouse, he saw the militia, as he expected, but immediately knew something was amiss.

About 100 yards from the square, he saw some men point at him and trot out to intercept his party.

Then he saw it. On a branch of a large tree that spread out over the square was a body hanging from a rope. Judging by his still gently swinging form, he was freshly executed.

"Who are you, sir?" the lead militiaman challenged.

"Daniel Shays, sir. And you? What's the meaning of this? Who is there hanging and what did he do to deserve it?"

"Ah, damn it all. I'm Jack Fisher. I'm captain of the company from Oxford."

"Are you in command here?"

"No, sir. There's... well, really no one is in command. We haven't taken a vote yet to elect a regimental leader."

"And the man hanging there, who is he?"

"Sir, I was just going to try to find out myself when I saw you riding up."

Shays frowned and pushed his horse past Fisher and his six of his men. Now red faced with rage he bellowed, "I'm Daniel Shays! Who hung this man and what was his crime?"

A man bundled up against the cold looking about 35 stepped forward, "We hung 'em. He was a lawyer. He was going to take our farms for the dandies in Boston."

"Not any more he ain't!" roared a man from the somewhere behind the tree. There was scattered laughter among the militia that melted away as Shays grew angrier.

"Who accused this man? Who hung him?" Shays demanded again.

The first man looked up at Shays and then looked at the frozen ground. "I did. We did. We did it to save our farms. We told him to leave for Boston. He refused. He insisted on going to the courthouse to file against us."

"You insufferable fool! You've brought ruin to our cause—to your cause…"

There was a shout at the edge of the square from the direction of the morning sun. "It's General Lincoln! It's the Boston army!"

Musket rang out. The Regulators had been completely caught off guard. They had no pickets, no warning, and most of them were milling about simply admiring the dead lawyer.

The militia panicked and ran.

Shays pulled out a pistol and shot the hangman in the head. The man crumpled to the ground a bloody mess with the men around him too terrified of Lincoln's onrushing legion to react.

Shays wheeled his horse around and rode hard for Palmer, 33 miles to the east about two-thirds of the way to the national armory at Springfield.

General Lincoln forced his hand and now the only hope of overthrowing the emerging tyranny out of Boston were the muskets, cannon, ball, shot, and powder at the arsenal. The Springfield armory must be taken.

A week later, after delays to prepare, Shays and his army were ready to seize the armory, attacking it from three sides.

After the defeat at Worcester, Shays had lost contact with the enemy. His forces had not developed an efficient staff system, reconnaissance, or spy apparatus. They barely had time to elect leaders and encourage them to institute discipline and drill. Time was running out.

Shays approached the armory from the east, keenly aware that General Lincoln was somewhere behind him with an unknown force. Colonel Parsons was to be approaching from the north from Chicopee. Colonel Day, from West Springfield.

Shays rode at the head of 800 grimly determined militia were just in sight of the armory when one of Parsons' men galloped up to signal that Parsons'

500 were formed up and waiting to converge on the armory. Still, no word from Day to the west. Shays frowned.

"Regiment! Form up in ranks!" Shays frowned again. He was never very good at formal drill. Still, enough of the men had served, either as militia or with the Continental Army, they formed into company ranks quickly enough.

"To the forward, march!"

A volley of musket fire and smoke emitted from the direction of the armory. None of Shays men fell, though there was some consternation. Most of the men thought—hoped—that the national government would remain neutral. The gunfire from the armory suggested otherwise.

Shays' men closed another 50 yards and then he saw it. A force of more than 1,000 men, with supporting cannon—no doubt from the armory—and they were militia, turned out with the same haphazard uniforms as his men. Boston beat him to it!

The Boston men, having first tried to warn off the Shaysites, now let loose with grape shot. Two dozen men went down. Shays' command disintegrated and fled, some south to Rhode Island, others to New Hampshire, but most rallied, first at Amherst and then Petersham. What else could they do? It was fight or lose everything to the lender or the state.

Lincoln and his 3,000 Eastern men came on in remorseless pursuit, not even stopping for a blinding snowstorm on the bitter night of February 3. Lincoln caught the Regulators on the 4th and achieved complete surprise, driving 1,000 rebels out to Vermont and states to the west, though many slinked home in the hope that burnt loan records would be enough to save their farms.

Back in Boston, the very day that Lincoln crushed the Shaysites at Petersham, the General Court was busy. Legislators passed a bill authorizing martial law, as well as appropriating funds to reimburse Lincoln and his wealthy supporters who had raised the money for his army. To curtail rebel political power in the rural areas, the legislature soon after passed the Disqualification Act which prohibited former rebels from holding public office.

Lincoln's victory over the rebels wasn't without a high personal cost—in the last skirmish at Williamstown in the northwest corner of Massachusetts, a Regulator's rifle round found the general. He lingered for six days in pain and delirium, victim of a gut wound.

Sympathy rebellions—no more than riots, really—sprang up in New York and a few other areas as well. But the crisis of Shays' Rebellion seemed at an end. In Massachusetts, almost 4,000 farmers signed confessions, and hundreds were indicted.

Some of the rebel leaders who might have been encouraged to return home saw the hardening attitude in Boston and decided that prudence dictated remaining out of state, with Vermont and Rhode Island being the main hideaways.

The four breakaway New York counties forming Vermont, a de facto independent republic, continued to hold their own against New York in the Green Mountain War. Ethan Allen and his Green Mountain Boys routinely expelled New York tax collectors and land surveyors, while few New York militia could be talked into confronting the large and irascible Allen.

When Massachusetts sent an extradition delegation to Rhode Island, the people's assembly there invited them to observe the proceedings as they debated whether to grant Massachusetts request. The men from Boston recognized two Shaysites on the floor of Rhode Island's upper house. When they asked Rhode Island leaders why these two ringleaders of the rebellion were on the floor, participating in the proceedings, the reply was that they were made honorary members of the Senate! The Massachusetts men went home without their quarry.

Governor Bowdoin requested extradition of the rebels from adjoining states, but only Connecticut, New Hampshire, and New York agreed. By spring 1787, hundreds of rebels had been convicted of treason and the gallows had claimed 45 Shaysites, some say in revenge for Lincoln's killing. Many of the men found it hard to get legal representation after the Regulators' hanging of the young attorney from Cambridge.

It was only John Hancock's return as governor after the April election that spared hundreds more rebels from the noose. Hancock's pardon was dimly viewed by his peers, with the commonwealth's chief justice, William Cushing, denouncing Hancock's clemency for "Evil minded demagogues and ignorant, unprincipled, bankrupt, and desperate rabble-rousers."

Cushing's anger could be well understood—some 4,000 rebellious farmers were still in Vermont and, to a lesser extent, New York, where they kept up a low-level guerilla effort aimed at making Boston miserable.

Chapter Twelve – Confederacy

September 1786, Wyandot village, Ohio Territory

Weyapiersenwah was impressed by the size of the gathering which included dozens of Iroquois chiefs who spurned his warnings 13 years ago, turning their backs on the Shawnee as they fought alone against the white man on the Ohio frontier. And now, here they were, some three dozen nations, meeting in council, with same British who defeated his tribe in what they called Lord Dunmore's War.

"Blue Jacket! An honor to see you."

It was an English officer who was present at the close of the Dunmore's War at the Treaty of Camp Charlotte in 1774. The Seneca-Cayuga chief, Logan, refused to attend the proceedings, blaming a white man for massacring his family. That man, Cresap, wasn't guilty; another white man was.

Simon Girty, a white man captured in a Seneca raid and raised in their ways, delivered a statement from Logan at the treaty meeting. For Weyapiersenwah, three poignant memories remain from Girty's speech on behalf of Logan. First, that Logan professed his love for the whites which caused him to remain idle in his cabin. Second, that Logan, when moved to revenge for the killing of his family, felt no fear. And third, the close of Logan's Lament, "Who is there to mourn for Logan? Not one."

Weyapiersenwah, known as Blue Jacket among the whites, turned to the Englishman, "And an honor to see you. Many nations are gathered today and you as well. I thought your king surrendered to the Americans. Why are you here?"

The officer clenched his jaw and then forced a smile. "We seek your friendship. We share an enemy. Unless we unite, the colonists will push into your lands, will take your lands, and will kill your people."

"And when the whites keep coming, who will mourn our passing? You?"

"There are 35 nations here. Some of them stood by and did nothing when you fought. They are here now. Together, you can defend your hunting grounds. Together, with our help. Please, follow me. There is something I wish to show you. A gift for you, Blue Jacket. For you and your brothers."

Weyapiersenwah expected the officer was going to show him blankets or farm tools—and then expect his tribe to fight the whites from the east. To color the Ohio red with his people's blood on behalf of a distant king who wanted his own revenge for the embarrassment of losing to his children.

The officer headed towards the river where there were eight large rafts. Weyapiersenwah saw Miami and Wabash warriors unloading the rafts and carefully stacking hundreds of muskets, kegs of powder, flints, and yes, blankets too.

Weyapiersenwah smiled at the sight. If only he had such support 13 years ago. Of course, he was then fighting the English king and his settlers. Now they split and have become enemies. "What do you want from the United Indian Nations? Such a great 'gift.' Your expectations must be greater."

The Englishman returned the smile. "It is not up to us to presume to tell the confederacy what to do. But we would suggest that you reject the treaty signed at Fort Finney. Agreeing to allow settlement north of the Ohio River will only lead to more violence, more death, and more settlers. You must make a stand if you are to keep your hunting grounds."

Weyapiersenwah knew the officer was right. He also knew that the English didn't really care if his tribe lived or died. They only cared that they would fight. And today they were providing the tools for him and many other nations to do just that.

Chapter Thirteen – Green Mountain Boys

March 1787, New York and the Republic of Vermont

Burr was in a quandary. He had left the New York State Assembly almost two years earlier to focus on his thriving law practice and his wife, Theodosia. His first child, named for her mother, was almost four and his wife was pregnant with their second child together. Further, Burr found his wife's chief servant, Mary Emmons, 27, originally from the opposite ends of the British Empire in Calcutta by way of Saint-Domingue, to be irresistible. Mary was pregnant too and Burr wasn't quite sure if Theodosia knew or, if she did, whether she simply accepted Burr for what he was, good and otherwise.

But Burr's attention wasn't fixed on his domestic complications, but rather on Vermont, Hamilton (*Hamilton!*), and Governor George Clinton.

Burr was closely following Hamilton's efforts to quench the Shaysites brushfire as his rival was rumored to be trying to broker a deal between New York and the would-be governor of Vermont, Thomas Chittenden, and Ethan Allen—the real power in the Vermont Republic. The deal was simple: promise to expel the Shaysites to face justice in Massachusetts and, in return, New York would relinquish its territorial claims and support Vermont's inclusion as the 14th state.

Hamilton had a few advantages in his efforts. First, he was the one who brokered the prisoner of war exchange that resulted in Ethan Allen's release from almost two years of brutal British captivity and had stayed in touch with the odd and mercurial man. Second, Hamilton was said to have secured the approval of his wealthy father-in-law, Philip Schuyler, to abandon his extensive land claims in Vermont. Third, Hamilton had already drafted a bill in the Assembly to formalize his scheme—Burr knew because he paid the clerk of the Assembly to keep him informed of such developments emanating from the Old Royal Exchange where it moved to after the Congress of the Confederation displaced it from the Old New York City Hall.

Lastly, Burr was aware of Hamilton's likely involvement in a secret convention aimed at overturning the national government. Hamilton's role in this effort furthered Burr's worry that it might impair his own political ambitions.

Burr resolved to put a fly or two in Hamilton's Vermont ointment. If he couldn't stop Hamilton from granting the Vermont Republic its legitimacy as a state, perhaps he could encourage Ethan Allen to continue to allow the Regulators to conduct their politics outdoors with shot and musket instead of quill and debate as with indoors politics. After all, the Vermonters were nothing if not conniving, as it was Ira, Ethan's younger brother, who almost negotiated Vermont's return to the crown with Frederick Haldimand, the British governor of Quebec, late in the war for independence—with negotiations only collapsing on word of the defeat and capture of General Cornwallis at Yorktown only six years ago in 1781.

As much as he hated to take time out of the city, Burr decided to risk a visit to Allen in his lair at the Catamount Tavern in Bennington, first traveling 150 miles up the Hudson by boat, then 40 miles overland to the east by horse. If he hurried, and the winds and road conditions cooperated, he could be there in three days.

Burr smiled, as he often did, when a plan came together.

Chapter Fourteen – The Federalist

October 23, 1787, New York City

Jeph looked up at the approach of footsteps down the hall at the law offices he managed for the four attorneys, Hamilton, Burr, Henry Brockholst Livingston, and Richard Harison. Burr squared himself in the doorframe, smiled, and started to speak as Jeph jumped to his feet, "Colonel Burr, sir, how may I help you?"

"Have you seen Mr. Hamilton? I've a case I wish to discuss with him"

"Colonel Hamilton has been entertaining a man from Virginia—a delegate to Congress I believe. I saw Mr. Jay there as well when I delivered writing supplies to them yesterday."

"Ah, our proprietor's brother-in-law," Burr said, referring to Livingston, "Perhaps that explains why Mr. Jay wasn't over for dinner last night as expected. Where are they? I need to speak to Mr. Hamilton."

"Yes, sir. They're on the second floor of the boarding house just down the street from City Hall."

"Oh?"

"31 Wall Street."

"Thank you, Sergeant Clark."

"Colonel Burr."

Three days later Burr's network surmised that the Virginian Jeph mentioned was James Madison, in town as a delegate to the Congress of the Confederation but more importantly, one of the architects of the Philadelphia constitution that was soon due up for ratification by the states. Of note, Madison, Burr discovered, had been absent from his duties in Congress for the past week.

It all made sense though—that Madison would be working with Hamilton and Jay to overturn the present government and replace it with something more to their liking. Burr admitted the present government was entirely unsuited to preserving the nation in the face of rapacious European powers. Further, he suspected the new form might check his own grand ambitions— besides, fear of Europe and chaos could be useful tools in his hands. Burr feared the proposed constitution would become a net cast to ensnare and enfeeble great men—as the thousands of tiny ropes the Lilliputians cast over Gulliver.

Burr knew that Governor Clinton had already started to write criticisms of the proposed constitution, writing under the penname "Cato" only four weeks earlier with another Clinton confederate writing under "Brutus" just last week. And now here was Hamilton—he was sure of it—writing as "Publius" in the *Independent Journal*.

Burr thought his own reputation was too important to dissipate in public debate. And, while ideas were nearly impossible to kill, he didn't need to kill an idea, he just needed to kill ratification.

Even so, Burr discovered that the trio intended to publish additional letters, not only in the *Independent Journal*, but also in the *Daily Advertiser* and the *New-York Packet*. Burr was close to the publisher of one and he had heard that the other was in a degree of financial difficulty—perhaps a degree of friendly persuasion might hobble Hamilton's effort. Or, perhaps a more energetic course of action was called for.

Chapter Fifteen – A New Nation?

January 1788, New York City

"Well, what's the word from the Coffee House?" said George Clinton, his pale blue eyes smiling over his reading spectacles. Clinton, governor of New York for the past 11 years, had many concerns, among them, staying in power with stopping the new national constitution a close second.

Burr guardingly returned Clinton's smile. "Hamilton is still holding court. McDougall's and Seton's Bank of New York continues strong. Most of the Chamber of Commerce has turned against your tariffs and especially against your paper money."

"You support the tariffs."

"I did. But New Yorkers see them as yours. The tariffs are crushing the city. The money you printed is a problem too."

"And are still popular in the rest of the state. Besides, we need the revenue as there aren't many Tory estates left to seize."

"True. But Hamilton has made inroads in your strongholds too. He's gotten the attention of the Van Cortlandts, the Schuylers, and even the Livingstons!"

One of Clinton's eight house servants, a Black slave woman of about 40 named Beulah, quietly entered the meeting room.

"Tea?" Clinton asked.

"Yes, please, thank you." Burr looked at the woman and nodded. She briefly returned his look and then looked down. Burr never quite understood Clinton's founding membership in the New York Manumission Society along with Hamilton and John Jay who owned five slaves himself. But Clinton was determined to maintain a base in heavily Dutch Kings, Richmond, and Ulster counties where slaves worked the farms. Even so, the legislature passed a gradual manumission bill two years earlier, only to see it quickly vetoed by the Council of Revision because it subsequently denied free Blacks the right to vote or run for office.

Burr turned to Clinton, "Your support in the city is almost gone. Hamilton has gathered the Tories to the Federalists. The residents suffer. Artisans, mechanics, and tradesmen are with him. The British continue to dump cheap shoes and hats into the city—some hatters have even given up and moved south."

"But—assuming we could raise the revenue overwise—how would lifting the import duty or the double duty on West Indies goods end English dumping? If anything, they could drop their prices even more."

"Since when has logic moved political thought among the people?" Burr said matter-of-factly.

"Hell, what if we doubled tariffs? Tripled? Eventually the English won't be able to afford to keep cutting prices, right?"

"True, but you wouldn't be able to get it past Hamilton and the Assembly."

"But Hamilton loves tariffs!" Clinton snorted.

"He does! He does... just not for the State of New York. He wants only the national government to have the authority to enact tariffs."

"All the more reason to oppose his Philadelphia constitution." Clinton gently smacked the table, but, as a big man at six feet tall, his beefy hand still caused a drop or two of tea to splash out of his cup. Clinton's ire was stoked by the fact that he had initially supported Hamilton's quest to revise the Articles of Confederation to forge a stronger national union—until he realized that Hamilton's tariffs would eclipse his own and leave him searching for another source of revenue that, falling on the people, would be politically unpopular.

"And that's what I've been working on while you've been playing 'Cato' in the newspapers," Burr said blandly.

Had he used a different tone in his house, Clinton would have had a right to be insulted, but it was Burr. Burr was practical. "I thought it important to continue to counter Hamilton and his band of federalist writers," Clinton responded, almost pleading.

"Words won't solve this challenge. Words rarely do... unless they're promises. Action is better. Money, better still," Burr was talking to the air as if the Governor of New York was a thousand miles away.

Clinton leaned forward, "Speaking of money, I heard you're buying property; a considerable amount of it. Are you speculating in the Northwest?"

"Ohio? No, too risky. The British still occupy the frontier forts. And Carleton in Quebec has increased shipments of muskets, powder, and clothing to the Shawnee, Miami, and other tribes. You can buy land north of the Ohio but try to farm it and you'll be scalped for your trouble."

"But you are buying land..."

Burr looked annoyed, "Yes."

"You're not stockjobbing are you?" Clinton briefly clenched his jaw.

"I'm doing no more or less than any other son of New York who has high confidence in your governorship."

Clinton seemed resigned, "So, soldiers' pay certificates and state bonds. Did you acquire any Tory lands?"

"A few modest parcels along the Hudson, nothing ostentatious," Burr was growing bored.

"Try to keep it that way. The almshouse is still overflowing. Hamilton is stirring up trouble over the number of debtors in jail. The Society's treasury is almost empty. The last thing we need is people starving and freezing this winter while one of my closest associates is out buying up land with the profits from stockjobbing."

Burr decided he had enough of Clinton's moral posturing. "I understand that 50 slaves were sold south out of the city last week. It seems there a fear that gradual manumission will lead to abolition. There are still almost 10,000 slaves in the city and up the valley. That's about a million and a half dollars' worth of slaves. There's talk that a few freemen are being kidnapped and sold south."

"I expect the Legislature to send me a revised slave code soon."

"But it won't close the harbor to slavers. At least that's my understanding," Burr now stared at Clinton with an uncomfortable intensity.

"One step at a time, Aaron. We can't afford to lose anymore Dutch votes," Clinton's eyes were tired, perhaps sad. "Let's talk about Massachusetts. Their constitutional convention starts in a fortnight. Do you have any word on how it will go? Can it be stopped?"

"Perhaps. I've put in motion some plans. I've been in touch with the Regulators and have encouraged them to give up on their politics outdoors and try some indoors now." Burr's countenance betrayed a barely concealed gleefulness.

"I see. But how can they participate? Even if they've been pardoned, they have no property. They can't meet the threshold." Clinton was puzzled.

"Stockjobbing, you say? Well, I call it a prudent investment in our future and the future of New York." Burr beamed.

"You didn't!" Clinton's look of astonishment was quickly overtaken by joy.

"Let's just say that there will be more farmers participating in the convention than Sam Adams, Hancock, and Bowdoin expect." Burr smiled broadly and then took a big gulp of the now-cooled tea.

"I hesitate to say that I underestimated you, Aaron." Clinton sat back in his ornate high-backed chair and stroked his chin once, looking at Burr with a sparkle in his eyes. The old politician had a few more tricks up his sleeve, even if most of them were named "Burr."

Chapter Sixteen – Practical Politics

June 15, 1788, Poughkeepsie, New York

Burr rode alone. He was heading north for a meeting at an inn, and he found his mind divided on a multitude of concerns.

The gathering darkness brought out the fireflies which were making a slightly early appearance this year.

Burr hadn't spent much time in Poughkeepsie, though it was on the northern edge of his last active-duty assignment in 1779. The most important thing about Poughkeepsie was that it was on the eastern flank of the Hudson River and only 60 miles away from Great Barrington where Burr had acquired a goodly number of friends who owed him.

Burr puzzled over his options.

Seven states had ratified the constitution, which specified that nine of 13 approving would activate it—quite contrary to the spirit of the Confederation, which operated on unanimous agreement among the 13 states. Although Burr had to admit, that was rather the point of the new system.

The Federalists clearly lost momentum in February when the Massachusetts convention unexpectedly voted to adjourn, 178 ayes to 176 nays, without approving the new constitution. His efforts to re-enfranchise a few strategically placed farmers worked, with just enough margin for safety that he didn't begrudge the investment.

Then, a week later, the New Hampshire convention convened on February 13. This was a chance for the Federalists to regain momentum. But the meeting broke up nine days later without ratifying. It served them right. General John Sullivan, the President of New Hampshire, and his friend and predecessor, Portsmouth shipping merchant John Langdon, schemed to call the legislature into session in January in Exeter, less than 10 miles from Portsmouth, to call for the convention when the roads in the Antifederalist western and northern parts of the state were encumbered with snow and ice. The stratagem worked. So did the effort to soften the state up with a major effort to encourage the public's patriotic sentiments. A large network of pastors, fearing sinful anarchy, helped. Yet, there was enough bitterness remaining from the Shays' business down south—egged on by Burr—that the meeting couldn't overcome its divisions.

Clinton was ecstatic and shed his politically tempered caution to boldly announce against the new constitution, rallying supporters to the status quo cause of maintaining the Confederation.

The third blow was expected when Rhode Island met in raucous town meetings across the state in late March. The state's growing reputation for lawlessness and violence aimed at Tories and Federalists caused the latter to avoid the town meetings for fear of tar and feathers—or worse. Rhode Island voters rejected ratification, 2,708 to 237.

So, now the score stood at seven approved to one rejected with three states yet to take a vote and another two that had adjourned without taking action. Approval from any two of the five would likely trigger the founding of a new governmental structure—one that would greatly disadvantage New York—and Burr's plans.

Burr ticked through the sequence: three in December with tiny Delaware on a unanimous vote, Pennsylvania where the Antifederalists, though strong, were outmaneuvered by the Federalists who used persuasion by force to bring the Antis to the chamber for a vote, winning a tainted victory 46 to 23, and then New Jersey, unanimous again; Georgia and Connecticut by wide margins in January; then New Hampshire and Massachusetts dealing the Federalists crushing twin blows in February; Rhode Island rejecting in March; then Maryland breaking three maddening months with no action, approving in April followed by a more contentious than expected ratification convention in South Carolina in May, approving on a vote of 128 to 94.

Seven states.

Now Virginia had gathered on June 2 in Richmond to consider the new form of government. Word had traveled north that Patrick Henry, leading the Antifederalists, challenged the very authority of those who met in Philadelphia the prior summer and their arrogant claim of speaking for "We, the people" instead of "We, the states." Fresh dispatches also cited George Mason's warnings that a stronger central government would crush Virginians with taxation, destroy liberty, and via the courts, eventually destroy state sovereignty. But to these encouragements, Burr also heard of troubling news that Virginians who had served under Washington had been forged into a cohesive Federalist army and were determined to sweep away Henry's passionate speeches and overcome Mason's warnings.

And then news arrived that Sullivan and Langdon had already arranged to make another run at it since New Hampshire didn't explicitly reject the constitution in February, they simply adjourned. It was set to start June 18, only a day after New York's gathering was scheduled to kick off. If both states ratified, the constitution would go into effect.

So, three conventions going simultaneously with Burr only able to truly influence events in New York, though he calculated that the narrow loss in Massachusetts would probably auger well for continued failure in New

Hampshire as some of his "friends" among the Regulators might be inspired to action.

The waxing moon was only three days from full, allowing Burr to see the inn's outline among the trees before he could see the dim candlelight casting through the windows.

He tied up his horse to a hitching post. There were three other horses tied up as well as a two-horse coach. The coach belonged to an owner of substance. Burr frowned in the dark and then quietly walked into the roadhouse.

Burr's eyes swept the room. There, a table with two somewhat rough men looking to be in their late 30s. There, a man dining alone. And... Damn! Zephaniah Platt, a Dutchess County judge and one of Clinton's Antifederalist allies! One of the two men looked up from his ale and started to motion at Burr who immediately turned around and exited the tavern.

Burr tended to his horse, splitting his attention between his mount and the inn's door. Seconds later, one of the two men from the table opened the door and looked around.

Burr hissed, "We can't meet here."

The man approached, looking quizzical in the pale light.

Burr passed the man some coins. "This is for your dinner and drink. Fetch your friend and ride north 100 yards and we'll talk," Burr said in a soft voice.

The man nodded and disappeared back into the roadhouse.

Burr mounted up and slowly made his way north, fireflies and occasional shafts of moonlight illuminating the heavily wooded road ahead.

Chapter Seventeen – Deliberations on the Hudson

July 2, 1788, Poughkeepsie, New York

Governor George Clinton still felt confident. Almost two weeks earlier, word arrived from Concord, the site of the New Hampshire's second attempt at ratifying the new constitution—the meeting site moved north and inland from Exeter as an olive branch to the more populous interior reaches of the state—failed again. The effort faltered when abolitionist and former Loyalist Joshua Atherton made a motion to make ratification take effect only upon amendments to the document, especially one that outlawed slavery. Federalists knew this to be anathema to the South—even delegates as far north as New York might balk at such a bold, absolutist move. After the convention rejected Atherton's amendments, he moved to adjourn the proceedings—and won.

Then, this morning, a dispatch arrived from Richmond: Virginia approved the constitution on a vote of 85 to 83. It would all come down to New York and North Carolina, though Clinton understood the North Carolinian effort to be doomed—the state did, after all, birth the original Regulator Movement to oppose corrupt colonial officials, with violent unrest lasting six years through 1771. The people of North Carolina, like Rhode Island, were highly distrustful of a powerful central government.

Still, there were a few things troubling Clinton. First, he hadn't seen or heard from Aaron Burr in three weeks. And second, and he prayed to God, unrelated to his lieutenant, there were whisperings of foul play. John Sloss Hobart, a New York Justice of the Supreme Court of Judicature and an ardent Federalist, was missing. He left New York by carriage on June 16 and never arrived in Poughkeepsie.

Could Hobart have been the victim of a violent scheme, or was he waylaid by a highwayman? Clinton knew the delegates—all of them. He was confident that Antifederalists held sway some two-to-one, which, he thought, would make a politically motivated attack on Hobart superfluous and even potentially deleterious to the Antifederalist cause if uncovered.

Even so, the Federalists, constantly seeking advantage, urged a full debate of the new constitution line-by-line, paragraph-by-paragraph by a committee of the whole—meaning all delegates could participate in the discussion. By this tactic, the Federalists hoped that word of the constitution's ratification in New Hampshire and Virginia would make it to Poughkeepsie in time to reverse the growing momentum in favor of the Antifederalists. With the eighth and ninth state in hand and the effort a fait accompli, the Federalists then expected their opponents would give in and allow the fifth-most populous state to join the new union. To ensure news of their success reached New York, the Federalists set up a special courier system connecting Concord and Richmond to Poughkeepsie. But news of the second failure of New Hampshire to ratify had the opposite of the intended effect.

Even so, the entire Federalist contingent operated as one while Clinton's Antifederalists split into four sides, roughly equal in strength: those opposing any new union and thus, in support of the status quo; those who favored ratification after a certain number of years, pending the adoption of amendments; those who supported ratification conditional upon the addition of a bill of rights; and those who were willing to support the constitution with a bill of rights merely recommended.

Clinton's fear was that the fourth group, when added to the Federalists, might equal a majority—especially if Hamilton dropped his opposition to a bill of rights.

Clinton's fears weren't realized. The Federalists, grimly shaken by the losses in Massachusetts and New Hampshire, and the near loss in Virginia, where the delegates demanded a bill of rights as a condition of ratification, dimmed their ardor. The Antifederalists' spirits were buoyed to the extent that, when Governor Clinton moved on July 12 to reject the new constitution, rather than merely adjourn without a vote, the convention voted 35 to 21 in favor of the motion. Insofar as New York was concerned, the Philadelphia constitution was a dead letter.

Chapter Eighteen – A Path Forward

July 19, 1788, New York City

Clinton and Burr settled down for their first meeting in almost two months. Clinton was cheerful, Burr, pensive.

Beulah poured their tea and Burr's face briefly relaxed as he nodded at her.

Clinton considered his friend and mused that Burr paid more attention to any woman in his presence than even to his precious schemes. His wife, Sarah, enjoyed the Burr's lavishments, as did all his five daughters, Catharine, 18, Cornelia, 10, Lizzy, 8, Martha, 5, and especially precocious three-year-old Maria. His son, George Washington Clinton, 10, usually took visits from "Uncle Aaron" as an excuse to absent himself from his studies and hunt frogs and squirrels.

Clinton started, "Aaron, we won. Enjoy the victory. I can't imagine how our friend Alexander is feeling right now."

"At best, we have a stalemate. If just one state that adjourned without a vote reconvenes, we're finished. We have a reprieve. We have not defeated the enemy."

Clinton, not wanting to confront Burr's harsh logic gradually realized he was right, his face slowly darkening. "What do you propose?"

"Roll back!" Burr said the phrase as if it were a command to a unit maneuvering in the field.

"Why would a state that approved the Philadelphia constitution now abandon it?"

"Money."

"Go on." Clinton stirred to interest.

"What were the main grievances of New Jersey and Connecticut that caused them to so overwhelmingly and quickly ratify?"

"Charging them to use New York's harbor. Certainly, you aren't proposing to eliminate our tariffs? How would we fill our treasury?"

"The contrary, the contrary. We should increase tariff rates to 20 or even 25 percent and then offer Connecticut and New Jersey a fair share of the revenue for goods destined to their states. We'll even invite them to send customs officers to the docks. If, and only if, they vote to rescind their approval of the proposed constitution." Burr sparkled as he did when explaining one of his plans.

"How can we strike a deal? We don't have friendly relations with our bordering brother states. And New Jersey's still overrun with Loyalists who now fancy themselves Federalist patriots."

Burr faintly smiled, then explained, "Remember three years ago when Washington hosted a meeting with representatives from Virginia and Maryland to iron out their shared interests regarding their waterways?"

"Yes, I recall. It resulted in the Mount Vernon Agreement."

"The Mount Vernon Compact," Burr corrected diplomatically, "Covered a host of issues beyond navigation—even toll duties, fishing rights, and collection of debts across state lines. I believe if we invite representatives of Connecticut and New Jersey to New York—and we do so soon—we can relieve some of the lingering irritants that make ratification more possible. Further, and this is important, we should assuage Hamilton and his Federalists at least somewhat. Give them something important. Hamilton wants higher import duties to encourage and protect manufactures. We can give that to him and perhaps other states with great ports will do the same. The merchants won't like it, but most everyone else will and you might earn back some votes from the artisans that the cheap British imports have thrown out of work."

"I like it!"

"Yes, and you should lead the conference, of course, but why not invite Hamilton to pay a role. It would be good to keep him busy on your behalf."

"Yes!" Clinton's pale eyes glowed.

"There is another thing, and it may be the hardest to enact. We should propose to share a portion of our duties with the Confederation and instruct our delegation to the Congress to try again on a national import duty. Rhode Island would likely reject, but it's important we try to make the national government work since we are viewed as having ruined an earnest attempt to address its defects."

"I'll get to work on a proposal to submit to the Legislature." Clinton was primed to act.

"Sir, I have drafts for you here." Burr reached into his satchel and handed Clinton two folders, one outlining his idea for an "Old Royal Exchange Compact" joining New York, Connecticut, and New Jersey in an import duty and toll road agreement and the other draft legislative language for a ten-fold increase in import duties to 25 percent.

Burr felt good about the meeting. Moreover, he was relieved that Clinton said nothing about the missing Hobart.

Chapter Nineteen – Rogues' Island Reds

August 1788, Boston

John Hancock was tired in his bones. Gout made every movement a weary chore. At 51, he'd already served as President of the Continental Congress twice, the first during those heady times when an impetuous new nation issued its Declaration of Independence, and he signed his name with a flourish to the parchment. He'd been Governor of Massachusetts, resigning on January 29, 1785, when he saw the storm clouds on the horizon that would billow up into Shays' rebellion. He didn't want to resign—he expected the General Court to beg him to stay on—and give him the means to defuse the coming crisis. They didn't. And Bowdoin's election ensured disgruntlement turned into violence. On his resignation, he once again took up his station as president, though that second effort was less auspicious, lasting barely more than six months and ending only two years prior as the Congress was drifting and rarely able to conduct business.

Now, he was back in office in Massachusetts. Bowdoin and his merchant supporters had made a complete mess of things. The entire state was seething.

He also kept dwelling on the winter's events. The ratifying convention only made the state's divisions worse. He'd taken ill the month before but still felt obligated as governor to accede to the delegates' desire that he be president of the convention. He rarely spoke. But, as the convention drew to a close, and the delegates from the western reaches of the state grew more contentious, a wave of melancholy suffused with his unshakable malady rendered him silent at the critical hour. His old friend and rival, Samuel Adams, gave an equivocating speech, trying to split the difference between the hardened factions, wealthy and poor, merchant and farmer, Bostonian and everyone else. Adams's words were like warm spit, satisfying no one. The convention voted to adjourn 178 to 176.

And now the braggadocio Bowdoin wanted to see him about Rhode Island.

Hancock winced as he rose and walked to the mirror by his powdered peruke. He carefully arranged his wig and prepared to meet his blood-stained predecessor.

"John," Bowdoin began, "We have a problem. Rogues' Island not only refuses to repay its loans, but its sheriffs are also expelling any debt collectors seeking to recover individual debts. If this is allowed to continue, some of our lending houses and merchant families will be bankrupted. Further, the state is issuing a flood of paper money—and then demands that it be accepted for the settlement of debt."

"So, you accuse Governor Collins of doing what he was elected to do?"

"Elected? He was voted in by a propertyless mob. And things are getting worse. Their paper money is worthless and becoming more so by the day and it's running down the state. People are idle. Homes and businesses are in disrepair. Newport is a shambles."

"Would you raise an army to collect what is owed you?"

Bowdoin looked at Hancock and sighed. "I fear you are right. But how do we collect? If Rhode Island is allowed to continue, I fear for our finances."

"Well, you have encouraged a boycott of their apples and other exports. What is it you say, 'Don't support Rogues' Island rag-money'? Though I am to understand you only made Red Island's goods more popular among in our western counties."

"I don't want to raise another militia, but I'll do it."

"And who will lead it now that the Regulators killed old Benjamin? And who will lend money for the cause, given I'll veto any funding bill that gets to my desk?"

"We must act!"

"James, do not presume to tell me to act!" Some color came back into Hancock's face.

Bowdoin sat back in his chair. He expected Hancock to be frail and sickly. Indeed, he started out that way, but his words only seemed to fuel the man. Bowdoin sighed and thought of different tack.

"Very well then, what if we reestablished the naval militia?"

Hancock started to reply and then, intrigued, waved Bowdoin on.

"Yes, the naval militia. In 1779 our commonwealth navy and privateers captured more than 180 prizes."

"True, and then we lost our entire navy at Penobscot."

"The Rhode Islanders aren't the British." Bowdoin countered, "We could outfit some merchants to serve as privateers, seizing cargoes bound for Newport and impounding them as payment for debt. We might even blockade Narragansett Bay."

"This idea does have promise." Hancock was surprised that Bowdoin forwarded a moderate, rational idea. If carried out, this plan would swing the Boston money back into his camp while at the same time not alienating his constituency in the west nor risk provoking a broader conflict on land. He doubted the people's legislature in Rhode Island would immediately be moved to action to defend the interests of their monied cousins.

Chapter Twenty – Rapprochement

August 1788, New York City, Bank of New York

Burr never sought out Hamilton's company. But, as one of the founders of the Bank of New York, he had to meet with him from time to time on the bank's business. And today, Burr needed Hamilton's full attention and support.

Hamilton walked in off the street. There was a steamy rain outside, and Hamilton's boots were caked in mud and horseshit. Burr smiled. He always took pleasure in seeing Hamilton look less than perfect.

"Aaron, good to see you." Hamilton wasn't as self-confident as he'd been in the months leading up to the failed effort to ratify the Philadelphia constitution. His ebullient nature suffered as a result.

"Hammy, likewise. Tea?"

"Please, thank you."

Burr poured them both tea, offering Hamilton sugar. Hamilton sprinkled in a teaspoonful and allowed the drink to linger on his tongue.

"New York has an opportunity. Since the Treaty of Hartford, the state has the first rights of refusal to purchase Massachusetts's land claims. But I understand that Nathaniel Gorham and Oliver Phelps and are intending to buy the six million acres for $1 million."

"So I've heard. How do they propose to get the Six Nations to agree?"

"The Iroquois in New York have been abandoned by the British. I'm figuring they'll be more than willing to accept a modest payment. What choice do they have?"

"Where do we get a million dollars to speculate in land?"

"That's just it, I'm not proposing that we buy it or that the bank purchases it. Rather, the state with the bank selling the bonds to facilitate the purchase from Massachusetts."

Hamilton stroked his angular chin. "And how will New York make good on the payments? Certainly not with paper?"

"Heavens no! With specie, if that's what Massachusetts wants. Hell, even Spanish gold, if need be."

"Again, Aaron, where does the state get its financing? My time in the Assembly informed me our coffers are almost empty."

Burr's brown eyes lit up. "When the 12th Legislature meets for business, Clinton aims to place before it a proposal that, I hazard, will enjoy your hearty approval."

Hamilton leaned forward. He needed a spark, a challenge.

Burr let his rival remain in suspense for an extra couple of seconds while his sipped at his tea.

"Governor Clinton will be proposing to increase the import duty by ten-fold. He will also invite Connecticut and New Jersey to a conference to come to an agreement regarding the disposition of our trade and tariff revenue. I think both states will find the offer very compelling. Further, I expect that the increase in duties from 2-1/2 percent to 25 percent will repopulate the city will artisans and craftsmen. You'll get your manufactures."

Hamilton narrowed his eyes, "The British will surely retaliate."

"Perhaps. But it is my understanding that Ambassador Jefferson has been working on trade agreements with the French. The British will soon no longer be our only option. Besides, even if trade fell by one-half, our revenue will still increase five-fold."

"Assuming purchases of imports remains at the same level. It won't. It will drop and local production will increase. The state derives no revenue from that."

"True." Burr should have anticipated that. He was on unfamiliar terrain—trade and manufactures—terrain Hamilton knew all too well. "Yet, the almshouse will empty, and the jails will no longer be crowded with debtors."

"Yes." Hamilton's look suggested Burr was coming up short.

"There is one other matter that ties into this. Something particularly suited to the Little Lion's nature." Burr thought Hamilton's other nickname was ridiculous, but he knew Hamilton liked the sobriquet.

"I have arranged for Colonel Hugh Maxwell to lead a survey of the tract and... You know Christopher Colles, the Irish waterworks man?"

"Of course."

"Well, when I was in the Assembly, he surveyed the Mohawk Valley and presented a report proposing a canal to connect Lake Ontario to the Hudson."

"That undertaking goes back decades."

"True, but unlike in Cadwallader Colden's time we have the ability—and the resources—to do it. Colles has even made extensive study of the Bridgewater Canal in England."

"The north is much larger, and its terrain is far more robust than in northwest England, no?"

"I don't disagree. But these things have been done. And, I'm told, shipping by canal can cut the costs of transport by 95 percent. We can open up the West, Hammy! Besides, even Washington is working on the same with his Patowmack Canal."

"There's one more consideration. The lands in the Northwest. Even if we can clear them of Indians and the British, why would anyone settle there?

How can they profit. The costs of shipping any surplus to the cities would more than eat up any money they'd hope to make from the sale of their grains and hogs. Without a canal, they'll be forced to sell their surplus down the Ohio and Mississippi to the Spanish in New Orleans. Without a canal, our settlers will find themselves increasingly bound to Europe, not the states. Oh, and with a canal being built, the land will immediately become far more valuable. New York will make millions on the effort. Perhaps even enough to quickly pay for the canal. New York City will benefit too."

"Aaron, this is the boldest scheme you have hatched since you conspired to make Theodosia your bride."

"I'm not done yet." Burr looked intently at Hamilton. "We—Clinton and I—want you to lead the canal effort. Our bank can issue the bonds and the state can purchase the land from Massachusetts. We can turn New York into an empire..."

Hamilton narrowed his eyes.

Burr quickly added, "An empire of commerce."

"Please let me have a day to consider your proposals. They are intriguing. I even think they may be workable."

Hamilton stood, at 5'7," just an inch taller than Burr. Burr fluidly rose to his feet and the two shook hands.

The last time Burr enjoyed himself this much was six weeks ago during his romp with the house servant Mary.

Chapter Twenty-One – Empire at Sea

April 1789, Haverford Township, Pennsylvania

From the two letters he exchanged with the with the 37-year-old naval architect, Joshua Humphreys, Burr knew him to be a visionary. A genius. Guided by the pull of their dreams, visionaries were the easiest to manipulate.

Burr swung off his horse in front of Humphreys' house, a stout, two-story stone manor. He walked up to the portico and was about to knock when the door opened to reveal a slightly surprised blue-eyed man with a weathered face.

"Burr?"

"You must be Mr. Humphreys." Burr stuck out his hand and Humphreys warmly shook it.

"Please, come in, welcome to Pont Reading. And please call me Joshua. It's an honor to meet you. Though, with your leave, I do have tasks requiring my attention at the shipwork. Do you care to join me?"

Despite his friendliness, Humphreys seemed a man thinking of a half-dozen matters at once, and Burr wasn't in the top six.

"I would be delighted to see your shipwork. May I ask, 'Pont Reading'?"

Humphreys showed Burr back outside and shut the door, "Named after Reading Pont, the family homestead in England. The shipwork is three miles distant." Humphreys made for the back of his house, letting himself in through a gate. He said over his shoulder, "Allow me to me fetch my horse."

It was just before lunchtime on a Wednesday and, judging by the horse's equipage, Humphreys was intending to leave for the shipwork anyway.

A large, shorthaired brown dog followed Humphreys' horse out the gate, trailing 10 feet behind.

The spring sun warmed the muddy trail leading to West Philadelphia and the Schuylkill River and Philadelphia beyond.

As they rode together, Burr heard the story of Humphreys' early entry into the shipbuilding trade. Apprenticed to a Philadelphia shipbuilder at 14, the builder died six years later, and Humphreys was left to run the business.

Burr could see the bones of a ship at the end of the street, partially obscured by a large wooden ramp and scaffolding around the bow.

"That's impressive. Is that yours?" Burr asked.

"Well, no, it's not and yes, it is. It's just a merchant brig. Its burthen is to be 100 tons with a crew of 11."

"Burthen?" Burr had been occasionally a passenger on small vessels but had not spent any time at sea.

"The carrying capacity of the ship. But this is just my trade and I've been at it 23 years. Let me show you what you came to see." Humphreys smiled and now the dog trotted ahead to a small office building with a large window that overlooked the shipwork. They tied up their horses and went in. There were carefully ordered stacks of papers everywhere. The dog was already laying under a table burdened with drawings.

"This, this is the Frigate." Humphreys' hands unrolled a six-foot-long scroll and then placed small lead weights at either end. "It's 50 to 1 scale. The ship is 300 feet long from bowsprit to spanker. She will carry 44 guns and weigh 1,600 tons. She will be able to outrun larger ships-of-the-line and out-gun anything smaller. I've designed her to clear the Mediterranean of its pirates, beat any British or French frigate, and run from anything else."

"How much to build it?"

"Her."

"Her." Burr corrected himself.

"$400,000 or so. Maybe less if more are made at the same time."

Burr whistled. "Why so much?"

"Here, see this?" Humphreys turned to a rack on the wall on which some long, rectangular strips of wood hung. "These are molds. Templates used to select trees fitting a specific need or shape in her construction. In this case, these are for the ship outside. But imagine something many times bigger and for trees found 900 miles down the coast in Georgia. They're called southern live oak and they're tough as iron. She'll have her framing made of live oak, cut specially for each part of the ship. We'll plank it with white oak. But the framing will be so tight that a cannon ball will scarce get through. Europe—England and France—can't compete. They have no such wood. Only we do and it's hard to get and hard to transport here. It won't be easy but when we launch her, she'll be the best in the world!"

"Would you make one for New York?"

"For the state or city?"

"The state. We are considering the formation of a naval militia to defend our commercial interests. The brigantine Betsey out of New York was taken by the Barbary pirates four years ago. Your frigate could put an end to their privations."

"She'll be good, but by herself, she'd be vulnerable—two for $700,000 would be better."

"The four pirate kingdoms only want $2-1/2 million in tribute." Burr stared at Humphreys with a bit of a grin, "$700,000 approaches the pirates' price."

"For today, maybe. We did purchase peace with Morocco, but Algeria remains belligerent. Their prices go up or down based on their estimation of our power and resolve."

"True. Is there a smaller drawing or sketch of your frigate I might have to take back to New York and make part of my recommendations to Governor Clinton and the Legislature?"

Chapter Twenty-Two – Disquietude Among the Merchants

April 1789, New York

Clinton's tariffs were very popular among all but the importing class—at first. The legislature, deciding that the proposed 25 percent import fee on British and other goods imported from Europe was too high, compromised on 20 percent. This made all manner of manufactured items more expensive as local manufactures increased prices to match the now more costly British goods. And then the smuggling started.

Since the economic pain was not uniformly shared, with New York City's artisans benefiting and everyone else paying the price, Governor George Clinton's fifth three-year term looked to be seriously contested. Of his last three elections, 1780 and 1786 were unopposed and he won with more than 75 percent in 1783.

This time, Robert Yates, a fellow anti-federalist, had signed up to oppose him. Even though Clinton had always been careful not to make a display of his wealth while never missing an opportunity to ally himself with the common folk, especially outside of New York City, Yates was the true article. A lawyer from Albany who supplemented his income by surveying, Yates came from an accomplished family. Most importantly, while Clinton was maneuvering to kill the Philadelphia constitution in Poughkeepsie, Yates had focused on ensuring that any national government would honor individual liberties. Yates saw the danger firsthand, having been part of the New York's three-member delegation to Philadelphia, along with Alexander Hamilton and John Lansing, Jr.

The election returns from the upper Hudson came in strong for Yates, and it appeared he won by 89 votes, 6,523 to 6,434. But Aaron Burr became aware of certain irregularities in the election, namely, that the ballots from some counties were not properly delivered by the sheriff or his deputy to the joint committee of the New York State Legislature per the state Constitution of 1777.

Legislative representatives from New York, while displeased with Clinton's tariffs, were nonetheless alarmed by Yate's appeal to the yeomanry and his opposition to Clinton's costly plan to build a canal linking Lake Erie to the Hudson River. When Burr gave them a way to reelect Clinton while banking political credit with the old politician, they took it.

Richard Varick, concurrently New York City's chief legal officer as Recorder, and the New York State Attorney General, was asked to arbitrate when Yates's supporters in the Legislature suggested that all three of the counties that transmitted flawed ballot tallies—Clinton, Otsego, and Tioga—should have their ballots counted. Clinton's allies, working with Burr, countered that only those from Otsego and Tioga counties should be rejected. A majority of the canvass committee, agreeing with Varick's suggestion, threw out the ballots from all three disputed counties, thus reelecting Clinton to his fifth term.

Even so, Clinton was on thin ice, with Federalists now controlling both houses of the New York Legislature. In gratitude, Clinton appointed Burr New York Attorney General for a three-year term. Importantly, the appointment came with a position on the three-member New York Land Board—a position which, if used properly, could purchase a lot of loyalty and new voters.

Chapter Twenty-Three – Revolution

July 13, 1789, Paris, France

Thomas Jefferson had been in France now for almost five years, working with Benjamin Franklin and John Adams as Minister Plenipotentiary for Negotiating Treaties of Amity and Commerce. Put simply, his mission was to establish the United States as an equal among the world powers. There, of course, was another reason why the 46-year-old main author of the Declaration of Independence was in France—his political opponents wanted him out of the way. Jefferson's ideas on liberty, when combined with Thomas Paine's powerful pamphlets and Patrick Henry's fiery speeches, threatened the social order with violent rebellion, something the weak and newly independent nation could ill-afford.

And now, as the French empire, though wealthier and larger than the British, had run out of money—the French king, Louis XVI, had the power to spend money, but only the Estates-General could raise taxes. As a result, the crown borrowed 4.5 billion livres. But debts must be repaid, and the provincial appellate courts, called Parlements, were unwilling to collect taxes. The inevitable result: terrible inflation that, when combined with poor harvests and a bitter winter, left the peasants with no food to sell and the city dwellers, assuming they even had work, with little to spend. In desperation, the king summoned the Estates-General for the first time in 175 years.

Jefferson was increasingly back in his element. He was holding court with aristocrats, thinkers, and radicals in Hôtel de Langeac, a new two-story rented house with a neo-classical exterior in the heart of a city of 600,000 people. Paris alone held one-fifth of the entire population of the United States, with only Jefferson's state of Virginia having a greater number of people, at almost three-quarters of a million.

The entertaining was painless—he had eight servants, five of them American slaves from his plantations in Virginia. Martha, his wife of a decade died seven years earlier and for the first time, he felt rejuvenated. The overseas posting kept him increasingly busy. But then there was the affair with Maria, the Anglo-Italian painter, composer, and musician three years ago. But Maria was married and back in London. Soon after, Jefferson sent for his nine-year-old daughter, Polly, chaperoned by 16-year-old Sally Hemings, one of Jefferson's 181 slaves. Sally was now his constant, if discrete, companion.

He was expecting an interesting assortment of company tonight, foremost among them, the 31-year-old hero of the War for Independence, Marquis de

Lafayette. There was change in the air, with conditions far worse in France than any American would ever tolerate for a week, much less several years. For Lafayette, knowing what he helped make possible in America demanded his action in France.

A servant announced Lafayette, the first to arrive. He was early. Jefferson rushed out to greet his old friend, speaking in near-perfect French.

Jefferson beamed, asking, "And how is little Georges? Polly was hoping he would be joining you today."

Lafayette's face betrayed exhaustion, "I sent Georges back to Chavaniac. Matters are coming to a head, I am afraid. The king is rejecting the reforms, urged on by that Austrian spy Marie Antoinette and his fool brother, Comte d'Artois. He only wants the Assembly to raise taxes for him. We met the entire day yesterday and into the night under threat of the Swiss Guards dispersing us. But the people filled the streets. The Guards Regiment refused to move on the people. I'm telling you, Thomas, never in my years of battle have I seen anything so likely to disintegrate into chaos and death. It's a miracle that no one was killed."

Jefferson had heard the rumors, but Lafayette's was the first eyewitness account of the prior day. "If the king opposes the reforms, then revolution seems probable, no?" Jefferson looked intently at his friend.

Lafayette set his jaw and was about to answer when two more guests arrived. The party had started, and Jefferson thought it best to allow Lafayette to take the lead on seditious matters given it was his life and his nation that were at stake.

Pleasantries and small talk, wine and good food, had been partaken of for almost two hours. James, Sally's brother—they were temporarily paid servants under French law—did an exceptional job as chef for the affair. His training in French cuisine was one of Jefferson's smartest investments.

Lafayette motioned for the 14 guests to be quiet. "I want to thank my dear friend, Minister Jefferson, for hosting us tonight. The food and the company were wonderful."

Jefferson nodded.

"And now, I apologize, I fear I must bring forward an uncomfortable, but necessary, conversation." Lafayette's dark green eyes smoldered under his white, powdered peruke. The room was silent. Two of Jefferson's slaves and one of his French servants stood at the edge of the gathering.

Lafayette gathered his lanky 5'9" frame—Jefferson was 6'2," and one of Jefferson's male slaves was almost as tall, but Lafayette was the tallest Frenchman in the room, "Three weeks ago, when the king forbade the

Assembly meeting in the Salle des États, we moved to the tennis court and swore an oath…"

"The Tennis Court Oath!" Catholic Abbot Emmanuel-Joseph Sieyès affirmed.

Lafayette allowed himself a slight grin, "Yes, and thank you for your vote. We swore an oath not to leave Paris until we had given France a constitution. Only four days ago, the Assembly disbanded. From that body, we created the National Constituent Assembly. In that capacity, I have been working with Abbé Emmanuel-Joseph and the comte de Mirabeau—and our American host—to craft the principles which shall animate our new constitution. We now have a working draft of what we call the Declaration of the Rights of Man and of the Citizen."

Jefferson smiled from his chair.

Lafayette continued, "Time is not our ally. Every day, the citizens grow more impatient, hungrier for liberty and bread. Without the hope of a new government, one that promises, liberty and equality, we may face violence in the streets and rebellion in the countryside."

Sieyès spoke up again, "Yes. But the king continues his obstinance. He continues to rebuff the people, to deny that the Third Estate has power. We, here, except for the Americans, are representatives of the First and Second Estates. But truly, what is Third Estate? We can say that it is all other Frenchmen," Sieyès gestured towards Jefferson's male French servant. "But I say the Third Estate is everything—everyone, even those of us in the First and Second Estates. The king sees this as nothing. Irrelevant. But, if we are to have a new France then, at the very least, the Third Estate must be something." Sieyès was paraphrasing from his political pamphlet that he had published six months previously. Everyone knew the words, but hearing Sieyès reiterate them added a certain clarity.

Count Mirabeau joined in, "I fear we may be too late to save the Ancien Régime, in any form, from the people—from the Abbot's 'Third Estate.' I hear that the mob may fill the streets tomorrow with the Bastille in their sights."

One of three female guests let out a barely audible gasp.

The gathering broke up just before midnight.

The next day, in late afternoon, Jefferson heard the news. The Bastille, a royal armory that also served as a small prison, had been stormed. It was taken after hours of fighting with the loss of some 100 people—including soldiers who joined them—who then started to pick apart the two-story stone structure by hand, tossing stone and beam into the street. The rage was personal and directed straight at the royalty. More disturbingly, Jefferson's informants told him that the armory's commander was taken to the Hôtel de Ville and then summarily executed with this head mounted on a pike and paraded around by a frenzied mob.

King Louis, terrified at the spiraling violence, turned to the only man he thought who could bridge the widening gulf between him and the now-awakened Third Estate: Gilbert du Motier, the Marquis de Lafayette. The French Revolution was now a deadly reality.

Chapter Twenty-Four – A Meddlesome Methodist Minister

August 2, 1789, Hagerstown, Maryland

Hagerstown, Maryland was only 100 miles from Bucks County, Pennsylvania, but it might as well have been a different world in some respects. In the wake of the Gradual Abolition Act of 1780, slavery, never as widespread as in Maryland or Virginia, dwindled to the point that fewer than one in 100 Pennsylvanians were black slaves. In Maryland, three of 10 people were enslaved, in Virginia, almost four of 10. But sin is sin, just as a little leaven leavens the whole lump—and that was one of the main reasons Reverend Jacob Gruber, a Pennsylvanian, found himself preaching at a Sunday evening revival tent meeting of the Methodist Society just outside of the town of 2,000—that and the preacher scheduled to speak had lost his voice and Gruber, as presiding elder, was obligated to fill in.

The fiery Methodist preacher in his gray suit and wide-brimmed planter's hat found a receptive, or at least curious, crowd this evening, some 3,000 men and women. Moreover, at the edges of the gathering were up to 500 Blacks, mostly slaves.

Gruber sized up his flock and began, "Righteousness exalteth a nation, but sin is a reproach to any people. What kind of righteousness exalts a nation or a person?" he asked. Gruber than answered the question, calling the faithful and the unsaved alike to live better, more Godly lives, eschewing cigars and strong drink while distaining the vanity of high fashion. When Gruber called out fancy men's walking canes and ladies' exposed petticoats, scores of people shifted nervously on their feet while others called out "Amens!" Gruber exclaimed that many stones blocked the path towards salvation, including profanity and infidelity.

"The indwelling presence of the Holy Spirit," he continued, "a spirit of grace, of peace, of adoption, of love, of liberty. This Spirit is not an end to itself, it is not to be understood as a culminating experience, but a beginning point for living the Christian life. Living your life right. Call it practical righteousness."

At this point, Gruber was about 50 minutes into his sermon. The sun was moving low in the horizon to Gruber's left, reddish rays streaming past the day's last billowing thunderclouds over the Alleghenies. But, just as the crowd was expecting Gruber to wrap up, his voice grew stronger and his manner more energetic. He now began decrying the deadliest national sin: slavery.

Gruber briefly took off his hat, showing a shock of red hair, and mopped his face before beginning anew, "Sin is a reproach to any people, nation, or person. Sin is the transgression of the law. The way of transgressors is hard. He that committeth sin is the servant of sin. He that committeth sin is of the devil. Sin is a reproach to any person, no matter what his rank."

Gruber was on safe ground so far. He made the plunge.

"The last National Sin I shall mention is slavery and oppression. This in particular, is a reproach to our nation. We pity other nations who are under the yoke of Emperors and Kings, who tyrannize over, and make slaves of their subjects. We are happily delivered from such bondage; we live in a free country; we hold self-evident truths, that all men are created equal, and have unalienable rights, such as life, liberty, and the pursuit of happiness. But are there no slaves in our country? Does not sweat, blood and tears say there are? The voice of thy brother's blood crieth. Is it not a reproach to a man to hold articles of liberty and independence in one hand and a bloody whip in the other, while a negro stands and trembles before him, with his back cut and bleeding?"

There were a few scattered "Amens" amidst an undercurrent of murmurs. Gruber was committed now.

"There is a laudable zeal manifested in our country to form Bible and Missionary Societies to send the Scriptures and the gospel to heathen nations. Would it not be well for some to be consistent? Instruct the heathens at home in their kitchens, and let them hear the gospel likewise. What would heathen nations at a distance think, if they were told that persons who gave money liberally to send them the Bible and the gospel did not read, believe, or obey it themselves, nor teach their own families to read that book; nor allow them time to hear the gospel of their salvation preached? There is some difference even in this country. We Pennsylvanians think strange, and it seems curious to read the public prints or papers from some states and find in those papers advertisements reading: For sale, a plantation, a house and lot, horses, cows, sheep and hogs, also, a number of negroes; men, women and children, some very valuable ones, also, a pew in such and such a church for sale, for life, a likely young negro, who is an excellent waiter, sold for no fault-or else for want of employment. These are sold for cash, for four, five, six, seven, or eight hundred dollars a head; soul and body together, ranked with horses and other livestock!"

A few people started to leave. They were angry, and, by the looks of them, wealthy.

"Look further in those papers and see this, fifty dollars reward, one hundred dollars reward, two hundred dollars reward! What for? Has an apprentice run away from his master? No. Perhaps a reward for him would be six cents. A man that ran off has, probably, gone to see his wife, or child, or relations who have been sold and torn from him; or to enjoy the blessings of a free country, and to get clear of tyranny. In this inhuman traffic and cruel trade, the most tender ties are torn asunder, the nearest connections broken!"

Gruber glared at his flock.

"That which God joined together let no man put asunder! This solemn injunction is not regarded. Will not God be avenged on such a nation as this?"

The stream of people leaving, some with angry shouts, had grown. Perhaps 500, maybe more. Gruber felt pity for their hell-bound souls.

"But some say, we use our slaves well; better than they could use themselves if they were free. Granted. But what assurance have you, or what security have they that your children, or those you will them to will use them as you do? May they not tyrannize over them after you are dead and gone, and may they not—the slaves thus abused—rise up and kill your children, their oppressors, and be hung for it, and all go to destruction together? The Lord have mercy on their souls!"

Many of those who stayed were now openly weeping.

"Such alarming and dreadful consequences may attend and follow this reproachful sin in our land and nation."

Gruber lifted his eyes and pushed his voice to one last exertion. "And to you, the Negroes in the back. To you men and women I say this, of all people in the world you ought to have religion. You have most need of it in order to enjoy some happiness or peace. Sin is a reproach to you. There is no peace to the wicked. Some of you have good masters; you ought to attend to religious duties; never be absent from family prayer when it is in your power to attend; discharge your duty and it may make your situation more agreeable, even here, and certainly hereafter. Some of you have cruel masters; are slaves to them, slaves to sin, and slaves to the Devil, and if you die without religion, you will be slaves in hell for ever; miserable, wretched, poor, and lost to all eternity. But if you repent, and get converted; be made free from sin; serve the Lord faithful unto death—however hard your situation may be in this world—your sufferings will soon be over; and you may have crowns and kingdoms in glory, where the wicked cease from troubling; where every tear is dry, and not a wave of trouble rolls across the peaceful breast, be happy in heaven forever; while wicked masters are turned into hell and damned forever."

That day, 22 of the 300 or so slaves who heard Gruber left for the north. Only two were recovered by slave catchers. The ones who escaped to freedom included a blacksmith and two artisans who lived independently in

Hagerstown on the condition of sending their masters a yearly fee. Escapees also included three domestics, and 14 fieldhands. Most of this group made for Albany, New York, where they had heard they might have opportunities to settle their own land.

Chapter Twenty-Five – Pushing into Ohio

August 12, 1789, New York City

Burr saw a problem with no immediate solution. There was a steady trickle of escaped slaves making their way up north, mainly from Maryland and Virginia. Judging by reports from the almshouse in the city, there were 300 since the beginning of the year. Most of these had no immediately useful skills, especially in a city. And, if there weren't some useful employment for them, they'd be readily picked off as slaves for the wealthy, Federalist-supporting Dutch estates up the Hudson—or victims of slavecatchers who stood to earn a bounty for their return south to their masters.

Yet, if they were allowed to ply the one trade most of them knew well—farming—they'd immediately garner the resentment of the yeoman farmers he—and Clinton—relied upon for their political power.

Burr struggled to see how this source of manpower might be used when, he sat back in his chair and by the light of the fading sun setting in the west it hit him.

The West!

His plans to settle the lands west of the Pre-Emption Line about 180 miles west of Albany between Lake Ontario and Lake Erie to the north and Pennsylvania to the south with farmers, many of them Shaysites, supportive of himself—and Clinton—was going well. More so since construction of the canal connecting the Hudson River to Lake Erie had commenced. Some 4,000 farmers had already moved into the area, displacing the remnants of the Iroquois who lived there. But, without commerce coming in from the unsettled Northwest Territories north of the Ohio River, the canal would be a financial bust and Burr's plans would suffer.

Yet, short of raising a professional army, something the Federalists in the Legislature would oppose so long as Clinton remained governor, it was difficult to convince men to settle beyond New York while putting their families at risk of attack, rape, scalping, and enslavement at the hands of the natives.

Further, the British, from their perch in Fort Lernoult, were steadily supplying the Indians with arms and other necessities, with the express intent of keeping the Americans from overrunning the continent—or at least making another go at Canada.

But a steady supply of self-freed slaves might be put to good use as a buffer against the so-called United Indian Nations and their English masters. The Negroes could carve out a living, trade with those further to the east and south along the Ohio, and boost cargo coming through the Erie Canal which was due to be finished—well, with some sections using temporary wooden sluices and locks—by 1795.

Burr resolved to speak to Clinton about his idea, as well as a proposal to end slavery in New York, with the discussion putting the now-ascendant Federalists on the defensive.

Chapter Twenty-Six – New England Quasi War

August 14, 1789, 60 miles ESE of Boston, Atlantic Ocean

The family business, slaving, was under pressure from Massachusetts—not out of any particular animus towards slavery from the merchants out of Boston, but because Rhode Island's governor, John Collins, wouldn't or couldn't make good on its public debts. As a result, James DeWolf, at 25 with more than a decade of experience at sea, was at the helm of his family's 18-gun brig looking for a prize.

Massachusetts had stood up its naval militia in an effort to squeeze Rhode Island of its considerable merchant trade, much of it based on the transportation and sale of slaves, sugar, rum and coffee—with his family dominating most of that business.

James didn't need a lot of convincing from his brother Charles, 19 years his senior, to go to sea as a privateer. Rather, adventure and the chance to impress young Nancy Bradford, the daughter of William Bradford, a man of considerable wealth and Rhode Island's deputy governor, was more than enough motivation. There was also a more practical matter: the Bostonians had captured the 40-ton schooner he bought the year before to run slaves and rum up from the family plantations in Cuba. Without his ship, his plans for life were dead in the water.

A salty spray broke over the brig's bow and wetted the fore sail and mainsail—along with 18 of his 120-crew working the rigging closest to the deck. The wind was freshening to his back, blowing out to sea from the west.

A crewman working the top gallant sail more than 80 feet up the mainmast called down, "Ship!" He pointed towards the east.

James called his helmsman to take the wheel, not releasing his large hands until the smaller man had fully gripped it. James walked a few steps across the quarterdeck and braced himself on the starboard side railing. His gray-blue eyes scanned the eastern horizon, squinting in the morning sun.

His crew was terrified of him. The old salt on the ship, a man of 59 and a veteran of 50 years of the sea, said master DeWolf was seduced by the Devil himself with no fear of God or man before his eyes. James had heard the whispering and found it pleasing to him. He did nothing to dispel the talk.

There. James saw a blot on the cloudless horizon. He lifted his brass spyglass and, with a practiced slouch, moved with the waves to capture a better glimpse of the oncoming vessel. He smiled broadly. The ship had two masts.

"Bos'n, call general quarters."

In half an hour the ships had closed close enough that James could see it was a merchant brig, likely out of Boston. He guessed that it held English manufactured goods—with luck, enough to make good his loss of the schooner.

The merchant kept coming on, tacking against the wind and making about three knots towards Boston Harbor. Sensing the wind, James timed his turn to port to come alongside his prize. Up until that turn, the merchant's captain had no reason to suspect his ship of ill-will—after all, his was Rhode Island's first effort to answer Boston's naval campaign to extract debts owed.

"Helmsman, West-Nor'-West, if you please!"

"Aye sir!"

James could clearly see the ship's name now, the Swan, as he put a copper loudspeaker to his mouth and called out to the other ship's captain now just 100 feet away, "Brail up and prepare to be boarded!"

There was a sudden commotion on the deck and in the rigging of the Swan.

"On whose authority?" the Swan's captain responded.

"The Colony of Rhode Island and Providence Plantations and her governor!"

James heard the Swan's captain order the ship to come about to starboard to escape with the wind. He had anticipated that and, not wanting to damage his prize, he ordered the swivel gun loaded with shot trained on the Swan's captain.

"Fire." James gave the order quietly while looking straight at the Swan's master.

The swivel gunner let loose. The blast caught the Swan's captain and the helmsman both, sending them to the deck. The gunner immediately swapped out the still smoking breech and placed a fresh one on the mount.

"To the new captain of the Swan, I say brail up and prepare to be boarded!"

A young man, almost a boy by the looks of him—probably the captain's son—looked up from his crumpled captain and, with a cracking voice, gave the order to surrender.

James had his first prize and Massachusetts now had Rhode Island's answer.

Collecting that debt wouldn't be so easy now.

Chapter Twenty-Seven – The Price of Peace

October 6, 1789, New York City

Alarmed that the outbreak of the so-called "Debtor's War" between Massachusetts and Rhode Island would renew efforts to ratify the Philadelphia constitution, Governor Clinton arranged for negotiations between the parties, with adjudication offered by himself and the President of New Hampshire and Governor of Connecticut.

To ensure success, Clinton directed Burr, whom he had appointed as his state attorney general the month before, to buy up as much of the wartime debt as possible—at a steep discount, of course. Burr jumped at the chance and, in so doing, meet the wealthy families of Boston, Providence, and Bristol while better understanding the lingering grievances of the common people.

With a large majority of the loans quietly purchased by Burr and his agents, the main irritant between Rhode Island and Massachusetts vanished. And, when word got out that New York, and not Boston, was holding the paper, its value quickly increased. Burr quickly resold half of the debt at a double profit, thus distributing the debt holders out of Boston, and then returned the capital to the New York treasury before Hamilton and the Federalists could make anything of it.

The crisis was defused, leaving Clinton, New Hampshire President John Sullivan, and Connecticut Governor Samuel Huntington to warmly preside over truce between Rhode Island's John Collins and John Hancock of Massachusetts, who complained bitterly about the ill-effect the coach ride out from Boston had on his gout.

Chapter Twenty-Eight – Admission

May 18, 1796, New York City

Burr desperately missed his Theodosia. She passed away two years ago on this date, and he felt an aching hole in his heart. Their daughter, named after her mother, was almost 13 and looking and acting more like her namesake every day. Burr thanked God for her.

Burr cleared his mind and focused on the present. George Washington was making trouble for him and there was little he could do.

Washington put all his prestige into admitting the state of Tennessee under Article XI of the Articles of Confederation, with nine states needing to approve the admission of a new state. New York voted "no", but it wasn't enough. Tennessee became the fifteenth state in the union after Kentucky's admission in 1792. And now, at least nine states were ready to overrule New York's claims on Vermont and admit that state too, making sixteen.

Thankfully, New Jersey had voted to rescind its ratification of the Philadelphia constitution, making it only seven states in support of that centralizing document: Delaware, Georgia, Maryland, Pennsylvania, South Carolina, Virginia, and Connecticut, which Burr still hoped to pressure into rescinding its support.

That two more states might make the nine needed to ratify would eventually become a mathematical certainty.

Burr had little idea of the sentiments in Kentucky and Tennessee—but Vermont, as much as the leadership there hated New York, was as radically anti-Federalist as Rhode Island.

He had to develop a plan to forge the middle states into their own union, else the votes of Kentucky and Tennessee or even New Jersey, if they again changed their minds, might provide the nine needed to ratify. Yet, if he made a public concern of it, he feared it might stoke the Federalists to new exertions. Best to let sleeping dogs lie.

Chapter Twenty-Nine – Death of the Father

December 18, 1799, New York City

For 10 years, New York Attorney General Aaron Burr racked up political credits—and considerable cash from his prodigious land dealings—so much so that Governor Clinton was growing wary of him. Further, Burr's membership on the New York Land Board, created in 1790, allowed him to be seen as the grantor of land titles to thousands of New York veterans of the war. And now, with both men sensing it was time for Burr to move on to new challenges, Burr was out of public office.

As fate's timing would have it, Burr was contemplating the news he just read that George Washington had passed away four days ago at the age of 67.

Burr put the paper down. The now fifteen states, held in loose confederation with a weak and ineffectual government, would fly apart. Washington, the man of mythical proportions, was the band that held the barrel together. With Washington gone, the barrel would soon burst. The questions for Burr were when and how to take advantage of the chaos.

Soon after revolutionary France revealed its radicalism, the monarchies of Europe went to war with it. America, desiring neutrality, tried to stay out of it, but the states pursued their own interests, even as the central government tried in vain to steer a cautious course.

With issues from the Revolutionary War still unresolved and the additional complication of much of Europe's war against France, the Confederation Congress dispatched a diplomatic team led by John Jay to London. Jay came back with a treaty, but Congress couldn't get the needed votes to ratify it, even after Washington paid a personal visit.

Boston soon swung towards England and, as a result, provoked revolutionary France to dispatch privateers to capture and harass American shipping, mostly without distinction between vessels out of New England verses vessels out of New York and points further south which were much more sympathetic to the French cause.

In late 1796 and into the spring of 1797, some 300 merchant ships were seized by the French in the Caribbean and nearby waters.

But soon, the two exceptional warships purchased by New York eight years earlier on Burr's strong recommendation and launched in 1787, the 44-gun frigates NYS *American Empire* and the NYS *Manhattan* encouraged the French to lay off the merchants from New York and other states more friendly to France. As well, Paris began to see the possibility of splitting America, which could have its advantages.

New England was hit especially hard and made arrangements to convoy with British warships whenever possible. New England's self-interested moves incensed the other states, further straining national relations.

On the other hand, Britain was angered at the provisioning of French privateers in American ports from New York down to Charleston. Further, there were rumors—likely true—that many of the French privateers were built in Baltimore.

Burr glanced back at the newspaper and it suddenly dawned on him: to become something more than merely the governor of New York, he'd need strong words written on his behalf—words written by Thomas Paine! He'd invite Paine back from his uncertain exile in France and press him into service to spark a second (or third) revolution, with Burr at the helm.

Chapter Thirty – Murder Most Foul

March 20 to April 2, 1800, New York City

"Does he have any money?" Burr asked.

"Is he guilty?" Brockholst Livingston queried.

"Does it matter?" Hamilton responded, "Levi Weeks deserves a fair trial. He has a solid alibi and, if convicted, stands to lose his life to the noose."

Jeph Clark stood on the periphery, being watchful to attend to the three lawyers' needs.

Burr rolled his eyes, though only Jeph saw it—the two exchanged a secret grin.

"Besides," Hamilton added, "The legislature continues its follies at so rapid a pace that it has afforded so plentiful a harvest to us lawyers that we have scarcely a moment to spare from the substantial business of reaping."

"Hear, hear!" Livingston said laughing.

"What does the state claim?" Burr asked.

Hamilton jumped in, "On a snowy night, December 22, Miss Gulielma Sands, 22-years old, a resident of a boarding house went outside. She wasn't seen until eleven days later when her fully clothed body was found in a well. Her fiancé is the accused, Levi Weeks. Of course, in these cases, the fiancé or other intimate male relation, is frequently the culprit. It doesn't help that there are rumors that Weeks found out they were to have a baby. But the coroner determined that the deceased was not pregnant."

Livingston added, "And since, our beloved city authorities determined that justice, or at least prurient interests, could be served by placing the body on public display, our task will be made the harder."

"At least it's been freezing most nights, otherwise, she might not keep," Burr quipped.

Livingston suppressed a chuckle.

Hamilton glared at Burr, "Please, we are speaking of the dead."

Burr secreted a glance at Clark, but this time Clark wasn't playing, instead, almost imperceptibly shaking his head, a rare rebuke from the help. Burr thought for a moment about the 38-year-old man who fought under his command 22 years earlier—seemingly a lifetime ago. He was competent, reliable, loyal, and passably literate, though he didn't spend much effort to get to know him and his family—he was just an employee after all.

"Lastly," Hamilton said, "Mr. Weeks claims to have an alibi, namely, that he was having dinner with this brother during the night of Miss Sands's disappearance."

"Is the brother credible?" Livingston asked.

"I don't know, I haven't met him," Hamilton allowed.

"Well, let's get to work, we have a case to win," Burr said without much apparent enthusiasm.

The People v. Levi Weeks started at 10 in the morning with the jury needing to be seated and scores of witnesses sworn. It was a packed courtroom, including a few writers for newspapers.

The court clerk addressed the prisoner, "Levi Weeks, prisoner at the bar, hold up your right hand and hearken to what is said to you. These good men who have been called, and who do now appear, are those who are to pass between the People of the State of New York, and you, upon your Trial of Life and Death. If, therefore, you will challenge them, or either of them, your time to challenge is, as they come to the book to be sworn, and before they are sworn, and you will be heard."

The Clerk then called the jury from the panel and gave the defendant a chance to challenge jurors, the Quakers being dismissed, as they refused to serve on juries wherein a death sentence was at stake.

The preliminaries dispensed with, the Assistant Attorney General addressed the court and jury. He looked nervous in the dim December light of the courtroom. He took a deep breath and began, "In a cause which appears so greatly to have excited the public mind, in which the prisoner has thought it necessary for his defense, to employ so many advocates distinguished for their eloquence and abilities, so vastly my superiors in learning, experience and professional rank; it is not wonderful that I should rise to address you under the weight of embarrassments which such circumstances actually excite."

Burr leaned to whisper into Hamilton's ear, "I think I'm rather going to enjoy this, poor man." The Assistant Attorney General was an aspiring Federalist.

The state's prosecutor gathered himself, picking up speed, "But gentlemen, although the abilities enlisted on the respective sides of this cause are very unequal, I find consolation in the reflection, that our tasks are so also. While to my opponents it belongs as their duty to exert all their powerful talents in favor of the prisoner, as a public prosecutor, I think I ought to do no more than offer you in its proper order, all the testimony the case affords, draw from the witnesses which may be produced on either fide all that they know, the truth, the whole truth, and nothing but the truth."

Burr looked at the jury, several of the men already looked distracted. The prosecutor's demeanor was suited for government work.

"If I had the power of enlisting the passions and biassing the judgment, which those opposed to me possess, I should think it unjustifiable to exert it on such an occasion."

"Spare us," Burr muttered.

The prosecutor went on, too long in Burr's mind. They finally got to the witnesses, and Burr saw an opportunity to deny some of the hearsay evidence. He made a procedural objection, urging the court, based on specifically cited precedence, to deny some of the testimony. The judge agreed.

After 12 hours of testimony and more than 50 witnesses deposed, it was Hamilton's turn for some courtroom theatrics, with someone present in the courtroom that the legal team had reason to suspect was the actual murderer. As Livingston asked a witness, William Dustan, about their recollection of events, Hamilton made his way into the audience with two lit candles. Dustin replied to Livingston's question, "Last Friday morning, a man, I don't know his name, came into my store."

Hamilton, now next to Richard Croucher, held the candles on either side of his face, and called out, "Was this the man you saw in your store?"

Croucher was horrified and quickly turning red.

Dustan responded, "Yes! That was the man!"

Livingston asked the witness, "What did he say?"

Dustin, now speaking with greater authority, replied, "He said, 'Good morning gentlemen, Levi Weeks is taken up by the High Sheriff, and there is fresh evidence against him from Hackensack.' He then went away and as he went out, he said, 'My name is Croucher." And this was all the business he had with me."

The prosecutor objected and was overruled by the judge.

Hamilton now had legal blood in the water and, after establishing Levi Weeks's alibi—having dinner with his brother on the night in question, he set about destroying the credibility of the main prosecution witness, Richard Croucher. His voice rising and falling as he spun Croucher's history as "a shady salesman of ladies' garments." Hamilton having set the scene, called Croucher back to the stand and got him to reaffirm that he was a tenant at the same boarding house as the late Gulielma Sands and using candles again to ensure the jury could see his face—Objection! Overruled!—he then got Croucher to admit that he had a strong argument with Weeks, the deceased's fiancé. Hamilton then paused, looked at the jury, and said to them, "Mark every muscle of his face, every motion of his eye. I conjure you to look through that man's countenance to his conscious."

At this point, Croucher broke down in tears plunging from one admission to another.

Now, 75 witnesses later, the prosecution's case was in ruins.

Closing arguments were anticlimactic and, by 1 a.m. on April 2, the jury was released for deliberation of their verdict. Only five minutes later they emerged, finding Levi Weeks not guilty. The trial concluded at 1:30 in the morning.

Chapter Thirty-One – Massacre

May 31, 1800, Ohio River

Lelewayou was born a Lenape, known as the Delaware among the white man; his tribe had moved from their ancestral lands on the Delaware River west to the Ohio. In 1782, as a young boy, he was almost killed at the hands of American militiamen led by Captain Williamson at the Gnadenhütten Village massacre south of New Philadelphia. All but two of his band, 96 in all, were wiped out as their professed neutrality during the colonists' war with their mother nation was viewed with suspicion. As fierce Indian raids on the frontier, encouraged by the British, were met with American reprisals, no tribe could remain neutral.

Now, adopted into the Shawnee, he was leading his first war party—48 warriors—against the white man. Success might even bring him to the attention of the great Shawnee chief Weyapiersenwah, known as "Blue Jacket" among the white settlers steadily encroaching on his tribe's lands.

The plan was simple enough. They'd set up an ambush along the trading path that led north to some new settlements up from the Ohio River from Kentucky. If the party was of the right size, they'd attack, taking captives and goods back to the tribe some three days march to the northwest.

Lelewayou and his men settled into the tall grass and bushes near a stream that fed into the mighty river, some two miles from the Ohio itself. The sun was almost overhead, now being covered by grey and white clouds, now not, when he heard a horseshoe strike a rock.

The wind freshened from the south, bringing with it the smell of burning tobacco. Lelewayou waited, confident that his men would remain hidden and would not act until he gave the signal.

He slowly raised his head. He saw a file of men, all mounted, all armed, heading north, two abreast, with each man about five horse lengths behind the other. The lead man had a rifle, perhaps a brace of pistols, and a sword. This was no group of traders. These were heavily armed Kentucky militia.

Lelewayou thought back to his youth. The top of his scalp was scarred and hairless, an embarrassing reminder of the scalping he received as a boy.

He waited. Counting. Ten. Twenty. Thirty. Forty. Fifty. He counted 100 soldiers. Then, at the end of the column came three large wagons each pulled by four horses. The wagons were heavily laden and covered with canvas. As they bumped along, their cargo made dull metallic sounds. Lelewayou reckoned they were hauling farm implements. Another 20 armed men followed the wagons. Counting the men he saw in the wagons, there were at least 125 men in this party.

There would be no attack today.

Lelewayou waited until the sun traveled half the distance to the horizon and then gave the signal to move to the rally point he set before the ambush. Each warrior silently rose and moved off to the east, eventually falling into single file column.

Lelewayou was the last to arrive. His men were drinking water and eating pemican. He motioned them to gather round. "Today was not a good day for a fight," he said quietly. The older braves nodded silent agreement. Several of the younger men looked angry, but not enough to speak out.

"There is something unusual about the party we saw. It's not a trading party. It's a war party. I wish to follow them to their encampment and then one day beyond." Lelewayou looked to his senior braves. One by one, they nodded agreement until he came to Chinkwe, the youngest of his war party leaders.

"What do we do then? Why not wait here until a trading party comes by?" Chinkwe asked.

"There are two reasons, Chinkwe," Lelewayou said patiently, "The men we saw are on horse and heavily armed. They stand between us and anything we might gain by our efforts. We don't want to fight twice. And, such a party is odd. They travel with a purpose. I want to know this purpose."

Chinkwe nodded.

Lelewayou stood taller, his eyes sweeping across the faces of his warriors, "John," he said, addressing a blue-eyed man with lighter skin and light brown hair, "You are our best tracker. You lead our party. We sleep a five-minute walk away from their camp tonight. We will then follow these men until the sun reaches noon. Then we will decide what to do next."

Lelewayou and his 48 moved stealthily through the night under a starry sky until John doubled back and told them to stop as they were nearing the militia encampment.

Lelewayou didn't sleep much. But at least he had no bad dreams.

They awoke before dawn, straining to hear any sounds from up the trail. John had gone ahead and, after a short time, he returned.

"They've broke camp," John hissed. "They continue to travel north, though they've left the three wagons behind with some men."

This was unexpected. Lelewayou narrowed his eyes in the faint predawn darkness that held just enough light that he could recognize each man by their profile.

The color that came with dawn was just being seen, first yellow, then green, when Lelewayou heard gunfire in the distance, to the north.

"John!" Lelewayou, said, "Take five of the swiftest, take care not to let the men with the wagons see you, and report to me what you see. I will be at the wagons on your return. Go!"

Lelewayou turned to the remaining 43 as John was already heading out, "We will take those wagons. Use knives. I want no sound if we can help it."

Lelewayou's war party trotted quietly along the trading path until it opened to a clearing. He could see the wagons. A man stood on one, looking north. Three other men moved about, though their attention was also fixed north. A fifth man was returning from relieving himself, his back to Lelewayou.

Lelewayou picked up the pace and his men followed. Within seconds, three men were dead, one man was racing north, screaming in terror and trying in vain to outrun four of Lelewayou's braves while the man on the wagon had drawn a pistol and was pointing it angrily at Lelewayou.

Using English, Lelewayou addressed him from 30 paces away, figuring that at that range, the man only had half a chance to hit him with a well-aimed shot. "Why are you on our hunting grounds?"

The man relaxed slightly, "We're not here to hunt y'alls' game, we're here to catch us some escaped slaves."

Lelewayou gestured to the north to the stiffening gunfire, "Do I not hear fighting? It sounds like your slaves wish to be freemen."

Lelewayou gave a signal and a dozen arrows arced through the air, eight of them finding their mark, including one arrow that pierced the man's throat. His eyes wide, he aimed at Lelewayou and fired, the ball whizzing harmlessly overhead.

Lelewayou saw the men returning from their chase, one triumphantly holding a scalp. "We now wait for John. Spread out. Do not be seen."

The sun was only a quarter of why through morning when John and his men cautiously appeared. Breathing heavily, with sweat drenching his buckskins, John found Lelewayou, "You were right!" John looked around the encampment and saw the four dead and scalped men, "These men are attacking a stockaded village. Whoever is there is fighting back. The men took some women and children. Black women and children. They're coming back this way on horseback and will be here soon. They're being pursued."

Lelewayou thought quickly, "You! Put those men on the wagons. Prop them up. You two, hide the man you slew up the trail and cover the blood." He turned to John, "Are the captives on foot?"

"Yes!"

"Good. They will be the first to arrive. Kill those guarding them. Take them to safety over there." Lelewayou pointed to the edge of the clearing to the west.

Lelewayou deployed his warriors in a sack, a dozen to each side of the trail and two dozen at the edge of the clearing behind the wagons. On his signal, his men would first fire their rifles and muskets, and then use their bow and arrow and then close in with knife and tomahawk.

Curious, Lelewayou pulled back the canvas on a wagon. It was piled high with heavy iron shackles.

Five men on horseback herding a group of ten women and eight children, all able to walk, came into the clearing. One man was yelling at the women, cracking a whip overhead. The captives, all with skin darker than his own, were crying. Lelewayou waited. The men came closer, the noise of gunfire echoing more loudly through the green leafy trees up the trail. He could see movement behind the men—perhaps more mounted soldiers. He fired his rifle at the man with the whip. The man clutched his chest, dropped his whip and rolled off his saddle, his right foot caught in the stirrup. His horse spooked and reared up as gunshots felled the remaining four men. The horse turned and charged back up the trail, dragging the man's lifeless body behind it.

Lelewayou jumped up and waved his arms to the captives, "Move! Move there! Now!" He pointed to his left. The captives looked stunned until a woman took charge of the group and led them to the western edge of the clearing. Lelewayou's men moved them into the trees and told them to get down.

Ten down, 115 to go. Lelewayou was thinking this was a rash mistake. His war party was about to lose many warriors, and this would not be easily forgiven by the tribal elders. The women who choose the chiefs would never elevate him if he lost more than a handful of braves—they had so few to lose, and life was precious.

Lelewayou's men were busy reloading their weapons. The sounds of battle grew louder as a mob of about 30 men, some bloodied, made their way into the clearing, eyes wide with confusion and fear.

"Where's Jake?" one called out.

"Jake's dead. I saw Jake's horse galloping north dragging him behind!" another yelled back." The men kept looking over their shoulders to the north.

Lelewayou carefully aimed and fired his rifle. Another man dropped as the edges of the clearing erupted in smoke. Ten men went down. The survivors drew their swords and yelled at each other as they tried to regroup.

None of them drew their pistols or raised their rifles—they hadn't time to reload.

The woods concealing Lelewayou's men were too thick to easily allow the horsemen to make a clean charge, even if a lieutenant did take command and order one.

Then the arrows came. Two more men fell, writhing in pain. A struck horse reared up, threw its rider, and then galloped south; an arrow having pierced its neck. The men struggled to load their pistols, their numbers dwindling by the second.

"Make a break for it!" a man screamed. A dozen mounted men spurred their horses to the south, the man who lost his horse was pulled up by a comrade and they joined the mad dash down the trail. Arrows followed them, finding the horse and its two riders. Bloodied, they drove on to the Ohio and safety.

Forty down, 85 to go.

Now a steady stream of riders would make it into the clearing, two or three at a time, some wounded. They'd pause in confusion, seeing the death in the camp they'd left hours earlier and then, gunshots and arrows from the trees, they'd urge their horses on down towards the Ohio. Some made it.

The gunfire slackened. Lelewayou could hear occasional screams and cussing. Then he saw them, black men with muskets topped with bayonets. Some of them wore faded blue uniforms.

Lelewayou ran out into the clearing in front of the wagons and motioned for his men to bring the captives to him. He called out to his men to stand down but stay hidden.

The men came marching, eight abreast, shoulders filling up the trail with ranks of bayonets seen behind. Lelewayou figured there were at least 80 of them, all armed.

Lelewayou stood in the clearing. The front row of men dropped to their knees, aiming their muskets at him, the men behind facing left and right. "Ambush!" someone yelled as the women and children stumbled out into the clearing next to Lelewayou. "Cease fire! Cease fire!" a uniformed man called out.

"Praise be to God!" he yelled, "Halleluiah! They're safe!" The men erupted in cheers and laughter.

Lelewayou remained standing as the former captives raced to be reunited.

Their captain strode forward, alone, to greet Lelewayou.

"My name is Ted White, thank you," he grinned broadly from under a well-worn cocked hat, his blue uniform faded and patched, but his buckskins were new.

Lelewayou took his proffered hand and shook it, "I am Lelewayou of the Shawnee. What happened here?"

White gestured around the clearing, "Raiders from Kentucky. They came up here fixing to capture some of us. Plantation owners in Kentucky will pay as much as $200 to recapture a slave in good health or any black man whether he was ever a slave."

"But you are an army," Lelewayou said admiringly.

"We are trying to become one, yes," White replied, "We were sent west from New York with some weapons and supplies. We've been here a month and did what we could to build some defenses and begin clearing and planting. Many of the men served with the Continental Army or even with the British. But now we fight for ourselves. We have wanted to meet with the Shawnee and arrange a truce. We just want to live free. Do you know Blue Jacket?"

Lelewayou nodded. Perhaps this day would elevate him in the eyes of his tribe. He killed many enemy, captured three wagons and some horses, and made a new friend who could prove to be helpful to the Shawnee.

Chapter Thirty-Two – Paine's Return

June 15, 1800, New Rochelle, New York

The 17-mile ride to New Rochelle from Manhattan invigorated Burr. The sky was clear, the day was mild, and the country was still festooned with flowers while corn stalks were already two feet high in some fields.

Burr walked up to the small, white, two-story cottage on the farm once belonging to Frederick DeVeaux, a Tory. The cottage was overgrown with trees and bushes—likely unoccupied for years.

The cottage and the surrounding 300 acres were seized from DeVeaux after he was convicted of treason against the State of New York and then gifted to Thomas Paine in 1784—though he had only just moved into the cottage a few weeks ago upon arriving from France. Unfortunately, the main stone farmhouse burned down seven years earlier while Paine was in France. Even so, Paine brought very little back with him from France beyond clothes, books, and unfinished manuscripts.

Burr dismounted, tied his horse to the hitching post, and knocked at the door.

He heard Paine call out from inside and waited. It was quiet for a time and Burr cocked his head in puzzlement.

"Aaron Burr! Is that you?"

The voice came from the side of the cottage. There was Paine, his head sticking around from the right side of the house.

"The one in the same. What are you…?"

"Can't be too careful, my friend, I've discovered that some people want me dead. It seems my pamphlets have angered too many kings and lords." Paine started walking towards Burr with a smile and an outstretched hand.

The men shook hands and Paine tried to open his front door.

"Damn!" Paine spat out and then muttered, "Old fool," before walking back to the side of the house and saying loudly before disappearing, "The door's barred. Just a moment…"

Burr shook his head and wondered if Paine had always been like this or if time's toll had dulled his considerable capacities. Seconds later the door opened. "There we go! Please, come in!"

Burr smelled no alcohol on Paine's breath and Paine seemed cleaner than the first and only time they formally met 15 years earlier in New Jersey.

"Have you thought about our last conversation?" Paine said, staring directly into Burr's eyes.

"How could one not? Not only have I thought about it, but I've also been doing all within my limited authority to address the shortcomings in our form of government. We've greatly expanded the franchise—30,000 voted in the election for governor two years ago, six times the vote in 1783."

"Good start, Aaron. How much has the state grown?" Paine wasn't fully convinced.

"Roughly doubled," Burr admitted.

"So, you still have property requirements?" Paine responded.

"We do. Though we have plenty of land and I've arranged for veterans of the war to easily acquire land to qualify them to vote."

"So, you're addressing the symptoms and not the disease, eh?"

"I do what I can. I'm not the Governor. I've only been appointed the Attorney General and with it, my position on the Land Board has allowed me to make thousands of men property owners."

"In your letters to me, you spoke of a new government. A new national government. One that would improve on the terrible Philadelphia constitution you almost adopted."

"Yes…"

"You know why that constitution was terrible? Three things. First, you assign the executive all the prerogatives of the Crown, including the negative power of vetoing the will of the people expressed by the parliament. This negative power was established by conquest, not by compact. Why carelessly copy it? Second, the terms of office were too long—especially the Senate— it takes its form the House of Lords, more properly, the House of Robbers. As the sage Franklin said, 'Where annual election ends, tyranny begins.' The third, the method of choosing electors was left to the states. All kinds of mischief could result from this. It must be specified! The fourth. Did I say three things? Four. The franchise wasn't made broad. Linking suffrage to property is absurd and it makes for artificial distinctions among men. Do not the rich become poor and the poor rich? Riches are not permanent and therefore, having no stability, cannot be the foundation of a right. Five. Slavery must be abolished. And lastly, there should be provision made for payments to persons dispossessed from land, some compensation to offset the system of landed property along with an additional payment to those of the age of 50 years and older. There was one thing right though—two houses! One house leads to too much precipitancy, as we see in your Confederation Congress. Two houses of equal size and power, lead to calm deliberation."

Burr waited to see of Paine would continue. Paine looked up from his thoughts and stared at Burr. "Are you ready for a real constitution, Burr? Are you ready for revolution? Certainly, Boston isn't ready for it—in thrall to

John Adams as they are. The slaveowners of the South? Nay! New York? A good start, but not a nation. What say you, Mr. Burr?"

Burr stared back at Paine. He was pleased that Paine had internalized his suggestions and entreaties in the ongoing correspondence he'd exchanged with the old philosopher and soul-stirrer. "Will you draft for us a declaration of independence? One of your own words, free from interference? New York, Pennsylvania, Delaware, and New Jersey for a start. Others may join as they may."

"Yes, yes I will. That is why I returned from France, is it not? And a constitution?"

Burr responded, "I was thinking of a simple order. Similar to the Council of Appointment in New York. We'd elect a president from among all the states by popular vote. He'd have one vote on the council and be commander-in-chief, but have no negative, no veto. And each governor, or their designated deputies, would have a vote as well. Simple."

"Yes, but legislative power needs to come directly from the people. Why not a congress of two houses? Each of equal size, apportioned by population serving for one-year terms?"

"After you draft a declaration, please send me your ideas on a new constitution. We've much work to do. England seeks to move on our weakness and the Tories lick their wounds in Canada seeking revenge. Who knows? The old Loyalist who owned this place might return someday to kill you and sleep in his old bed!"

Chapter Thirty-Three – A Secret Alliance

October 12, 1801, Manhattan, New York City

Burr had a lot riding on a successful. Times were hard, harder than in '89 and, for most, the hardest they'd been since the War for Independence. The Federalists and old Loyalists were, of course, carefully hoarding their fortunes and recalling their loans. Rebellion was in the air again, helped along by Thomas Paine's new pamphlets, and Burr aimed to make good use of the unrest.

Being president of a rump republic of four or five states would be a start, but only so. To truly become master of the continent he needed help, and France, in the form of First Consul of France, Napoleon, was the one to help him.

Burr's plan was simple and bold: First, convince Napoleon's representatives that he was on the verge of unifying America under his leadership; Second, offer to help France recover Canada or, at least, certainly French-speaking Lower Canada, formerly, the French colony of Quebec; Third, secure military assistance from France to increase his odds to achieve his foremost objective.

Burr thought it a mixed blessing that the War of the Second Coalition against France was grinding to a close after French victories last year in Piedmont at Marengo and in Bavaria at Hohenlinden. And now, with William Pitt the Younger out as British Prime Minister, replaced by the diplomatically minded Henry Addington last February, Britain was prepared to listen to Napoleon's peace offers. More so that Napoleon wasn't as revolutionary as was the Directory overthrown by Napoleon and his Consulate two years before. Plus, it didn't hurt that British belligerence was damped by Austria's surrender in February and the successful Franco-Spanish expedition that knocked Portugal out of the war four months later. Lastly, rising British fears of a Russian declaration of war tempered even the most ardent voices for war in Parliament. While peace, however temporary, might make Napoleon more likely to think once again about North America, peace also meant that both France and Britain might consider plucking the indolent American states—so rich, but so negligent in their defensive preparations.

Burr's plan for the day was to meet with Louis-André Pichon, France's ambassador to America, and Edmond-Charles Genêt, the former French ambassador from the early days of the revolution in France. Genêt ended up marrying one of Governor Clinton's daughters and stayed on in America due to his well-founded fear that the Reign of Terror would remove from him his head. With the fall of the radical revolutionaries, Genêt was rehabilitated. Most importantly, he now had a firm grasp of American politics and was a Burr ally.

Then, depending on how those discussions unfolded, Burr hoped to dissuade Napoleon from carrying out what were rumored to be plans to crush the nascent republic in Saint Domingue. For that purpose, he invited Saint Domingue to send a representative for discussions.

General Jean-Jacques Dessalines, the deputy to General Toussaint Louverture, sailed the 1,500 miles from his island to New York. General Louverture had named himself governor-for-life of the America's second republic, after helping to lead a massive slave uprising in French Saint Domingue in 1791, said to be inspired by the French Revolution in 1789.

Burr did admit to himself a measure of jealousy towards Louverture in his proclamation of lifetime tenure.

After the French revolutionary government issued a decree abolishing slavery throughout the French realms in February 1794, General Louverture thought it wise to proclaim his allegiance to France. Just before the British, seeking to weaken France and capture what had been France's most-profitable colony, invaded in 1793, and then escalated their effort significantly three years later. By 1798, tropical diseases and General Louverture had inflicted 100,000 casualties on the British.

Having defeated his internal and European enemies, Louverture turned on the Spanish, his former allies on the eastern half of the island, and overran Santo Domingo in January, announcing an end to slavery there.

Burr thought it obvious that Louverture and his men could not be conquered and forced back into slavery—no matter the terrible lure of the colony's massive profits from the export of sugar. Plus, and here was a bonus only an American could truly understand, Louverture's successful revolution horrified the states to the south where there were twenty times more black slaves than were in New York and the other northern states. Burr's task was to convince Napoleon that the long-term rewards of aiding him outweighed the costly but likely short-term gains of reestablishing slavery in Saint Domingue.

There was a knock at the door. Burr rose to open the door to his office. It was Genêt. His blue eyes set below a tussle of brown hair and a nose that time was rendering increasingly beak-like.

Burr smiled and grasped Genêt's hand with both of his, "Citizen Genêt, how are Cornelia and the children today?"

"Little Maria is now nine weeks old. Henry is hale. But, junior, I worry for him," Genêt looked away.

Burr pulled the man closer and squeezed his right arm with his left hand, "It is never easy to have a sickly child. I shall commend little Edmond Charles to my prayers."

"*Merci mon ami, merci.*"

"When was the last time you spoke with Pichon?"

"A month ago. We haven't kept in touch as frequently since the naval conflict was resolved a year ago. I understand he's been spending more time in Baltimore, meeting with Jefferson and others."

Burr's face darkened slightly for a brief moment. Genêt likely didn't notice.

"Please, sit. Coffee?" Burr gestured to an upholstered wingback chair. There were three, as well as three more modest chairs up against a well-stocked bookcase.

"Please…"

Another knock at the door suggested the ambassador's arrival.

Burr rose to let him in. He and Pichon met a few times socially and had informal contact as they worked to end the Quasi War in a manner more favorable to New York and France than to Massachusetts and England.

"Ambassador Pichon, welcome!" Then shifting to French, Burr said, "I trust you know Citizen Genêt well?"

The Ambassador smiled at both men and greeted them with kisses on each cheek. "Good to see you both well!"

"Coffee?" Burr asked, preparing to pour it himself. No servants were visible.

"Please, thank you."

They engaged in a few minutes of obligatory small talk before Genêt viewed it time to break the ice, "Ambassador Pichon…"

"Please, call me Louis." Pichon's eyes sparkled. He was clearly interested in what this conversation might hold.

"Louis. My friend asked you here today to lay out for France a proposition that would clearly be in your interest."

Burr smiled, "Louis, thank you again for making your way here. First of all, I wish to convey my congratulations to France for its victories on the battlefield. I understand that your enemies, England chief among them, are seeking peace even now."

"Yes, thank you." Pichon nodded, sipping his cup of coffee.

Burr continued, "As you are no doubt aware, the United States is on the verge of breaking its bonds—at least the governmental bonds. New England is chafing for closer relations with Britain. They resent our policy of selling warships to any bidders."

"So do the English," Pichon broke in.

"Especially the English," Burr allowed. "Meanwhile, New York, New Jersey, Pennsylvania, and Delaware are increasingly interested in manufactures and developing the Northwest. Boston would rather trade and import. Further, we are encouraging more farming. Boston is embarrassed of their farmers. And the South with their slaves seem content to live in the past. They refuse to spend money to defend themselves."

"Yes…" Pichon confirmed, signaling he knew and agreed with Burr's assessment.

"It is time for a new order in America. Just as Napoleon overthrew the Directory without blood, the people are ready for change. They chafe under the rule of the rich—the American aristocracy. I will run for election as President of a new federal order, joining four states under my leadership with New York as its capital. I will win and assume office by next spring."

Genêt nodded and said, "And he has my father-in-law's support and that of my cousin too." Genêt was referring to Governor George Clinton and his nephew, DeWitt Clinton, the Mayor of New York.

"What do you propose?" Pichon said with only a diplomatic hint of suspicion.

"Three things. First, a formal defensive alliance with France upon my taking office. Second, the provision of Gribeauval cannon, including at least forty 12-pounders and a dozen 24-pounder siege cannons…"

Pichon interrupted, "Our army is only new receiving the new 12-pounders, you may have to settle for 8-pounders."

Burr smiled, "It never hurts to ask for the best. As I was saying, in exchange, I will arrange for the shipyards of New York and Pennsylvania to build for France four of our 44-gun frigates. France will provide the cannon to outfit these ships. And third, the stationing of up to 20,000 French regulars on our northern border with Lower Canada. You will pay for the soldiers' upkeep and supplies. We will ensure that they receive good food and any logistic support you deem needed and pay for in gold."

Pichon's eyes widened at the last part of the proposal. 20,000 regulars with accompanying artillery could be enough to reconquer Quebec and firmly reestablish France on the North American continent. And, with French regulars already in New Orleans after the secret transfer of Louisiana back to France from Spain last year, France would be in strong position to frustrate English ambitions. Everything lost in the Seven Years' War 38 years earlier would be regained. Pichon would go down in history as a hero and, more importantly, be well-rewarded by Napoleon.

"Of course," Burr added with a grin, "We might accept additional French forces if France was to consider allowing Saint Domingue to continue as a republic."

Pichon sat back. He was dumbstruck that Burr obviously knew of the plans to retake Saint Domingue from the slaves. He frowned at Genêt who simply shrugged in return.

Burr smiled reassuringly, "I understand that this may be a sensitive topic. But allow me to provide a few items for consideration. First, your deployment of soldiers to New Orleans has unnerved my southern brothers. They think you might spread your revolutionary Rights of Man to their negroes. They don't yet know that you intend to reimpose slavery on your large sugar plantation. Second, France cannot post soldiers in northern New York, mostly out of sight of our people for the purposes of a defensive alliance and invade Saint Domingue and keep a large garrison in New Orleans. To do all three will leave me vulnerable to charges of being an agent of France. I will be removed from power and France will lose an ally. Third, those slaves on Saint Domingue are now free. They beat you, they beat the British, and they beat the Spanish. You cannot defeat them—unless your scientists can develop cures against the yellow fever and malaria. Just as we are learning not to listen to the greedy entreaties of the estate holders, slave owners, and merchants, so too will you discover that the people are more numerous and powerful than the plantation owners."

Pichon exhaled, puffing out his cheeks, "Ah, Mr. Burr, perhaps you may be excused in not knowing that Joséphine de Beauharnais, Napoleon's wife…"

"I know who she is…"

"Then you may know she owns slaves through her estates and has many friends among those who lost their plantations in Saint Domingue. She has frequently reminded her husband that it was our most profitable colony."

"And what good is it if it cannot be possessed? The British tried and failed mightily. Think about it. Canada will fall into your hands like a ripe apple. Saint Domingue will kill your sons and give you only grief."

"As you say…"

"General Louverture is a leader as any other. He wants to keep the power and wealth he's fought for. Same with his princes. It's the same with all men. Louverture cannot eat Saint Domingue's sugar, he must sell it. Why take on the burden of overseeing so many slaves? How do you think Louverture grows his sugar? Forced labor, merely slavery by another name. And, because of the disease and harsh working conditions, Louverture must import more labor from Africa, the same as the French plantation owners. The only difference, and it's an important one, is there is the impression of freedom, of self-determination. The reality is that the slaves of Saint Dominque simply exchanged white masters for black masters."

"What are you driving at, Burr?" Pichon was growing weary of the lecture.

"Merely this: you don't need to conquer Saint Dominque, you simply need to make money off of it. For that, you only must control the ports and the export of sugar—to extract an export fee. Boston and London traders won't like it, but they'll still make money on the sugar. Let Louverture grow rich and he'll keep the island in line. No French need die. Now, Louis, I have arranged for General Louverture's deputy, General Jean-Jacques Dessalines, to meet with us tomorrow. Would you be willing to meet with him?"

"That butcher?" Pichon spat out.

"Horrors of war," Burr replied casually.

"If need be, of course. I'd be *honored* to meet any representative of a government that has killed so many British."

Burr chuckled. "More than I have."

"Yes." Pichon smiled and raised his cup in a toast-like fashion, sipping the coffee.

Burr and Genêt returned the smile and did the same.

Burr then leaned forward, "I understand practical decisions. Here is what I propose. You inform First Counsel Napoleon of our offer. He provides guidance to the invasion force that you are no doubt preparing for Saint Domingue and your other lost possessions in the Caribbean. Your fleet sails west and reprovisions in New York. We will open our harbor to you and you may use it as a base for your operations up until the day you decide to invade Saint Domingue. If, on the other hand, you determine it to be in France's greater interest to become reestablished in North America, then execute the provisions of our agreement."

"Assuming you have correctly surmised France's intentions, what if we arrive off of New York and you are not yet First Counsel yourself?"

"Then I only ask for your government's honest assessment of the situation and a modest amount of patience. At the least, you can repair your ships, take on fresh supplies, and be able to gather a significant amount of intelligence while making the English very concerned at your presence. We may even allow your soldiers shore leave and, if agreements can be made, we may provide training grounds so your soldiers can freshen their skills before being committed to retake hell."

At this last Pichon snorted. Burr was right. But, if hell itself was to be taken, then Napoleon was the man to do it.

Chapter Thirty-Four – A People's Republic

December 14, 1801, Manhattan, New York City

"Thank you all for coming," Burr said warmly. The men in the meeting were wigless. Burr thought the ongoing revolutionary sentiment remarkable. The old ways were passing, and they were passing quickly.

There were five of them in the room, all Democratic-Republicans, all equally suspicious of the British and of the Federalists: George Clinton, governor of New York, Thomas McKean, president of Pennsylvania, Joseph Bloomfield, governor of New Jersey, and David Hall, president-elect of Delaware, and Aaron Burr.

Burr got to the point, "Two years ago yesterday, the great patriot and father of our independence, General George Washington left us. Since then, the Confederation Congress has become an even more useless shadow of itself. European nations, Britain chief among them, mock our weakness and seek to reassert their primacy at our expense."

Burr paused and sipped a cup of black coffee and sugar. He briefly held the eye of each of the four men.

"While Simcoe departed Canada seven years ago, the lieutenant governors of Upper and Lower Canada continue his policy of providing aid to the Indians in the Northwest, stymying our westward settlements and threatening our development of Ohio and northwest New York. Further, they still hold four forts in New York, as well as Dutchman's Point in Vermont, and Fort Miami in Ohio.

Burr lowered his voice a bit, "Further, the Federalists have a stronghold to our east: Trumbull Jr. in Connecticut, Tichenor in Vermont, Gilman in New Hampshire, all led by the Anglophile monarchist Adams from his perch in Boston."

"Well," Clinton broke in, "At least Rhode Island remains defiant."

"True," Burr allowed, "Arthur Fenner and his Country Party remain fierce opponents of the Tories and Federalists. Even so, without an organized army and navy, we are at grave risk. Only six years ago, the British set about to conquer Saint Domingue and take for themselves all of the French possessions in the West Indies. They mustered 30,000 men in 200 ships. Imagine…"

Bloomfield broke in, "But they lost 100,000 men in five years and wasted four million pounds! What did it profit them? Beaten by slaves!"

"Joseph, I'm afraid you miss my point. Most of men lost in Saint Domingue were lost to Yellow Fever, not to General Louverture, though he has been extraordinarily effective. My point is that the British pushed in more than 100,000 men to take a small island that, when properly managed, generated enormous wealth in sugar. Their effort was more than double what they committed to try to force us back under the King's rule. Counting the Germans and the Tories, they lost four times more soldiers in the effort than they did here in more than eight years of fighting." Burr stared at Bloomfield and then said a little more slowly for emphasis, "Do not underestimate the capacity or the willpower of the British Empire to engage in conquest. They have only gotten more powerful in the last 20 years while we, we have allowed our strength to atrophy."

Clinton cleared his throat, "And, we have reason to believe that Adams is conspiring with the British to cut off our trade routes."

McKean spoke up, "Perhaps our allowing the French to commission privateers out of your shipyards is an irritant."

"They pay in gold," Clinton replied. "And besides, Baltimore does it as well."

"I wouldn't make too much about that, Tom," Burr smiled, "I understand Mr. Joshua Humphreys is building a special frigate for the French even now in Philadelphia."

McKean started to respond, then, flushing, thought better of it.

"Gentlemen, we are surrounded on three sides by the British and their sympathizers while the South isn't a threat, they've invested even less in their army and navy than have we which, I'm afraid, will invite trouble." Burr looked quite grave.

Hall finally entered the conversation, "What do you propose?"

Burr solemnly looked at the four state leaders, "We propose a simple democratic military alliance with three components. First, a formal exit from the Confederation. Second, a common election for President within the following context: the President will be commander-in-chief and will have an equal vote at a council of five, with each of you having a vote, majority rules. Third, we expand the franchise to all men not in bondage to end, once and for all, the threat of a Loyalist resurgence under the guise of the Federalists."

McKean furrowed his brow, "What about taxes? How will you raise an army and build a navy?"

Burr knew he had won the argument now that McKean, whose Pennsylvania was slightly more populous than New York, was asking a question about details rather than fundamentals. "Simple," Burr responded, "They'll be set by majority vote among the council."

Hall spoke up again, "What if we expand? What if other states want to join our compact—do we keep the same form?"

"Yes," Burr said, eyes glowing, "Each state gets a vote as does the President, with a simple majority deciding, thus addressing the main defect of the Confederation: unanimity."

"I have a state run govern," Bloomfield said, "How can I be expected to vote at this council of yours if I'm in Trenton?"

"You will send deputies who will vote on your state's behalf if you are not present," Burr assured the men.

Bloomfield persisted, "What about the courts? How do we resolve disputes? And who manages the treasury? How can we ensure its integrity?"

Burr smiled, "Joseph, these are exactly the sort of practical issues we should be discussing. Any minister must be approved by a super majority of two-thirds, so, four votes out of five at the start. Disputes will be settled in the same fashion, by the five of us."

"Us?" Bloomfield winked at Burr, "That's rather presumptuous of you, isn't it? I was unaware that you were a governor or president, and we haven't held an election as yet."

Burr laughed, "Fair enough, though I presume you four would rather remain at your posts, since governing a state is still the bigger, more prestigious public office."

"So, when is the election for president? That's what we're calling the office, right?" Bloomfield had made his decision.

Burr had an answer, "Ask your legislatures to approve the arrangement and, two months after the last of you signs the enabling legislation into law, we'll hold an election. I reckon by June of next year should be sufficient. The new president will take office within a month, pending the certification of the results, with the national vote winner being declared President."

Clinton lifted his right hand and said, "Also, the vice president, we'll have a vice president, selected from among the governors and presidents," he first nodded at Bloomfield and then McKean and Hall. "The vice presidency will rotate among the four of us for one-year terms, the president having a five-year term."

"And rights, what about rights?" Hall insisted.

Burr quickly responded, "The people retain all their rights as citizens of the states. We don't want to create a national government that intrudes on your citizens and your powers—we only wish to defend ourselves."

"Should we issue a declaration of independence from the Confederation?" McKean asked.

Burr replied, "I've asked Thomas Paine to draft one, though I'd say his pamphlets have already made the case to our citizens."

"How long has he been back from France? Is he here to stay?" McKean asked.

"A year-and-a-half. And I'd say so. He wants to have a hand in finishing our revolution," Burr said.

Burr handed a parchment with the proposed constitution to every man. "June, earlier if possible. We have work to do."

"So, you're running?" Bloomfield asked.

"If called, I will serve," Burr said with a smile.

Chapter Thirty-Five – Tammany

January 2, 1802, Manhattan, New York City

"Welcome to our wigwam, Chief Burr!" said William Mooney, the Society of St. Tammany's Grand Sachem. He still appeared rough around the edges from year-end celebrations, no doubt.

Burr warmly shook Mooney's hand and dispensed with the pleasantries as quickly as possible. The old war veteran was not whom he was here to see today. Burr stalked down the hall to the room reserved for the planning meeting. The door was already open and Burr quickly scanned the room. There were four men present. John Pintard, a wealthy merchant, was seated at the chair to the right of the chair at the of the table head. Matthew Davis, a newspaperman and Society sachem sat next to Pintard. John Swartwout and William Van Ness sat opposite the two men and, with their backs to the door, turned in their chairs and rose to greet Burr. Pintard was smoking a cigar. The other men were helping themselves to the port wine and apple cider.

"Are we expecting DeWitt?" Pintard asked.

Burr shook his head, "He says we have his support, but we can't trust him or his uncle. If we're going to win this election, we need to take measures outside the Clinton political operation. Now, to the point, to win, we must ensure that everyone who wishes to vote for us can do so. It's too late to change the enfranchisement rules and we don't have a large enough majority in the Legislature to do so anyway, but we have money, and we have land."

Isaac Ledyard, a member of the legislature, walked in with Anthony Lespinard, a Democratic-Republican operative. "Sorry we're late, gentlemen."

Burr nodded, he was especially pleased to see Lespinard and said, "I was just explaining that we need to ensure we have enough voters. In last year's gubernatorial election, there were almost 46,000 votes, with Clinton getting just over half. That's means about one in three men voted in the election. We have about 132,000 men in New York. The legislature selects the governor in New Jersey. How many voters were there in 1801? Anyone know?"

Lespinard cleared his throat, "There are about 50,000 free men in New Jersey. Voter eligibility there is £50 or 100 acres. About 15,000 votes with about 8,000 of those being Democratic-Republicans."

"And Pennsylvania?" Burr asked.

Lespinard was ready, "Pennsylvania allows anyone who pays tax to vote. Just over 70,000 votes in Pennsylvania for governor in 1799 with McKean getting about 38,000. There were about 7,000 votes in Delaware their last elections. You may recall that ten years ago, Delaware emulated Pennsylvania and removed its freehold qualification—any man who pays tax can vote there."

Burr was taking notes, "So, we can expect 95,000 votes—call it 100 for discussion, in the three states plus about 50,000 votes in New York." Burr frowned.

"But," Lespinard continued, "You only need to get a simple majority, assuming anyone prominent runs against you."

Burr looked up, "So, call it half of 150,000 votes—75,000. It seems, though, we may have a threat from Pennsylvania. What if McKean runs and the Federalists don't put up a candidate? If he gets 70,000 votes out of Pennsylvania, he wins."

Ledyard joined in, "Well, you'd get some votes there."

Burr stared at his notes, "We must ensure victory, but not overdo it. We can't have our rivals credibly accuse us of manufacturing victory."

Lespinard smiled, "Easy enough. We need 10,000 new votes out of New York. How much do we have to make that happen? And are we using eligibility rules for the Assembly at an £20 freehold or the Senate's £100 threshold?"

Burr responded, "It's the lower. I've reserved enough land in the north for veterans that we could enfranchise up to 7,000 in time for the election. They'd have conditional titles that they could present to the registrars."

"And the other 3,000?" Lespinard asked.

"The Society can issue loans," Burr said.

"Our treasury can only fund 2,000 voters before we'll run dry," Pintard said reluctantly.

"Gentlemen?" Burr looked around the table, "We're £20,000 short."

Davis immediately jumped in, knowing that to be first might also lead to his not having to lose too much, "I'm in for £1,000."

Burr, knowing what Davis was up to was nonetheless grateful, "Good! Thank you."

Swartwout quietly said, "I can put up 5,000."

"Excellent, thank you, John!" Burr smiled.

There was an uncomfortable silence of three seconds. Burr needed another £14,000.

Van Ness spoke up, "Times are very difficult for me right now, I put up £500."

"Thank you, William, much appreciated!" Burr seemed genuinely moved.

"I can do the same," Senator Ledyard said.

"Same here," Lespinard followed.

"Isaac, Anthony, thank you gentlemen, thank you both!" Burr thought he might get through the meeting without having to dip into his own savings.

Pintard sighed, "Oh hell, Burr, I'll loan the Society £15,000 and the Society can chip in the rest. You'll have your election. Just don't forget your friends when you make that climb to the top!"

"Why climb otherwise, friends?" Burr was beaming. He and Lespinard would now be able to generate an additional 10,000 unexpected votes to ensure the election, scheduled in the four states for March 9, would go completely as planned.

"A question though," Pintard said, "What's to keep New Jersey from changing their enfranchisement rules? What if they dropped the property requirements? Wouldn't that put our plans in jeopardy if they could put up more votes?"

Lespinard had an answer, "No, I don't think so. Of the four states in play, New York has the highest bar for enfranchisement. Some 90 percent of New Jersey men can vote. Hell, even women can vote there if they own their own property."

"90 percent?" Pintard looked skeptical, "Why so high? You said New Jersey requires £50 or 100 acres to vote, that's more than double our requirements."

"I should have elaborated," Lespinard allowed, "During the war, New Jersey broadened their £50 requirement to include paper or proclamation money…"

"Paper money!" Pintard laughed. "Damnit, Burr, figures your election requires real money!"

Chapter Thirty-Six – Code Duello

February 15, 1802, Weehawken, New Jersey

This would be Burr's second duel, though he'd threatened a few other times—his opponents deciding that their lives were worth more than their honor, they withdrew after formal apologies to Burr in writing.

Burr's first duel was fought with John Church less than three years earlier. Church accused Burr of political corruption, alleging he took a bribe from the Holland Company. Both men missed their shots and Church apologized afterwards, saying he shouldn't have accused Burr without evidence. The apology was especially useful for Burr politically: Church's wife, Angelica, was Hamilton's sister-in-law.

William Van Ness, Burr's second and close political ally, inspected the pistols chosen by Harry Croswell, a newspaper publisher. Croswell's second was Morgan Lewis, like Burr, a lawyer and war veteran as well as a signer of the Declaration of Independence. Lewis was also close to John Jay and a Federalist opponent of Burr's.

The duelists crossed the Hudson River from New York to face off in Weehawken, New Jersey, on a narrow strip of wooded land next to the 100-yard-high cliffs of the New Jersey Palisades. Burr hoped Croswell would select this spot. He felt it particularly propitious. For here was where, less than three months prior, Hamilton's 19-year-old son was cut down by George Eacker. Eacker, a lawyer, Antifederalist, and supporter of Burr's through his membership in the Tammany Society, gave an Independence Day speech for a militia brigade and Tammany where he said that Hamilton was opposed to democracy.

Hamilton's son, Philip, took umbrage and demanded Eacker apologize. When Eacker refused, the younger Hamilton demanded a duel. He got it, was shot, and died the next day. Hamilton's family was devastated, with Burr satisfied that Hamilton's political effectiveness was diminished by grief.

On this occasion, Burr wanted to put opposition newspapers on notice.

Croswell published a Federalist paper called *The Wasp* under the pseudonym of Robert Rusticoat, Esquire. The paper, with a masthead that proclaimed its mission was, "To lash the Rascals naked through the world" was founded in opposition to the Antifederalist paper *The Bee*.

Burr didn't mind opposition newspapers—so long as they didn't resort to smearing his honor. In this case, Croswell crossed the line with a scandalous story claiming Burr had several illegitimate children with a negress. That the story was more-or-less true—he had had two children, now 14 and 10, with Theodosia's East Indian servant, Mary—was beside the point. The story was libelous and, as he was running for President, he had to defend his honor and put a chill into the opposition. Especially so as he had ambitious plans and didn't need the press poisoning his relationship with the people—even though few of his base among the common people read Federalist papers.

The men faced off In the early morning light that cast half their faces in shadow and half in the warm morning glow.

Croswell was visibly shaking and his looked as if he was about to vomit.

On the signal, both men lowered their pistols. Croswell fired wide and missed. Burr smiled.

Croswell stood, helpless, arms at his side, only 45 feet away. He dropped his piece.

Burr considered the consequences of killing the newspaperman outright and slowly lowered his pistol. He fired at Croswell's feet and hit.

The pistol's bullet, just over half-an-inch round, bore through Croswell's boot and shattered his right heelbone.

Croswell cried out has he hit the ground in agony.

Van Ness ran out of the woods at the base of the cliff, followed by Lewis.

Burr said, "Morgan, I believe your man needs a physician. If you don't have a good one, I believe I do. If he's lucky, Croswell might even keep his leg."

Lewis glared at Burr and called for Van Ness to help him get Croswell back into the boat they took across from New York. Lewis worked frantically to stanch the blood flow with a tourniquet.

Again, Burr smiled, but only inwardly. He strode forward and helped the other two men carry a writhing Croswell to the river.

Burr looked to his right, to the south and downriver out to the Upper Bay and saw what appeared to be a warship at full sail making its way up the Hudson. He looked back down at Croswell whom he had gripped under each knee as they sloshed into the river next to the boat.

With Croswell safely aboard, Burr climbed back on the rocky bank and looked again at the ship. It was a brig. It was flying the French colors. Burr nodded. The timing was perfect.

Chapter Thirty-Seven – National Popular Vote

March 24, 1802, New York

The French fleet showed up in New York a little more than five weeks earlier with dozens of ships of the line and frigates and scores of transports carrying some 40,000 troops.

Soon after, British ships showed up to shadow the French fleet. British warships were sighted off the coast of Boston, New York, and at the mouths of both the Delaware Bay and the Chesapeake Bay.

That the British appeared was serendipity for Burr. Within days, pro-Burr newspapers were breathlessly publishing stories about the imminent threat of British invasion. Burr expected the voters, whipped into a patriotic fervor, would flock to his banner, seeing Pennsylvania Governor McKean—68-years-old a week before Election Day—as too phlegmatic to lead the new nation, while John Jay, the Federalist candidate, was too pro-British.

Burr expected the results from Election Day, Tuesday, March 23 from New York City, Brooklyn, western Queens County, and Staten Island to foretell his chances. And the results were far better than even he expected: he received 20,280 votes to Jay's 4,333 to McKean's 511.

Of equal importance was the overwhelming support of the plebiscite to create a new nation and approve the new constitution. That vote was running 21,002 to 4,151.

Results would start trickling in from up the Hudson over the next week as county sheriffs certified the vote and transmitted it to Albany for formal tabulation and, in about 10 days, word from New Jersey, Pennsylvania, and Delaware would make it final: Burr would be the first directly elected President in North America. The prize was sufficient, for now—he was not entirely satisfied with the arrangement of a collective council with votes from the four governors and himself constituting legislative power. But, in time, and with ample fear of foreign invasion, he was confident his position as commander-in-chief and president would allow him to consolidate power. In fact, he was sure the people would demand it.

It was now just before noon. Burr had stayed up late the night before with his Tammany Hall lieutenants, dispatches coming in via horse and rider—a technique he gladly adopted from the Federalists' failed effort to ratify the Philadelphia constitution.

In a few minutes he expected the generals Leclerc and vicomte de Rochambeau to arrive as his guests for lunch. General Charles Leclerc—

whose wife was Napoleon's sister—and his deputy, vicomte de Rochambeau, son of comte de Rochambeau, the French hero of the American Revolution and the victory over the British at Yorktown, had been anchored in the Lower Bay since February 28.

At Burr's suggestion, Donatien-Marie-Joseph de Vimeur, the vicomte de Rochambeau, was feted at what, for a normal man, would have been an exhausting series of dinners and speeches with old heroes of the Revolution—Rochambeau having accompanied his father on the Yorktown campaign (and even fathering an illegitimate child in Williamsburg in late 1782). In this, Rochambeau was a more than willing participant in Burr's electoral schemes, cementing good feelings between revolutionary France and revolutionary America—and showing the public that Burr had a strong ally against any British attempt to subjugate the new American Republic.

Further, Burr invited the French army offshore—with some Polish Legions and even some soldiers from northern Italy—to train with the New York militia, thousands of whom spontaneously swarmed to Long Island to see their revolutionary comrades who, much like the Americans, fought the British virtually nonstop over a decade to create a new regime. Though, after only four weeks, Burr's Tammany machine encouraged the militiamen to return to their home counties in time for the vote.

Burr, officing at Tammany until the election was certified, heard the French officers in the hallway and walked from behind his desk to greet them. Generals Leclerc and Rochambeau were both compact men, Rochambeau being a little shorter than Burr at about 5'4." Both men wore black boots that came almost to their knees with white breeches, thick golden sashes around their waists, high collars of red and gold, and dark blue jackets. They left their large black felt and gold-trimmed bicorne hats and swords in the entrance—these being very impractical to wear inside. Leclerc, being the senior, stepped forward, his grey-blue eyes intensely searching Burr for any hints of news.

"Monsieur Burr, are you yet President?"

Rochambeau's dark brown eyes also bore into Burr. These were men of action and Burr knew they were growing tired of being entertained by the Americans.

Burr stepped forward and firmly shook both men's hands and then offered them tea, coffee, whisky, or cider. Rochambeau asked for whisky, Leclerc, coffee. The fully stocked and well-staffed Tammany Hall operation efficiently made it so and Burr invited the generals to take a seat while stepping behind them to close the door to the office.

Burr turned to Leclerc and spoke in French, "We only have the election returns from the immediate vicinity of New York so far. I have about 20,000 votes to Jay's 4,000. Our lead suggests that we should win New York State with more than enough votes to carry the election. Though, to be sure, I would very much like to see some returns from New Jersey or Pennsylvania first."

Leclerc nodded slightly and asked, "When do you expect the first results from those states?"

"Within a week to 10 days."

Rochambeau looked at Leclerc, briefly clenching his jaw. Leclerc waved him off and replied, "We've waited more than a month, we can wait another week. In the meantime, you've been most hospitable, and our soldiers are greatly enjoying the time ashore."

Burr asked Leclerc, "What of the British fleet? There are reports of British ships from Boston to Chesapeake Bay. Do you have additional information? Have any transports been sighted?"

Asked a military question, Leclerc responded with a relaxed tone, "Off the coast of North America, we have only seen what you have seen. So far, we believe there are two squadrons shadowing our force, one to the north, consisting of three ships of the line and four frigates, and one to the south consisting of six frigates. British activity in the Caribbean is not alarming, at least as of two months ago. We dispatched Captain Willaumez with a force of two frigates to scout up to the Gulf of Saint-Laurent as we arrived. We expect his return shortly and will inform you if Captain Willaumez saw anything unexpected."

Burr turned serious, "General, once my victory has been confirmed, I propose we move quickly. I understand you brought the Gribeauval cannon I requested?"

"Yes, of course, to be provided upon a formal agreement after your election."

"Excellent. Then, have you also brought the cannon to equip the 44-gun frigates we have already started to construct for you in New York?"

"Enough for one ship. We can easily bring more cannon from France—after all, they are one of the last items needed to complete a warship."

"Fair enough. And the gold for payment?"

"I was authorized to pay for the first ship and to advance a payment for the second. Payment for additional ships will be dependent on the quality and delivery of the first ship."

Burr smiled, "Again, reasonable. Good. And my proposal to discretely station 20,000 troops on our border with Quebec?"

"Yes, we agree. Again, on confirmation of your victory and subsequent passing of a defense treaty with France. We will dispatch the remaining 20,000 troops to reinforce our colonies in the Caribbean, New Orleans, and Saint Pierre and Miquelon. We intend to fortify the latter for use as a supply base for potential operations up the St. Lawrence."

"Excellent. One hopes that any commencement of hostilities comes at a time when the weather in Quebec is amenable to offensive operations."

It was now Leclerc's turn to smile, "I understand you know something personally about campaigning in Quebec."

Burr beamed, "Yes, I was in Colonel Benedict Arnold's command. We set out in September 1775 with 1,100 regulars from Massachusetts, sailed to the mouth of the Kennebec River, traveled upriver as far as we could, then traversed over swamp, broken terrain and raging rivers until 600 of us arrived, starving and half-naked, to the gates of Quebec City in November. If we dallied, the winter would have killed the rest of us."

"What do you recommend?" Leclerc intently looked at Burr.

"The best overland route is up the Hudson, to Lake Champlain, the Richelieu River then 40 miles up the St. Lawrence to Montreal and 190 miles downriver to Quebec. If a force moved quickly enough, it should be able to concentrate at Montreal, invest the city, and rally support from the French-speaking population before moving to take Quebec before the British could reinforce by sea. With Montreal and Quebec in your hands, Upper Canada would be cut off and at your mercy. Further, the St. Lawrence is less than 2,000 feet wide at the citadel at Quebec. Provisioning the old fortress with new cannon and building a fort on the opposite bank would prevent the Royal Navy from easily getting upriver. They'd have to disembark troops to take the forts first. Lastly, once you take them, even if the British obtain superiority at sea and blockade the St. Lawrence, we could ensure you remain supplied with food and ammunition. Further, there are only about 5,000 British regulars in all of Canada, about 1,200 to the west in Upper Canada and 3,800 in the east in Montreal, Quebec City, and the Maritimes with many garrisoning Halifax. Upper Canada's population is what, 40,000 to 70,000? But only about one in six are truly loyal to the Crown, the rest are recent American arrivals, interested only in their 200 acres. They won't fight. The Indians are another matter. They'll help the British in the west so long as they think they have a chance. If you take Lower Canada though, you'll cut them off. And Lower Canada has more than 100,000 French-speaking subjects, no? As for Upper Canada, they won't be able to produce enough food to feed their armies. I'd give them a year at the most. And one last consideration," Burr's eyes were gleaming now, "Timber."

"Timber?" Rochambeau asked.

"Timber. Most timber used to build the Royal Navy comes from the Baltic. Napoleon threatens this. If Napoleon cuts off the supply of fresh timber to England, then the only remaining source of timber is North America. If you are serious about defeating Britain and not just forcing temporary armistices, then you must starve the Royal Navy of its timber. Taking Quebec, then, is of strategic import."

"Well then," Leclerc replied, looking first from a skeptical Rochambeau and then to Burr, "We must pray you win."

"I intend on it."

Burr saw the two generals out and immediately began caucusing with his Tammany lieutenants. Things were looking good, very good.

Chapter Thirty-Eight – Pushed into a Corner

March 28, 1802, Monticello, Charlottesville, Virginia

"Thank you for seeing me on a Sunday, Thomas. I wouldn't have imposed unless I thought the matter urgent," Hamilton was wearied from the weeklong ride south from Manhattan—350 miles with increasingly alarming reports of the vote for Burr and the plebiscite carving a new nation of out the United States.

Jefferson's house slaves took Hamilton's coat and offered him refreshments. Normally, this would have made the abolitionist Hamilton uncomfortable, but he had far heavier concerns on his mind.

"The honor is mine, Alexander. It's been too long. So, does Burr win?"

"He's won. New York, Pennsylvania, New Jersey, and Delaware will be a new nation in weeks. Napoleon has even landed 20,000 troops in support."

"20,000…"

"I don't know if they'll be aimed at Canada, Boston or Virginia, but that army is like a poison dagger in Burr's hands." Hamilton's crisp blue eyes flashed an urgent intensity.

Jefferson, melancholic, looked at a favorite painting of his on the wall behind Hamilton, "The French revolution turned out so different from our own."

"Indeed. The question for us is Burr going to be a Napoleon or a Robespierre?"

Jefferson turned back to Hamilton and sat a little straighter in his chair, "Likely a pale reflection of both. Burr, so great in the small things, and yet so small in the great."

Hamilton pressed, "I have an idea to rescue the republic—to rescue us from Burr."

Jefferson pressed back, "Perhaps you could have spared us this point if you hadn't insisted that your perfect constitution didn't need a bill of rights."

"Point taken. I was in error, though I'm not sure that would have made a difference after Bowdoin's reprisals against the Shaysites and Burr's machinations. You do know he had Justice John Hobart killed to ensure the Antifederalists won in Poughkeepsie?"

Jefferson raised an eyebrow. He was less surprised by Hamilton's accusation against Burr than by his ready admission of fault. "Robespierre…" Jefferson said to himself.

"Once Burr's election is certified. I believe within two weeks; I think he'll move swiftly to consolidate power. How is your relationship with Governor Monroe? Would he call out the militia if you asked him to?"

"Not without a clear threat," Jefferson was growing animated, being drawn into Hamilton's dread.

"You must lead the nation, Thomas. You must step up. Republicans trust you and the Federalists have no strong alternative. Other than Massachusetts, the opposition to Burr resides in the South."

"Yet the Articles require unanimity to amend and nine for action. I'm suspicious of a strong, national government, but I don't see how I can get all the states to act as one accord until, as you fear, it is too late."

"That's it, you don't have to. You're popular throughout the South. Even in Tennessee and Kentucky. The Philadelphia constitution only requires nine states to ratify for it to go into force. After Burr pressured New Jersey into rescinding, seven states have ratified. If you could get North Carolina to reconsider and either Tennessee or Kentucky, we'd have a new government capable of defending itself against Burr's designs."

Jefferson was fully engaged now, "Ah, you Federalists, always so crafty with the rules yet so dismissive of the principles. You can't legitimately include Pennsylvania or Delaware—their people voted to form a new nation and to leave the old. You have five states and need four."

"If you get Tennessee and Kentucky and convince North Carolina to reconsider, I'll get Massachusetts. John Adams is as alarmed as I regarding Burr."

"Then what?"

"It's a race, Thomas. Our ratifications and elections against Burr's army. He'll likely seek to attack Massachusetts first. It's closer and he needs to secure his flank."

"What about the British and the French? My influence in Paris isn't what it used to be under Napoleon. Though I still am on agreeable terms."

"Not agreeable enough to have Napoleon forsake landing 20,000 soldiers on your doorstep. As for the British, they will be quite concerned about the threat to Canada and their Caribbean colonies. If you were to agree to having John Adams as your vice president, I think we can expect some measure of British support against Burr and Napoleon. Of course, slavery will be an issue for both Adams and the British."

"I've been pressuring Monroe to agree to end the slave trade into Virginia. He's with me. North Carolina too. South Carolina resists…"

"We can't just end the slave trade. We must develop a plan to end slavery itself. At least be open to it."

"I agree in principle. I did in 1776 and I do now. But perfect principles are hard to put into imperfect practice." Jefferson was again looking at the painting—John Locke in a reddish-brown robe.

"Ha! And you accused the Federalists of being wed to rules, not philosophy." Hamilton smiled gently.

"True enough. Slavery is how we grow our rice, tobacco, and indigo."

"Thomas, your lands are more productive than those in the north. The South has greater abundance. But this won't last long. Either Burr's army will complete what Cornwallis failed to do in 1781 or manufactures will supplant and then eclipse your yeomanry. In any case, that issue can wait. We have an adequately crafted constitution that only awaits approval from four states to become law. If it does, will you agree to allow your name to be put forward for President?"

Jefferson stared at Locke's portrait. "Life, liberty, and property…"

"Locke," Hamilton said and turned in his chair to see the portrait. "Ah, Locke! I envy your collection, Thomas. But don't forget your Montesquieu. Therein is the danger from Burr. He's managed to forge a government that has no real check against him. Once the governors in his council realize that he can have them arrested at a whim, their fears will make his power near-absolute. He'll become a tyrant on his way to an emperor!"

"I will, I will serve, if called. And I will urge ratification—with amendments to follow specifying rights. You must be exhausted. Please, stay a night and allow us to wash your clothes and prepare you for your return journey."

Hamilton breathed a sigh of relief, "Thank you."

"What will you do, Alexander? Where will you go when we have two nations?"

"We'll have two in form, but not in spirit. I'll stay. I can be of greater use fighting Burr from within."

Jefferson's mind drifted back to the rivers of blood in Paris during the Terror. "Perhaps. Though I should think that you have a higher purpose than being a spy and a troublemaker."

Hamilton looked at Jefferson with determination, "You don't know Burr like I do."

Chapter Thirty-Nine – President-Elect Burr

April 15, 1802, Manhattan, New York

The votes had come in and were certified in all four states. The plebiscite creating a new republic won with 59% of the vote. Aaron Burr also won a majority of votes, capturing 50% with Pennsylvania Governor Thomas McKean came in second, with 26%, but winning his home state, and John Jay, third, with 24%. Burr would be sworn in in a month in Manhattan, in the same hall now infrequently used by the Convention Congress—which hadn't achieved a quorum for a year.

And, Burr reckoned, he hadn't a moment to spare, now that the British fleet had arrived in numbers equal to the French fleet, with British ships frequently shadowing their French counterparts.

War hadn't been declared by either the French or the British, but war was in the air. And, at home, he had powerful people aligning against him. But he had an idea to enlist one to his side—or at least keep him occupied.

There was a knock at the door of his office in Tammany Hall. He heard the familiar voice of one of his personal guards say through the door, "Sir, you have Mr. Hamilton here to see you."

Burr grinned, "Thank you, send him in." He rose from behind his desk and made his way towards the door to greet Hamilton who walked in with a strained smile.

"Good to see you, Aaron. Or, should I say, 'Mr. President-elect.'"

"Thank you. Good to see you're well. I understand you've been travelling," Burr said it just so with a tone that wasn't overtly accusatory.

"Yes. Many old friends to see. Some I haven't seen since the war." Hamilton did not seem defensive at all.

"War, yes. That's what I wished to see you about."

"Oh?"

"Yes, you see, I am very concerned about the British. Their fleet off New York grows by the day. I fear they may decide to make war on our new republic before it has a chance to establish itself."

"Perhaps you should have thought of that before you broke the union in two," Hamilton sharply replied.

"The union! When was the last time the Confederation Congress met to consider attending to its own defense?" Burr snapped back. Burr took and breath and said in a quieter voice, "Alexander, the union was sick and weak. We're making a new start. I need you. New York needs you."

Hamilton stared at Burr wondering what the old schemer was up to now. "What do you have in mind?"

"I'd like to appoint you my first ambassador. Ambassador to Britain. You can stop the war. We need you to stop the war. You'd be able to talk sense into the British." Burr looked at Hamilton plaintively.

Hamilton wasn't expecting this. His gaze softened. "It is a great honor. May I think about it for a few days? I have much put in order, both in my practice and with my family."

"Of course, please. But I ask the honor of your reply in two days. I'm afraid we have no time to waste. If you accept, I'd propose asking a British frigate to convey you to London—it might keep the fleet off us for a time."

Hamilton's mind was elsewhere—the Confederation Congress had one last act it must complete before being split asunder by Burr's machinations.

135

Chapter Forty – The Last Congress

May 16, 1802, State House, Philadelphia, Pennsylvania

Burr had been sworn in days earlier as the first president of the new United Republic of America. But the Confederation Congress had yet to formally acknowledge the dissolution of the perpetual union—of course, they hadn't even achieved quorum since March 1801, when they convened to authorize payments on the national debt and to, once again, unsuccessfully take up the issue of Vermont, which was again threatening to declare its own republic if it wasn't granted formal independence from New York.

But the delegates assembling for one last time in Philadelphia, with the quiet approval of Governor McKean—still smarting from his electoral thrashing at the hands of Burr—had other plans.

Hamilton was present, claiming to represent New York. No one from the Burr-Clinton faction was there to dispute him, as they boycotted the proceedings. So did New Jersey. Two delegates from Delaware showed up, one Federalist, the other Anti. And, a full contingent from Pennsylvania was present as well. Connecticut, Massachusetts, New Hampshire sent their representatives. Rhode Island's members were said to be on their way. Lastly, every southern state was represented as well, having been encouraged into coming by Jefferson and a team that included James Madison, James Monroe, and Andrew Jackson.

Burr, focused on his own plans from New York, was unaware of anything unusual. Even if he was suspicious, his only solid intelligence on the South came from his daughter Theodosia—just last year she married Joseph Alston, a wealthy and prominent South Carolinian who, Burr surmised, was destined for elected office.

Congress achieved a quorum and gaveled in. Andrew Jackson, leading Tennessee's three-member delegation asked to be recognized. Jackson, at 6'1," about three inches taller than the average American man, stood above most members present.

"Mr. President, Members, it is with great humility and honor that I rise to announce that Tennessee has become the sixth state to ratify the constitution reported out of this very city in which we convene almost 15 years prior!"

There was silence, then a growing murmur.

"Mr. President, Mr. President!" It was John Fowler, a member from Kentucky.

"The gentleman is recognized," came the reply.

"Mr. President, I too, have news of import, the people of the great Commonwealth of Kentucky also convened a convention to consider ratifying the 1787 constitution. As with our neighbors to the south, we too saw fit to approve the document!"

The murmurs grew into a buzz of excitement, though several of the members from Pennsylvania furrowed their brows and spoke quietly to each other.

"Mr. President, I wish to be recognized." It was John Stanly, a Federalist from North Carolina.

"The gentleman from North Carolina is recognized."

Stanly cleared his throat, "It is a high honor to report that the citizens of North Carolina, convened at the request of the legislature, have once again considered the Philadelphia constitution and in their wisdom, they have approved this new mode of government!"

"Mr. President," It was John Adams from Massachusetts.

"The gentleman from Massachusetts is recognized."

"Mr. President, the Massachusetts Legislature, on behalf of the people, convened a convention to ratify a new constitution and did so, not four days earlier."

The state house chamber filled with shouts of acclamation, though two of Pennsylvania's members ran from the chamber.

"Mr. President, with ratification of the new constitution by the ninth state per Article VII of the same, I move that this body set a date for national elections as set forth in the constitution to commence on Friday, October 31, 1802."

"I second the motion!" bellowed Jackson.

"Call the question, roll call by states, Connecticut?"

"Connecticut, aye!"

"Delaware?"

"Delaware not voting."

"Georgia?"

"Georgia, aye!"

"Kentucky?"

"Kentucky, aye!"

"Maryland?"

"Maryland votes aye!"

"Massachusetts?"

"Massachusetts, aye," Adams, looking tired, quietly responded.

"New Hampshire?"

"New Hampshire, aye!"

"New Jersey? New Jersey? New Jersey not present. New York?"

"New York did not send a complete delegation, Mr. President," Hamilton responded.

"North Carolina?"

"North Carolina votes aye."

"Pennsylvania?"

"Pennsylvania abstains, Mr. President."

"Rhode Island? Rhode Island is absent. South Carolina?"

"South Carolina, aye!"

"Tennessee?"

"Tennessee proudly votes aye!" Jackson yelled from the back of the room to the amusement of many delegates.

"Virginia?"

"Virginia, aye, Mr. President!"

"There being 10 votes in the affirmative, no nay votes and four abstentions or absences, the measure carries."

The chamber erupted in cheers. It was clear many of the delegates met beforehand. This was a coordinated action.

Adams rose again, "Mr. President, I request that this Congress's resolve be sent to the printer and distributed to the states."

"Without objection."

"Mr. President, I move to admit Vermont as the fifteenth state."

"I second!" it was Jackson again, red faced and clearly enjoying himself.

An hour later, after minimal debate, the measure carried with 10 votes.

Adams rose one more time, "Mr. President, I move to adjourn, sine die."

"The motion is not debatable. All those in favor?"

The room roared "Aye!"

"Opposed?" There were a few feeble "Nays" from the Pennsylvania delegation. And, with that, the Confederation Congress met for the last time.

America had two national governments, the United Republic of America, a union of Delaware, New Jersey, New York, and Pennsylvania led by President Aaron Burr, and the United States of America, purporting to represent all 15 states, though not even yet formally operating.

Chapter Forty-One – Opening Moves

May 18, 1802, Manhattan, New York

Burr was furious. He was angry with Hamilton and angrier with himself. Hamilton tricked him, spurring his generous offer of an appointment as Ambassador to the Court of St. James's, citing concerns over family and finances—all the while working to reanimate the moribund Philadelphia constitution. But he saved his fury for his personal failure, brought on by his greatest weakness: arrogance.

Yet, Hamilton's effort was too little, too late. Within days, the Republic's army would mobilize and move on Boston—and there'd be no United States of America to oppose it until at least next spring. The timeline of creating a new government—a government under pressure of invasion—would be too great.

Virginia and Maryland might mobilize their militias, but there was scant chance they'd send them north. Rather, they'd be content to protect their hearth and home. Massachusetts would stand alone.

In the meantime, the French army would head north, marching up the well-trod invasion path: the Hudson River to Lake Champlain, and down to the St. Lawrence to Montreal and then Quebec, only 150 miles distance. By the end of the summer campaigning season, Burr expected his eastern front, Boston, and his northern front, Canada to be secured. The British in Upper Canada, and their Indian allies in the Northwest, would be cut off from all assistance and unable to mount any serious operations along the Erie Canal, which, daily, was being improved, with the temporary wooden locks and sluices being replaced with stone and iron. Burr's sole remaining concern was protecting New York, Philadelphia, and Boston, once liberated, from British bombardment, blockade, and invasion. But additional Gribeauval cannon from France would make any direct assault very costly in men and ships.

Lastly—and Burr was truly excited about this development—French military engineers were working with local artisans and mechanics to construct what they called an "optical telegraph" system. By a chain of signal towers, each within line-of-sight of the next tower, critical communications could be sent during good visibility in daylight hours, greatly speeding military movements, improving logistical efficiency, and allowing Burr and the French commanders to quickly respond to British threats by sea. The first leg of the optical telegraph system would link New York to Quebec, then New York to Philadelphia, then New York to Boston, once that city was taken. Burr marveled at what such a system would have meant for either side during the war for independence.

Chapter Forty-Two – Lean Times

June 3, 1802, Manhattan, New York

Hamilton smiled at Jeph Clark, his longtime legal assistant and office manager he shared with Brockholst Livingston and, before he was elected president of the United Republic of America, Aaron Burr. "Jeph, I'm terribly sorry there hasn't been much work for you in the past year, I'm afraid that Burr has let it be known that I should not be consulted for legal work."

"I understand, sir. Is there anything I can do?" Jeph replied, knowing full well there was nothing a man of his station could do for Hamilton.

"No. It's kind of you to ask." Hamilton paused, thinking. "There is something, something that I'd like you to consider doing for yourself."

"Sir?"

"I don't see my business getting better anytime soon. In the meantime, you have six children at home. May I make a suggestion?"

"Please, sir," Jeph was starting to feel sorry for his boss.

"Squab. Pigeons. You ought to consider keeping some. You can sell the meat. They are easy to raise. And, I fear the price of meat will go up soon. War always does that to food, and, with the British fleet to contend with, I'm guessing our catch will be scarce as well."

"All well and good, sir, but I have no place for them. We barely have room as it is for the children."

"I can help with that."

"Sir?"

"I own a property in New Rochelle. It's a home with three bedrooms and ten acres of land. It's 20 miles away so I'm guessing you'll not be able to spend every night at home, but, if you promise to keep pigeons, I'll sell it to you."

"Sir! Well… Thank you, sir, but I don't have money for such a purchase…"

"Of course, you do, I'll lend it to you. And, if you keep pigeons, I'll forgive the loan in five years."

Jeph was completely puzzled by Hamilton's odd request. But a home! Molly would be thrilled, even if it meant that he'd spend many nights away from home. "I'd be honored to accept your offer, sir," Jeph replied after a few seconds.

"Good, I'll work up an agreement." Hamilton's countenance grew distant as his thoughts drifted back to more weighty concerns.

Chapter Forty-Three – Quebec

July 3, 1802, Quebec City, Canada

The French set off in two divisions of 10,000 soldiers each in late May. Through careful movements of transport boats in full view of the British fleet, the French presented the impression that they were merely embarking and debarking their troops to conduct training on Long Island. In reality, the French were gradually building up their forces in New York and, by small groups of 50 to 100 soldiers, were heading up the Hudson via boat and reassembling out of sight north of Albany. By mid-June, the complete force was in place and the French fleet departed south—a portion with 2,000 soldiers headed for New Orleans, with the majority carrying 18,000 soldiers headed for French possessions in the Caribbean.

General Charles Leclerc led the overall force while General Rochambeau led one of the two divisions. A small French staff contingent remained in Manhattan, the terminus of the newly established optical telegraph system, to liaise with Burr and his War Bureau as well as to send messages to the fleet and back to France.

By late June, the divisions were ready to strike. It was then that the new British ambassador to the United Republic of America paid President Burr a visit. It was a contentious hour during which he expressed his grave concerns over growing rumors of a large French force ranging somewhere in New York. Burr assured him that the French were nowhere in sight, having left for the Caribbean weeks ago. The ambassador, unconvinced, threatened Burr with unspecified consequences if the French were to harm British interests due to Burr's assistance. Burr sarcastically asked what His Majesty's government under Prime Minister Addington would do, given its financial exhaustion and back-to-back failed harvests—rent out the army to harvest corn and potatoes?

Then, on June 27th came the welcome news that France's Le Corps Canadien stormed Montreal and forced the surrender of the British garrison of 500 with little damage to the city of 18,000. The French heavy artillery army made short work of the fortress's northeastern stone outworks while the inner citadel's wooden palisades were quickly splintered. Meanwhile, French artillery, nimble gunboats, and bateaux manned with soldiers blocked any word from traveling rapidly down the St. Lawrence River to warn the 1,500-strong Redcoat garrison at Quebec City.

Within a day after securing the Montreal, the French vanguard moved rapidly downriver by boat, leaving only 500 soldiers behind as a garrison. By July 2, they arrived at Quebec.

The British knew Quebec's fortifications needed significant improvement—after all, they captured the city in 1759. The French tried to retake the city the following year, but the siege only lasted 19 days until the British fleet showed up and sank or captured the six French ships supporting the siege. Since then, there had only been modest improvements to the fortifications that, by European standards, weren't terribly impressive.

The French benefited from agents within the city who opened a disused gate in the moonless night, allowing advanced elements from the French corps access to the city. The British discovered the betrayal and tried to retake the gate, but French reinforcements showed up at an increasing rate and by noon, there were already 5,000 French regulars within the outer walls. Siege batteries, including four modern M1795 Long Porte howitzers with bores of almost 6-1/2 inches showed up the following day. The French heavy cannon holed a British frigate anchored in the St. Lawrence and drove the warship off with a growing list to port while the obsolete and motley collection of British guns were unable to answer the French barrage.

Without naval support, outnumbered more than 10-to-one, and hearing news of Montreal's fall, the garrison commander surrendered by Saturday afternoon.

In only eight days, Napoleon's Le Corps Canadien erased much of the national embarrassment of the loss of New France in the aftermath of the Seven Year's War 39 years earlier in 1763. The challenge was keeping the gains—starving out the small British garrison of 1,200 in Upper Canada, turning their native allies against them, and clearing the Maritimes, especially Halifax and St. Johns. The latter were problematic, for if the British retained the bases they could, at any time, mount an operation against Quebec City or, at the very least, blockade the waterway. Even so, active logistics support from New York would replenish the French forces, allowing them to stay in Quebec indefinitely.

Chapter Forty-Four – Rumors of War

July 10, 1802, Manhattan, New York

John Bentley served as a captain in the Malcolm's under Burr back in 1778. He was now 48 years old to Burr's 46. But whereas Burr's wife died eight years ago, Bentley never married. Burr and Bentley kept in touch after the war and, when Burr was elected President of the United Republic of America, Bentley asked for a job and Burr was happy to appoint him as his executive secretary upon taking office two months ago. Burr wanted his Tammany Society associates to remain clear from the new national government—at least one step removed from the temptation to enrich themselves. And Burr preferred a veteran he could trust. Being unmarried like himself was, he thought, a benefit as well, given the long and irregular hours he worked. Bentley tapped at the massive oaken door, barely audible, but Burr knew the pattern. "Enter," he said.

"Mr. President, the British ambassador demands to see you."

"Demands?"

"Sir."

"Please tell the ambassador that I have no openings today."

"As you will, sir," said Bentley as he closed the door.

Burr had just returned his attentions to bids on upgrading a section of the Erie Canal when he heard Bentley knock once more, "Enter!"

"Sir…"

"It's not the ambassador, is it?"

"No sir. The French military liaison is here to see you."

"Lieutenant Colonel du Vignaud?"

"Yes sir."

"Well, show him in. Please bring us refreshments and stay to take notes, Bentley."

"Yes sir."

Burr heard the early French revolutionary politician turned military officer approach down the hall, his knee-high boots thudding as he walked. Speaking French, Burr said, "Rivaud! Please, Colonel du Vignaud, it is wonderful to see you. Do you have news?"

Vignaud could barely contain himself, "Monsieur President, I have three developments for you. All good."

Bentley entered the room with a tray holding carafes of wine, cider, and whisky and three glasses. The men helped themselves and Vignaud looked at Bentley.

Burr, continuing in French said, "It's fine. He can stay. He doesn't know French, but I want to him to take notes in English as needed."

"I can speak English if you prefer," Vignaud said in passable English.

Burr responded, "Thank you. That would ensure clarity."

Bentley's eyes lingered on the whisky as he readied himself to take notes.

Colonel du Vignaud started slowly, looking at his own notes, "As I said, three, ah, developments. One. We have completed the permanent telegraph towers to Montreal and brought on the temporary towers between Montreal and Quebec City only four hours ago."

Burr's eyes widened. Quebec City? The must mean the French had already taken the city under siege! Remarkable!

Vignaud smiled broadly, "Two. Quebec City is ours. It fell seven days ago. We took 2,000 prisoners in the operation."

Burr stood up and shook Vignaud's hand, "Congratulations! Please extend my congratulations to Generals Leclerc and Rochambeau and First Consul Napoleon."

Vignaud poured himself some whisky, took a pull, and then, smiling even more broadly said, "Three. The British fleet arrived three days ago and landed 10,000 soldiers. In a battle lasting an entire day, the British force was defeated with heavy casualties. We captured another 2,000 men and sunk two ships-of-the-line. There was no sign of the British fleet by sunrise this morning. Quebec remains ours."

Burr looked at Bentley, slightly raising an eyebrow. Bentley nodded, indicating he captured the information.

"Any additional details, Colonel du Vignaud?" Burr asked.

"None yet. The telegraph system is only capable of sending basic information in code. We'll have to await a courier from the corps headquarters before we know more."

Burr sat back and considered the news. It really couldn't have gone any better. He manipulated Napoleon into securing his northern flank without the loss of a single American soldier—and did so while diverting Napoleon from wasting his army on the diseased-plagued isle of Santo Domingo. And, more importantly, leaving the freed slaves on that island as a potential mortal threat aimed at the slave holders in the south. The sole irritant was the telegraph code. He wasn't happy that he didn't know it, yet. But, with patience, he was confident his agents would find and copy the cipher book, rendering him able to know what the French knew when they knew it—and know whether they were telling him the truth of things.

Burr grabbed a box of cigars from his desk and offered one to the French officer who gladly took it. Bentley reached behind him to grab a burning candle to offer Vignaud a flame. Within seconds, Vignaud was leaning back in his chair, sipping whisky, and puffing on his cigar. "Monsieur President," he began in French, "First Consul Napoleon will, no doubt, be sending additional instructions. These rapid victories change everything. Of course, a formal declaration of war will be forthcoming from the British. I surmise they will declare war on both France and your United Republic of America. May I suggest the formal creation of a joint allied headquarters here in New York. Our actions must be coordinated."

Burr was both excited and anxious over such a move, though he expected it would come eventually. America was far from France, but France's population was more than five times that of America's and their ability to use conscription to generate large armies dwarfed his own. Americans were still too cantankerous and commercially minded to readily submit to a draft even if it meant national greatness. Promise of land was another thing—and he had plenty of that, especially north of the Ohio River—which, once the British and their Indian allies could be starved out, would quickly become more valuable.

Chapter Forty-Five – A Free Press

July 14, 1802, Manhattan, New York

Hamilton walked into the office carrying three newspapers and a smile.

Jeph, worried about finances, looked up from the ledger, wondering which past due accounts might be collected upon to fulfill this year's property tax levy of 12 dollars.

"Jeph! Have you seen these? Little Burr will be apoplectic."

"Sir? Sorry. My concerns are more urgent. We have no funds to pay the land tax due next week." Jeph immediately regretted his unusually acid tone with Hamilton. But Hamilton's continuous political battles with Burr had crossed the line from being merely pointless to harmful—Hamilton hadn't landed a paying case in three months.

Hamilton, seeing Jeph's face quickly turned his attention to away from the newspapers, "How much? How much do we owe the taxman?"

"12 dollars."

"How much do we have on hand?"

"Five dollars and twenty cents."

"Well then. That and fifty dollars should be enough for taxes and for your month's salary." Hamilton reached into his coin pouch and placed a dozen gold British guineas and two Spanish silver dollars on Jeph's work desk.

Jeph sighed with relief and looked up at Hamilton. "The papers, sir? What's in them?"

Hamilton immediately beamed, laying the papers on the desk. Jeph only recognized the masthead of one of them. The other two he was unaware of. The papers were already opened to the stories that had excited Hamilton's interest.

The headlines blared:

Burr Risks War

Napoleon's Army In New York

Burr Threatens British Ambassador

"Is any of it true? Is Britain going to attack?" Jeph asked. It was one thing to fight as a 16-year-old boy with nothing to lose—another thing entirely at 40 with a wife and children to look after.

Hamilton looked up from admiring the newspapers and replied, "True? Likely so. How often am I wrong?"

Jeph paused, "You wrote these, sir?"

"I wrote two of the three. I own the printing presses too, though both my ownership and authorship are a matter of secrecy and rank speculation. The third…" Hamilton tapped the "Burr Expels…" headline, "This one was completely unexpected. It looks like I'm not the only one concerned about Burr's recklessness."

"Do you think Burr will seize your presses?"

"Of course, he will!"

"Why do you do it? Why provoke him?"

"Because he wants to be a tyrant. Every day we publish is a day we can warn others about Burr's plans. Every day makes new friends of liberty and new enemies of Burr. And, when he comes to seize the press, or smash it into pieces, or burn it, he'll create an enemy regiment in his midst. Either way, Little Burr loses."

Jeph was silent. He admired Hamilton's convictions but was no longer confident in his strength. Burr had outmaneuvered or outmuscled Hamilton at every turn. And now Burr was president and Hamilton was a failing lawyer.

Hamilton stood back away from the desk and walked back towards the door. He stood still for a moment and then turned to face Jeph, "How's the business going? How's squab sales these days?"

Now it was Jeph's turn to smile, "We're sold 11 dollars' worth in the past two weeks. Our costs in feed and supplies were six dollars. We spent another four dollars for space at the market for a month. I expect that once the flock is established, the profits will be just enough to employ two of my children and keep them at home and pay for their books and education."

"Excellent! Keep it up! With some work, if your flock stays healthy, you should be earning enough to make up for my being such a poor lawyer." Hamilton walked back to the desk and snatched up the three newspapers and spun about sharply and let himself outside while whistling Yankee Doodle.

Jeph marveled at the man's energy and optimism.

Chapter Forty-Six – The Best Defense

July 22, 1802, Allied Liaison Headquarters, Manhattan, New York

After French military liaison Lieutenant Colonel du Vignaud suggested formalizing an alliance, Burr immediately moved to secure a building on the Hudson close to docks large enough to accommodate a frigate. It was also adjacent to the terminus of the optical telegraph system, though the tower's signals weren't visible from the building, as they were facing upriver and were perpendicular to the place.

Burr, and his aide John Bentley walked into the headquarters, pausing to let their eyes adjust. The French had blacked out the ground floor windows and only a modest amount of light on the heavily clouded day came in through the upper windows of the recently former warehouse.

Burr saw Henry Dearborn, his newly appointed general and hero of the War for Independence, standing next to colonel du Vignaud in an animated discussion. Burr thought for a moment of the wisdom of Dearborn's appointment. On one hand, he was a reliable Antifederalist and, with strong roots in Massachusetts, would be invaluable in Burr's plans. Weighing against Dearborn were two factors—he was self-taught in warfare and didn't know a lick of French. Still, Burr was able to appoint and remove officers at will as President. Dearborn would be a general until Burr decided he wouldn't be.

Dearborn turned towards Burr, "Mr. President," he nodded at Bentley who nodded back. "We were just discussing developments from Quebec City."

Vignaud tightly smiled and dismissed two French junior officers who both walked to the back of the building and let themselves out, their forms briefly silhouetted in the doorway.

"Colonel du Vignaud?" Burr asked with raised eyebrow.

Speaking English so as not to exclude Dearborn, Vignaud started hesitantly, "Yes, well, umm, err, after our victory over the British two weeks ago we have started build a new fortification on the south bank of the river. Our fleet arrived with new heavy cannon and material for upgrading the fort. Military engineers as well and artillery officers."

"Excellent!" Burr responded, "Why the concern when I walked in?"

Dearborn spoke, "When the French arrived to provision Quebec, they also gave word that a large British force appears to be assembling at Halifax. This force could make another attempt to retake Quebec, or it might be sent to New York or Philadelphia. We don't know and we don't have the strength to repel them yet."

"And what is our strength, excluding militia in service of the states?" Burr asked, though he knew the answer day-to-day.

"We've raised one brigade in New York and one in Philadelphia, each containing an authorized strength of 2,000 men organized in two regiments, one regiment in New Jersey with 1,000 men, and the Delaware battalion with 500. They have trained now for five weeks. In addition, we have our dragoons. They are 500 strong and have been recruited from all four states. Most of them are militia veterans. So, in all, 6,000 soldiers. We also have two 44-gun frigates with one nearing completion and two more in construction with four smaller sloops as well as three revenue cutters. Additionally, there are the two frigates we're building for the French to the same specifications. Mr. President, we have much coastline to defend."

"General, the state militias will handle any British invasion, just as they did 20 years ago. We must prevent the British from establishing a permanent presence close to New York. The best way to do that is to secure our eastern flank and the best way to do that is to take Boston before John Adams can invite the British in—or they invite themselves in."

"I can assemble the Army in New York in a month," Dearborn said without much conviction.

"General Dearborn. I want you to continue training and equipping the Army. I expect that the council will approve another brigade soon. I will personally lead the New York brigade and our dragoons into Massachusetts three days hence. We have no time to waste." Burr turned to Vignaud, "Colonel, please inform General Leclerc of our plans and ask the general if he would march a division of his army back to New York so as to secure my base while I take Boston. Word of his victory should be reaching London in a week. We can't expect Prime Minister Addington to remain passive in the face of such a defeat, else be at risk of being replaced by a more energetic man. Depending on how swiftly the British act, we could see naval forces and raiding parties as early as the first week of September with an army as soon as October."

Dearborn betrayed a slight frown, "Do you think the British will declare war?"

Burr considered Dearborn. He looked like he was losing his elan. Perhaps the man's courage had dimmed since the Battle of Yorktown almost 21 years previously.

Burr responded casually, "On France, most certainly. On us? Perhaps. We've done no direct harm to British interests—none that could easily be proven, anyway. Of course, that may change. In any event, perceptions matter more than fact and preparedness is never wasted."

Chapter Forty-Seven – On the March

July 28, 1802, Western Massachusetts

Burr grinned broadly. It felt good to be back in the saddle in command of men. He wore a simple uniform for the occasion with the rank of lieutenant general. Instead of a cocked hat, he wore his favorite black presidential top hat—the crown only some three inches above the brim.

Puffy white clouds dotted the sky propelled south by a cool breeze from the north. The road to Pittsfield was wide enough to march in columns six abreast. They passed well-kept farms and patches of woods as they marched east. The two regiments, artillery, and their baggage train stretched back half a mile, 2,500 men in all. The dragoons, almost 500 of them, ranged ahead on horseback about a mile and on smaller parallel roads to the north and south.

Burr shifted in the saddle. He had a simple plan: march east across the middle of Massachusetts, from Pittsfield to Northampton, cross the Connecticut River and split his forces, one regiment taking Amherst, the other, accompanied by most of the dragoons, taking Springfield, then recombining his force at Worcester and at that point, deciding whether to take the northerly approach to Boston via Concord and Lexington or the southerly approach via Brockton.

Based on information from his network of spies, Burr surmised that he would pick up support along the route from old Shaysites and their still-bitter sons.

To further increase his odds, Burr also carried along what he thought as a secret weapon: $200,000 in newly minted gold coin—7,500 twenty-dollar pieces and 10,000 five-dollar pieces. He received a shipment in gold bullion from France and, having already made arrangements, began stamping out the coins over the past month.

Burr viewed the United American Republic's coinage as essential to his plans. North America was still chronically short of coinage. Circulating coin in gold and silver would go a long way towards showing his citizens that they had a part in a legitimate—even superior—government as compared to the confederation or what might soon be the United States of America under the Philadelphia constitution.

In any event, the gold coin was enough to pay for three months of operations with his infantry paid five dollars per month, his dragoons, eight dollars, supplies, and five dollars per month for any Massachusetts, Connecticut, Rhode Island, or New Hampshire militia that fought alongside him. That he could pay in gold, not paper, would make all the difference.

His last stroke of genius—the coin featured a profile of Liberty with the motto, "Liberty, Equality, Unity" on one side, and a profile of George Washington on the other, thus, establishing a link with America's founding independence from Britain while distinguishing the new republic as an endeavor for all the people, not just the well-to-do.

Burr's thoughts were interrupted by a young dragoon officer galloping down the road, kicking up dust clouds with every hoof fall. The dragoon's horse skidded to a halt in front of Burr. Burr looked back to the brigade commander who called the column to halt.

"President Burr!" the lieutenant was out of breath. His horse was starting to lather, and dust caked his face which was streaked in some places with rivulets of sweat and mud.

Burr urged his horse forward to receive the man's report out of earshot.

"Take your time, lieutenant," Burr smiled, "But don't take all day."

The dragoon's uniform was resplendent with a blue blouse and white trousers—made in New Jersey—topped with a black jacked leather helmet with brass accoutrements—made in Pennsylvania.

The young man inhaled deeply and then spoke in a conversational tone. Burr approved. This man knew how to read his surroundings. "Sir, the Pittsfield militia has mustered and won't let us pass."

"I see. How many of them are there?" Burr was not anticipating resistance so early.

"We counted 150 with more arriving by the minute."

"Any cannon?"

"None we could see."

"Anything else?"

"Sir, it seemed odd, they were led by an older officer on horseback. He was turned out in uniform from the war."

"Hmmm." Burr stroked his chin. "I wonder…"

Burr had resumed the march and expected to reach the Pittsfield town square in an hour, leaving another three hours of daylight.

Traveling at the head of the column with his dragoons screening out ahead and to his flanks, Burr caught sight of the town's church steeples, and then rooftops, and finally, the militia formed up in lines facing west. There were 200 of them and they looked ready to fight.

Burr told the brigade commander to halt the column and rode ahead with the dragoon lieutenant. He saw a man on horseback—a bit soft in the middle, he looked to be in his mid-50s with curly white hair pushing out from his cockaded hat.

"Who's in charge here?" Burr bellowed from about 50 yards away, his column about 50 yards behind.

The man cleared his throat and started to speak, his voice cracking at first, "I am. Major General Jackson!"

"General Jackson? Henry? Henry Jackson of Monmouth?" Burr called out cheerfully.

"The same. Who are you? Why are you in Massachusetts?"

"It's Colonel Burr, Henry, President of the United American Republic. We aim to restore liberty to these lands just as you aim to stop us."

"Liberty? Ha! You're a tyrant in the making, sir!"

"Is that so, Henry? Where is the militia commander? Assuredly you don't live in Pittsfield. What happened to the man these men elected as their captain? Boston doesn't trust him?" Burr jeered.

Jackson glared at Burr, pushing his horse past the two ranks and stopping about 30 yards from Burr.

"A 'tyrant'? You dare call the elected president a 'tyrant?' Let me assure you and your men that I am no tyrant. Tyrants care not to liberate the oppressed."

Burr surveyed the men. Some were looking very nervous. Many were no older than 20.

Burr took a deep breath and called out loudly and clearly. "Listen to me! We are not enemies, we are friends. This man, Henry Jackson, was sent here by your lords in Boston to ensure you fight on their behalf—to keep you in chains—in bondage to heavy taxes and debt. Ask yourself this, men, if Boston trusted you, would they not allow you to muster under your own captain?"

Burr heard a few grumblings from the militia as four more men joined the muster. Jackson looked over his shoulder with a mix of annoyance and fear.

"You there, Jackson! You insulted me. Rather than our men spill each other's blood, let us settle this here and now, man-to-man! If you win, my men will return to their homes, if I win, I will continue to march on Boston until every man in Massachusetts is the equal of the other!"

There was more noise in the ranks and Jackson turned around in his saddle to stare down his men.

"Go home, General Jackson!" said a grizzled farmer.

"Go home Henry!" this time in a mocking voice from an unseen man in the back rank.

"Order!" Jackson bellowed.

"Henry, if I were you, I'd leave. I'd ride and not stop until I hit Boston and then I'd catch the first ship to London. That's where your friends are, right Henry?"

There were scattered guffaws among the militia.

Jackson turned around in his saddle to face Burr. He quickly pulled out his pistol and spurred his horse forward. Burr drew his own pistol, urging his mount forward a few steps and then halting.

Jackson pressed on, red-faced and enraged.

Burr raised his piece and brought it down smoothly on his target.

Jackson, suddenly realizing the rashness of his charge unloosed his shot at Burr, the ball whipping past low and striking a soldier in the column behind.

Burr fired, hitting Jackson square in chest. Jackson, wide-eyed, looked down at the blossoming blood streaming out from his overly tight uniform. He wheeled his horse around and goaded it to flight. Horse and rider smashed through the militia, trampling one citizen-soldier and then, three seconds later, Jackson toppled off his horse, his right boot still stuck in the stirrup. Jackson's hat quickly came off and a moment later his head struck a rock, and his body went completely limp. The foot came out of his riding boot and his lifeless body lay in the dirt lane.

The Massachusetts Minutemen stood, looking at each other, back to Jackson's body and ahead to Burr.

Burr trotted closer to the men. "Gather 'round, gentlemen, let's talk."

Burr dismounted and took his hat off, walking towards a small monument in the town square. He stepped up on the base to give himself two feet of height and surveyed the anxious men.

"I know you are doing nothing more or less than what I myself would do—defending your homes. We have no quarrel with you. Our enemy is the same as your oppressor: Boston's bankers, Boston's merchants, Boston's lawyers. Those who would rule over you and surrender your liberties to King George." Burr looked at the men. He had them.

"Not to be chuffy, sir, but how are we to know you're not going to make a cat's paw of us?" It was a man of his mid-40s, about Burr's age, and clearly a veteran as he betrayed no fear of Burr.

"That's a good question. It's right to question those who would ask for your support. I do intend to march on Boston. I'd be honored to have your help…"

"What do we get in return?" Burr recognized the man as one of the first to grumble against Jackson. "The last time any of us served, we ended up gut-foundered with a pile of worthless Continentals."

"That's an honest concern, good sir. Freedom is one thing. Putting food on the table can be just as important. For those who volunteer with their own serviceable kit—and are accepted into service—we'll pay five dollars a month in gold for a three-month enlistment."

There were several approving nods among the militiamen.

"I have to give you fair warning though. If you sign up, discipline will be to regular Army standards. Desertion is punishable by death. You're free to go or free to join us. Either way, you're free!"

The men cheered, though Burr noticed a few in the back who remained sullen faced.

"If you wish to join us, report here in an hour and you may enlist."

Burr rode back to his lines with the dragoon lieutenant who saw everything. He reached down and drew a long pull of water, thankful that Jackson was both impetuous and a poor shot and doubly thankful that the weather remained mild.

Chapter Forty-Eight – Siege of Boston

August 10, 1802, Boston, Massachusetts

Burr's march on Boston went faster than he expected. His army hadn't seen one serious confrontation with the Federalist holdouts in Boston. All along his route of march, yeoman farmers, chafing under Boston's yoke, rallied to his banner—so much so that after Pittsfield, he had his choice of recruits, turning half away as being too old, too young, or lacking in a good musket or rifle.

By the time he put up lines to besiege Boston, his 2,500 regulars and 500 wagon drivers, cooks, and other camp followers had been augmented by 4,000 Massachusetts militia who had signed up for three-month enlistments—the total force coming close to the number of patriots who laid siege to the British in Boston in 1775.

Yet Boston showed no signs of giving up despite their stunning lack of support in the countryside. Their ships were able to come and go at will and, infuriatingly, a robust trade in black market goods occurred throughout the Massachusetts coast. Boston's elite, their traders and merchants, could hold out for longer than Burr's supply of gold which, if not replenished, would be exhausted by the end of September, leaving his enemy intact and looking for revenge.

To force an end to the threat from Massachusetts and the newly proclaimed United States of America, Burr would need more French siege artillery and the French fleet, both of which he had no control over. It was 1781 all over again, with Washington and the Continental Army reliant on the French army and fleet to tip the scales against the British.

Burr looked up from his presidential correspondence inside the canvas field tent he made his home for the past two weeks. It was already uncomfortably hot. He felt a sense of dread—the heat, his old enemy since Monmouth, was threatening him in ways Boston and the British never could.

Burr pushed outside the tent into the bright sunlight. The air was stifling and still. Sweat had been dripping off his face and onto the documents he was reviewing but now his face felt drier. He mopped his brow and realized he was likely to faint. He took a step and all went black.

Chapter Forty-Nine – The Trap Closes

September 23, 1802, Manhattan, New York

Burr was simultaneously frustrated and relieved. On one hand, his weakness in the face of hot days was embarrassing. It humbly reminded him why he cut short his service as a field commander after Monmouth. On the other hand, his swift march through Massachusetts while suffering only a handful of injuries and no battle deaths was widely reported throughout his republic.

And the story of his face off against General Jackson had already reached legendary proportions. It was being said that his personal courage saved the lives of thousands by preventing a bloody war between neighbors. That the more than 50 newspapers in New York—about half of the total publishing regularly—were owned by his friends and allies amplified the praise. Even some of the papers generally in opposition reported favorably on his bravery.

Still, he was feeling fatigued by the campaign and was happy to be inside, working out of the sun and with plenty of water to be had.

Portions of the French fleet were reassembling in New York's harbor. The squadron that carried 2,000 of Napoleon's soldiers to reinforce the garrison at New Orleans was the first to arrive, with the transports sent on to France with a light escort. But, the two ships-of-the-line and four frigates were deemed inadequate, even when reinforced with Burr's two first rate frigates, to effectively and safely blockade Boston.

Bentley knocked at the office door and announced the arrival of Lieutenant Colonel du Vignaud. Burr, responded with a simple, "Enter!"

Vignaud stepped in, his knee-high riding boots sporting a high polish, "Mister President," he said in English, then switched to French, "You wish to have Citizen Bentley for notes? It may be a short meeting; I was hoping to see you at the headquarters."

Burr had avoided the dusty warehouse since his return from Boston. He didn't feel strong enough to appear among soldiers, though he did miss his almost daily meetings with the French military attaché. "I'm sorry I haven't visited. I've so much to attend to. The paperwork really piles up with you're fighting in the field."

"I can only imagine. I hear Napoleon complains of the same."

Burr smiled at the comparison. "To what do I owe the pleasure of your visit?"

"I thought you should know; the rest of the fleet arrived this morning from the Caribbean. I invited the admiral onshore for a conference. You may wish to request formal naval support for your blockade of Boston. Also, I regret to inform you that Britain has declared war on France."

"I expected as much. I suspect we'll be next. Of course, if you help us in our blockade, the remaining states will declare war on France."

"Of course. The United American Republic is our ally. The United States of America is merely a plan that hasn't come to fruition."

There as a short knock and Bentley poked his head in the door, "Sorry to interrupt, sir. A development." Bentley looked at Vignaud, then at Burr.

Burr responded, "Proceed."

"Sir, a rider just arrived from East Hampton Town. Montauk was raided three days ago by the Massachusetts naval militia. They set fire to the village and killed several of the local militia, carrying off others as prisoners. They also took ten head of cattle. Some warriors from the local tribe, the Montaukett's, joined with the militia and drove off the raiding party."

"Is that all?" Burr said flatly, looking at a document he still had to read and sign.

Bentley's face flushed and he stuttered in reply, "I-I-I thought... I thought you'd want to know."

Burr looked back at Bentley, who was still poking his head into the room, "John, we're at war. This is a small skirmish in a far larger contest. Please arrange for relief wagons of food, clothing, and construction materials to be sent out to the Sheriff in Suffolk County. Winter will soon be upon us, and we don't need our citizens dying in the cold."

"Yes sir!" Bentley quickly disappeared.

Burr returned his attention to Vignaud, "Now, any word as to my siege guns? We need to finish this."

"General Leclerc needs every gun he can spare to properly secure Quebec from British threat. I believe that the next fleet that arrives from France may meet your needs. We must wait and see what was sent," Vignaud said hopefully.

"We must wait and see what gets across the Atlantic past the British," Burr replied, "You're at war now."

Vignaud wryly replied, "How are those new frigates coming?"

"The first is being outfitted with 44 cannon in Philadelphia. The second won't be ready for launching for about a year. Though, importantly, we have secured enough live oak timbers from Georgia to complete five additional vessels."

"Excellent! Though I suspect the fleet in the harbor is enough for our immediate needs in Boston. Presuming the admiral agrees."

"Yes, well, we'll just have to convince him that blockading Boston would be worth his time." Burr pushed back his seat and stood but he quickly put his palms on his desk to steady himself. He looked at Vignaud who appeared not to have taken notice.

Chapter Fifty – Heroes Again

October 18, 1802, New York

The French fleet had commenced the blockade of Boston almost three weeks previously. Even more importantly, Burr was now in possession of his own French manufactured Long Porte howitzers, six of them, adequate, along with the French fleet, to begin to bring Boston under bombardment.

Fortunately, along with the siege cannon, the French fleet delivered another almost one ton of gold bullion, which his mint rapidly stamped out into twenty- and five-dollar coins. This would allow him to keep his army in the field for another couple of months while the increasing circulation of gold coin would further cement the legitimacy of the United American Republic in the eyes of the people.

Burr had recovered enough from his heat apoplexy that he was visiting the allied military headquarters again on an almost daily basis. It helped that the days were cooler now.

Burr was approaching the converted brick warehouse that housed the headquarters when he heard the voice of the British ambassador calling, "President Burr! I was told I'd find you here. I'm afraid I have terrible news. Can we go inside?"

Burr, surmising what was about to be said replied, "No, I don't believe that it would be appropriate for you to enter this building. What you say can be said here."

The ambassador was well-dressed, but not so much as to attract attention in New York. He handed Burr a scroll sealed with wax, "I regret to inform you that His Majesty's government has declared war on the United American Republic." He looked down and then looked straight into Burr's eyes. "You can't admit to being surprised about this. You allowed your nation to be used as a base to host a surprise attack on British soil. I know you were part of a failed attempt to take Quebec. I can…"

Burr cut him off, "Mr. Ambassador, you've done your duty. Return to London and Godspeed. Someday our relations will be reestablished, though on equal terms, I reckon."

The ambassador nodded, turned on his heels and quickly made his way down the street.

The news was welcome to Burr, after a fashion, as it was one less unknown for him to consider. The two guards outside the main entrance, one French, one American, looked more serious than usual. They saluted him and he returned their salutes as he walked into the dimly lit building. He could immediately tell something different, something more urgent was going on.

General Dearborn saw Burr and quickly walked over to him. His blouse was unbuttoned, and he was animated, "Sir, the British have landed a force at Gravesend Bay. It's a repeat of 1776. I recommend we consider evacuation. We have no regulars on hand, only militia."

"How many?"

"We don't know."

"How many ships are supporting the landing?"

"We know of five ships."

"Five? Only five? What classes?"

"One appears to be a ship-of-the-line. We don't rightly know yet of the others."

"General Dearborn, this is a raid. The British only formally declared war on us today…"

"Wait, sir? Why was I not informed?"

"General, the British ambassador only informed me himself just minutes ago. After the British defeat at Quebec in the first part of July, we knew that a force of some 10,000 or so British regulars was likely assembling in Halifax. But General Howe had 20,000 men under his command in the battle of Long Island. There is little chance that the British, after losing the war to keep us in the empire, are going to invade New York with anything less than 20,000 men. It's a raid. I suggest you mount up, rally the militia, and take charge yourself before they leave."

Dearborn stared at Burr for a moment and then buttoned up his blouse, called for his aide and left in a rush.

Hamilton heard about the British landing party at Gravesend 12 miles and a ferry away from his office in Manhattan and immediately went for his horse, yelling to Jeph to follow, stopping only to strap on his sword and grab a pistol, shot and powder. The two called out for the militia to muster on their way to Gravesend. By the time they approved the docks in Brooklyn they could see three distinct columns of smoke rising to make one growing brown cloud over the bay. Beyond, barely visible through the pall, were the masts of ships, though it was impossible to tell if they were British warships or American merchant ships at dock.

Hamilton saw a group of 50 militiamen milling about, "Who's in command here?"

The men looked up at Hamilton with a mixture of indifference, defiance, and, in a few faces, awe. One young man stepped forward, "No one, Colonel Hamilton."

"Men! Listen to me. This is Sergeant Clark. He's a veteran of Monmouth and more battles than either of us care to remember. Follow his lead. Now, who here has a rifle?"

"I do, sir!" called a young man with a broken complexion who looked no older than 17. He had a small caliber piece more suited for squirrel hunting.

"Have you ever killed a man?" Hamilton queried.

"N-no, sir."

"You may today. Anyone else?"

"Here, sir." A man of about 50 raised his American longrifle.

Hamilton eyed the man, "Can you see well enough to hit anything?"

"If'n I could read, I'd reckon I'd need glasses, but I can still kill a man. Killed me a few in the last war."

"Right. Have you all brought your bayonets?" Hamilton asked with impatience.

Half the men raised their hands. Out of the corner of his eye, Hamilton saw another four men quietly slip into the crowd.

"Sergeant Clark!" Hamilton barked out.

"Sir!"

"Sergeant, organize these men into four ranks, first and second ranks with bayonets. You two with the rifles, stay close to me. We'll going to march down to the docks and stay on the lane, buildings to the flanks. Riflemen, you're going to aim for the officers. I'll point them out. The rest of you, you'll hold your fire until the British charge. Understood?"

There were scattered "Yes sirs!"

Jeph tied his horse up and started to form the men. The smoke coming from the docks thickened and blew past the men, adding to their unease.

"Alright, men. Let us defend our freedoms, defend our homes, defend New York. To the front, march!"

The militia, now swollen to 65 men, unsteadily marched towards the smoke, the lane gradually curving until the docks came into view.

Hamilton, still on horseback, the riflemen close behind, led the way. Through watering eyes he scanned the scene. *There.* A group of 10 redcoats carrying torches were coming out of a warehouse next to the docks. In the distance, a ship-of-the-line was firing at will, shots ringing out every few seconds. Three merchant vessels were aflame and two more were smoking. *Heated shot.* Hamilton noticed a group of five soldiers who were likely posted as pickets at the same time they noticed him. One of them called out an alarm and the other four leveled their muskets at Hamilton from 100 yards off. Smoke rose from their flash pans and Hamilton heard the familiar sound of musket balls whizzing by.

Hamilton turned around in the saddle, "Hold your fire, men!" And, as he turned back to survey the docks, the young rifleman fired at the pickets. One of the men fell in pain. The militiamen cheered "Huzzah!"

Jeph was facing the men, his back to the action, his arms outstretched, with a pistol in his right hand.

Hamilton scowled at the young rifleman. "Reload. Make it sharp. And next time," Hamilton paused, "What's your name, soldier?"

"Keaton, sir. Jeramiah Keaton."

"Very well, Private Keaton. You've shot your first man. Next time, shoot the man I tell you to shoot."

"Yes sir."

The older rifleman never stopped surveying the waterfront.

"Sir!" he called, pointing to the left.

"Yes?" Hamilton squinted in that direction.

There. About 200 yards away through the smoke was a patch of red above which was the headgear of an officer on horseback, a red and white plume, like some tropical bird, atop a black cocked hat.

"Keaton, you almost reloaded?"

"Working on it, sir!"

The young private was starting to set his patch and ball.

"And what's your name, private?" Hamilton turned to the older man.

"Daniel Eastwood, sir."

"Well, Private Eastwood, do you think you can strike that officer for me?"

"Yes sir!"

Eastwood moved over to the corner of the wooden building to his left to steady his rifle. Hamilton looked down on his right to see Keaton furiously ramming home the ball.

Eastwood fired just as smoke from the burning merchantmen obscured the assembling British troops. Hamilton strained to see through the billowing smoke. *Damn!* He could see the officer's plumage, red topped by white. They were a little closer and marching towards their position. Though it was impossible to see how many ranks there were. Twenty men? Eighty?

"Keaton?"

"Yes, sir, ready sir!"

Keaton dropped to one knee and steadied his piece. Though from the lower vantage, he had more smoke to contend with.

"Take your time, boy. Steady. Squeeze gently." Hamilton saw Eastwood methodically reloading.

For a moment the onshore breeze stopped and shifted, blowing towards the British. At that moment, Hamilton could see a force of at least 200 men bearing down on the militia, bayonets flashing in the sunlight in front of two officers on horseback.

Keaton fired.

An officer clawed at his chest and then slumped in the saddle, disappearing from view.

"Huzzah!"

Hamilton allowed them this celebration, this brief moment of triumph, knowing full well that if the British ordered an infantry charge from 150 yards out, they'd be bayoneting these half-trained militia in less than a minute.

Eastwood rammed his patch and ball home, tamping it several times for good measure. He brought his rifle up horizontally and charged the flash pan. He calmly raised his piece and pulled the set trigger. Hamilton's eyes shifted quickly from Eastwood to the oncoming British and back to Eastwood. The old man pulled the second trigger, now turned into a hair trigger by activating the set trigger. Smoke and flames erupted from his flash pan and Hamilton was rewarded with the second officer grabbing his right arm in agony as he dropped is saber. Still, the British came on, now at 100 yards.

Hamilton eased his horse behind the densely packed ranks of men, four deep. "Eastwood, Keaton, follow me and reload. As he started to squeezed past the first rank, he called out, "Sergeant Clark! Commence volley!"

Jeph felt as if he was still a 22-year-old sergeant. It was comfortable, familiar. He had organized the men into four ranks of twenty, "First rank, kneel! First and second ranks, make ready! Take aim! Fire!"

Hamilton had passed through the men now and was assessing the effect of the volley—some 10 men fell at about 80 yards out. Almost 200 pressed on, outnumbering his militia by more than two-to-one.

Jeph called out, "First and second ranks, to the rear, march. Load! Third rank, kneel! Third and fourth ranks, make ready! Take aim! Fire!"

This time, at least a dozen men fell. The British line started to waiver. Hamilton saw the British sergeants encouraging their men. "Eastwood! Keaton! Redcoat sergeant on the left of the formation! Shoot him!"

Jeph ordered, "Third and fourth ranks, to the rear, march. Load!"

Eastwood pushed his way through the ranks, followed more tentatively by Keaton.

The British paused to close ranks. The sergeant was started to command them to prepare to fire with a bayonet charge sure to follow. It would be a slaughter as the militia would stumble over each other in panicked flight.

The sergeant fell, shot in the back by Eastwood. The redcoats wavered and looked at each other when three of them pointed down the street adjacent to the docks to the northwest.

Jeph continued, "First rank, kneel!" Eastwood dropped to one knee and flattened himself against the building. Keaton, more exposed, went to a prone position while picking out a target. "First and second ranks, make ready! Take aim! Fire!"

Almost twenty men fell not 40 yards away. But more British were pointing down the street, out of view to Hamilton's right. Hamilton urged his horse forward, past the reloading militia and craned his head around the corner of the building on his right.

Reinforcements! He could see a large mass of militia—at least 200 men— with a uniformed general behind them on horseback.

The British broke and ran, heading for the docks while the closest supporting warship, about 600 yards off, shifted its fire from the docked ships to the onrushing militia, dropping several with cannon shot.

At that moment Jeph cried out, "Arrah now!" while he grasped his left hand and added, "Sonofabitch!" for good measure.

Jeph looked up at Hamilton, "Sorry sir," he said as he held up his left hand where, at Monmouth, he lost two fingers to the British. The same old wound was bleeding.

"What are the odds, Jeph?" Hamilton laughed despite himself, "Had you still your fingers, you wouldn't anymore. Bind it up and tell the men to holdfast, the smoke is too thick to see anything now anyway." Hamilton looked behind him to see a dozen militiamen had broken ranks and were running away.

Hamilton looked at his troop, "Anyone else injured?"

Nothing but smiles returned his question. "Well, then, very well. Give yourselves three huzzahs for a job well done!"

Up the lane, already 50 yards off, the deserters skidded to a halt, looking at each other. Two of them started trotting back to the formation, looking sheepish, one called back to his shaken companions, and most of them turned around and started running back.

The militia down the lane to the right had stopped and taken cover, cannon balls passing overhead and smashing into the shops and warehouses along the docks every few seconds. In a few hours' time and at the cost of maybe 30 men and a couple of officers, the British had drawn first blood and exacted a modest toll in property damage in their second war against their American cousins in 25 years. Hamilton expected much worse to come, though he felt powerless to stop it in the face of Burr's determination to forge an empire.

Chapter Fifty-One – Fake News

October 26, 1802, Manhattan, New York

Jeph walked in on Hamilton sitting back in his chair, two weekly newspapers arrayed on his desk.

Hamilton looked up with a grin and asked, "Did you see these, Jeph? I'm wagering it will give Burr pause. It may even bring in a little business."

Jeph walked over to see the papers opened to the news.

Colonel Hamilton Fights at Gravesend

And,

Ham'ton Wins Fight

"That's fine, sir. But the *New York Post* just published." Jeph handed Hamilton the paper which featured a rare front-page headline amidst the advertisements.

General Dearborn Defeats Redcoats
-
Hamilton Routs

Hamilton snapped forward and groaned. "Damn Burr, damn him to hell." Hamilton cradled his head in his hands. Then, looking up at Jeph, he said with resignation, "You know, Burr pays 180 of 200 newspapers in the state a subsidy of five dollars a month, more if they print advertisements from the government? This story will be spread by his optical telegraph up the Hudson and down to Philadelphia."

Hamilton started to read the article.

A British force of 300 landed on Long Island at Gravesend, site of their 1776 victory. The militia mustered to meet the British threat at which point Col. Hamilton appointed himself their leader and went forward to meet the enemy. But after firing one volley, he and his force fled at the sight of British bayonets, according to eyewitness accounts of two of the soldiers who were there.

The timely arrival of gen. Dearborn at the head of 200 militia saved Hamilton's force from capture and annihilation and forced the British to retreat with heavy losses.

"It's fake news, sir," Jeph moaned, "I know what we did." Jeph's left hand was still bandaged from his fresh battle wound.

"It's not 'fake news' unless the people think it is, Jeph, otherwise, it's just news."

Chapter Fifty-Two – First Election

November 2, 1802, Boston, Massachusetts

John Adams's clothes were fitting loosely now, and he had a toothache. He figured that since the French fleet's blockade was added to Burr's siege on October 2, he'd lost ten pounds, half of that to worry and half of that to eating little more than salted cod washed down with ale.

He was hopeful that the election returns would be favorable—though he was increasingly questioning whether it would make a bit of difference. And, with food supplies running low now that the fishing fleet was bottled up, he wasn't even certain that people vote for him or would even vote at all. At least his second cousin, Samuel Adams, the former governor, was not in any physical condition to agitate against him, were he so inclined. Though, he had heard that even Samuel had dim views of Burr's growing tyrannical proclivities.

Prior to Burr's invasion, the plan was to have two presidential Electors chosen by the state legislature with the other Electors chosen by the state legislature from a list of the top two vote-getters in each of Massachusetts' 14 Congressional districts as apportioned by the most recent census in 1800 authorized by the Confederation Congress in 1799 before Washington died. But now, only a rump of the legislature was in session in Boston to receive the vote and the vote would only be coming from Boston—though arrangements were made for refugees from other parts of the state to vote as if they were voting from home—there were a handful of them—in some cases, no more than three men would vote for one of them to be a congressman while also voting for president. War caused all sorts of improvisations.

Unfortunately, Connecticut and New Hampshire, cowed by Burr's show of force, had declared their neutrality and were said to be in negotiations to join Burr's union. Vermont, well, they'd redeclared their independence as a separate republic. Other than a few wealthy shipping families in Providence and Newport, Rhode Island was openly supporting Burr's aggression. This would reduce the legitimacy of the national election but, with New England's most-populous state participating, at least the election would be more than merely confined to the South.

It was almost Noon when the first election results came in. The votes being almost unanimous. If things went as planned in the Legislature, he should get 16 votes and Thomas Jefferson of Virginia should get 15. The national unity ticket would then commence the immense task of containing Burr and reclaiming the nation under a more energetic government—assuming, of course, he survived the siege long enough to become the United States of America's first Vice President.

Adams just finished looking at the tally sheets when he heard the unmistakable sound of cannon fire—though, unlike the desultory fire from Burr's besieging army answered by the occasional counterbattery fire from Boston's lines, this was different. It was like a continuous roll of thunder.

Adams mounted the stairs to the house he was staying in—Peacefield, his home in Quincy, was overrun weeks ago. Adams labored to the third floor and opened a dormer window that faced east with a commanding view of Boston Harbor.

A bitter wind blew in, chilling Adams to the bone and numbing his face. The sky was slate gray with little sign of the sun. The rumbling of cannon fire was even louder and clearly coming from the harbor, not from the surrounding siegeworks.

Adams frowned. He dare not hope that this was a rescue. Massachusetts's own naval militia was anchored close to the city and under the protective watch of the city's own guns. And the rest of the confederation hadn't attended at all to naval preparations—one of the first orders of business Adams hoped to encourage if he made it to Virginia to assume office.

Adams dropped his head in prayer, occasional bits of sleet bouncing off his bald crown.

The cannon fire grew louder and then stopped. He looked up. Squinting, he could just make out two vessels, so close they might have been grappled together but too far off for his old eyes to determine what flag they flew. Even so, *something* had happened. And, given that it was the French fleet that was blockading them, some vessels must have challenged that blockage and, were either victorious or themselves vanquished.

Adams again looked the distant ships. *There!* He could see two more ships under sail approaching Boston.

Nightfall was approaching when a captain of the Massachusetts naval militia knocked at the door. Abigail let him in and called for her husband, "John, please come here. You'll want to see these gentlemen."

Adams was of a mind to go to bed early, his stomach was growling, and his legs were shaky from lack of food. "Can it wait 'til morning?" he called from the room where he was reading his Bible.

"John, come."

Adams groaned and shuffled towards the door.

There, arrayed on the doorstep and stairs below, were four naval officers, one was a naval militia officer he recognized and the other three were British. *British!* Adams eyes went wide, and he cleared his throat, "Please, gentlemen, please come in out of the cold and rain. I wish I could offer you more than cider and salted cod, but, alas, our supplies run low with the unpleasant circumstances."

The officers tramped into the house and introduced themselves. The first one was a slight man with grey-blue eyes, though one of the eyes looked dead, and entirely missing his right arm. He stood at least three inches shorter than Adams, who, at 5'7," was below average for an American man. The short man was obviously the highest ranking one. He was crackling with energy and even gave a rakish nod to Abigail who duly returned it.

"Sir, Vice-Admiral Lord Nelson at your service. If we are to be friends, you may call me Horatio."

"Admiral Nelson?!" Adams sputtered, then quickly regained his composure, "We've heard of your exploits even here. With all that racket I heard earlier, I can only assume that the blockade is lifted?"

"Indeed. We even gained two ships out of the exchange. Though, I must say, we had a nasty encounter with a beastly frigate flying the colors of your American rival. The damn thing seemed as if it had a hull of iron. Thankfully, there was only one of them."

"May I offer you some cider?"

"Please, though I regret we cannot stay. As you may know, His Majesty's government has declared war on the United American Republic as well as France. I'm under orders to offer your safe passage to points south. I recommend Charleston. If you refuse, we'll do what we can to reprovision you, but I cannot guarantee that the French fleet won't return. We only sank two vessels, damaged others, and captured two before the rest fled. I cannot linger more than two days. I won't risk my ships to the French long guns that have been known to operate in North America for the past six months."

Adams stared at Nelson. He had expected to move to the new nation's capital, likely somewhere in Virginia, but he hadn't considered the possibility of asking the entire city to evacuate. There were some 25,000 living in Boston in normal times. The siege saw an exodus of some of the lower classes, but even larger numbers of well-to-do families replaced them such that there were likely 26,000 people in the city. Boston's merchant fleet could likely accommodate all of them—if they left most of their belonging behind. Adams breathed a heavy sigh.

"There are some 23,000 people in this city and 3,000 militia. Evacuation, without being overrun, is going to be very difficult. Do you have and soldiers who may assist? Plus, I'm sure you don't wish for our cannon to fall into their hands. That and other military material should be recovered or rendered unusable."

Adams showed the men to the dining table while Abigail served them hard cider.

"I agree, yet we must evacuate in two days. I'll send General Moore to coordinate our efforts. We have enough soldiers to cover a retreat, but I cannot risk my ships to the cannon surrounding Boston."

John and Abigail Adams spent the next hour with Admiral Nelson and his officers, long enough to be mesmerized with his tales of battle and exotic places, but not so long for Nelson to experience John Adams's self-important cantankerousness.

Chapter Fifty-Three – Plans

November 4, 1802, Manhattan, New York

Burr walked into the allied military headquarters in Brooklyn and sensed he had walked in on a stiff argument. General Dearborn and Lieutenant Colonel du Vignaud were standing toe to toe with Vignaud pointing his finger in Dearborn's chest.

"Gentlemen?" Burr interrupted, "May I inquire as to the nature of your discussion?"

Dearborn spoke first, "We are simply having a discussion over the likely disposition of the British fleet and where the British might first attack in force. I believe they'll try to recreate their success of 1776 in New York as that is where our capital is, they land in Long Island or Staten Island and develop a base of supply, and then take Manhattan. As a result, General Leclerc's command should be in Manhattan."

"I disagree," Vignaud began slowly, being careful to enunciate his English, "The British have contempt for American armies. They have been fighting, you have not since 1781. They will land at Long Island, emplace their artillery on Vinegar Hill and Brooklyn Heights and quickly force their way across the River East, er, the East River. They will support the crossing with the fleet. They'll want to move fast and try to capture or destroy the seat of government—to put a swift end to you. But we must decisively end the British threat to North America, at least for a time. We can only do this by drawing the British into an open battle and annihilating their force. Therefore, we should place Leclerc's division in Brooklyn and move swiftly to engage the British force when it lands, forcing their defeat and surrender."

Both men looked at Burr. "This decision is best made between General Leclerc and me. When is he due to arrive from Quebec? I expected his return a month ago. We are exposed with the army in Boston."

Vignaud responded, "The general and his staff should be here in two days. They've reached Albany. The division is a day behind them and should be fully assembled in New York within a week."

Dearborn had been distracted by a note handed to him by one of the American signalmen.

"You have news to share, General?" Burr asked.

"Sir! Boston has fallen. But I regret to say that the British fleet arrived in strength and broke the blockade. It then evacuated the city with the evacuated covered by British soldiers. Only 5,000 people remain in the city."

Burr contested with conflicting emotions. The fall of Boston was wonderful news, but the evacuation of his foes meant they'd survive to fight another day. And the large and successful British intervention was a particularly unwelcome development.

"Colonel du Vignaud, please convey a message to General Leclerc and his staff to meet with me in two days. General Dearborn, please follow me." Burr walked towards his personal room in the old warehouse, refurbished only a few weeks ago, spartan, but clean and equipped with a good writing desk and ample light.

Burr walked in and sat behind his small desk, waving for Dearborn to sit as well. "Henry, with Boston ours, I have another assignment for you."

"Oh?" Dearborn allowed a hint of concern to creep into his reply.

"Yes, I want to appoint you military governor of Massachusetts. Will you accept?"

"Yes sir, of course. Will I remain the commanding general?"

"No, I need you more as governor of Massachusetts. You have extensive contacts in Massachusetts that will be useful in raising a brigade for the army there and surveying the shipbuilding facilities. Also, your vote on the council will be of even greater importance."

"I'll have a vote on the council?" Dearborn was surprised and pleased.

"All governors in the United American Republic have a vote on the council. You'll have the same vote that Clinton, McKean, Bloomfield, and Hall have—at least until you decide to recommend an election. Also, two more things."

"Yes?"

"I want you to bring New Hampshire and Connecticut over to our side. You'll have some support in the newspapers. I can see to that. And you can have the army at Boston—though I must let the militia go—though, you may recruit the best among them to form your Massachusetts brigade. You will be commander-in-chief of this new formation. Once you gain control of Connecticut and New Hampshire, plan on raising a regular regiment of 1,000 in each state. I will also need your recommendations for military governors for those states as well."

Dearborn finally understood Burr's plan for consolidation of government power onto himself, but he said nothing, he had work to do.

Chapter Fifty-Four – Warning

November 16, 1802, Manhattan, New York

Jeph was returning to the law office with supplies as a few clients came in for Hamilton after the fight against the British raid. Even Henry Livingston and Richard Harison picked up new clients. He was opening the door when he heard a familiar voice behind him, "Here, let me help you with the door, Sergeant Clark."

It was Burr. He was wearing a black beaver felt top hat with a three-inch crown, a black coat and grey trousers with knee high riding boots polished to a high sheen. Jeph's own boots were covered with mud and horse droppings. Burr's were immaculate. Jeph lifted his gaze to see the official carriage behind Burr, driver and two guards armed with unusual looking muskets. The day was dark and the sun, low, with what little light there was imbuing the guards with a sinister form as they were silhouetted against the gloomy sky.

"Colonel Burr! What an honor to see you, sir, thank you."

Burr opened the door for Jeph. Burr looked back briefly and motioned the guards to stay put.

"Is Mr. Hamilton here?"

"I don't rightly know, sir. I went out to purchase paper, quills, and ink this morning and haven't yet been inside the office."

"May I?" Burr smiled.

"Of course, sir. Is there anything I may do for you? And I know it may be above my station, but I think of you frequently, sir. I pray to God that he may bestow His wisdom on you and for the success of our nation."

"I thank you, Jeph." Burr seemed moved momentarily and then asked, "Would you please see if Mr. Hamilton is in, I need to speak with him."

"Yes sir. Of course." Jeph set his supplies down and walked a few steps down the narrow corridor to Hamilton's office. He knocked softly. "Mr. Hamilton?"

"Yes," said Hamilton softly, absentmindedly.

"Sir, you have a visitor. Colonel Burr is here to see you."

Jeph heard a start, as if Hamilton suddenly sat up in his chair. "Please, send him in and please, fetch us the usual refreshments. Tea or hot cider would be nice on such a dreary day."

Jeph turned to Burr who was already advancing down the hallway, "Sir, Mr. Hamilton will see you. I'm going to get some refreshments, anything in particular, sir?"

"Thank you, I'll have whatever Mr. Hamilton is having."

"Right sir." Even though Jeph and Burr were both compact men, the hallway was narrow enough that they had to turn their shoulders sideways to avoid brushing past each other as Jeph went to the tavern across the street to buy some hot tea, as he hadn't stoked the fire yet this morning.

As Jeph came back a few minutes later, he could hear an intense exchange between the two former army officers.

Hamilton was speaking, his voice raised, "...dangerous tyranny. Making enemies when we should be making friends."

Burr's response was calm, deliberate, "The old system wasn't working. Our weakness was attracting enemies. It was only a matter of time before Europe saw we were incapable of defending ourselves."

Jeph lightly tapped on the door, "Gentlemen? May I?"

Hamilton said, "Come in! Thank you, Jeph."

Jeph saw Hamilton standing behind his desk, Burr was seated comfortably, his right hand on his chin, his hat on his lap.

Jeph said, "I'm sorry it took a few extra minutes, I hadn't been in to start the fire yet this morning and had to visit the tavern for some tea." Jeph served the men, taking measure of their faces. Burr's was impassive, Hamilton's fully engaged as if he was making an argument before the jury in a capital offense case.

Hamilton addressed Jeph, "Have you been able to collect on the Jones case? I understand he was just paid his judgement. Please attend to this now. You should find him at this store."

Jeph knew that was Hamilton's way of getting him out of the office; of protecting him. From exactly what, he didn't know.

An hour later Jeph returned with two of the new twenty-dollar pieces minted by Burr's government. They were impressive coins. And, unlike the paper dollars issued by the Continental Congress and enthusiastically counterfeited by British engravers, gold was not yet liable to the alchemy of replication.

He walked into the office building and saw that Hamilton's door was open and walked down the hallway towards the office. He knocked on the doorframe without peering around it. "Sir?"

An exhausted Hamilton replied, "Come in, Jeph."

"How was the rest of your visit with Colonel Burr?"

Hamilton looked up from his desk, "He warned me to stop undermining him."

"Well sir, are you?"

"Jeph, I'm trying to save this nation... save it from a tyrant who would be emperor."

"So, President Burr has a legitimate concern?"

"I resist his political ambitions. I haven't taken up arms against the man— only words. That he cannot brook dissent shows that arms will inevitably come next. As Jefferson reminded me in his letter of last September, 'The tree of liberty must be refreshed from time to time with the blood of patriots and tyrants.'"

"Sir, I don't mean to be argumentative. But given you're a lawyer and I work for lawyers, perhaps I've picked up an inclination to argue."

Hamilton laughed.

"So, you called Colonel Burr a tyrant twice now in the last minute. What do you mean to call him that? By that, I mean, sir, what has he done to be a tyrant?"

"Done? Done? He gathered and army an invaded Massachusetts, for one."

"Well, sir, with respect, Massachusetts—really the United States— threaten to overturn our independence. They threatened to void Colonel Burr's election as president. So, under the doctrine of the right of self-defense, we marched on Boston to secure the peace... At least that's what I've read in the newspapers."

"Very well. I might have done the same were I in Burr's shoes, but there's an even graver sin against the rights of man that Burr is about to commit."

"Really, sir? But, and again, no disrespect, sir, I'm trying to understand what's at stake here, sir"

Hamilton smiled at Jeph, "I don't blame you for questioning me, Jeph, you should. This is life and death. This is the future of your family—of the nation. Likely the world of man. Let me be clear and succinct. Burr's election as president came with no safeguards. No constitution. No restraints. In this, Burr is emulating Napoleon and his elevation as First Consul three years ago. Napoleon has already quenched the chaos of the revolution and with it, any real republic, and is on his way to being emperor."

"Yes, well, sir, Americans aren't the French. We still have our state governments and state constitutions. Colonel Burr may be president, but he can't do anything in the states that the states don't have the power to do."

"Really?" Hamilton arched his eyebrow at Jeph, "You really think that Burr will be restrained by state power? By a governor? Do you really think old Governor Clinton is going to stand up to Burr? Burr has the Army, what does Clinton have?"

"The Governor has the power of the purse and the militia..." Jeph protested.

"And Burr already has the power of the purse and a national army. His vote, as the first among equals, and that of two more governors, and he can do—will do—whatever he pleases. And, if the governors don't like it… Well, I'm afraid they won't be in office for long. Burr created for himself the shell of a monster. The vote of the people breathed life into it. Burr operates it. It will continue on a path of destruction until the people turn on Burr or it's defeated in battle. We are facing grave times, Jeph. Grave times."

Chapter Fifty-Five – Phony War

February 28, 1803, Manhattan, New York

The British landed 10,000 soldiers on Staten Island in New York on November 24, with the fleet blockading New York Harbor since.

The French still held Montreal and were busy fortifying Quebec to prevent any sizable fleet from sailing up the St. Lawrence waterway.

A small British and allied Indian attack on Montreal was beaten back in early November with light casualties on both sides.

And the tiny French colony of Saint Pierre and Miquelon, just off the coast of Newfoundland—and only just returned to France as the result of the Treaty of Amiens with Britain—was promptly sacked again by the British, with the small population of would-be colonists shipped back home to France.

Importantly for Burr and his United American Republic, General Leclerc returned to New York with 10,000 men, 2,000 of them French Canadians who volunteered, allowing Leclerc to replenish his campaign losses.

British intelligence must have been sufficient to know that they faced a peer army of a similar size. The British stayed on Staten Island and the French eyed them from Manhattan and Long Island.

In the meantime, Burr's newspapers made hay out of the British occupation of Staten Island, building up the new nation's ability to defend itself while praising the French as steadfast allies.

Then, on the last day of February, the British left, and with them, their fleet as well.

There was no damage to structures on the island and the population reported that they were treated well.

Only later was it learned that Napoleon was assembling a huge army of army of 200,000 men, known as the Army of the Ocean Coasts, to invade England and put an end to the rival that could strike at France at any time wherever there was salt water to convey a force to land.

But Burr used the interlude well. Slowly expanding his army, improving its training, and receiving more cannon and muskets from France. The United American Republic even built up its own musket manufacturing—almost 200 muskets per month patterned off the French Charleville—at the Springfield Armory in Massachusetts, now under the watchful eye of Governor General Dearborn. With the addition of recruits from New England and the pacification of New Hampshire, Rhode Island, and Connecticut— Vermont was still a problem that Burr promised himself to resolve as soon as he dealt with Jefferson in the South—the Army grew from 6,000 to 10,500, not counting the state militia or the Navy.

And soon, Burr would commence conscription, doubling the size of the Army to 21,000 with the veterans training the new recruits. Then, after two months of training, Burr would consolidate the 10,500 veterans in Philadelphia, forging them into a fighting Army, a true national force, rather than a collection of scattered full-time state units. With this Army, Burr would move south and force Jefferson to abandon his pipedream of a new republic to rival Burr's.

Chapter Fifty-Six – The (dis)United States of America

March 4, 1803, Richmond, Virginia

Thomas Jefferson and John Adams were formally sworn in the as the first president and vice president of the United States of America as reorganized under the constitution that was drafted in Philadelphia in September 1787. It had been a long and fraught process and now the nation was effectively torn asunder. Aaron Burr's United American Republic controlled all land from Pennsylvania and Delaware north, comprised of eight states with Vermont still a holdout self-proclaimed republic. In the South, Jefferson led a fragile new national government, born in war and representing eight states: Maryland, Virginia, Kentucky, North Carolina, Tennessee, South Carolina, and Georgia with a government in exile from Massachusetts in residence in Charleston, South Carolina.

The first order of business was setting up a national capital. The largest city in the South was Baltimore at 27,000 people, the third-largest city in America after New York and Philadelphia. But Baltimore was deemed too close to Burr's armies to be readily safeguarded. Charleston was next, the fifth-largest city after Boston with 19,000 people, recently swelled by the addition of some 20,000 refugees from Massachusetts, delivered there by the British fleet after the evacuation of Boston. But memories were still raw over the six-week British siege of the city in 1780 that culminated in the surrender of almost 5,500 American soldiers, leaving the South denuded of troops. Charleston was considered too susceptible to rapid attack from the sea. Jefferson argued for his familiar Richmond. Richmond featured a beautiful state capitol that Jefferson himself conceived of, patterned on an ancient Roman temple he visited in Nîmes, France. And while Richmond was only the thirteenth-largest city in America and the second largest in Virginia, at almost 6,000 people, it was deemed more defensible—plus, Virginia was the most populous state at 880,000 inhabitants, though 350,000 were slaves. So, Richmond it was.

Jefferson and Adams, though normally not seeing eye-to-eye on the need for an energetic national government, cautiously papered over their differences to face Burr's threat.

Jefferson selected fellow Virginian James Madison as his Secretary of State. Charged with seeking foreign support and, if possible, turning Napoleon away from helping Burr, Madison was the chief architect of the Philadelphia constitution and, in the months leading up to the formal inauguration of the new national government, of a Bill of Rights to restrain the government from abridging the people's natural rights.

James McHenry of Maryland was asked to be Secretary of War. McHenry, a federalist, was a supporter of the constitution when Jefferson was a skeptic—albeit, from a distance in France.

Recognizing the dire need for financial strength, Jefferson reluctantly extended an offer to Alexander Hamilton to be Secretary of the Treasury. Hamilton begged off, saying he was better employed trying to free New York from Burr's grip. Next was Albert Gallatin, but Gallatin, from Pennsylvania, had already been recruited by Burr for the same task. With most southerners' wealth tied up in land and slaves, finding a qualified leader of the Treasury was difficult. Jefferson eventually settled on former South Carolina governor Charles Pinckney for the task.

Levi Lincoln, Sr., who accompanied Adams during the flight from Boston, was appointed Attorney General, thus further cementing the government's claim to represent all of America.

Marylander Robert Smith was appointed Secretary of the Navy—he had the herculean task of organizing the naval yards in Baltimore, Norfolk and Charleston to create a navy from scratch.

With the government in place, the cabinet soon confirmed by the new United States Senate and its 16 members, Jefferson set about to ensure the nation would survive its first two challenges: Burr and bankruptcy. And though Adams urged him forward against Burr, Jefferson was content to build on the status quo—even, frankly, to abandon the Massachusetts exiles if a peace treaty could be worked out with Burr. Though that latter consideration he kept to himself.

Jefferson figured he had time on his side, if he could survive the first year. The South was richer than the North—with longer growing seasons, more fertile soils, and valuable export crops: tobacco, sugar, rice, indigo and, increasingly, cotton. And the South's population was even with the North's, with Tennessee and Kentucky rapidly growing while the threat from the British and Indians in the Northwest had kept that region from attracting settlers as rapidly as those lands south of the Ohio. Though, there was that troublesome colony of escaped slaves in Western Ohio—a colony that also threatened to empty plantations of their labor throughout the South at Burr's encouragement.

Lastly, as distasteful as it was for him, Jefferson had to agree with Adams that his most pressing task was to forge an agreement with Britain. Napoleon's ascent and alliance with Burr had put his preferred friendship with republican France out of the question. Besides which, he had to grudgingly admit that Napoleon was busy burying the last vestiges the revolution's rights of man on his tyrannical quest.

Burr's attack on Massachusetts did confer two windfalls. First, Boston's considerable merchant fleet—some 500 ships and the knowledge to build them, man them, and trade with them—came south to Charleston. Thus, in one movement, the South's merchant marine jumped from 700 ships, mostly based in Baltimore, to 1,200 while the North's dropped from 1,600 to 1,100. Second, allying with Napoleon and drawing a declaration of war from Britain meant the latter's reimposition of its blockade of France while making Burr's ships subject to confiscation by the Royal Navy. Thus, Burr's ability to trade or generate naval power would degrade over time—unless Napoleon was successful in his rumored cross-Channel invasion. The fact of British naval supremacy and its de facto protection of the U.S. merchant fleet allowed Jefferson the luxury of opposing a blue water navy, preferring instead to request Congress fund harbor gunboats manned by local militia. Of course, privateers were another matter—and Jefferson didn't have to request taxes to pay for those.

Chapter Fifty-Seven – Build-Up

May 19, 1803, Philadelphia, Pennsylvania

Most of Burr's regular army, now just over 20,000 strong, almost half of whom were veterans of the siege of Boston, was assembling in Philadelphia. Burr ordered his generals to forge one division along the lines of France's Le Corps Canadien. This unit was to have a strength of 10,000 infantry organized in three brigades, each having two regiments. The division was supposed to be supported by an artillery brigade of 32 guns, though only 21 serviceable guns of a standard caliber could be assembled so far due to competing demands from the navy and the need to emplace artillery at New York and Boston to keep the British at bay. This unit had been drilling for almost a month. An additional 2,000 men were formed into a cavalry brigade. These practiced charges against the infantry, as well as scouting and screening techniques, all under the watchful eye and guidance of French officers detailed to assist the Americans.

In the meantime, Burr's growing network of spies reported that fortification efforts were now underway in Baltimore, with a trench line supported by strongpoints running from Ridgley Cove in the west, north about a mile, then east almost a mile, and then south to anchor at the Patapsco River. The Locust Point peninsula jutted out eastward only 1,000 feet of open water to the south of the shore. At the end of this finger of land there was a poorly maintained wooden stockade officially known as Fort McHenry but known locally as Fort Kindling. This fort stood on the grounds of old Fort Whetstone; an earthen star fort quickly built in 1776 but allowed to decay over the past 20 years. There were plans to upgrade the stockade to a real fort in 1798. City fathers even commissioned Jean Foncin, a French fortress architect, for a design. But when the British never followed up on threats to put the privateer shipyards to the torch, interest in the costly fort waned.

In Richmond, 150 miles to the south of Baltimore, the new federal government of the United States of America was very busy, passing laws, including a tariff on imports and exports reluctantly signed into law by President Jefferson. It also sent a Bill of Rights to the states for ratification into the Constitution. With great reticence, Jefferson even allowed Secretary of State Madison and Secretary of the Treasury Pinckney to negotiate with the British for a line of credit to ensure the new government would remain solvent. The louder of Tennessee's two senators, Andrew Jackson, threatened to scuttle the arrangement, but when asked which new taxes he'd be willing to support in lieu of a loan, he stalked off muttering about the English being the spawn of Satan himself.

By mid-March, Congress sent President Jefferson bills to authorize an army and a navy, including marines. But the appropriations bills for the same took another six weeks to hammer out, with one bill making an appropriation of $1.3 million to construct two 44-gun frigates, pay for sailors and marines to man the warships, and underwrite a naval arsenal in Richmond. The other bill made appropriations for the army, setting aside $350,000 for 5,000 regular army soldiers and officers, $500,000 to fortify Baltimore, Charleston, and Richmond, $200,000 for coastal gunships, and another $500,000 for a series of armories, and supply warehouses for a total of $1.55 million.

For Jefferson, the almost $3 million was double what he would have otherwise been willing to spend absent the threat from Burr and Napoleon. But he would cease being a statesman if Burr put his head on a pike. Out of an abundance of caution, Jefferson sent letters to the seven state governors—ignoring the Massachusetts government-in-exile—asking them to mobilize their militias to meet the threat from the north.

When Senator Jackson, who also served as the elected general of Tennessee's militia, got wind of Jefferson's call, he eagerly rode out of Richmond for Knoxville to assume his martial duties.

Now, eleven weeks after being sworn in as President, Jefferson believed he had done all that he reasonably could to safeguard the new republic with which the people had entrusted him.

Chapter Fifty-Eight – Clouds of Oppression

June 5, 1803, New Rochelle, New York

Jeph's mind weighed heavily this bright and cool Sunday morning. He was fretting over his finances. The legal support work he did for Mr. Hamilton was half of what it was in prior years. Colonel Burr no longer had need of him now that he was President. Taxes were going up on his house. His oldest daughter, Jenny, age 19, was due to be married in a month. And his wife, Molly, was expecting their sixth child in a month, adding to the family of three daughters and two sons.

Yet here he was in church, seated one pew up from the back in a wooden Presbyterian that held about 80 congregants, and he was fretting over things of this world. Jeph frowned and then considered that his one-year-old squab business was doing well and that he should be thankful for that.

Molly shifted uncomfortably on the wooden bench and then lightly hit his ribs with her elbow, motioning with her eyes that the sermon had started, and he should be paying attention.

Jeph snapped back to the present, smiled at Molly and looked up at Reverend John McLachlan.

"…Therefore the Psalmist says in the fifth and sixth verses of this psalm, 'The stout-hearted are spoiled, they have slept their sleep. None of the men of might have found their hands. At thy rebuke, O God of Jacob! both the chariot and the horse are cast into a deep sleep.' And then the Psalmist reflects, 'Surely the wrath of man shall praise thee; the remainder of wrath shalt thou restrain.' What does he mean here? The fury and injustice of oppressors shall bring in a tribute of praise to thee; the influence of thy righteous providence shall be clearly discerned; the countenance and support thou wilt give to thine own people shall be gloriously illustrated; thou shalt set the bounds which the boldest cannot pass."

Reverend McLachlan surveyed his flock, and then noted, in the back right pew, sitting alone, was none other than Thomas Paine—though he doubted Paine had come for the spiritual sustenance; rather, Paine was likely here for the same reason another man was, also sitting alone in the back left pew—a man McLachlan surmised was there to report back to the authorities the nature of today's preaching.

He took a deep breath, "I am aware, my brothers and sisters, that this psalm may seem, at first, to be ill-suited to our trying times. It was composed after a victory; whereas we are now but putting on the harness and entering upon a terrible trial, the length of which is unknown but to God. But know this, all the passions of men, whether exposing the innocent to private injury, or whether they are the arrows of divine judgment in public calamity, shall, in the end, be to the praise of God. Or, to bring us to America's present state and the plague of war: The ambition of mistaken princes, the cunning and cruelty of oppressive and corrupt officials, and even the inhumanity of brutal soldiers, however dreadful, shall ultimately promote the glory of God, and until then, while the storm continues, His mercy and kindness shall appear in prescribing bounds to their rage and fury."

The man in the back pew cleared his throat a little too loudly and Paine shot him a wicked grin.

McLachlan continued, "But where revelation allows discovery of the wisdom and mercy of divine providence, nothing can be more delightful or profitable to a serious mind, and therefore I beg your attention. In the first place, the wrath of man praises God, as it is an example and illustration of divine truth, and clearly points out the corruption of our nature, which is the foundation stone of the doctrine of redemption. Nothing can be more absolutely necessary to true religion, than a clear and full conviction of the sinfulness of our nature and state. Without this there can be neither repentance in the sinner, nor humility in the believer. But where can we have a more affecting view of the corruption of our nature, than in the wrath of man, when exerting itself in oppression, cruelty and blood? All the disorders in human society, and the greatest part even of the unhappiness we are exposed to now, arises from the envy, malice, covetousness, and other lusts of man. But war and violence present a spectacle still more awful driven by the universal lust of domination. Men are rarely be satisfied with their own possessions and acquisitions, looking instead upon the happiness and tranquility of others, as an obstruction to their own? Yet for what? Is it not the great law of nature, that 'Dust thou art, and to dust thou shalt return'? Yet history is filled with the wars and contentions of princes and empires. And further, that of all wars between man and man is not a civil war between citizen and citizen all the more abhorred? How deeply affecting is it, that those who are the same in blood, in language, and in religion, should, notwithstanding, butcher one another with unrelenting rage, and then revel in the act? That men should lay waste the fields of their brothers, with whose provision they themselves had been fed, and consume with devouring fire those houses in which they had broken bread."

The man in the back scribbled a few notes as McLachlan gathered himself, "Nations and people grow lax in prosperity but when earthly comforts are endangered, they seek something better. It is proper here to observe, that at the time of the reformation, when religion began to revive, nothing contributed more to facilitate its reception and increase its progress than the violence of its persecutors. Their cruelty and the patience of the sufferers, naturally disposed men to examine and weigh the cause to which they adhered with so much constancy and resolution. At the same time also, when they were persecuted in one city, they fled to another. How have we benefited at the pain of Boston and of the looting of its wealth? Is this not sinful envy? To take that which is not ours? If our cause is just—we may look with confidence to the Lord and intreat him to plead it as his own. Yet, as you all know, this is the first time of my introducing any political subject into the pulpit—and in these times, it is not only lawful but necessary as we find America now in arms with one side warring against the cause of justice, of liberty, and of human nature and for power, and tyranny, and greed."

And then, looking straight at Paine, McLachlan, voice rising, concluded, "These are the times that try men's souls. Tyranny, like hell, is not easily conquered; yet we have this consolation with us, that the harder the conflict, the more glorious the triumph."

Paine resisted the urge to applaud just long enough for the congregation to start singing a hymn. He was thinking it might be time to revisit his studied hostility to faith.

Chapter Fifty-Nine – The Battle of Baltimore

July 4, 1803, Baltimore, Maryland

Burr let his new professional army train while he awaited a new shipment of French cannon to round out the 1st Division's artillery brigade. The division had 31 operational bronze Gribeauval pattern eight-pounders with another six 24-pounder siege cannons, also bronze—half of his total inventory—brought down to Philadelphia from New York. Burr had wanted to go earlier, but his senior officers warned him that the muddy conditions would slow the artillery and baggage train while the lack of a full artillery brigade would mean the army couldn't fight as it had trained. And so, he waited.

But on June 30, the French ambassador gave him the bad news that, due to preparations for the invasion of England, the approval for additional French cannon export were suspended. Instead, the French would send a team of engineers to supervise the construction of two armories in New York, one for the manufacture of the newer, larger 12-pounders, the other to manufacture Charleville muskets along with 20,000 francs in gold coin to underwrite the effort. Once the armories were up and running, France reserved half of the production for themselves, which, of course, they'd pay for.

Time, no longer an ally, Burr immediately set out for Philadelphia with Captain John Bentley, his executive secretary, and a major from France's military mission. He sent orders ahead via optical telegraph for the army to begin moving on Baltimore. Every evening for four days, Burr retired at an optical telegraph station to read the daily dispatches from his army and every night he'd feel mixed emotions at the ease with which the army moved, thinking he should have ordered it to action far sooner.

And now, three-and-a-half days' ride later, Burr had caught up with his army's baggage train as they were crossing Herring Run only a half mile from the northeastern extent of Baltimore's outer works.

It was almost noon, the sun unobscured by any cloud. Burr could feel the coming heat with the air thick with humidity. He mopped his brow as he made his way past the long file of supply wagons that were slowing down to cross a modest wooden bridge over a stream. The trees along the creek's edge grew high and strong, meeting in the middle to completely shade the water, lending Burr welcome relief from the sun.

Burr paused at midspan and inhaled deeply. Behind him, he heard the snort of the two-horse team drawing a powder supply wagon. The bridge groaned. Then ahead, he heard a nearby cannon volley. Bentley's horse seemed disquieted at the cannon sound. Burr looked back at Bentley, "Is your mount a war horse?"

"No sir, she's not," Bentley responded with less confidence than Burr would have liked.

"Well, no time like the present to break her in!" Burr straightened his coat and adjusted his black hat and urged his horse towards the sound of the guns.

The dusty road edged up from the stream and back into bright sunlight. Burr reached to retrieve the canteen of water and took a pull—draining it. There was only enough water for two gulps.

Bentley drew even with Burr and held out his own canteen, "Sir?"

Burr ignored his old captain as he crested the stream's bed, surveying treeless fields stretching out to the west, laden with corn, wheat, and barley. He could see the tracks of his deploying army radiating out like spokes from a wheel reaching out to Baltimore. He smiled and mopped his forehead again. "Magnificent, isn't it?"

"Sir?" Bentley said, still holding out the canteen.

Burr, deep in thought, spurred his horse to a gallop, heading to the nearest artillery, the smoke from their volleys just visible above the corn stalks.

Bentley chased after him with a visibly excited French major just behind.

Just over a minute's ride later, the supporting ammunition wagons were in view and Burr reached the crest just as a battery of two 24-pounder siege cannons let loose, belching flame and smoke. Bentley's horse reared, but the captain maintained control and leaned close to the horse, speaking to soothe it.

If this gun crew could see the enemy lines, Burr couldn't. He scanned left and right, looking for ranking officers. He addressed the battery's commander, "Lieutenant! Where's the General Lewis?"

The lieutenant looked up, soot and sweat dripping down his smiling face, "Sir?"

Burr started to ask again and then could see the look of recognition flash across the young officer's face.

The lieutenant saluted, "Colonel B-Burr, P-President, sir!" he stuttered, "General Lewis's command should be 500 yards to the south along this crest. Just follow the gun line, sir! Sir, very glad to meet you, sir. I'm Lieutenant Halsey, Mark Halsey. From Brattleboro, sir!"

"A Green Mountain Boy, eh? Very glad to meet your acquaintance, Lieutenant Halsey, now, attend to your guns, if you will." Burr saw that the gun crew had stopped to gawk at their commander-in-chief and, looking over his shoulder as he rode off south, he could see the men laughing at their lieutenant. Burr smiled and spurred his horse to a gallop again.

Less than a minute later, Burr saw a cluster of horses topped by men in blue jackets topped by impressively tall black bicornes. "General Lewis!" Burr called out.

Morgan Lewis, lowered his spyglass and looked towards Burr, disappointment briefly on his face before he forced a smile, "President Burr, a pleasure to see you, sir!"

"I'm supposing Gertrude would not approve of this." Burr swept his hand towards the enemy lines some 400 yards distant.

General Lewis retorted, "Mrs. Lewis doesn't approve of much." The crow's feet framing Lewis's dark brown eyes deepened as he broke out in a genuine grin.

Burr lifted his hat to wipe the sweat off his face, though it wasn't as sweaty as before. Burr absently ascribed it to the gallop. Bentley again proffered his canteen, but Burr was focused on General Lewis, "What's the situation, General?"

"We've deployed the division to about 300 yards from the enemy earthworks and put them to prone as we were receiving some casualties from rifle fire." Lewis shifted his gaze from Burr to the enemy lines and back again. "I estimate the enemy strength at 5,000 militia and 20 supporting cannon. There is no sign of the national army. I've issued orders to destroy the enemy cannon with counterbattery fire and, once their cannon are out of action, to assault their earthworks. If we can do that in the next two hours, I'm inclined to storm Baltimore. If it takes longer, we will consolidate on their works and then take the city on the morrow."

Burr nodded at Lewis, "Excellent. Carry on, General."

Lewis nodded back and, looking relieved, turned his attention to his staff. "Captain Brown! Order the batteries to move up 100 yards, they're wasting ammunition and time."

Burr's face felt hot and he looked around for Bentley and his water. He saw his secretary speaking with a colonel—by the looks of it, an old colleague. "Bentley! I'll have some of that water now."

Bentley broke off his conversation, shook hands with the mounted officer, and trotted over to Burr, hand outstretched with the canteen. Burr winced at his gathering headache. *Not again.*

A mile to the north of Belair Road, the right extent of the United American Republic's battlelines, a force of 508 mounted Tennessee militia made their way to the northeast in the direction of Philadelphia. Many of the buckskin-clad warriors sported hats fashioned from racoon, or beaver, or bear—even a wolf—while others wore old, ill-fitting Continental Army uniforms. Almost half carried saber or sword and a brace of pistols, the rest being armed with Kentucky rifles, tomahawks, hatchets, and large knives.

Major General Andrew Jackson, 36-years-old, on self-leave from the U.S. Senate, rode a few yards behind his scouts, wearing a deep blue jacket with high golden-yellow collars that came up to his jaw line and gold epaulets that undulated in the intense sunlight at every hoof fall. Riding alongside was Jackson's aide-de-camp. A captain, the youngest son of a well-known plantation owner from just south of Nashville, wore a similarly immaculate uniform that—if the truth be told—cost nearly double Jackson's own. The mounted Tennessee division featured only four other officers identifiable by their uniforms, two led the cavalry of 197 men and the other two led the mounted riflemen of 309 men.

Jackson arrived in Baltimore two days earlier after a fortnight's trek of some 530 miles up the Great Valley from the Great Smokies, transiting one river valley to the next, gliding past the Blue Ridge mountains and finally reaching the Shenandoah Valley before turning east at Winchester, Virginia. There, he was told that a force of 10,000 men and supporting artillery was rapidly making its way south towards Baltimore from Philadelphia. Sources in Pennsylvania suggested that their objective was the capture of Baltimore in the opening act of Burr's final war of conquest to unite America under his leadership.

Jackson learned that there was, as yet, no effective federal army, the appropriations for which had only been approved just over two ago with five Army regiments of 1,000 soldiers each approaching completion of their training. Even so, there was only one training regiment in Maryland and its commander was under strict orders to avoid fighting until it was ready for action.

Instead, Maryland's governor had called out the militia with 7,500 answering the call and concentrating in Baltimore while the residents of that city, freeman and slave alike, furiously constructed earthworks. The new federal government's work could be seen in three places: work was commencing on the construction of a new masonry star fort in place of old Whetstone along with four lesser fortifications to the west along the neck of Locust Point; an odd assortment of 31 cannon had been delivered by ship a month before with more promised; and work was starting on a proper frigate in the port's largest shipyard.

Jackson was asked by his Maryland counterpart to scout the advancing army and send reports back as to its disposition so the Marylanders could anticipate where the invaders might first attack.

Jackson agreed to the request but only to get out of the stuffy room the Marylanders had made their headquarters.

Jackson viewed his plan as a wartime adaptation of the Maryland militia commander's request—a reconnaissance in force. He didn't leave his post in the Senate to travel back to Knoxville, gather all the militia he could, and then race north to Maryland just to sneak around in the brush and send reports back to Baltimore.

And now Jackson heard the unmistakable sound of artillery to the south. He turned to his aide-de-camp, "Captain Campbell."

"Sir!" the blue-eyed youngster was set for action.

"Captain, fetch me my regimental commanders. We're fixing for a fight."

"Yes sir!" Campbell wheeled his horse and charged down the loose double file of horsemen.

Five minutes later Jackson's regimental cavalry commander, Colonel Baker, rode up. Jackson told him to relax until his colleague arrived and another ten minutes passed before Colonel Wright galloped up, horse in a lather.

"Glad you could make it today, Colonel Wright," Jackson ribbed.

Wright edged his horse close to Jackson and said in a low voice, "I thought it unwise to shit in my hat before battle, so I wrapped up business as fast as nature allows and made my way here."

Jackson laughed and cuffed the officer on shoulder, "I thought I smelled the remains of last night's dinner on the air as you approached!" Jackson looked at his two commanders, "Now, let's get to fighting. Wright, I want you to take your mounted rifles and make your way behind the enemy infantry and bring the northern-most enemy cannon crew under fire. I reckon there will be about 30 men, maybe 40. Fire a volley and charge. Reload and fire on the next battery you see then get the hell out, following Belair Road until you get to the creek about a mile or two up the road. Put up pickets and wait for me to return from my excursion down the Herring Run." Jackson's blue eyes glittered with anticipation. "Now, Colonel Baker, I have a proper cavalry mission for you. We're going to find that Yankee supply train and we're going to break it, burn it, and relieve it of its horses. We'll frolic for half an hour and then we'll make our way back up the eastern side of Herring Run and link back up with Wright's men and swing northwest of the Yankee army and then back to Baltimore to swap stories."

Jackson looked at his two commanders, Wright was an old frontiersman, some 10 years his senior. His face was creased, and his forehead sported a knotty scar, a memento of a Creek Indian arrow. Baker was barely older than his aide-de-camp and, like Campbell, came from a prominent plantation family who owned more than 200 slaves. "Now, I want to be clear as sky above us. We're in a bad mess right now. The Yankees have raised a real army with proper artillery and help from France. We're on our own. No one's coming to help us. On this day, 27 years ago, we declared our independence from the British and their bastard king—you might have even been suckling on your mother's teat by then Baker—though I'm pretty sure Campbell there was just a gleam in his father's eye."

Baker and Campbell just grinned sheepishly as they were both under 27 years of age. Wright laughed and spat a big wad of well chewed tobacco at Baker's mount's front hooves.

"Today's battle belongs to us. I can't vouch for tomorrow but let us bestow on our brother militia one more sunrise of freedom. Now, Wright, you get your men at the ready as soon as you get back and speak to your officers. By the time you tell them your intent, we'll be making our way down the run. I don't want you to attack too soon, so try not to be seen. It will be best if we can find that supply train before you attack. I'm sure the Yankees have some cavalry of their own and, as much as I'd like a fight with those devil-spawn, I'd rather keep things on our terms today. Let's go! I'll be damned if I'm going let some New York dandy licker march onto our soil and order us about!"

Burr rode ahead with his party, keeping pace with General Lewis as the general stayed about 300 yards behind his advancing troops.

The Maryland militia, now virtually stripped of their cannon after a three-hour artillery duel, had a stark choice: they could stand and fight toe-to-toe with the United American Republic's 1st Division; or they could flee. In the grand tradition of the militia, many of whom lacked proper bayonets, Lewis calculated they would flee and, that's when he planned to unleash General Stephen Van Rensselaer and his 2,000 cavalrymen.

Lewis's artillery was now trained on the militia in their earthworks, pouring cannister into their positions at oblique angles to the advancing infantry. This didn't kill many of the enemy, but it did keep them pinned down and decreased their rate of musket fire.

The lead lines of Northern infantry were only 200 yards from the earthworks when the call went out to double-quick time march at the enemy lines.

Burr rode up behind Lewis who was carefully surveying the battlefield with his binoculars. Burr considered saying something, but his head was pounding, sweat saturating his clothing.

"Van Rensselaer! Send in your boys! They're breaking. Charge, man, charge!"

"Rensselaer is here?" Burr slurred.

Lewis twisted in his saddle just to see Burr swoon. Lewis bellowed, "Surgeon! The President's been hit! Surgeon!"

Bentley hopped off his mount, barely having time to break Burr's fall. Burr's face was ashen and clammy.

"General Lewis! General Lewis!" A breathless lieutenant galloped up to the general's staff.

"Yes?" Lewis took his eyes off of Burr. "Lieutenant?"

"Sir, sir," the lieutenant gasped for breath atop is lathered horse.

"Slow down, son," Lewis admonished, looking back down at Burr as Bentley was pouring water from his canteen onto Burr's face.

"General Lewis, 2nd Brigade's supporting C Battery has been taken under fire by sharpshooters. The crews are dead or driven off."

Lewis looked at the lieutenant, blinking, he looked back at Burr who appeared to be speaking, and then back at the junior officer. "When did this happen?"

"Sir? Um, about a quarter-hour ago, sir. D Battery has oriented its guns north."

Lewis considered the news—half of his artillery was now out of action or focused away from supporting his infantry. But the enemy was fleeing. The attack would continue.

"Commit the reserve. Send them north and retake that battery, we can't allow the enemy to capture or damage those guns!"

Lewis saw another rider heading for the command group from the east, the rider whipping his horse vigorously. This man was a sergeant. He looked to be about 40 years old.

"Permission to address the General?"

"Speak."

"Sir, the enemy is attacking the baggage train. The teams have laagered and are holding them off, but we've lost several wagons, including two powder wagons. There are said to be 200 or more enemy cavalry in the area of where Philadelphia Road crosses Herring Run."

Lewis looked down at Burr who was wide-eyed and motioning the general to him. General Lewis locked eyes with an aide, a captain with a large black mustache in the style of the French officers, "Fetch me Van Rensselaer! Recall the charge and order him to secure our baggage train. Go! Make haste!"

Lewis motioned two more aides to his side, telling the mounted officer to the left, "Go to the 2nd Brigade, tell General Wesley to pull back to the crest and secure his right flank immediately!" And then the other officer, "Order 1st Brigade to secure their sector of the earthworks and consolidate on the position."

Lewis swung off his mount and knelt by Burr. Burr weakly grabbed Lewis's right collar with his right hand and slurred, "Attack… drive home the battle… as at Gaugamela, the Persians and Indians are in the camp. Parmenion is saved. Pursue Darius. Nothing else matters."

"Surgeon! Get Burr to shade immediately. The heat has struck him down."

Burr mumbled, "Darius. Attack." And then his eyes rolled back and he passed out.

General Van Rensselaer's 2,000 cavalry ran down almost 100 militia and captured a couple score before being recalled only to fruitlessly chase Jackson's Tennesseans until nightfall. Jackson and his men slipped back into Baltimore just past sunset—to a massive Independence Day fireworks display—and proceeded to drink heavily until two hours before dawn.

Unnerved by the loss of a third of his supplies and wagons, General Lewis destroyed or captured what enemy cannon he could, secured his 43 prisoners, and withdrew 40 miles to Havre de Grace on the west bank of the Susquehanna River, leaving the field of battle to the Maryland militia and granting President Jefferson a few more precious months to organize.

Chapter Sixty – Fear and Loathing in New York

September 12, 1803, Manhattan

From a military standpoint, things were going well for Burr's United American Republic. The army firmly held the approaches to Baltimore, entrenching only a day's cavalry ride from Baltimore at the Susquehanna River. The entire Delaware peninsula—the eastern extant of Maryland and Virginia were secured. This area was placed under the military governorship of Morgan Lewis whom Burr appointed to ensure he kept out of New York politics as well as to remove him from command after he failed to follow up on his initial victory in Baltimore. The Cumberland Valley was secured down to the Potomac River and all the myriad finger-like valleys running to the northeast through the Blue Ridge Mountains were made secure from cavalry raids. And to the west, Pittsburgh was garrisoned and fortified. In short, the United American Republic was in no danger from the so-called United States of America. To the north, France remained firmly in control of the St. Lawrence from Quebec up to Montreal and was gradually squeezing the British and their Native allies in Upper Canada. This, while in Europe, France kept Britain tied down with its threat of invasion from its 200,000-strong *Armée "Angleterre.*

There was hopeful progress with the integration of New England into the Republic, with Connecticut on track to elect a governor who would have full voting rights on the Republic's council as it transitioned back to civil rule from General Henry Dearborn's military governorship. In short, President Burr should have been very pleased with the progress of his not even 18-month-old project. Only Vermont continued to bother him, like a cankerous sore that never quite healed, yet too small and poor to waste the 5,000 men and treasure it would take to truly defeat them. Even so, the Vermonters who left for the opportunities to be found in the Republic outnumbered the knaves, highwaymen, and malcontents to moved there by the necessity to avoid Burr's growing numbers of national police and gendarmerie.

But there were signs of trouble. Politicians worried at Burr's growing assumption of power were pushing back in the state legislatures. County sheriffs complained of the erosion of their responsibilities by unelected officers of the Republic. And the economy was not growing as it should be due to constant British harassment of his merchant ships as they tried to trade with French possessions in the Caribbean as well as continental Europe—and it didn't help that most of the merchants and sea trading families of Massachusetts and Rhode Island fled to South Carolina.

As a result, Burr's Republic was in need of more revenue to expand the navy as well as a larger army to defeat the threat from the South and become the undisputed master of America.

But raising that revenue and building an army, difficult enough on its own, was now consuming almost all his time as he found himself having to counter Hamilton and his allies at almost every turn. Something would have to be done about Hamilton and, ideally, that something should not openly implicate the Republic's President. And then there was Thomas Paine, who had finally outlived his usefulness.

Chapter Sixty-One – Invention, Cotton, and Slavery

October 2, 1803, Richmond, Virginia

President Jefferson settled in for a task that he had been looking forward to for weeks after the Patent Office, created in Congress's first weeks in April, was expected to send over its first applications for Jefferson to review. Given the President's keen interest in invention, the Superintendent of Patents himself would convey the 17 approved patents to the President. They filed through them: potash, steam power, an improvement on optical telegraphs and then they came to a filing from Eli Whitney, one of the refugees from Boston.

It was for a cotton engine or simply gin, that could clean some 50 pounds of short-staple upland cotton a day—50 times the output of one person doing the work by hand.

Jefferson put the patent application down. "Do you realize what this means?" Jefferson wasn't really addressing the Superintendent who, previously a merchant from New Hampshire, had no clue as to the implications of the invention anyway.

Jefferson, staring at the design, spoke his mind out loud, "Long-staple cotton only grows well on the coast where the air is conducive to it. Short-staple can grow most anywhere in the South, but there are no mechanical means suitable to remove the seeds from the bolls. This invention, if it works as this Mr. Whitney claims, will revolutionize cotton production."

The Superintendent nodded.

But then Jefferson's face darkened as he continued, "Which, of course, will mean an increased demand for African slaves just as rumors of Britain ending the slave trade are gathering and our own Constitution foresees that Congress may ban the importation of slaves in only five years and as Burr's government strives to entice our labor away to forge them into an armed buffer against the hostile tribes of the Northwest…"

Jefferson looked down and then looked at the Superintendent who stood in stunned silence, thinking that, even were Jefferson to dine alone, it would be the greatest assembly of intelligence in America.

"This little invention may be more trouble than it's worth," Jefferson sighed, but then quickly added, "Yet, the boost in our cotton exports may bind the British more closely to our interests while providing revenue for our defense against Burr's ambitions."

Chapter Sixty-Two – Politics and Power

December 10, 1803, New Rochelle, New York

Thomas Paine was feeling all his 66 years—that and not a small amount of alcohol, spite, and hate over the decades. It was said that in politics, friends come and go but enemies accumulate—and he excelled in making enemies, so much so that if he had one friend for every 1,000 people who wished him ill, he'd have more friends than faces he could remember. He had an arrest warrant issued for him in England 11 years earlier, fled to France and was arrested by French revolutionaries where he believed he was disowned by George Washington, whom he subsequently criticized bitterly.

And now, back in America, he saw the forces for liberty of all men, rich and poor, that he helped unleash being harnessed for tyranny by Aaron Burr whom he once viewed as a pupil.

Paine sipped on a glass of port and fondly recalled that June sermon preached by the Scottish Presbyterian minister in the church not far from his farmhouse. He resolved to attend again tomorrow and to consider more diligently the state of his soul.

The sun had been down for an hour and the fire needed some more logs before he would retire for the night. He painfully rose to his feet when he heard something outside his door.

"Who's there?" he called. Silence.

He padded over to the log carrier next to his Franklin stove—given to him by Franklin himself—and grabbed a log to put into the stove when he heard a voice just outside his door.

Paine started to ask, "Who's…" just as his front door splintered into pieces with a large log landing with a thud a couple of feet into his house. Behind the wreckage of his door, he could see the shadowy outlines of two men. Paine tossed the log at the doorway and lurched for the pistol he tried to always keep nearby.

There was a flash of light, and a deafening bang and he felt as if his left side was on fire. He tumbled to the ground; his left arm useless.

He heard heavy footsteps coming for him as his wooden floor creaked and moaned and his field of view was filled by a large man with blue eyes and a black beard who then smiled, revealing two broken front teeth. The man reached down and clamped his hands around Paine's throat. Paine weakly tried to resist and then, choking, gasping for air, thought about what Sunday might have beheld for him.

Twenty miles to the southwest in Manhattan, a Senior Inspector of the Gendarmes of the Republic visited Alexander Hamilton, handing him an official order restraining him from leaving the city or having any contact with current or former elected officials or military officers, either in person or by post. The man was friendly enough—he could afford to be, given the power he knew he had.

As the man left, Hamilton thought about what he could have done differently.

Chapter Sixty-Three – Exile

December 13, 1803, Richmond, Virginia

Even though he viewed his Vice President's manner too self-important and prone to complaint, President Jefferson had to admit that John Adams was a dedicated patriot, brilliant lawyer, and an astute student of government and man. Adams was shown into Jefferson's office and, after a short exchange of pleasantries, got straight to business.

"Thomas, we have a problem in the maintenance of our Union, and I propose a solution—one that may also aid the war effort through politics."

"Please, continue."

"The last election in Massachusetts cannot be replicated next year. There's no chance that Burr would allow an open election anywhere his armies control. Yet, we now have some 20,000 Massachusetts citizens in and around Charleston, and many thousands of others from Rhode Island, New Hampshire, and Connecticut. Article IV, Section 3 of the Constitution sets out how new states may be created. This got me to thinking that we might prevail upon the Congress and the government of South Carolina to set aside—temporarily, of course—a parcel of land east of Charleston across the Cooper River for purposes of erecting and maintaining a government-in-exile for Massachusetts. As such, the area would not necessarily need Congressional approval, though that would be preferred. This would allow Massachusetts to maintain, perhaps, a member in the House of Representatives as well as to reappoint one of its senators when the term of the first senator expires next year. It will also provide to us an enticement for the people of Massachusetts to more fully join our Union, providing they vote in the election for the House."

"Interesting. Though, what happens if Burr relinquishes the military governorship there and reestablishes the state government?"

"Yes, that could be a problem, having two competing state governments, but, as you know, each house is the final judge of their membership. The House could allow members to be seated and participate in the House's affairs in Richmond while the Senate could determine to recognize the senators appointed by the Massachusetts government-in-exile."

"I presume you have already spoken to Governor Richardson?"

"I have."

"And?"

"He'd rather not have 25,000 Yankees diluting the votes of 194,000 South Carolinian citizens."

"Ha! Smart man!" Jefferson smiled, crow's feet radiating out from his blue-grey eyes until they smoothed out into his freckled temples.

"Of course, this is only a temporary wartime measure. If, God willing, we prevail and reintegrate the North into the Union, we can readily retrocede the land back to South Carolina. If the arrangement meets with your approval, we might consider expanding it to the Rhode Islanders as well, as they're the next largest group of exiles with about 2,100 people sheltering around Charleston." Adams allowed himself to look relieved, a major looming political crisis had been adverted.

"Yes, interesting. I think, perhaps, we can readily justify a member in exile for the House since each House member in Massachusetts would have represented about 30,000 people. It would be a stretch that might give aid to our enemies if we go further than that. Let Massachusetts continue to have her representation in the national government while enticing the rest by our salutary example to join our project."

Of course, one thing Adams didn't mention to Jefferson was that Massachusetts law regarding slavery would hold sway on the territory, specifically, that the Commonwealth's 1783 Constitution no longer extended legal protection to the right to own another person, a decision arrived at through judicial review in the state courts. With this, Adams intended to give his remnant two opportunities: the ability to reestablish their dominance in sea trade and a way to reinvest the profits into manufactures that might provide employment for former slaves that Massachusetts abolitionists might purchase from their masters.

Chapter Sixty-Four – Consolidation

May 1, 1804, Manhattan, New York

Burr frowned at the report from his Finance Minister, Abraham Alfonse Albert Gallatin, or, as Gallatin himself preferred, just Albert. The Republic and its constituent states owed some $20 million; $2 million was owed to British creditors, mostly individuals, half of which was owed by Massachusetts, $5 million was owed to the French government, $4 million to the Dutch, and $9 million of debt was held by domestic creditors, most of whom Burr counted as enemies.

By exiting the United States of America and its weak, debt-ridden national government, Burr escaped responsibility for some $60 million in debts—now Jefferson's problem. But the move had a negative side in that it showed Americans and the world that Burr was leading a breakaway effort rather than the successor government to the United States.

Even so, the Republic was rich in people and land, but poor in gold and silver. As a result, the payments due in gold or foreign currency were set to exceed current sources of income for the Republic and its states. Tariffs from trade out of Boston, New York, and Philadelphia were significantly below expectations as the Royal Navy continued to seize and harass the Republic's shipping due to its alliance with France. Worse, hundreds of ships went with the Boston exiles down to Charleston, leaving the Republic's shipping far smaller than before the siege of Boston. And, of course, Burr had the army and the navy to pay for.

Burr agreed with Gallatin's recommendations to prioritize repayments to creditors in the Batavian Commonwealth, the successor state to the Republic of the Seven United Netherlands and one of Napoleon's client states and to suspend payment to British creditors, but not renounce the debt entirely. Gallatin recommended renegotiating payment to France and staying current on payments to the Republic's own creditors. Burr had other ideas.

First, he didn't think it wise to renegotiate his debts to Napoleon—it would show weakness and unreliability at a time he needed to show strength and steadfastness.

Second, Burr personally knew many of the holders of the debt issued by the states and to a lesser degree, the Republic and they were an increasingly troublesome lot—especially the extended Astor, Church, Fish, Schuyler, Stuyvesant, and Van Rensselaer families.

John Barker Church was particularly problematic. Hamilton's brother-in-law, Burr dueled with him in 1799. Only three years before the duel, Church had been a member the British Parliament. Church had moved back to the land of his birth after he finished his time as one of the American envoys to the French government after the war. As soon as he returned to America in 1799, he helped found the Manhattan Company with Burr and others as well as the Bank of North America.

But Church, and his wealthy peers, had two fatal weaknesses—they weren't popular among the common people, and they were too close to the British. And, as Church helped dozens of French exiles who fled the French Revolution and its Reign of Terror settle in New York, he wasn't particularly liked among some of his more republican-minded French allies.

Fortunately, Burr had set in motion a plan—one that would solve two pressing problems—his finances and his growing political opposition. Months earlier, Burr's agents had begun intercepting and opening the inbound and outbound mail from a select number of his opponents, specifically those holding substantial loans. Soon enough, Burr had what he needed.

To validate and manage the financial aspects of his plan, and to keep Gallatin in the dark, Burr even bailed a very grateful Robert Morris out of Philadelphia's Prune Street debtors' prison, where he'd been locked up since defaulting on his debts just over six years earlier. At one time, Morris had been one of America's wealthiest men. He nearly singlehandedly financed the final years of the War for Independence, but a series of business miscalculations and a financial panic that led to deflation caused him to lose his vast land holdings as he couldn't raise the cash to pay his loans. Much of his land went to the men whom Burr intended to liquidate. Morris, now 70, would be Burr's avenging angel and financial inquisitor. And, when the task was complete, Burr calculated that the Republic's finances would be secured for at least a decade.

Chapter Sixty-Five – Traitor

July 9, 1804, New York City

Alexander Hamilton, Jeph's sole employer now, after Brockholst Livingston vanished, swept into his office Monday afternoon, just as Jeph was ready to lock up and go home to Molly and his children. Speaking urgently and softly, Hamilton told Jeph that he was expecting to be arrested for treason by Burr's new Public Safety gendarmes.

The next thing Hamilton told him hit like a thunderbolt: He wanted Jeph to inform on him—to turn him into the authorities for sedition and treason. Hamilton pressed two opened envelopes and letters into Jeph's trembling hands. "These letters," Hamilton said, "Are from Thomas Jefferson and John Adams. I am confident that they were intercepted and read before I received them yesterday. I have additional reasons to believe that Burr is preparing something terrible."

Jeph stared at Hamilton, lightly clutching the two letters that were still mostly in Hamilton's hands, "You... want... me..."

"I need you to turn me in. You must. I am lost. Burr is going to arrest my wife's family too. I've heard rumors they even have guillotines sent from France to carry out the executions."

"Executions?" Jeph said unbelievingly.

"That's the penalty for treason," Hamilton replied flatly.

"You think you will be executed?"

"I will be executed. The only question is how soon and how soon before they come for me. I tried to convince Burr's executive council—the governors of New York, New Jersey, Pennsylvania, and Delaware to depose Burr. I failed. David Hall of Delaware even asked for a bribe. But without another two votes to override Burr, Delaware was a worthless prize and Hall knew it. He was just squeezing me for gold." Hamilton paused and then looked at Jeph, saying, "Have you read Machiavelli?"

Jeph recognized the name from the books in both Hamilton's and Burr's offices. Machiavelli's "The Prince" was common to both men. "No sir, I have only read Blackstone's Commentaries as it helped me better support the practice."

Hamilton pushed the letters fully into Jeph's reluctant hands and pulled a book from the shelf. He opened it up and, in his courtroom voice, though quietly, he read, "If you take control of a state, you should make a list of all the crimes you have to commit and do them all at once. That way you will not have to commit new atrocities every day, and you will be able, by not repeating your evil deeds, to reassure your subjects and to win their support by treating them well." Hamilton flipped through some pages and found another passage, "If an injury has to be done to a man it should be so severe that his vengeance need not be feared." And again, "It is much safer to be feared than loved."

Jeph shook his head, "That's just an old book," he protested.

"So's the Bible, Jeph. Burr knows the Bible, but he follows The Prince. Dare I say it? The Prince is Burr's bible. Burr is preparing to commit great crimes and I need you to not be murdered because of my employment of you."

"I was Burr's employee too!" Jeph was wide-eyed.

"When was the last time he paid you? Since he was elected? Two years ago? No, you're my employee. Guilt by association. Your life is in danger too. Unless... unless you take these letters and turn them into the Committee on Public Safety. Even better if you could arrange to deliver them to Burr himself."

"And then what? Lie by saying you're a traitor?"

"It's not a lie, after a fashion. I am trying to overthrow Burr. He's become a tyrant and he's not content to lead only the North. He wants to rule all of the states."

Jeph stared at the ground, his head spinning. He was suddenly resentful of Hamilton for putting him and his own family in grave danger—and then giving him a coward's way out.

Jeph sighed, "I'll do as you say, sir. I don't like it, but I'll do it."

"Jeph, I don't often speak of this, but I didn't know my father either. I'm proud of you—what you made of yourself." Hamilton allowed himself a grin, "It's never easy for us bastards."

Jeph was taken aback for a moment, and then chuckled.

Hamilton lifted his lips briefly in a tight smile, "I must go now. Be swift. We don't have much time. Oh, and one more thing, you may be asked to testify at my trial. You should do so if asked."

Jeph's knees started to shake and his left hand, with the two nubs of fingers torn off by that British musket ball 26 years ago, ached terribly.

Jeph waited for quarter hour after Hamilton left the office. He locked the door and, letters in his breast pocket, he made his way for Old City Hall where Burr made his office. It was already past 5 p.m., but Burr was known to work long hours.

Jeph walked past four blue-clad guards armed with bayonet-topped muskets and walked into the main entrance. There was a large desk there, behind which sat the captain of the guard, flanked by two soldiers, each of them armed with a sword and pistol.

The captain looked up with annoyance. "Your business, citizen?"

Jeph looked down at the captain, "My name is Jephtath Clark. I was an employee of President Burr when he practiced law. Alexander Hamilton and Brockholst Livingston as well."

"So?" the officer said with the impatience of a bored bureaucrat.

"I must see President Burr on an urgent matter."

"I see. Why don't you come back tomorrow and ask for an appointment with his secretary?"

"It can't wait, I'm afraid. I... I have direct evidence of treason and I believe it must be acted upon immediately, else the security of our nation would be at great risk."

Now the captain looked ill at ease. If he told this unimportant citizen who claimed to know President Burr to go away and he actually held evidence of treason, it could mean the end of his career. If, on the other hand, this slight man with a scarred hand and threadbare clothes was a crank, and didn't have evidence, and he allowed him entrance to see the President, his career would also be at an end. He hesitated, "I must see your evidence."

Jeph gathered himself. He was well-acquainted with creatures of this sort from his three years in the Continental Army. "No. I will only present the evidence to President Burr as it involves his old friend and colleague, Mr. Hamilton."

There was a stir to the right of the captain's desk where, out of the shadows came a familiar voice, "Citizen Clark, so pleased to see you! Captain, you may let him pass."

Burr stepped forward to shake Jeph's hand. He was plainly dressed in black trousers and a jacket with black boots. He wasn't wearing a wig. Nobody wore wigs anymore.

"Sir, I need to see you about an utmost matter of urgency and delicacy," Jeph said quietly.

"Please, follow me," Burr said. There were two guards posted just outside the open double doors to his office and two inside, facing Burr's desk. "Please, leave us some privacy," Burr said. The two guards inside the office moved quickly to shut the doors behind the two men, leaving them alone.

Jeph started to pull the envelopes out of his left breast pocket, conspicuously showing Burr his battle wounded hand.

Burr smiled and touched Jeph's hand. Burr's hand was cold, though the day was still warm. "You fought bravely at Monmouth."

As the envelopes came out, Burr pulled back his hand. Jeph wondered if Burr thought he was going to take out a dagger and stab him.

"Sir, I believe you need to see these letters. I... I am embarrassed to say that I read them. They are the private correspondence of Mr... Citizen Hamilton with John Adams in Boston and Thomas Jefferson in Virginia. I... I read them because I suspected Citizen Hamilton of plotting against our government. Given your past association with Citizen Hamilton, I thought it best to give them to do directly."

Burr accepted the envelopes but wasn't particularly interested in their contents. "You've done well, Jeph, thank you for your diligence. This is a most unwelcome development. Hamilton! Who would have ever believed that Hamilton would betray his country?" Burr turned and put the letters on his desk.

Jeph stood, feeling queasy. His knees were weak.

Burr turned back to face Jeph and putting both hands on Jeph's shoulders said, "Once again, you've done your duty. Thank you."

"The letters, sir?"

"I will have the Committee on Public Safety look at them. That's their job. Now, if you please, I'm late for dinner."

Burr walked for the double door and pulled the right side open. "You may go now, Citizen Clark," Burr said loud enough for the captain to hear, "Thank you for your information. Please see the captain on your way out and he'll make sure you are rewarded accordingly and make arrangements should we wish to see you again."

Burr walked past Jeph and made his way outside, leaving Jeph with a visibly relieved captain.

"Congratulations, Citizen Clark. Please sign this register and indicate your home address and, if you have a fixed place of employment, that address as well." The captain made an entry into his own registry and then pulled out a drawer and removed a leather bag, he counted out six stacks of five bright new silver dollar coins—minted only last year on the order of President Burr. "Here," the captain said, turning his registry around to face Jeph, "Please sign here acknowledging payment for your services."

Jeph swallowed. He took the quill from the captain and dipped it into the ink well, the first half of his signature started as a large ink blot, which was his intent. He didn't want his treachery recorded forever—a new Benedict Arnold. He turned to go.

"Aren't you forgetting something, Citizen Clark?"

Jeph turned back to face the captain, who was now standing, his right hand stretched out to shake Jeph's hand, his left had now holding that stack of 30 coins.

Jeph's face reddened as he mumbled, "Yes, thank you. Of course."

Jeph walked out of the Old City Hall and struggled to think of what he'd tell Molly.

Chapter Sixty-Six – The Court of Justice

July 11, 1804, Old City Hall, New York City

The past day-and-a-half was a blur. Jeph was numb.

In the morning, Jeph made his way to Old City Hall again, where two days earlier in the late afternoon, he'd met President Burr, his former employer, and handed him two envelopes and letters addressed to Alexander Hamilton from John Adams and Thomas Jefferson. Jeph pushed his way towards a guard and presented the guard with his witness summons. The guard looked it over and motioned for Jeph to enter the Old City Hall.

Jeph walked in and let his eyes adjust for a moment. The captain's desk was gone and the central meeting room had been reconfigured into a courtroom. Only, instead of a jury box and a judge's bench, there was a larger judge's bench with room enough to accommodate three judges.

A sergeant waived him over, "You a witness?"

"Yes, sergeant."

"Please sit here."

There were already a dozen people seated. Hamilton was nowhere in sight.

An hour later, there was a minor stir in the crowd as a shackled Hamilton was led out to stand at the dock. His face looked swollen, as if he was captured in a struggle.

A major, acting as bailiff, called out, "All rise!"

Three judges entered the room. Two of them wore the uniform of a general, and one, the chief judge by the looks of him, a simple black robe. Their faces were grim. Two judges were gray haired—the one seated to the left had a full head of ink black hair.

The bailiff faced Hamilton and said, "The accused will enter a plea."

"I do not acknowledge the authority of this so-called court!" Hamilton yelled.

The chief judge glared at the bailiff who advanced on Hamilton, holding a leather strap and gag. "You will address the court with respect and enter a proper plea, Citizen Hamilton, or it will be done for you by your counsel."

Hamilton stared up at the bailiff who towered over him by six inches.

Hamilton started in again, "I will not comply. My rights are being violated! All men's…"

The bailiff jabbed Hamilton in the stomach with a thick wooden shaft, knocking the air out of him and sending him to his knees. While Hamilton was stunned, he and placed the gag in his mouth and secured it with a leather strap.

The judge in the black robes looked satisfied, as did general black hair on the left, but the general seated to the right—Jeph thought he recognized him—now looked ill at ease.

They were only minutes into the proceeding when Jeph realized that this trial was like nothing he'd seen in more than 20 years of supporting Hamilton, Burr, Livingston, and others. There was no jury of peers and, it was becoming obvious that Hamilton's fate would be decided by these three men. And, further, Hamilton had the burden of proof to prove his innocence! This was a new and terrifying court of law.

After two hours, 10 witnesses had been sworn and appeared. Under questioning by a uniformed lawyer, a colonel, they each gave brief testimony that they'd overheard Hamilton making seditious remarks critical of President Burr. One witness even claimed he had heard Hamilton plotting with someone else to overthrow Burr and his government. Hamilton was left to simply stare at the witnesses. Hamilton's attorney was silent the entire time.

Jeph was then called to the witness stand. The colonel started to question him, "Do you recognize Citizen Hamilton in this room?"

"Yes, sir, he is there," Jeph said, pointing at Hamilton.

"Do you know the accused?"

"I do."

"Please explain how you know him."

"Since the end of the war, I worked for him as a clerk in his law practice."

"So, you know him well?"

"I do."

"Please tell the court what you found."

"Last Monday, I noticed two opened envelopes on Citizen Hamilton's desk in his office. Normally, I would not pry into the mail of my employer, but I had overheard some conversations he had had with others that made me suspect his loyalty to New York and to President Burr. So, I removed the letters and read them. I was shocked to see correspondence from two prominent opponents of President Burr addressed to Citizen Hamilton, in which they urged action against our government and asked Citizen Hamilton how they could be of assistance. Naturally, I took the letters and immediately brought them…"

"You brought them to the authorities."

"Yes sir."

"Are these those letters and the envelopes in which you found them?"

"Yes sir. It looks like them."

"That is all, Citizen Clark. You may go. May it please the Court, these letters are entered into the record as exhibits X and Z."

The proceedings only went on for another hour—about three-and-a-half hours total. The whole affair appeared to be rushed, as if they had many more cases to try.

With the completion of the testimony, the three judges conferred briefly and then signaled the bailiff.

"All rise!" he shouted.

Hamilton had been standing the entire time and had been held up under his armpits by two large guards for the last hour.

"The People's Court has come to the decision that the accused, Citizen Alexander Hamilton, has committed high treason against his nation and against his fellow citizens, the sentence for which is death. The penalty will be carried out expeditiously. Citizen Hamilton, having previously shown contempt for this court, is to remain gagged until his execution tomorrow." And with that, the chief judge of the People's Court smashed down his gavel and adjourned for lunch.

Jeph locked eyes with Hamilton who slightly nodded back. The guards steadied Hamilton and marched him off out of sight to the right.

The bailiff ordered the room cleared and the witnesses and spectators made their way for the exit.

Jeph kept his head down and moved through the crowd as inconspicuously as he could. The last thing he wanted was to be recognized, especially by any newspapermen.

Chapter Sixty-Seven – Execution

July 14, 1804, Gansevoort Street, Manhattan, New York City

The infernal guillotines had been busy for three days now. Only yesterday, the Chief of the New York Directorate for Public Safety approached Jeph with an opened letter in his hand. "Are you Citizen Jephtath Clark?" he asked menacingly.

Jeph nodded. The Chief of Public Safety was flanked by two giant men wearing tall black leather hats.

"Is this your letter, Citizen Clark?" The Chief's face twisted into a smile.

"I…"

"Or does this letter belong to your wife, Citizen Molly Clark?"

Two guards, dressed in dark blue with red cuffs, topped with black shakos appeared, tightly gripping Molly by each arm. She was ashen faced.

"Molly!" Jeph started forward, but the Chief's guards lowered their muskets on him, bayonets painfully poking his chest.

The Chief bellowed, "Or did one of your children write this letter? This letter is proof of treason, Citizen Clark! Answer me!"

Helplessly, Jeph saw six more guards, each with a child, including his baby, Theodosia. Behind them were the three guillotines. His wife was strapped to one. And his oldest son too. He was led up the stage, his knees buckling. The mob started to roar. He looked back over his shoulder to the left. Burr was in the dignitaries' stand smiling.

Jeph awoke with a start. The light of the waxing half-moon streamed in through the open bedroom window. His body was covered in sweat. He looked at Molly, gently sleeping with Theodosia snuggled next to her. Jeph slowly exhaled. He held his left hand out, palm down, the moon showing his battle wounds: thumb, index finger, calloused nub, calloused nub, little finger. He slowly inhaled through his nose and silently said a prayer, asking God for strength and wisdom.

Chapter Sixty-Eight – The Second Oldest Profession

July 17, 1804, Manhattan, New York City

Jeph had only seen his brother William—his half-brother—once before when William was 13. It was months after his mother died and his father, John, asked his oldest son Jonathan, one of 10 legitimate children and, at 34, a veteran of the war who rose to the rank of colonel and fought at Monmouth as well to see to his needs. Jonathan gave Jeph a modest payment of 10 Spanish gold pieces worth about three months' salary. As part of the young man's education, Jonathan brought William along for the journey.

Jeph thought the money dirty—a guilt payment from the man who made his mother pregnant but didn't marry her and never provided support, leaving the two of them to make their way in a harsh world of revolution and scarcity. Jeph, apprenticed to a British-born lawyer in New York (only years later did he surmise that his mother became his mistress to advance the interests of her only child), ran away and joined the Continental Army just before his 16th birthday in the bitter winter of 1777. His mother died shortly after the British evacuated New York in 1783, a gaunt, former shell of herself. Still, the money was sorely needed as he had his eye on Molly and the Continental Congress's promises of pay for his time in service were not worth anything at the time.

William was everything Jeph wasn't. Just over six feet tall, he was powerfully built and topped by a mop of red hair. His voice was deep and sure. He was eight years younger than Jeph and had been too young to fight against the British, but he had been active in the Kentucky militia fighting Indians and he had even visited Spanish New Orleans.

The letter he received from William a week ago suggested they meet in Hamilton's law office. Jeph was still tidying the place up after the toughs from the Committee on Public Safety ransacked it, making a show of looking for additional evidence of treason. Burr's office next door, which hadn't been used in years, was untouched. H. Brockholst Livingston was still practicing law in the third office but for how long, Jeph didn't know; he hadn't seen him in a week. Livingston was, at least formally, a Democratic-Republican and should have been politically allied with Burr, but he distrusted Burr and his brand of populism and had been corresponding with Jefferson and other Virginians. Thus, a threatening message was sent when Livingston's office was gone through as well, though not as thoroughly or violently as had Hamilton's. Unless other attorneys could be convinced to rent a space at the building, the owner would soon find other tenants and Jeph would be out of a job.

The door was already open when William quietly rapped on the door frame, "Mr. Jephtath Clark?"

Jeph looked up from a stack of law books as he carefully put one of Hamilton's heavy books—one of the four volumes of Blackstone's Commentaries on the Laws of England—back on the shelf about where he remembered they had rested, though their value was soon likely to be no more than a curiosity as Burr was rumored to be working on adopting Napoleon's new civil code, in effect in France since March.

"William, I didn't expect you so soon!" Jeph did his best to feign warmth.

William looked at his older brother and said with concern, "I am so sorry to hear about Hamilton and the others. I saw the newspapers on my ride up."

"I hope your travels were pleasant."

"Well, other than having my papers checked every five miles as soon as I left Wilmington…"

Jeph looked up at his younger brother and shook his hand, "Welcome to Manhattan. Should I ask to see your papers?" William's clothing was first rate, though Jeph noticed a hole in the right elbow of William's coat. He was conscientious of the condition of his own threadbare and carefully mended clothes.

William laughed. "Perhaps you should. But let's talk first."

"Please, sit. You weren't particularly specific in your correspondence to me. Is our father alive?" Jeph moved Hamilton's chair out from behind his desk and placed it a couple of feet from the chair William was using.

"I'm sorry to say, he died five years ago in Kentucky."

Jeph stared at William, "I'm sorry to hear that. It would have been good to know that."

William took a breath, "Perhaps I should leave."

"No, you came a long way to see me, and, at a minimum of courtesy, I should hear you out."

"Thank you. Are we alone here?"

"Yes. I know the building. Were someone here, I'd know it."

"I wrote to you because of the things your employer wrote to my employer. I was asked to see you."

Jeph blinked at William and suppressed a wave of fear.

William leaned forward and said quietly, "Hamilton wrote to Jefferson about you two months ago. He knew what was coming. Hamilton said we could trust you. He said you would fight for liberty."

Jeph was simultaneously shocked, honored, and terrified. He swallowed, and said in a raspy voice, "Hamilton fought. He's dead."

"Indeed. Hamilton was obvious and too prominent, too dangerous to leave alone."

Jeph furrowed his brow and said, "And you speak of liberty, Burr abolished slavery. What of you, do you have slaves?"

William hesitated, "I own 13. I inherited them from our father five years ago."

"Inherited. Are slaves not human? Are they not made in God's image? Liberty!" Jeph snorted.

"You're right. We live in a fallen world. We are all sinners deserving of death…"

"You just accept it?" Jeph cut him off.

"It's wrong. Slavery is evil. Ridding ourselves of the institution would be better for both slave and master, I agree. But before you give too much due to Burr, let me ask you this? Where are the negroes? New York had more of them when I last saw you 16 years ago. I would have thought that with the additional thousands who have escaped and made their way north, I'd've seen many more."

"What is your point?" Jeph was now being combative for its own sake, driven by resentment of his late father.

"You know very well that Burr has sent his negroes to Ohio. He's using them to subdue the Indians."

"You've fought the Indians, have you not?"

"I have. The British have been arming them and training them—encouraging them to raid our settlements, rape our women, scalp and slaughter, and enslave the rest. The difference is we can fight the Indians on equal terms and win more battles than we lose. Burr's negroes are like sheep to the slaughter. He's using them."

"They have their freedom," Jeph retorted.

"The ones that manage to survive do, after a sort. How long do you think that will last? How long will Burr, and the people supporting him, allow the negro to keep the lands they cleared and defended at great cost?"

Jeph looked down. He enjoyed tangling with William, man to man. While working for Hamilton, Burr, and Livingston, he often heard the three argue, but it wasn't his station to participate. Debating William made him his equal.

"You asked about liberty and you tout your Burr. It's important that you know that Jefferson has consistently called slavery a 'hideous blot' on our nation and a 'moral depravity.' Before Burr aspired to be dictator—that's what he is—Jefferson called slavery the greatest threat to our national survival because it's contrary to the laws of nature because everyone has a right to personal liberty. Burr pushes the negroes out of New York into near certain death in western Ohio, but it was Jefferson who drafted Virginia's law that stopped the importation of African slaves in 1778 and it was Jefferson who first proposed the ban on slavery for the Northwest territories—the signal accomplishment of the Confederation Congress 17 years ago. I can't argue with you that it's a horrible contradiction. We're men. Men are flawed. But if you truly believe for a single instant that Aaron Burr is a defender of liberty and not a dictator hellbent for empire, then we have no further business." William started to get up.

Jeph sighed. "I fear you are right."

William settled back into the walnut chair.

"Men are flawed. So, William, tell me, what is it that my late employer and you want from me? I am a nobody, the bastard child of a dead man."

Now William sighed. He reached into his pockets and removed a flask and a plug of tobacco. "Care for some?"

Jeph rarely used either, seeing all too clearly the effects of drink on those at the margins of society and, with six children, thinking tobacco a vice he didn't need to waste his meager wages on. He reached over and accepted the flask and took a pull. It was whisky, as he expected. Good whisky.

William said, "I made it myself. This too." He extended the plug of chewing tobacco to Jeph.

Jeph retrieved the spittoon from the room's corner and chewed a bite off the plug. His mouth immediately filled with saliva and he quickly spit.

"You don't chew—at least not much—do you?" William said.

"No, I never developed the vice."

William smiled. "You are my brother. Are you willing to listen to me? If you don't like what you hear, you can give me up to the Committee on Public Safety—just do me the courtesy of a day's head start."

"Go ahead." Jeph was now curious, especially given Hamilton had written to Thomas Jefferson about him.

"Do you remain friendly with Burr?"

"Yes."

"Does he suspect you?"

"I've done nothing wrong."

"That's not what I asked, does he suspect you, whether he has reason to or not?"

"I don't believe so."

"Could you... would you work for him again?"

"What do you have in mind?"

"You clerked for him since the end of the war."

"And for Hamilton and Livingston too."

"Yes, and might you be willing to work for him again?"

"Doing?"

"Burr needs a secretary; someone he can trust."

"He does? He already has a secretary. He was a captain with the Malcolm's. Served under Burr. I was only a private."

"You were 16. Besides, you already worked with Burr for a dozen years."

"Thirteen," Jeph corrected.

"Thirteen." William replied.

"Again, Burr has a secretary, why…"

"Burr may need a new one soon. If he does, will you apply? After a modest interval, of course, you don't want to appear too opportunistic."

"Opportunistic?"

"Suffice it to say that Citizen Bentley may fall terribly ill after enjoying himself at the pub."

Jeph's eyes widened and then quickly narrowed. "How unfortunate for Citizen Bentley. He wasn't kind to me during my time in the Army anyway. So, let's say I agree and let's say I get the position, what then?"

"How well do you memorize?" William asked as he removed a two-foot by two-foot map from a case. He spread it out on Hamilton's desk. From his inside coat pocket, he removed a scroll of translucent vellum and set it next to the map.

Jeph looked at the map and the vellum, covered with letters and numbers.

219

Then William overlayed the vellum onto the map. "Were you to have knowledge of Burr's military designs, you would be able to transmit them to us via a simple code. This intelligence would help us greatly."

"To what end, William?"

"To have another chance at liberty in a proper nation. To have a second chance at creating the nation we should have created 16 years ago. But to do that, we must stop a tyrant." William looked at Jeph. His eyes held a mixture of compassion and intensity.

"If I were to have access to such information, how would I send it to you?"

"Carrier pigeon."

Jeph thought about this for a moment and then asked, "And how do I obtain birds that will fly to your outpost? And, assuming I do agree to accept these birds and send you intelligence, how do I avoid the Committee for Public Safety?"

William smiled, "I think you'll need a lot of birds. People eat squab, don't they? Times are hard, you'll start a new business. No one will notice a dozen extra birds that disappear from the flock on a regular basis."

Jeph smiled and shook his head, "As fate would have it, I started keeping pigeons at the insistence of Alexander Hamilton two years ago. I have a

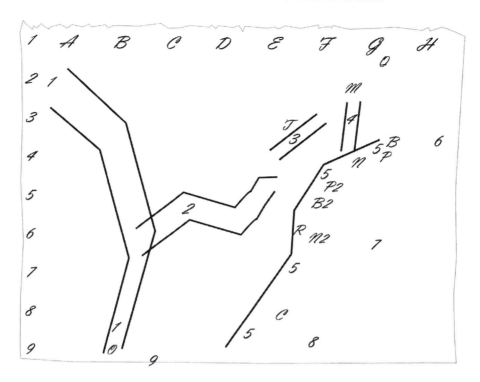

large flock now out at New Rochelle. In a good month, I make 80 dollars over expenses.

William laughed, "Amazing. That man was amazing."

Jeph nodded in response and then looked at his feet and then at Hamilton's desk. Hamilton. Executed five days ago. It was a new and dangerous world now.

"Now, I can't leave you with the map and vellum, it will kill us both. Memorize the overlay. From north to south, 1 to 9, from west to east, A to H. The Mississippi is 1, the Ohio is 2, the Lakes are 3, the Hudson, and Lakes George and Champlain are 4, the Atlantic coast is 5. Major ocean areas are 6, 7, 8, and 9. Major cities are indicated. B for Boston, P for Providence, N for New York, P2 for Philadelphia, B2 for Baltimore, R for Richmond, N2 for Norfolk, C for Charleston, O for New Orleans, T for Toronto, M for Montreal, and Q for Quebec."

William spent another 90 minutes going over the map code system and how Jeph could report the intention to move a certain type of force, such as 12,000 regulars, 2,000 cavalry, 3,000 militia, and 20 cannon in a certain direction in a certain month.

When he was done, he took both map and vellum and walked over to the fireplace, soaking both in whale oil, burning them and then stirring the ashes.

"Now," William said, "If you'll excuse me, I must go buy some drink for our dear friend Citizen Bentley. I understand he is not to be denied his whisky."

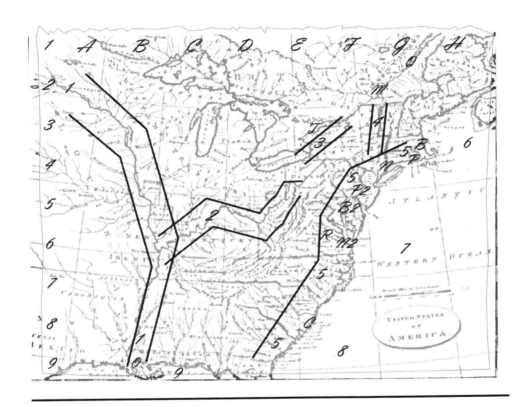

Chapter Sixty-Nine – Secretary

August 1, 1804, New York City

"President Burr will see you now," said the sergeant of the Presidential Guard. He wore white gloves and was armed with a brace of pistols and a sword. His unform was dark blue with gold trim and buttons and he wore a black leather shako cover with a large, polished brass insignia of an eagle.

Jeph nodded at the sergeant who stared blankly ahead, and walked in. Burr quickly rose from behind his massive, dark, red-brown wood (mahogany?) desk.

"Jeph! A pleasure to see you! Especially under different circumstances. How are Molly and your children?"

"Fine, Colonel Burr, thank you for asking. I trust your daughter is doing well. Do you hear from her?"

"Yes! She writes often. She had a son two years ago."

"Congratulations, sir."

"So, Jeph, how may I repay your service?

"Well, sir, I very much miss our time working together. The law practice has collapsed and frankly, there hasn't been as much law work since, since…"

"Since I became President?" Burr smiled.

"Well, yes, I suppose since then."

"Plus, it doesn't help that the last employer you had committed treason." Jeph looked down.

"Jeph, I know you weren't involved in Hamilton's schemes."

"I wasn't, sir."

"As I said, I know. We investigated. I'm quite sure you were not a party to Hamilton's treason."

Burr motioned Jeph to sit and Burr sat down behind his desk. Burr steepled his hands and looked over them at Jeph, thinking. "Jeph, are you still in the militia?"

"Well, yes sir, I am now. It's a requirement."

"I know, I signed the decree. What rank do you hold?"

"I'm a corporal now, sir. Though I'm afraid I'm getting a bit on in years to be serving in the infantry."

"As we all are, Jeph. I have an idea, Jeph, one that Molly may like. I have an opening on my personal staff. You intimately know my requirements and I trust your diligence. Why don't you become by personal secretary? The pay would be better than what Hamilton and Livingston were likely paying you before."

"Yes, sir, kind of you to offer. Thank you, sir. Umm, may I ask, what happened to your previous secretary?"

"He liked drink more than was good for him. He died two weeks ago."

"I'm sorry to hear that, sir."

"I feel obligated to warn you, Jeph, the hours may be long, and you'll have to accompany me most everywhere I go. But your supplies will be paid for. Is your right hand free from the gout? I suspect that by day's end, your hand will be sore."

"Yes, sir, I'm ready and willing to serve my President."

Burr smiled, rose, and extended his hand. "You're hired Mr. Clark. Also, tell your company commander that your militia obligations are now attached to the Office of the President. I can't have you mustered out from under me or arrested for desertion."

Jeph thought this last comment odd. The militia hadn't been called out and there was no conscription… yet.

Chapter Seventy – Birds

August 15, 1804, Dobbs Ferry, New York

William's last words to Jeph as he left the city were to travel to Dobbs Ferry on the east bank of the Hudson, just across the river from New Jersey's northern border with New York on August 15. There, he was to pick up a shipment of pigeons from his slave, York.

There wouldn't be a lot of negroes in the area, Jeph reckoned, even so, how would he easily recognize the man?

William replied that York was about 30 and handsomely built and would be wearing good, though worn, clothing.

Jeph rolled into Dobbs Ferry just before noon with a borrowed horse and wagon and headed for the docks. It had been a muggy night and it was already warm, though occasionally, a cooling breeze blew off the river. The New Jersey side of the river was mostly trees, with the opposite landing dock and dirt road the only sign of civilization.

It didn't take him long to see someone he thought was York. He was sitting on his own horse pulling a white, though mud-splattered, two-wheel cart. He was eating a large green apple. There were box-like outlines under a white canvas in the cart—likely two or three boxes about three feet wide, Jeph figured.

"Mr. York?" Jeph inquired.

York turned in the saddle and smiled broadly, "And may I ask your name, sir?"

Jeph didn't expect such caution, but readily replied, "Jeph, Jephtath Clark."

"Ah, I understand y'all are the son of my first master, Mr. John Clark."

"Yes, I am."

"Well, sir, you are to have these birds, compliments of your brother, my master."

"Thank you. I'm happy to receive them. May I ask, are you hungry? I brought enough food for both of us to sup. Will you join me? I'd like to ask you a few things." Jeph looked York up and down. His clothes were of a higher quality than his own, but they were threadbare in spots. There was a patch on one knee, though expertly repaired.

"I can do that. Happy to join you."

The two rode about a half mile together until they found a shaded spot for themselves near a portion of the road with a fair amount of grass for their horses. The pigeons cooed much of the trip, only stopping when the cart hit ruts.

"How do you keep them fed and watered?" Jeph asked?

York tethered his horse to a tree and peeled back the canvas to reveal two cages that held at least 20 birds each and a third box. He said, "I have chicken scratch, water, and four pans in the box next to the cages. You must be quick! You put pans with food and water into one side of the cage here," York pointed to a long, thin door in the cage that was wide enough for a hand and forearm, but difficult for a bird to sneak past and escape. The other side of the cage had a larger door. York then poured some water into the pans, put the pans in the cages, and then covered the cages again with the canvas. He then measured oats into a feedbag and hung the bag on his horse's head.

York accepted bread, cheese, and apple cider from Jeph and the two settled down with their backs to a large oak tree. A few flies had gathered on horse droppings on the edge of the road some ten feet away, and the two men would shoo them away every few seconds. It was a pleasant break otherwise.

York cleared his throat, "This here's good cheese and cider, thank you, sir."

"You're welcome, Mr. York."

"Massa Clark told me to tell y'all to send two pigeons, at least every week. Or, as soon as what he called 'significant movements.' He said it is best to let them fly in the morning. We should next meet in two months at Sneden's Landing on October 14 at noon and then again on December 10 at Kings Ferry at noon. I'll bring new birds. Massa Clark said we need to change our meeting locations for safety. I'll also bring messages, though never written. I will tell y'all myself what Massa Clark says."

"May I ask you, why are you doing this? It could be dangerous."

York paused, and then said, "My massa ordered me." There was a resignation in his voice.

Jeph pressed, "You're by yourself. You could just not go back."

York said reluctantly, "My wife's in Kentucky, in Louisville. Massa knows her owner. If I didn't come back, I'd never see her and it could be bad for her, real bad."

"Do you want to be free?"

York silently took a bite of bread.

"Does my brother beat you?"

York helped himself to the jug of apple cider and looked at the flies in the road.

"Mr. Clark, I enjoyed my journey, and I am honored to meet you. I hope to see you again, the good Lord willing. Now, let's load the birds on your wagon and be off on our ways."

Jeph brooded over York's words on the road back to Manhattan, the birds occasionally cooing in the back under the canvas. His younger brother, William, was probably mistreating York and yet, in their last visit, had proclaimed the basic evilness of slavery. Jeph buried the contradiction and focused on his next steps. His life—and the lives of his family—were about to become far more perilous.

Chapter Seventy-One – Evacuation

August 19, 1804, Eleutherian Mills, Brandywine Creek, Delaware

Éleuthère Irénée DuPont de Nemours gathered his family after church. At 33, DuPont had a personal brush with revolutionary "justice," spending a night in prison with his father as the family's home and printing press business was looted at the direction of the French government. Two years later, they sold everything and moved to America in 1799. And now it was happening again.

The execution of wealthy opponents to Burr's regime shook DuPont to his core. And, while his powder mill had only just produced its first batches of high-quality gunpowder, the risk of staying in Delaware was simply too great.

DuPont looked at his beautiful and pregnant wife, Sophie, carrying little Eleuthera and comforting toddlers Evelina and Alfred, shushed the other two children. There were no servants or slaves in sight.

"We must leave, Sophie. We have no choice. America seems set on its own Reign of Terror. These things, once started, take a life of their own and cannot be easily extinguished."

Sophie's face blanched, but she said nothing.

Victorine, their eldest at 12, protested, "Papa! I don't want to leave! My friends…" she started to cry, upsetting the other children.

DuPont reached out to console her and pulled her to his chest, silently hugging her. Her sobbing subsided, "You'll make new friends, I promise. But it's not safe for us here. We must leave."

"Where will we go?" Sophie asked.

"You will take the children to Wilmington. There's a carriage waiting for you. There, you will board a ship that will carry you to Charleston, South Carolina. There's a community of emigres there from Boston. We'll start over."

"And you? Our servants?" Sophie pressed.

"Many who wish will follow. Some, I suppose, won't. It's hard to tell after I do what must be done." DuPont gravely looked at his wife from over Victorine's shoulder.

DuPont's family had left for the docks on the Delaware River at Wilmington four hours ago. He had already arranged for his most trusted servants to pack up important items, starting with Sophie's cherished harpsichord.

With luck, a second shipment of household goods would follow in a week. And, with even greater luck, he'd find a buyer for his house and 95 acres—though, if he did it right, there wouldn't be much left of the powder mill.

DuPont rode at the head of two wagons burdened with his growing family's possessions. The waxing gibbous Moon was overhead, generously illuminating the way on the cloudless and starry night. DuPont reckoned it was about 9 O'clock. He was midway on the four-mile journey to the docks and would arrive in less than half an hour.

The last of the items were stowed on the ship by midnight, everyone was safe on board, including his father Pierre Samuel DuPont, and his stepmother, Marie. He hoped his brother Victor would soon join them from New Jersey.

The lines were cast and the ship slipped it moorings, heading south. DuPont made his way to the stern of the ship and watched the northwestern horizon. There! A red flash of light followed seconds later by a small clap. DuPont frowned. Surely that wasn't enough to destroy the powder mill? Then the horizon blossomed in fiery yellow fringed with crimson. The ball of light rose and faded to orange and then red. Seconds later, the explosion swept over the ship, sounding like dull thunder as the planks under his feet jumped.

DuPont smiled grimly and went below decks to join his family.

Chapter Seventy-Two – Raid

August 20, 1804, New Rochelle, New York

Jeph calmed his nerves as he strained to write his first pigeon post message clearly in small print. Based on the conversation he overheard between President Burr and an officer in his general staff, he knew there would be a raid in three days on the town of Norfolk in Virginia. The Moon would be full in one night and, presumably, the raid would take advantage of the waning Moon's illumination to be conducted at night.

He wrote: "100 R – 7 – N2 – 23 AUG" for 100 regular soldiers coming from the sea at at Norfolk on 23 August. And then, thinking that no one would view 100 soldiers as important, he added "RAID" at the end of the strip of paper.

100 R – 7 – N2 - 23 AUG -RAID

Jeph then copied the message onto a second strip and went to the separate loft where he kept the message birds separate from the birds he raised for sale. He carefully grabbed a bird and restrained it with a cloth so it wouldn't struggle so much and then scrolled the paper strip around the pigeon's leg and tied it with twine.

Jeph shook his head that such a scheme could even work or be of help and then he repeated it with the second bird, then, taking both birds to an area between the house and the small barn containing the bird lofts, he released them into the cloudy afternoon sky.

The pigeons circled around four times, gaining altitude, and then set off to the south. Jeph watched them until they disappeared behind the roof of his two-story house.

As he walked through the back door movement caught the corner of his eye. On the road, slowly heading north, were two cavalrymen about 50 yards off to the left, their distinctive shakos just visible above a hedge.

Jeph's hands started to shake as he went inside for dinner.

On the morning of August 22, the first bird arrived in Richmond at the home loft. The message—the first ever received—was excitedly conveyed to the Secretary of War James McHenry who summoned Commanding General of the Army James Wilkinson and his colleague, Secretary of the Navy Robert Smith. The three men agreed the message seemed plausible and dispatched a mail sloop from Richmond to ply down the James River and alert the town's militia. A few hours later, the second bird arrived, but the message was missing from its leg. With luck, the sloop should pull into Norfolk by nightfall giving the town from a few hours to just over a day to make ready.

Two 10-gun schooners ploughed through the moon-kissed waters between Cape Charles at the southern tip of the Delaware Peninsula and Norfolk, five miles to the southwest. The crew, experienced New Englanders, numbered about 50 on each vessel, and inside each, were 50 infantry armed with muskets and incendiary devices. If things went according to plan, by night's end, the naval shipyard at Norfolk would be aflame.

Just upwind of the Republic schooners, yet unseen by the crew fixed on the dim lights on the coast outlined in bright moonlight was the *Nonsuch*, a 12-gun Baltimore schooner captained by Thomas Boyle, a 28-year-old seaman who captained ships since he was 17. Boyle was aggressive and was eager to be the first captain to take advantage of the letters of marque issued by President Jefferson against the Republic and the French empire.

Once Boyle could see the Republican flag—a square of blue joined to a square of red with one large white star in the center—he rapidly closed in, planning to surprise the vessels, disabling or sinking one and capturing the other.

But after his first shots tore away the mainmast of the nearest vessel, he discovered to his dismay that both ships were carrying a platoon of marines who managed to rake his deck with musket fire, killing four of his crew. Allowing discretion to get the better of valor, he turned about and headed back to Baltimore.

By August 26, it became apparent that the forecasted raid never materialized, reducing the enthusiasm among the local militia for the venture. Several of the prominent citizens of Norfolk—officers of the militia—complained that their new federal government kept them up and away from their families and businesses for no reason. Though, others claimed that they had heard a naval battle off the coast the night of August 23, so, perhaps the raid was somehow intercepted.

By September 1, word made its way back to Richmond from Baltimore about the *Nonsuch's* night engagement with two Republican schooners-of-war and confidence in the United States' first high-placed spy was restored.

Chapter Seventy-Three – Conscription

August 23, 1804, New Rochelle, New York

Jeph arrived home wondering if Molly had heard the news. The sobs that greeted him indicated that she likely had. In an effort to win the war against the competing republic in the South, Burr ordered a second round of conscription. All 18- and 19-year-old men, whether in the state militia or not, were to report for 18 months of duty. In New York, this was expected to raise 8,000 for the army. Jeph's oldest son, Alexander, was 19. His younger son, Aaron, would have a year before his obligation would start.

As Jeph consoled Molly, he thought about the message he sent by bird earlier in the week and dreaded that it was now inevitable that he would send a similar message that might contribute to the death of his oldest son and, in only a year, his second son.

Jeph prayed that the war would be over before his son tasted battle. He then excused himself from Molly, his shoulder moistened from her tears, to write up two messages for the birds to carry as today he had the responsibility of drafting orders for Burr for five exhausting hours, conveying to him an intimate knowledge of the Republic's dispositions.

Alone, he started in listing both Republican and French forces as he remembered them, "10000 R 4000 M 4000 C 35 CN B2/P2 – 5000 R 1000 M 10 CN B – 15000 R 4000 M 20 CN N – 8000 R 1000 M 40 CN Q – 4000 R 500 M 10 CN T – 10000 R 1000 M 1000 C 12 CN O." In all 57,000 regulars of which 5,000 were cavalry with some 30,000 were Republican soldiers and 27,000 allied French plus another 11,500 local militia. The strip of paper was a foot long and Jeph labored to copy it, with his quill bleeding ink all over the copy forcing him to start over, carefully cutting the strip and starting again on the message.

With the ink still wet on the ruined copy, Jeph used a fork to hold it over a smoky candle, burning it to ash.

After the strips dried, he made his way back to the bird lofts, selected two birds from the 14 he had remaining, gently restrained the birds and carefully rolled up the long strip into a scroll on one bird's leg before tying it off with twine and turning to the other bird. Then, making it outside as the sun was an hour from setting, he looked around, looked around again, and then released the birds. One broke left around the house and quickly disappeared while the other landed on his roof and looked around from the crest, uninterested in taking flight.

Jeph was frowning at the bird's inaction when he saw a shadow cast upon the bird followed by an explosion of feathers as a hawk snatched the pigeon and made off with it. Jeph yelled, pumping his fist in the air and then fell silent, once again looking around to see if anyone saw him. He doubted the hawk would consume the message. That small strip of paper would remain out there, waiting as would the Accuser for the time to emerge. Jeph set his jaw and walked back into the house to speak with Alexander about army life.

Chapter Seventy-Four – Power

September 3, 1804, New York

Jeph hadn't seen Burr this energetic—even in the middle of Monmouth. The man was verging on frenetic, taking meetings one after the other, issuing orders, and drinking copious amounts of coffee. A week ago, Burr accepted Jeph's recommendation to bring in an assistant to ensure that everything was being properly recorded and letters drafted and sent in a timely manner, for which Jeph's increasingly aching fingers thanked him.

Moreover, Burr confided with Jeph that he was thankful for his having replaced the deceased Mr. Bentley, who too frequently showed signs of hard drinking from the night before. So, Jeph's position seemed secure. Well, at least as secure as someone committing treason on an almost daily basis could be.

The next meeting was to be with Burr's new commanding general of the Army. Burr felt burdened with lackluster talent. Henry Dearborn was a better politician than general, so Burr kept him at arm's length as the military governor of Massachusetts and New Hampshire with Connecticut's gubernatorial election due in a month. Morgan Lewis showed hesitation before Baltimore, but he was a sound logistician, and, a year senior to Burr and well-connected politically in New York, Burr needed to keep him busy and allied, so Lewis it was.

The central challenge was finding competent and aggressive field commanders for the arduous task ahead, the conquest of the South. And Burr admitted to himself, an even more urgent challenge in light of his own clear frailty during hot weather. Reconciling himself with giving up personal command of soldiers in battle was bitter, but at 48-years-old and President of the Republic, he had to focus on where he could be most effective. Command was a vanity he could no longer afford. Still, he was jealous that Napoleon could effortlessly combine both—and at 35!

General Morgan Lewis was led into the office by a young aide. Coffee service was provided by a free black woman. Burr thanked her, leaving Morgan to appear slightly squeamish.

Burr cleared his throat, "How is Mrs. Lewis? Has she yet forgiven me for abolishing slavery?"

Lewis was thrown off by Burr's opening, "I, ahh, we…"

Gesturing to the servant, Burr said, "Mr. Lewis, this is Miss Washington. She was born on one of General Washington's plantations and came north for freedom with her mother the day General Washington died."

Washington gave a modest curtsey and nodded.

Lewis ignored her and answered Burr, "Well, Mrs. Lewis is fine, thank you. We now have six out of the eight who worked in our household. One passed away and we could not afford to employ more than six, so we let the other one go. I understand he went to Ohio."

Burr's temperament immediately shifted, "You just came from the headquarters, I want to know about the state of mobilization and the French. I understand we may be seeing some change with Le Corps Canadien."

Lewis looked relieved to be getting to military business, "Yes. Both Generals Leclerc and Rochambeau are being recalled to France to aid with preparations for the invasion of England. Napoleon values their reputation and sees their notoriety as a morale booster as well as a threat to Britain."

"Of course, besides, Charles' wife's brother wants him home."

"Right, it doesn't hurt to be married to the Emperor's sister."

"Any word from Colonel du Vignaud on replacements?"

"Vignaud says we should expect Joseph Bonaparte, one of Napoleon's older brothers, to be installed as the King of Quebec."

"Yes, that comports with what Ambassador Pichon told me yesterday. Though it seems odd to have a kingdom to our north. A kingdom in name only though. Fascinating how Napoleon rules, building an empire. Central authority with far flung departments ruled by trusted family members. And what of the military command?"

"I'm told it's Marshal Louis-Nicolas Davout. He is to be named commander of French forces in the Americas."

"Davout?"

"Yes, he's a veteran of the Egyptian campaign, though captured by the British at sea and held for a time. His wife is General Leclerc's sister."

"Of course, another trusted family member!" Burr idly wondered if Napoleon had a suitable sister and how the people of the Republic would view a marriage to European royalty.

Jeph was silently taking notes in the background, all of which Burr would review and determine what would be memorialized into the Republic's official record.

"Yes, well, he's known for two things: discipline and, paradoxically, his slovenly appearance," Lewis added.

"So, now, what of your preparations. What is the state of mobilization and training?"

"Sir, we expect 20,000 conscripts to be added to our forces by the end of the month. Perhaps more, depending on the success of the levies from New England. Our current force stands at 19,545 after our losses in the Maryland campaign. Of this, some 5,000 are veterans of the first call. They signed up for two years and their enlistments are due to expire in December. Another 4,000 are of the second call for volunteers. Their enlistments expire on June 30 next year. Of the remainder, only 10 percent are conscripts as most men were motivated to join for the higher pay. The volunteers in the third cohort have three-year enlistments that run through March 31 of 1806 while the conscripts, about 1,000 of them, have two-year obligations that run through March next year. The fourth cohort now being raised will have the same terms, three years for the volunteers and two years for the conscripts."

"How many volunteers are signing up?"

"This round it appears that two of every three are volunteers."

"What is being done to convince the veterans to stay?"

"We are offering reenlistment bonuses of $50."

Burr paused, "What about an elite unit, open, at first, only the veterans of the first call and, if the ranks cannot be filled, of the second call. It will be a guards unit. A Republican Guard. Special pay and honors too. Land in the West."

"Yes, but it will harm unit cohesion. Many soldiers in our first-formed battalions will join."

"After December, none of those battalions will exist anyway."

"True. Perhaps we announce word of the Guard in mid-October. Shall I draft the proposed regulations for your approval?"

"Yes." Burr was looking distant, he was already thinking about the next pressing topic, "Tell me about your promising officers. We need generals."

"We have many talented men who, I am confident, can lead a battalion or a regiment, but I've seen few who can yet be trusted to maneuver and sustain a brigade. What about Colonel Spencer of the Light Dragoons? He served under Van Rensselaer," Lewis offered.

"We need an infantry or an artillery officer, not a cavalry officer. This war will be won with the cannon and bayonet." Burr didn't want to admit to Lewis that he didn't trust anyone connected to the Van Rensselaer family, whose 1,200 square mile estate he had seized upon Stephen van Rensselaer's execution for treason in July. He cut the rent to the 50,000 tenants, binding them to him, though he wasn't yet certain if he would have the state loan the tenants the money to purchase the land from the Republic or whether he would promise to give them the land and have them pay rent for a certain period before owning it.

"I'll continue to review our officer corps."

"Have you considered a training regimen? Something that might both improve our officer corps and show who might have talent for command?"

"Sir?"

"Are you familiar with Königsspiel?"

Lewis looked at Burr blankly, which didn't surprise Burr as almost all American officers were self-taught and far more familiar with fighting Indians than with fighting European armies.

"It's German for 'The King's Game.' Invented by a man named Weickmann about 140 years ago. It's not very complicated. Played on a chessboard. Some 20 years ago another German developed a more realistic game with 1,666 squares and just a few years ago I read that a Prussian, Viturinus, developed a tool with 3,600 squares but the rule book runs to almost 100 pages and it's so complex that no one can use it to any practical effect. You might ask the French what they recommend—though I suppose their true answer would be that they just fight so much that the good generals are the lucky ones who survive. The point, Morgan, is that Republican lives are precious, we don't have as many as do the French and we can't afford to lose too many men or to have too many defeats as either will shake faith in the government. We need to be confident that our generals are up to their responsibilities before they fight."

"Yes, Mr. President."

"We're likely going to get only one opportunity to unite America while the British fleet is focused on the Channel. I can't conceive that this state of affairs will last beyond a year."

Chapter Seventy-Five – Surveillance

October 14, 1804, Sneden's Landing, New York

Jeph's second meeting with York was to be in Sneden's Landing on the west bank of the Hudson River about eight miles northwest of his home in New Rochelle. He wasn't particularly keen on the meet, given he'd only used eight birds so far out of the 40 York brought him in August, and one got sick and died, leaving 31—enough to send 15 messages at two birds per message.

There wasn't much in the way of horses and wagons on the road—it was a Sunday after all—and Jeph had to wait longer than usual to board the ferry across the Hudson with two other men with small wagons like his.

Jeph looked down the slate gray river towards Weehawken, New Jersey, clouds on the southern horizon blending almost seamlessly with the river with the bright yellows, oranges, and reds of autumn providing a fiery frame to the dull waters. This was where one of Colonel Burr's allies shot and killed Philip Hamilton in late 1801. Jeph shook his head. So much tragedy in the Hamilton family—completely shattered by its deadly encounters with Aaron Burr.

As the ferry pulled next to the dock, the deckhands jumped off and moored the vessel, and then dropped the small ramp onto the sandy embankment. Jeph scanned for York's big frame among the five wagons and a dozen passengers waiting to cross over to the eastern side of the river.

Jeff led his horse and wagon off the ferry and looked around again. There were a few small homes, built in the Dutch style, with well-tended gardens. Two of the homes betrayed the occupation of their owners who had spread fishing nets out to dry. There was no road along the water. A marsh along the banks of the river lay north to Jeph's right only a couple hundred feet distant while to the south a few hundred feet, the palisades dove down to the river's edge around the New Jersey line making a road impractical. Ahead, the rutted dirt track rose steeply about 50 feet and then dipped out of sight.

Seeing York nowhere, Jeph decided to take the road up and out of the close shelter of Sneden's Landing. Jeph's horse pulled the empty wagon easily enough, though she was moving slower than her usual pace as she picked her way up the hill. As the road came up against a 15-foot rock face, it took a sharp left turn and gradually climbed up to the top of the palisades overlooking the Hudson. Jeph only caught glances of the river between the intense colors of the hickories (bronze), dogwood (purple), black locust (yellow), willows (yellow), and maples (bright red, orange-red, or bright yellow, depending on the variety).

Jeph was lost in thought when he was startled by a familiar voice from the brush, "You need a man, sir?" It was York.

Jeph halted his horse. "Y-Yes. Why, yes, I do. Hop on up."

York bounded up onto the wagon and sat in the back with his back to Jeph, "Keep riding south, don't say nothing, I'll explain. I was followed. Two militia stopped me. They wanted to see my load. They saw the birds. I told 'em I was a runaway. Which, after a fashion, I is—'cept I'm fixin' to run back."

"There's two men on horse up ahead. Were the militia on horse?" Jeph felt the wagon shift and he looked back to see York's back disappear into the brush.

Seconds later, the two mounted men—militiamen by their haphazard uniforms—rode by Jeph's wagon, one man on each side, looking, with visible disappointment, into Jeph's empty wagon.

"Pardon me, sir, I don't recognize you, are you from these parts?" The one Jeph's right said. He was young and had likely never shaved.

"I am. I'm from New Rochelle," Jeph replied.

"I need to see your curfew paper, sir."

Now this was a new development. For the past two months, the national government of the Republic had pushed for security, encouraging citizens to carry an identification document stating their age, eye color, hair color, height, gender, address, and occupation. The system was supposed to be voluntary through the end of the year, and, after that, if one was travelling during times of darkness, mandatory.

Jeph heaved a sigh, not only because he viewed this request as an imposition, but also because his occupation would make it clear to these low-ranking militiamen that he worked for President Burr—something that they might repeat to their commander which then might make its way back to Burr.

The man nearest Jeph took the paper. It was folded twice into a square and, as he unfolded it, he squinted and frowned at it. Jeph doubted he could read, though now he was nodding seriously while staring at the document.

"What's your occupation, sir?"

Jeph decided that the man definitely couldn't read, and neither could his partner, "I'm a squab seller."

"Oh? What a happenstance, there's a wagon up the road with a couple of cages of pigeon. Some runaway slave was driving it, but we haven't seen him around for an hour. Those wouldn't be your birds, would they?"

"I don't know. They might be. My flock was struck by fever, and I lost my birds. I made arrangements to buy birds from a reputable breeder in New Jersey—birds that are supposed to be immune to bird yellow fever," Jeph lied. He would have felt bad about that a few months ago—but times were rapidly changing for the worse.

"Well, that boy was with the wagon an hour ago, but when we rode past it a few minutes ago, that slave wasn't in sight."

"What did he look like?"

"I don't know. He was black. He's a big man. Nice clothes but patched."

"That's the man I was looking for! His master is the one I'm buying the birds from. Mercy, I hope the birds are fine and he just didn't run off and leave them."

"Well, sir, you'll find his horse and wagon on the side of the road just beyond the rise about 100 yards yonder. Perhaps you can wait for him. Do as you wish. You have your curfew papers, and we haven't had any reports of highwaymen since our river road patrols started in the spring so you're safe."

Jeph thought that he was rather safer without these two poking into his business, but he held his tongue, tipped his hat, and urged his horse forward.

Soon after, he found York's wagon and transferred the birds to his wagon and covered the cages with a canvas tarp. He then headed back to the ferry.

At the spot where he thought York jumped off, he spoke loudly to the bushes. "I got the birds." He paused, and then added, "Thank you, York. I'll see you eight weeks."

Chapter Seventy-Six – The Northwest Question

October 17, 1804, Richmond, Virginia

John Adams fidgeted outside of Thomas Jefferson's office. Being Vice President to Jefferson provided little responsibility and, with the 16-member Senate consisting of the representatives from seven southern states and his own Massachusetts in exile, opportunities to break ties were few and far between. Still, Jefferson seemed to invite his advice and take it seriously, and, along with Virginians James Madison and George Wythe, he was one of a small circle of men whom Jefferson engaged in philosophical debate.

Adams heard the distinct Boston voice of Jefferson's Attorney General, Levi Lincoln, Sr., as the meeting was breaking up. Jefferson's door opened and Adams, 13 days shy of his 69th birthday, painfully got to his feet and extended his hand to his old acquaintance and former political opponent, now bound together by the trials of war and exile. "Mr. Attorney General," Adams nodded.

"Mr. Vice President," Lincoln smiled back.

Jefferson cleared his throat, "Gentlemen, if I may interpose, I wish to see the Vice President."

Lincoln laughed and Adams smiled, his blue eyes twinkling.

Adams walked into Jefferson's office and study, books everywhere, including five on his desk.

"Tea?" Jefferson asked, knowing full well that Adams would likely turn him down, not wanting to be served by one of Jefferson's slaves.

"No, thank you kindly."

The two friends discussed their children and grandchildren, Jefferson still mourning the loss of his daughter, Mary, who died six months earlier, only months after the birth of her third child.

A few minutes later, Adams broached the reason for his visit. "Thomas, I think we—by that I mean you, of course—should request that the Congress consider the readoption of the Northwest Ordinance."

Jefferson's eyes narrowed and then looked past Adams, thinking through the political and policy implications of the matter. The old Confederation Congress had passed the Northwest Ordinance in 1787 before that body gradually ground to a halt. The law needed to be renewed if it was to have any effect in the new national government. While largely symbolic, given the effective control over the territories by Burr's Republic, the British, and their Indian allies, the law would provide for the division of the Northwest

Territory into three to five states, specify an admissions process, and guarantee a bill of rights, most importantly forbidding slavery.

"An interesting idea, sir," Jefferson said after several seconds, adding, "Why now?"

Adams looked at Jefferson, "I believe it helpful in our war against Burr. It would show the residents of the Northwest Territory that we intend to preserve their natural rights. It would show good faith."

Jefferson quickly retorted, "Yet the territories have continued to develop at a slow pace under the constant threat of Indian raids under the encouragement of the British. Ohio is up to what, 30,000 settlers of whom some 10,000 are runaway slaves? The rest of the territory only has fewer than 2,000 settlers—hardly worth a fight over in Congress."

"I disagree. First, only about half of the negroes are escaped slaves. Many of them are freemen, having been manumitted by law in the Northern states or having purchased their freedom…"

"Still, I have many planters in Kentucky complaining that Ohio stands beyond the reach of the law. If a slave escapes across the Ohio, they're long gone and free. Assuming, of course, the Shawnee, Delaware, or Miami don't scalp or enslave them first."

"Yes, I can see how the negro colony in Ohio is an irritant. But consider this, the British are likely to be far more amenable to providing assistance to us if we can swing Ohio over to our side and open up the Mississippi and the Ohio to trade with the cut-off portion of Upper Canada. Further, if we can made entreaties to the Northwest, I'm sure the British will more actively work to convince their Indian allies to raid New York for the recovery of their lands there, rather than raid settlements in Ohio."

"Do you really think Upper Canada will survive much longer? They've been cut off from England for two years now. Certainly, they must be running low on shot, powder, and coin?"

"I understand there's growing trade between Upper Canada and the negro settlements via the Native trade routes. It's not much, but some gets through. And, I understand, Burr is reluctant to enforce any sort of embargo. His power doesn't extend much west of the Pennsylvania border and he may see any tariff enforcement expedition as not worth the risk." Adams was gently pressing Jefferson as much as he dared.

Jefferson considered Adams' proposal and answered slowly while looking at a well-worn Latin text, *Tusculanarum Disputationum*. "That and Burr reckons that the magnet to draw our slaves to Ohio is worth far more than any effort to choke off the last of the trade with the British outpost in Upper Canada."

Jefferson paused and then finally returned his gaze to Adams, speaking quickly now, "I'd like to speak to Madison about this. I'm inclined to support it, but I'd like his opinion as to its effects on Britain. If I'm going to rally votes, I'd like to know it will have the intended outcome."

"Thank you, Thomas, you won't be disappointed! I'm certain that it will have a salutary effect on the war and on our development as a nation. Further, it will encourage British investment. As scarce as specie was in Massachusetts, I've noticed coin is even more rare in the South. Your capital is largely held in plantations and slaves. Raising the funds needed to fight Burr is going to be very difficult without borrowing money from Europe. And, if we must resort to paper money to pay our army, it will mean the utter destruction of our nation."

Jefferson's mind had already fleeted elsewhere. Adams knew Jefferson was done with him and he slowly rose to his feet, his knees painfully complaining.

Chapter Seventy-Seven – Troubles

October 18, 1804, New York

Jeph thought Burr's countenance was off. He was usually upbeat prior to a meeting with the French ambassador but today, he was brooding. More than likely, Jeph thought it was due to the almost constant disappointment the French had been for the Republic over the past year. British naval patrols and Napoleon's own ongoing buildup of forces across the Channel prevented additional French supplies from reaching New York—Europe was the priority and America was, at most, a distraction.

Burr was also troubled about the unexpected loss of the new powder mill in Delaware. It wasn't just that the mill was destroyed by a catastrophic explosion, it was that DuPont and his family disappeared without a trace two at the same time. And now the Republic's only supply of high-quality gunpowder had to be imported past the British blockade from France. Was DuPont kidnapped by the South? Did British agents abduct him?

Though, Jeph did note that Burr was pleased with the progress of the French cannon and musket armories situated at Port Henry on Lake Champlain. There, the French engineers supervised the construction of a large charcoal-fueled pig iron blast furnace where iron from nearby mines in the Adirondack Mountains was melted into ingots to be used in making cast iron 12-pounders and Charleville muskets. The French would have preferred that the cannon be made from bronze—and there were reliable supplies of copper to be had nearby, but none of tin, meaning that the cast iron guns were all that could be made with the supplies at hand. Unfortunately, unlike bronze, cast iron cannon were uncomfortably prone to catastrophically explode in action.

Ambassador Pichon arrived with former French ambassador Genêt, a close Burr advisor. The two Frenchmen laughed at a private joke as they were let into Burr's office, Jeph standing to Burr's left. "Messieurs ambassadors," Burr rose and warmly greeted the men.

After the obligatory talk of family was dispensed with, Pichon got down to business.

"You are familiar with how the spark of our revolution inspired rebellions in Santo Domingo and Eire?" Pichon asked, knowing the answer.

"Yes, of course."

"And that our comrades in Santo Domingo are restless, but poor. They seek a greater glory in the West. More autonomy. Louverture fancies himself the Napoleon of the Caribbean."

Burr considered that preposterously pretentious, given Louverture commanded the loyalties of an island of a half million people, mostly illiterate recently freed slaves who still did the same brutal manual labor required to grow and refine sugar, but now working under Louverture's guns, with voodoo cocomacaque sticks wielded by largely mulatto bosses replacing the whips of French plantation owners. Burr grunted softly and waved Pichon on.

"As you know, the plantation masters in the South greatly fear the slave uprising on Santo Domingo. They fear it may happen to them next."

Burr responded, "Fear is a powerful tonic—though I understand that before the uprising, there were about 10 slaves for every free person on the French side of the island—and less than half of the free population were Europeans. In Virginia east of the Appalachians, the ratio is about one-to-one. Sustaining a rebellion with those odds would be difficult."

"Yes, but what if the object wasn't a successful rebellion, but rather an attack on the South's economy and on their ability to raise a national army and oppose your own offensive?"

Burr nodded, his left hand stroking his chin and his eyes narrowing in thought.

"Santo Domingo owes France millions of francs for lost property."

"You mean people; slaves..."

"Yes, of course, lost slaves and land that was seized. Yet they need the protection of France. They fear Britain might try another invasion. So, here is what we have arranged. We have forgiven Santo Domingo $5 million francs of their $100 million debt and we have advanced to Louverture 500,000 francs in gold in return for which Louverture has agreed to assemble 5,000 of his finest infantry under the command of General Dessalines. This force will constitute an expeditionary army for the purpose of attacking South Carolina, sacking the plantations, and freeing the slaves. France will provide the transportation and a small number of horse artillery, cavalry, staff, and necessary supplies. Altogether, a force of 5,500 men. We are even carrying 1,000 extra muskets and uniforms to arm any slave who wishes to join the army."

Burr sat back in his chair, "Carrying muskets? This is happening now?"

"Yes. I suspect the forces will land on the Carolina coast in a month. The question is, are you able to exploit this? Can you restart your offensive?" Ambassador Pichon stared at Burr and offered a tightlipped smile.

Genêt looked from Pichon to Burr and back again.

Burr fixed his gaze on his desk and then raised his eyes to Pichon, "We need powder. Our best powder mill was lost in an explosion two months ago."

Pichon replied, "Powder mills explode. Is it repaired?"

"No. The proprietor disappeared," Burr wasn't going to offer that it was DuPont, a man of high esteem in Napoleon's circles. "Are there shipments inbound from France?"

Pichon shrugged his shoulders, "I do not know. The British blockade makes everything uncertain. Even so, I am to understand that Quebec is the priority. If a shipment does arrive, it will be at Quebec."

Jeph, taking his usual notes at a small work desk behind and to Burr's left, was ignored by the three men.

Burr was working long hours, meaning Jeph was working long hours. It was Thursday. Burr didn't work on Sundays—or, at least, didn't ask Jeph to work—but this information was too vital not to try to send. Yet, the Republic's Public Safety patrols were becoming thicker, and, at night, a traveler had to show his papers to proceed. Were he to try to ride the 18 miles home, his absence would probably be noted by the authorities. He had to sit on this information and wait until Sunday to send it.

Jeph rode back home on Saturday night, a bitter rain soaking him to the bone. The storm was bad enough that Jeph only ran into one Public Safety patrol and the two men didn't even ask to see his papers.

Jeph trotted up to his house near midnight, the horse accelerating towards its familiar stable. Jeph stiffly climbed off his horse, removed the bridle and saddle, and drew a bag of oats for the animal. He then woodenly walked towards his back door, quietly letting himself in.

Jeph saw Molly by the guttering flame of a smokey tallow candle—one he knew she made herself from hog fat. She had fallen asleep in her rocking chair in the sitting room.

"Molly, I'm home, let's go to bed."

Molly rolled to her feet and kissed Jeph, then exclaimed, "You're soaked! Freezing! Some hot soup for you first, then bed."

Early Sunday morning before church, while it was still dark outside, Jeph got up to stoke the fire in the Franklin stove. In the wake of the storm, the temperature had dropped to just-above freezing and the house was barely warmer than that. Jeph lit a costly spermaceti whale oil candle and started writing, his right hand aching from the cold. "5,000 R, 200 C, 10 CN – 8 –

C – NOV – Fm S. Dom. / 20,000 R, 4,000 M, 5,000 C, 40 CN – 5 – B2 – NOV."

It was just past eight o'clock as the sun rose into a crisp, clear Sunday morning, the night's rain still lazily dripping off the bright reds, yellows, and oranges of the trees on Jeph's property. Jeph made his way back to the pigeon loft, selected two homing birds from his replenished stock of 51, secured the duplicate notes to the birds and let them fly south.

Jeph figured he had just enough time to wash up and get ready for church with Molly. He wondered if he'd see an agent from Burr's Public Safety network again—the last one he saw made an appearance just before Thomas Paine's murder 10 months ago and he now realized the two were likely connected.

Chapter Seventy-Eight – Confederacy of the Eight Nations

October 27, 1804, Huron River on the Shore of Lake Erie

Ted White had never seen so many Indians. Gathered in a colorful array of feathers, body paint, necklaces, and various combinations of Native American and European clothing, hats, and weapons, representatives of the six United Indian Nations had gathered to meet with the British of Upper Canada and the newly prominent Black tribe of western Ohio.

White had caught a glimpse of the famous Shawnee chief Blue Jacket. Buckongahelas of the Delaware was there. Little Turtle, also known as Michikinikwa, the war chief the Miami, canoed east 60 miles from his lands along the Maumee River. Joseph Brant, or Thayendanegea, the great Mohawk, now a wise 63, arrived on a British sloop from the Grand River Valley with his friend and ally, the Irish-born ranger Major William Caldwell. Roundhead or Stayeghtha of the Wyandot, whom White had ongoing trade relations with, camped next to White's delegation. And Wequetong of the Detroit Odawa rounded out the six nations present. Altogether, they represented 10,000 warriors—if they could cooperate.

Caldwell, who represented the interests of the Crown, came with a mixed company of backwoodsmen militia, redcoated British regulars, and Royal Navy sailors, about 110 men in all. White knew that the Indian leaders, while historically sympathetic to the British allies, were also acutely aware of the British setbacks against the French in Montreal and Quebec and the deteriorating position they were in, having been cut off from their base of supply via the St. Lawrence River. Caldwell was circumspect, but most of the Native chiefs thought him capable of contributing no more than 1,000 warriors. More important was his connection to Britain and the diplomatic leverage he could bring.

And then there was White, the newest of players, but in many ways, the strongest. He was the elected governor of the Ohio Territory of Freemen, a rapidly growing community of 25,000 with 10,000 trained militia, though with no cannon and no trained cavalry. Some three in four of the territory's citizens were escaped slaves while the rest, already free, settled there mainly from Massachusetts, New York, and Pennsylvania. It was the latter group who formed the natural leadership of the territory, as, for the most part, they were literate and had managed their own affairs as farmers, shopkeepers, mechanics, and seamen. Even so, one in ten of the escaped slaves from the South were artisans—blacksmiths, coopers, and wheelwrights were common professions among the former slaves who were allowed to work independently so long as they paid a portion of their wages to their masters.

On the first formal day of the gathering, there was, for White, a confusing array of ceremonies—dancing, pipe smoking, prayers, bonfires, and feasts. This was replicated on the second day, with hosting nations vying to impress their tribal peers. Roundhead suggested to White that he arrange something for the third day since he, as the Big Chief, would be expected to have the greatest feast of all. Fortunately, White anticipated this, and had brought 20 fattened hogs, each more than 200 pounds, for the occasion. He had them slaughtered the night before and placed into pits, by Noon the following day, they were ready. Along with the corn and cured tobacco he brought, the assemblage had never seen a feast as generously provisioned.

By five o'clock, the sun hanging low, its golden rays streaming through the warm leaves of fall, White mounted a large stump on the shore that had been tossed there by a prior season's storm, his back to the lake. White looked into the expectant faces of some 2,000 men, warriors all, assembled in a great semicircle on the light tan sands of Lake Erie. White had purposefully brought 500 of his best men, heavily muscled and tall and asked them to spread out in the crowd with no more than three standing together. The effect was impressive. Everywhere among the 1,400 Indians and 100 British, for every ten warriors, there were two or three men from the Territory of Freemen. The effect was as White thought it would be—morale soared, and with it, his own standing.

As the last rays of the sun cast upon his face, White began, knowing all the leaders present knew English.

"As we know, the world is at war. France and Spain are fighting England and much of Europe. But that is far away across a great ocean and does not concern us directly. In the lands of our ancestors, the United American Republic makes war on the United States. Soon, this war will come to us. We will be forced to take a side, or we will be killed, and our women and children made slaves and our lands will be taken." Hearing murmurs, White paused.

"Unless! Unless! Unless we band together and declare ourselves independent. Declare our lands to be ours. I propose a confederacy of the eight nations gathered here today. This nation, our nation, will defend its territory. We will work together to preserve our families, our tribes. And we will negotiate as one with both the Republic and the United States!"

At that, White's men started cheering and then then entire mass joined in, a mix of applause and war cries.

While Brandt and Caldwell would determine the northern extent of the eastern boundary, it was White's intent to suggest that his territory would start at the Black River on Lake Erie, extending south to Killbuck Creek, and then the Muskingum River to the Ohio. This would cede the first 100 miles of coast along the lake from Pennsylvania to the Republic and in the south, 130 miles along the Ohio bordering Virginia. These were the lands most thickly settled, with about 12,000 farmers, most of whom owed allegiance to the Republic in the north and about 9,000 who looked to Virginia in the south.

White believed he had the start of a new nation—if those here today would stand fast.

Chapter Seventy-Nine – Agents of the Republic

October 28, 1804, New Rochelle, New York

When Jeph rode home Saturday afternoon, Molly was more agitated than he'd seen her in a decade. On Monday afternoon, she was visited by an agent of the Republic's Ministry of Finance. The revenue agent had reason to believe that Jeph's squab business was not properly remitting all of the new, one percent wartime sales tax. He demanded to see the operation's books. Molly refused and told the overbearing man to come back on Sunday when Mr. Clark would return from his job in the city.

Then, on Tuesday, she learned that Alexander, their oldest son, was moving south with his infantry regiment.

Jeph consoled Molly as best he could, and then set about to review his books and the last two quarters of his tax payment receipts. Satisfied that his affairs were in order, they walked to church in the cold, misty morning with Aaron, 17, Amy, 15, and Faith, 10, while Jeph carried little Theodosia, 15 months.

Jeph's family filled half of the pew in the third row from the front on the right side. They were just in time. The minister took his place behind the pulpit. But just as he was about to start, Jeph noticed something distracted him. Jeph looked over his left shoulder, but he could see nothing but familiar faces. He raised himself a few inches off the pew and then he saw him—the same man who attended the service just before Thomas Paine was killed. Jeph slowly sat back down before the man looked his way.

The pastor cleared his throat and then commenced to deliver a forgettable sermon on the need for repentance and redemption. Jeph got the distinct impression that the pastor didn't preach the message he'd planned to.

At the end of the service, Jeph and Molly chatted with their friends, passing Theodosia back and forth between them while their three older children played outside with their friends. Half an hour later, they started for home, their kids running to catch up from behind. Aaron and Amy pulled up alongside while Faith called out, "Wait!"

Jeph looked back to see that the stranger was following them from about 50 yards behind.

"Molly, it appears we may have company," Jeph said quietly.

"Oh?"

"Don't look," Jeph said and then motioned with his head and eyes.

Molly just looked at Jeph and shrugged.

Jeph continued in a low voice, trying to keep his children from hearing, "When we get into the house, bolt the back door. Aaron and I will arm ourselves. I don't know whether he's a murderer or a government agent."

"There's a difference these days?"

Jeph chuckled bitterly.

About 100 yards from their home, the man had closed the distance to about 30 yards.

"Molly, children, run along home, I'm going to see if I can help this man," Jeph said, turning to face the stranger.

Aaron paused and turned back but Jeph glared at him, and he quickly joined his mother and siblings.

"May I help you, sir?" Jeph said, facing the man, his family disappearing into the house.

"Yes, may we speak?" the man said, gesturing towards Jeph's house.

"Have we met?" Jeph asked, extending his hand, "My name is Jephtaph Clark, whom do I have the pleasure…"

Jeph reckoned the man to be just a few years younger than himself—in his late 30s. Of average build and height, clean shaven, and wearing a worn black tricorn and tattered black cape but his jacket, pants, and boots looked new. His eyes were grey blue under brown eyebrows. The hair on his temples had a reddish hue. His nose was flattened and slightly crooked to the left as if it had been broken once.

The man extended his hand and said, "Ulysses Proctor, good to meet you, Mr. Clark. Might we speak in private?" He gestured again to Jeph's house.

"We can speak on the street for now," Jeph replied.

Proctor walked past Jeph and headed off the road for the back of the house. "I prefer we conduct our business privately," Proctor said, heading towards the pigeon lofts.

Jeph's eyes widened as he trotted after Proctor.

Proctor stopped behind the house. Jeph could hear his pigeons cooing in the rookery next to the stable.

"Mr. Clark, I must speak with you about John McLachlan."

"The Reverend?" Jeph was simultaneously relieved and suspicious.

Proctor looked over Jeph's shoulder, "One of your birds?"

Jeph stepped away from Proctor and briefly looked behind him. There was a pigeon. And it had a message tied to its leg!

Jeph turned back to Proctor and narrowed his eyes, "Hard to tell," Jeph replied. "I raise 'em for food and we frequently see wild birds that fly in to eat some of the feed that gets scattered outside of the rookery."

Proctor took a half step towards Jeph, "About McLachlan…"

"Sir, you told me your name, but why the interest in the Reverend? Whom do you work for?"

The man started to reach into his pocket.

Jeph could see Aaron's shadow behind the panes of glass on the window overlooking the stable and rookery. "Slowly, sir, you're still a stranger to me."

Proctor nodded slowly and smiled, "Do you want to remove my papers to see for yourself?" He started to raise his hands.

"No, that's not necessary. Just, if you please, remove them yourself slowly," Jeph responded, not wanting to earn an enemy within the ranks of the Republic's gendarmes.

Jeph resisted an urge to look back at the bird.

Proctor extended his documents and Jeph cautiously took them and looked them over, his eyes glancing from the papers to Proctor and back again. Jeph handed the documents back—Proctor was with the Republic. Oddly, Proctor didn't ask for his papers, meaning, he already knew who he was or he didn't care. Jeph prayed it was the latter.

Proctor coughed twice and then spoke quietly, "Now... about McLachlan..."

Jeph heard his back door open and glanced to the right, it was Molly, carrying out two cups of tea followed by Aaron who rushed past Proctor and Jeph, headed for the pigeon loft.

Molly approached, "Beg your pardon. If you gentlemen prefer to conduct business outside, you can at least enjoy some tea." Molly smiled and handed a cup and saucer to Proctor and then turned to Jeph, privately glaring at him.

Proctor chuckled and Jeph turned to see Aaron with a weighted bird net. His son cast it over the bird, trapping it to the ground. Seconds later, Aaron returned the bird to the rookery.

Jeph figured Proctor hadn't seen the message tied onto the bird's leg on account of his being near-sighted.

Proctor lifted his steaming cup to Molly and said, "Thank you, Mrs. Clark," and then took a loud sip before turning again to Jeph, "As I was saying..."

Jeph said, "Thank you Mrs. Clark, would you please excuse us?"

Molly shot Jeph one last cold look and turned to go into the house, followed by Aaron.

Jeph waited until they were alone again and then asked, "What would you like to know, Mr. Proctor?"

"Does Reverend McLachlan support the Republic?"

"I haven't ever asked him. Have you?"

Proctor raised his cup to lips and swallowed his annoyance. The tea was good—he could taste some honey in it. Proctor sighed, "Mr. Clark, I don't need to tell you that we live in troubled times. The Republic is at war…"

"Yes, I know this. My oldest son is serving in the army…"

"Then you will be most interested in assuring that he comes home safe, sound, and victorious." Proctor sipped again.

"The Reverend has often been critical of government. He calls out corruption and abuse and does with equal scorn for any official," Jeph allowed, trying not to sound defensive.

"Has he criticized President Burr?"

"No sir, not that I've heard with my own ears."

"Has he called for insurrection?"

"No."

"Does he support the war?"

"Likely not. I should imagine that most men of God look with disfavor on war."

"Of course." Proctor gulped the last of his tea and handed his saucer and cup to Jeph and then pushed back his worn black cape to reveal a pistol strapped to each hip, quickly bringing his arms back to his sides and letting cape cover his weapons. "It is my duty to inform you that as a citizen of the Republic, your truthful cooperation is required and that if Reverend McLachlan is plotting insurrection, a people's tribunal may well find you liable as an accomplice."

Proctor aimed a steely glare at Jeph. Jeph looked back, unblinking.

"If you do hear something, Mr. Clark, you are obliged to report it." Proctor handed Jeph a card, "Here is my address at the Directorate for Public Safety. You may report in person or by letter."

Jeph consolidated the cups and saucers in his right hand and reached out to take the card with his left.

Proctor glanced at his crippled hand and looked away.

"Monmouth, courtesy of the British. Did you fight in the war?" Jeph suppressed a grin as he had his suspicions.

"Good day, Mr. Clark. Let me know if you see anything."

Thought so.

Jeph walked a few paces behind Proctor until he reached the road and then he returned to the back door and let himself in to Molly's ire.

"Mr. Clark, what is this?" she snapped, holding up the message that had been on the pigeon's leg. Molly glared at Jeph as he'd never seen before in their 20 years of marriage.

Jeph looked back at Molly, holding her gaze, and replied quietly, "I was going to ask you the same thing, Mrs. Clark."

Molly stopped, momentarily at a loss for words, and looked carefully at the message. The ink had run some and the edges of the strip of paper were battered from the bird having pecked at it. Molly wasn't literate, but she knew Jeph's hand—which is one reason why Jeph wrote the messages in the German hand rather than the traditional Round hand. The script didn't look like his own.

Jeph reached out to examine the paper. "This isn't my hand, Molly," he lied to his wife for the first time. "Where did the bird come from? Was it a stray?"

Molly thought. "There was a thunderstorm last month. The rookery was damaged, and a couple of birds got out. I had Aaron patch the hole. He caught one of the birds and he put it back."

Jeph thought for a moment. If Aaron put one of his breeding birds in the message bird enclosure, that would explain why this bird never traveled south! "So, this bird might have been one of ours or it might have been someone else's—though that doesn't explain the message."

Jeph squinted at the message. "I see numbers, letters, and what look like dates. I've heard of such a thing used by stockjobbers—people who use information about trading in company stocks in Manhattan. This might be evidence of a criminal enterprise. The best thing we can do is to destroy it before Mr. Proctor returns."

"And what about Mr. Proctor? He looked like the Devil himself."

"Mr. Proctor is an agent with Public Safety. He's suspicious of Reverend McLachlan and wanted me to inform on him. The Reverend's life is in jeopardy."

Molly shook her head in disgust. "How can you work for Colonel Burr? He's the one responsible for this!"

Jeph walked past Molly, opened the Franklin stove, and tossed the message into the flames. Jeph turned to Molly, "It's a job. We need the money..." Jeph knew he sounded less than convincing.

Jeph moved to kiss his wife and then hug her, "Molly, I must return to the city. Colonel Burr's busier than ever and needs me. I love you, Molly."

Chapter Eighty – The Second Battle of Baltimore

October 30 to November 11, 1804, Valley Forge, Pennsylvania to Baltimore, Maryland

The march from Valley Forge started well enough. Spirits were high as the previous day's frost had given way to a warm, hazy mid-morning—not too hot for marching. Alex heard one of the corporals refer to the weather as an "Indian Summer." He decided he liked the term.

After two days' march due west covering 20 miles, they made it to Downing's Town midway between Philadelphia and Lancaster. They trained on security with the sergeants explaining the importance of picket duty and stressing the severe consequences of finding any soldier asleep or absent from their posts. Five more days' march to the west brought them to Lancaster where they made a proper camp five miles to the west of the town. They feasted on salted pork, beans, bread, and coffee. They even had an hour to mend their uniforms, with some soldiers being issued new boots.

The army crossed the Susquehanna at Columbia under the banner of the Republic and made for York, where again, they bivouacked under a starry sky, leaving the tents in the baggage train.

The morning started with the manual exercise. Under the watchful eyes of the battalion lieutenant colonel, sergeants put their platoons through the motions, "Poise-firelock! Cock-firelock! Take aim! Fire! Half-cock-firelock! Handle-cartridge! Prime!"

Alex had almost committed the motions to memory, though from his father's descriptions of combat, he knew that practice prior to battle was a good thing. He bit the paper off the end of the cartridge and shook some powder into the pan and then started to shut the pan as the sergeant cried, "Shut-pan!" Alex slapped the pan closed and turned the musket around with the muzzle level with his chin. "Charge with cartridge!" Alex shook the powder into the barrel. "Draw-rammer!" Alex pulled the ramrod out, flipped it around and started to ram the ball and cartridge paper down as the sergeant bellowed, "Ram down-cartridge!" was issued. The soldier next to him, Jacob, struggled to seat his cartridge and ball while juggling the rammer. "Return-rammer!" Alex fluidly thrusted the rammer home, lifted the musket up to this shoulder with his left hand and his right hand grasping the weapon under the cock. "Shoulder-firelock! Order-firelock!" The butt of Alex's musket was now resting on the ground at his right side. Jacob was still a few seconds behind. "Ground-firelock!" Alex took a big step forward with his left foot, laying the musket on the ground pointing to the front while his right knee hovered above the ground.

Alex found himself thinking of home. The sergeant's commands became second nature. Musket to the shoulder, aim musket, fire, load musket, etc. They fired two volleys with actual shot. The sergeants, carefully watching their men, then called out a few soldiers who needed additional practice. Alex wasn't one of them. Jacob was. He and the other laggards went through the fifteen motions of prime and load with blanks—cartridges issued without balls—loading and firing three additional times.

At that, the battalion formed up into a column with its regiment and turned south to Baltimore, some 55 miles away—depending on the pace, weather, and if the enemy made an appearance, it would take five to six days to make Baltimore after eight days of continuous march from Philadelphia.

By the second days' march south they crossed the state line into Maryland. The weather held the first three days of the march out of York. But on the fourth night, again, sleeping in the open as they did more than half the nights, the stars disappeared as a brisk north wind set in.

Alex had the morning watch, but a cold rain had already awakened him minutes before. He welcomed the excuse to get to his feet and stand guard as he could no longer sleep anyway. The grey dawn started to break as the temperature was still dropping. Alex reckoned it was in the 40s. His fingers were stiff and he stamped his feet to keep warm.

The regiment formed up with each man issued a hardtack biscuit while topping off their canteens. They had 10 minutes to eat and relieve themselves before moving south just as the morning sun dully glowed through the clouds and the rain stopped.

They had marched for two hours on the York turnpike when Alex heard the crack of a firearm. A captain on horseback fell like a sack of potatoes, making a terrible thud as the wind was knocked out of his dying body. An officer called "Halt!" He then commanded "Right face!" his voice betraying a crack with the second word of the command.

Alex faced a stand of young, mostly leafless trees, their trunks about 30 feet apart. Some 40 yards away Alex spied movement behind a large, downed trunk. "Sergeant Wilson! There!" Alex got the attention of his platoon sergeant, pointing at the trunk.

Captain Wright yelled, "Standfast! Good eyes, Private Clark."

Moments later, five men on horseback rode between the halted double column of troops and the bare forest. The captain pointed at the log and the horsemen went in, sabers drawn, two to the left, and three to the right of the moss-covered log. Seconds later, Alex saw a man's back as he made a break for it, running at a crouch to a fallow farmer's field beyond.

A second shot rang out, but the five cavalrymen drove on, weaving and ducking between the trees. Alex saw a second man, yards in back of the first man in the clearing, also start to run, heading for the dark forest beyond. Two cavalrymen caught up with the first sniper and cut him down from behind, not even pausing to look back. Barely visible through the trees, Alex caught a glimpse of the second man. He had made it to the clearing, but there, the cavalrymen easily overtook him. He threw his weapon to the ground and raised his hands. A cavalrymen shot him with his pistol, and he crumpled to the ground. The other dismounted to inspect the fallen man.

Alex had just seen his first combat. His knees started to shake, and he wanted to vomit, but his stomach was empty. He grabbed his canteen and took two swallows. Captain Wright ordered the formation to left face, and they returned to the march south, the quickening north wind at their backs.

Two hours later Alex thought it was about noon, though clouds still obscured the sun, making it impossible for him to tell. The road to Baltimore rose and fell, constantly undulating as it coursed over hill and stream. Whenever they came to a fast-moving creek, the soldiers were told to top off their canteens in the clear waters upstream of their march.

As they closed on Baltimore, the surrounding countryside started to flatten out, with the route seeing fewer wooded ridges and more well-tended farms.

The sun had completely disappeared, and the rain felt like it would soon turn to sleet when Alex heard the rolling sound of cannon fire.

An officer rode up, splattered in mud, and called out for the regimental commander. Alex could see the two exchanging words and moments later, the entire regiment continued in route step—each soldier taking steps as needed to keep up with the man in front of him. But some five minutes later, the column was ordered to quick time, now marching slightly faster but in unison—left, right, left, right—the regimental drummer keeping pace to the south down the York turnpike, with the city of Baltimore clearly visible through the pelting rain some two miles distant.

Alex marched past three batteries of four guns each posted to the right along the finger of a ridge that pointed south. It was there that he saw his first enemy earthworks—sharpened logs pointed north. But here and there were gaps in the logs, with splintered wood and mud everywhere accompanied by channels dug through the earth likely minutes ago by cannonballs.

They quickly marched by a deep trench behind the smashed wooden abatis that stretched along on either side of the turnpike. Alex caught a glimpse of dead, blue-coated Republic soldiers, some laying on top of enemy militia. On the left, he heard a man cry out for his mother, on the right someone begged for water. His unit, marching a column of fours, then parted, two files on either side of a dead horse, its bowels spattered across the muddy road with the bloody stump of a booted leg lying next to a silver stirrup—the only material thing that wasn't wrecked.

Alex's stomach started to grumble, and his legs were getting a bit wobbly from only eating a single hardtack in what seemed like a month ago when he heard the command to double time.

The regiment picked up the pace and Alex could see a thickening array of bodies. Some bleeding, some missing limbs—one corpse, militia, judging by the uniform—was headless.

He heard a terrible thud. A moment's march later, he realized a cannonball must have hit the colonel's horse square on, as the animal was torn apart just ahead of Alex on the right side of the column. The colonel's left leg was taken with the shot, and he lay helpless under the remains of his mount, his right leg pinned under the gore.

They were called to quick time and slowed just before the command, "column left march!" was issued. The two right-most columns were halted and ordered to right face, the other two columns continued to march to the east.

Alex suddenly realized he was in the first rank of soldiers facing the enemy not 100 yards distant in a second trench line constructed at the outskirts of Baltimore—though this one with only a few protective logs sharpened to a point here and there ominously pointing his way.

Alex heard, "Fix bayonet!" and as one, more than one thousand men used their right hands to remove their bayonets from their scabbards and then twist them secure on their musket's muzzle.

Somewhere in the back of his mind Alex thought about the fact that the men weren't issued additional cartridges—they each had no more than two to three reloads on hand.

His thought was interrupted by Sergeant Wilson barking out, "Front rank! Make ready!"

Alex took a knee, brought his musket up to his shoulder and looked for a target. They weren't terribly hard to see—the heads and shoulders of the enemy 100 yards' distant, puffs of smoke randomly spouting up from the line only to be slowly wiped away by the rain and then carried south towards Baltimore's silent steeples.

"Take aim!"

Jabob, who was late in fetching his bayonet was just raising his firelock to Alex's left when Alex head a dull "smack." Jacob whipped around to the right, his musket flying from his hands while Alex's uniform was spattered with his friend's blood.

"Fire!"

Alex fired down the slight, grassy incline, seeing nothing of his target through the smoke.

"Rear rank! Make ready! Take Aim! Fire!"

Fire and smoke belched out over Alex's head in a roar.

His gaze sweeping right and left as he automatically reloaded, Alex saw a mass of blue charging down the slopes towards the trench line, great bloody gaps being blown into the lines by grapeshot fired at close quarter from cannons positioned between buildings.

Alex heard a distant command picked up by Sergeant Wilson, "March! March!" The fife and drummer picked up the order and called the tune, the regiment marching forward at the quick step.

"Charge, bayonet!"

The drums beat out the long roll and the regiment wheeled towards danger.

A few ragged puffs of smoke emitted from the enemy lines and Alex heard two of his comrades cry out.

Seconds later, Alex saw some of the militia break and run. One dropped his weapon. Others looking to the left and right, saw that they were being deserted and they, too, turned and ran.

Alex weaved to avoid a cluster of abatis stakes and leapt over the trench, almost catching up with a gray-haired militiaman when he heard the command, "Battalion! Slow step!"

Winded, knees shaking, Alex slowed to fall back into line. As he did, more than two dozen cavalrymen swept by, looking for fleeing prey.

A sergeant—not Wilson—called out, "Halt! Dress to the right!"

Alex realized he was shaking as the rain turned to sleet. He coughed twice and then coughed again three times as he struggled to get his breath.

He looked around and realized there were bodies strewn everywhere. Southern militia. Republic soldiers. Just ahead lay the outskirts of Baltimore, a wooden, two-story building aflame. There, a brick building with a hole smashed in its wall. Flames and smoke in the distance as the bitter evening gloom gathered.

After initial elation at reports that his army took Baltimore, Burr's subsequent thoughts bordered on depression. Of the 25,000 men committed to conquer the South's northernmost and largest city at more than 27,000 people, he lost 905 killed and 3,632 wounded with another 102 missing to the enemy's 200 dead and 2,500 captured. Maddeningly, everything of value in the city—its famed privateer shipyards, its naval stores manufacturers, and a powder mill—were all lost to fire. It was unknown as yet whether the fire was intentionally set by the retreating defenders or whether it was result of the battle—though the thoroughness of the destruction suggested to Burr it was planned.

Even so, it was clear that his army could move no further south in the winter, especially as many of the remaining soldiers had also taken ill. The army needed time to lick its wounds and bring on new recruits.

Still, there was one big advantage to a position astride the South's third-most-populous state with almost 320,000 residents, of whom just more than 100,000 were slaves. Burr could now set in motion his plans to destroy the South's economy by removing slaves from the plantations and farms where they labored and then send them to Ohio. His agents would also spread the word that any slave presenting himself to the Republic's army would automatically be granted freedom and his own land in the Northwest territories—assuming the new freedman could survive the Indian massacres and the Kentuckian slave raids.

Chapter Eighty-One – Attack

November 14, 1804, Charleston, South Carolina

On Thursday, word first arrived by packet boat of a fantastical threat from Santo Domingo. Two days later, via relay horse, the same message arrived from Richmond: an army of self-liberated slaves from the former French sugar colony of Santo Domingo would arrive off the shores of Charleston and invade, battling and pillaging their way to New Orleans. In this, the French would aim to repeat the stunning success of the British in the second Siege of Charleston when a force of 17,000 soldiers, militia, and sailors landed in 1780 and in six weeks dealt a devastating blow to the American army in the South.

The Santo Domingan force was said to consist of 5,500 men, most of whom were veterans of the remorseless campaign to rid the French colony of all of its white sugar plantation owners, leaving some hundred thousand dead slaves and masters in its wake and utterly terrifying slaveowners throughout the South—though few stopped to consider that the ratio of slave to master was some 10 to one in the profitable but brutal French colony whereas in Virginia and South Carolina, slaves made up just under half of the population.

That Santo Domingo under Toussaint Louverture reinstituted its own version of slavery and sought to remain in the French empire under Napoleon didn't lessen the fear of the havoc that such a force operating in the South might wreak.

With a small force of 50 Marines and two frigates from the U.S. Navy, Governor James Burchill Richardson knew his state's defense would be up to the militia. He immediately ordered a full mobilization and called for 5,000 men to report to Charleston and restore the city's Revolutionary War-era defenses that had been allowed to fall into disrepair.

Day broke on Wednesday, November 14 with a dense sea fog bringing visibility down to less than a quarter mile. Only 2,500 men had trickled into Charleston by then, though the Yankee exiles on the east bank of the Cooper River had quickly fortified their settlement, not wanting to be put to flight a second time in as many years. They even sent a company of riflemen over to assist in Charleston's defense.

By noon, an alarm was raised throughout the city of 19,000 when it was reported a French ship came ashore. The ship, a two-masted schooner rating 10 guns, got lost in the fog and was separated from the fleet. It ran aground on the north-facing shores of James Island, less than a mile from Charleston's South Bay and was only discovered when the fog began to lift at about two hours after sunrise. One of the U.S. Navy frigates carried a boarding party of Marines and quickly forced the vessel to strike its colors. The crew was French with no Santo Domingans aboard. As the tide came in, the captured vessel was refloated and taken up the Ashley River to be relieved of its cannon for use in the city's northwest defenses on the neck of the peninsula.

But the elation of this early victory was short lived as five French triple-deck ships of the line supported by five frigates slipped past Sullivan Island and its incomplete defenses, driving the U.S. Navy frigates upriver. These were followed by 42 transport ships. As three 80-gun third-rate ships of the line poured fire into Charleston's modest South Bay battery, the 42 transports sailed by, escorted by the remaining two ships of the line and the five frigates.

The Ashley River was navigable for some 20 miles past Charleston, all the way up to Dorchester. Within hours, the Santo Domingan force deployed across The Neck, the peninsula's narrow point before extending to the mainland. Having established his camp, General Dessalines fought off some inbound militia coming from the north and decided to call it day.

The night was cool and clear. Charleston's defenders could see the flickering glow of the Santo Domingan campfires some two miles distant.

The following day, the Santo Domingan army probed Charleston's lines, setting up a sharp artillery duel between French-manned batteries and a motley array of militia cannon, including a few of the guns taken off the captured schooner.

General Dessalines decided he neither had the force nor the time to set up a proper siege of Charleston and left his artillery and a force of 3,000 infantry to dig in at The Neck, with lines facing north to the interior and south to the city. Then taking his 2,000 remaining infantry and his 400 cavalry, he boarded his flotilla and sailed upriver. They quickly engaged the two American frigates that had retreated upriver the day before, sinking one and capturing the other—though it was so badly damaged that it was decided to scuttle her after removing her 34 guns.

Dessalines' real target—one that he didn't entirely reveal to his French "allies" who had a more conventional view of the operation—were the thousands of slaves laboring on the plantations along the Ashley, the largest three being Drayton Hall, Magnolia, and Middleton Place.

Carried by transports and largely unopposed as the local militia had been concentrating in Charleston, Dessalines spent three days raiding along the river, putting plantations to the torch, and taking slaves onboard his transport ships under the promise of freedom.

By November 18, Dessalines' foray had rounded up almost 8,000 slaves. He ordered them onto his transports, with 5,000, mostly men in prime condition. These he dispatched to Santo Domingo to replenish the sugar plantation labor force which had been depleted by years of war, disease, and now British interdiction of the slave trade from Africa. The other 3,000 slaves, mostly women, older men, and children, he sent to New Orleans where they would be conveyed up the Mississippi to the colony in Ohio to spread the impression that the French and Burr's Republic were actively working to free the South's slaves.

Then, on November 19, Dessalines abandoned his siege and took his war booty home. The French fleet split, some making for New Orleans, the others, escorting the transports back to **Santo Domingo.**

Chapter Eighty-Two – State of the Union

December 20, 1804, Richmond, Virginia

Jefferson intended to deliver his first State of the Union as a letter to the Senate and House of Representatives of the United States, as the Constitution doesn't specify the form of the address. Adams prevailed upon him, especially in the wake of the loss of Baltimore and the South Carolina plantation raids, that a speech was needed—a rousing, visionary speech in a time of peril. Jefferson reluctantly agreed and then set himself to writing, only showing Adams a very early draft.

Jefferson surveyed the assembled Congress. There were 80 men present: 16 senators and 63 representatives, and his vice president, John Adams.

Jefferson's blue eyes swept the chamber, briefly coming to rest on the tall, lanky, scowling visage of Andrew Jackson under his shock of red hair—Jefferson, at 61, was 24 years his senior and had long ago seen his red mane fade to grey and white. But, at 6'2," he still had an inch on Jackson, which annoyed the younger firebrand to no end.

Jefferson put on his glasses and started to read his speech, the papers covered with margin notes and cross outs. Jefferson expected to speak from memory, but he flipped through the pages just in case he stumbled, which he didn't expect to do.

"In calling you together, fellow citizens, I am aware of the difficulties of travel during this time of year. But matters of great public concernment have rendered this meeting necessary.

"Our new nation is buffeted by great winds in its infancy. We once again face a threat to our liberties—one from our brethren and one from our former ally, France, who seeks to reestablish an imperial presence on our continent.

"In recent days, we have learned of the loss of Baltimore, our preeminent city, to the enemy of liberty in the north, that would-be great despot, Aaron Burr. While in the south, Santo Domingan savages, conveyed to our lands by the French fleet, have plundered our farms, raped our women, and slaughtered our children. Further, Spanish outposts in Florida harass our citizens in Georgia with constant, almost daily raids.

"And, while the militia of freemen has admirably rallied to defend his land, it is with great reluctance that I come to Congress to ask for funding to create a national army of 20,000 men."

A murmur swept the chamber, but Jefferson saw that Jackson nodded his head in agreement.

"The sovereignty of the Mississippi and its waters have been contested, with our farmers in Kentucky and Tennessee unable to freely profit from the fertility of the country.

"Further, the tribe of Muscogee Indians has been stirred to agitation by French agents and armed by them, threatening settlement in the Mississippi Territory and even into Western Georgia.

"In normal times, separated by a wide ocean from the nations of Europe and from the political interests which entangle them together, with productions and wants which render our commerce and friendship useful to them and theirs to us, it should not be the interest of any to assail us, nor ours to disturb them. Yet, here we are, at war with the French and Spanish empires and the so-called United American Republic.

"We must endeavor to achieve victory—for only in victory are we able to enjoy the singular blessings of the position in which nature has placed us, the opportunity she has endowed us with of pursuing, at a distance from foreign contentions, the paths of industry, peace, and happiness, of cultivating general friendship, and of bringing collisions of interest to the umpirage of reason rather than of force.

"To that end, I have transmitted to the Senate a request to ratify a treaty with Great Britain."

Jackson shifted in his seat; a scowl now implanted on his face.

"This treaty has three objects. First, it secures a formal alliance with Great Britain until peace is agreed between all of the belligerents. Second, it provides for a favorable trade and credit terms for our new nation, ensuring that we can pay our bills and sell our produce. Third, it formalizes an offer from Great Britain to encourage Irish emigration to our shores where they will agree to terms of seven years of indentured servitude after which they will be granted 100 acres of land in the West and the religious freedom to worship as they deem fit to their traditions and practices."

Another murmur rattled through the chamber. Jefferson expected this— even he didn't like or trust papists, seeing them as enemies to liberty and reason. But wartime necessities warranted wartime measures—and Burr's active encouragement of slaves to move to Ohio was starting to put a strain on the nation and fear in the hearts of the most prominent citizens.

"And lastly, in concert with these policies, I am asking Congress to recognize the practical situation we find ourselves in. Until the raid on the plantations in Georgia, we had lost about 12,000 slaves, 10,000 to Ohio and 2,000 to the Spanish, who merely put them to work in Cuba. The attack from Santo Domingo snatched up 8,000 in only a week. Thus, in only two years, we have lost 2-1/2 percent of a vital workforce. And, under the strain of war and the enemy's designs, we can expect more, crippling our ability to defend ourselves and to win this contest.

"Therefore, I am urging this Congress to trade in reason and wisdom and consider a constitutional amendment to gradually abolish slavery."

Jefferson had already discussed this proposal with key members of Congress, so the reaction was, for the most part, silence.

"Twenty-eight years ago, America declared its independence from Great Britain. I see two of you with us today who were present then to pledge your lives, your fortunes, and your sacred honor." Jefferson stopped and looked behind him at Adams seated in the Senate President's chair next to Nathaniel Macon of North Carolina, the Speaker of the House. "Vice President Adams," Jefferson nodded, and Adams returned the acknowledgement. Jefferson then surveyed the chamber, and nodded to his left, "And Mr. Gerry of Massachusetts." Three members clapped the back of the New England exile.

"At that key moment in the history of Man, we declared that 'the Laws of Nature and of Nature's God' entitled our nation to a 'separate and equal station' among the nations of the earth. Further, we held that self-evident truths showed 'that all men are created equal'—not that all men have equal capacity for work or the acquisition of wealth—but that all men are equally men as they've been 'endowed by their Creator with certain unalienable Rights."

Jefferson paused again and made eye contact with prominent members of Congress. "We knew this to be true, yet, in creating a nation, we were also bound by practical considerations. We understood that trying to rid ourselves of the institution of slavery—sanctioned by the King of England—would have consigned our infant nation to a stillbirth. Yet, the promise and the contradiction remain. If the rights of Man include 'Life, Liberty and the pursuit of Happiness' then that includes all Men, South and North, free and slave."

Jefferson drew a breath and gathered himself, "And now here we are, amid a great civil war, battling against a man who would make slaves of us all as he has made slaves of his brethren. The government of the North has become destructive of the purpose of government—to secure natural rights. And it is our right—our duty—to abolish it and free our brethren so they may enjoy their 'safety and happiness.' Yet, our task will not be complete until we also address our own moral depravity, the hideous blot on our honor. The North would make slaves of us all but how much less is it that we only make slaves of some?

"Recall, if you will, the events of four years ago here in Richmond, when a slave by the name of Gabriel Prosser came within hours of organizing a rebellion that might have killed many of those seated with us today. And can we blame them? Can we blame a fellow man for also seeing the self-evident truth that all men are created equal?" At this, some members murmured their disproval.

Jefferson looked up from his prepared address and gazed out at a few specific representatives and senators—there, South Carolina's Thomas Pinckney, Tennessee's Andrew Jackson, and then Kentucky's John Breckinridge. He continued, now speaking off script, "Yes, equal. All equally human. All equally deserving of life and liberty. Not that all men are equal in the attainment of happiness. Not all men are equally strong, or equally smart, or equally diligent—but all men are equally deserving of the pursuit of happiness."

"As a consequence, and due to the exigencies of the great conflict in which we find ourselves fighting once again for our freedom," Jefferson returned to his speech, "I propose to grant all those laboring in servitude today the following terms: after 14 years of work starting at age 12, a servant will be freed with credit for up to one year for every two years already labored to a maximum of ten years' credit meaning that in four years' time, we will start a gradual emancipation.

"It is our anticipation that the importation of the Irish will more than make up for the loss of our present servants. Importantly, it will help to open up new lands to the west—lands needed to continue to expand cotton production.

"If this amendment is not passed by this Congress and subsequently ratified by three-quarters of the states now in this union, then it is my considered opinion that the formal alliance with Great Britain will, as a result, be a dead letter."

Jefferson knew that the bloody and intense 1798 Irish uprising by the secret republican group known as the Society of United Irishmen, had rattled the British. That revolutionary France provided assistance made matters worse, as up to 50,000 perished in the violence. This led to the Acts of Union in 1800 which merged the Irish parliament into the parliament of Great Britain while merging the Kingdom of Great Britain and the Kingdom of Ireland into the United Kingdom. The violence in Ireland had much the same effect on the minds of the British elite as did the revolt on Santo Domingo in preying upon the fears of Southern slaveowners—heightened even further by the raid up the Ashley River in South Carolina last month.

The most important part of his remarks delivered, Jefferson transitioned to the workmanlike portions of his address, summarizing the new republic's financial condition, and proposing various initiatives. Jefferson then finished his address, the nation's first, "I anticipate with satisfaction the measures of wisdom which the great interests now committed to you will give you an opportunity of providing, and myself that of approving and carrying into execution with the fidelity I owe to my country."

Jefferson surveyed the assembled representatives and senators, wondering if they, and he, were up to the task of building a nation dedicated to liberty and self-governance while fighting tyrannical powers at home and abroad— or whether their government of the people, by the people, for the people, would soon perish from the earth.

As Jefferson sighed. He felt a reassuring hand on his right shoulder. It was Adams. Adams leaned forward and spoke quietly in his high, raspy voice, "We beat King George and we damn well will beat Napoleon and his little Emperor Aaron." Adams paused, "We must."

Historical Timeline and Departures (Spoilers)

1778
June 28—Aaron Burr did fight at Monmouth and was injured when his horse was shot out from under him. He also suffered from heat stroke. (Historical)

1779
July 5—Aaron Burr led a contingent of Yale students to confront the British raid on New Haven, Connecticut. (Historical)

1783
November 22—James Duane became New York's first mayor after the British occupation ended on Jan. 1, 1784. He donated 20 guinea gold coins to the New York Almshouse in early 1784—money that was allocated for his inauguration party. (Historically based)

December 4—Cuffy Cockroach was a slave from the Guinea Coast who was widely known in Rhode Island as a master chef of turtle feasts. His owner, Jaheel Brenton, was a Royal Navy admiral and father of a Royal Navy admiral by the same name. The family fled Rhode Island for England in 1780. And, since slavery was never specifically legalized in Britain, the courts ruled it wasn't allowed. In the British case of Shanley v. Harvey (1763) it was noted that "soon as a man sets foot on English ground he is free." Thus, it is likely that Mr. Cockroach was sold before the family left Rhode Island. Of 68,825 people counted in Rhode Island for the 1790 census, 948 of them were black slaves. (Historical connection)

General Knox lost two fingers to a hunting accident. (Historical)

1785
July—Aaron Burr was elected to the New York State Assembly in 1784. (Historical)

"Those who own the country ought to govern it." Is a historical quote from John Jay. He would become the first Chief Justice of the United States and later, the second governor of New York.

Some historians believe Thomas Paine had a role in the early drafts of the Declaration of Independence.

Thomas Paine feuded with many of the leading lights of the American Revolutionary War, including John Jay, Silas Deane, and Robert Morris. He accused Silas Deane of war profiteering and his friendships suffered as a result. Years later, after Paine returned from France around 1803, Deane's corrupt practices had become exposed, and Robert Morris apologized to Paine for doubting him.

In 1787, a bridge of Paine's design was built across the Schuylkill River in Philadelphia.

1786
August—Most of the events depicted in Shays' Rebellion are historical. The modest deviation in this book is that the contest was more slightly more violent than historical with correspondingly greater reprisals in return.

A privately financed militia of 3,000 was in fact raised out of Boston to confront Shays' Rebellion. The financiers of the effort would later be reimbursed by the state government—who looked to raise revenue to finance it.

September—Logan was a prominent Cayuga leader. Logan's Lament is historical.

British support for the tribes of the old Northwest—Ohio and adjacent areas—led many to try to resist American settlement by force of arms, leading to reprisals and massacres committed by both sides. Ultimately, the new American nation raised a professional army and defeated the indigenous tribes in the Northwest Indian War lasting nine years from 1786 to 1795.

1787
January—This is a historical deviation in the timeline. There is no record of the Shaysites executing anyone, though passions were high, and they did burn courthouses and court records, and intimidated judges and lawyers who sought to foreclose on the farmers' defaulted loans.

February—General Benjamin Lincoln was not wounded in the battles against the Shaysites and would later vote to ratify the Constitution.

The Rhode Island Legislature was taken over by people who sympathized with Shays' rebellion and who invited some of the ringleaders to serve in the state's upper house.

March—This is a historical deviation in the timeline. Historically, several hundred Shaysites were indicted, but most of these were pardoned by John Hancock under a general amnesty after he replaced Bowdoin as governor on May 30, 1787. Eighteen men were convicted and sentenced to death but only two were hung on December 6, 1787, only three months before Massachusetts ratified the Constitution.

Vermont really did look to return to the Crown in 1781 while at the time, operating as a de facto independent republic. The American victory at Yorktown put an end to their negotiations.

May—Historically, the Massachusetts legislature passed the Disqualification Act which prohibited former rebels from holding public office. This aimed to curtail Shaysites' power in the rural west—but it came at the cost of increasing resentment.

1788
February—Ratification of the Constitution was stalled in New Hampshire to the horror of George Washington, even after the Federalists conspired to hold the ratification vote in the winter to make it difficult for the anti-Federalist farmers in the north and west of the state to make it to the convention. The vote was put off until June but the anti-Federalists almost scored an absolute rejection of the new Constitution.

The story takes a historical deviation in Massachusetts where the actual vote for ratification of the Constitution on February 6, 1788, was 187 to 168 with the resolution including a demand that the new constitution include a bill of rights.

March—Rhode Island held a referendum on the Constitution and it was rejected by voters.

June—South Carolina approved the Constitution 149 to 73 on May 23, 1788—a wider margin than depicted here, but momentum in politics, like momentum in sports, is a very real phenomenon.

272 Crisis of the House Never United

Virginia's ratification convention approved the Constitution on a vote of 89 to 79 on June 25 with news reaching New York a week later on July 2.

July—Historically, New Hampshire ratified the Constitution 57 to 47 on June 21, 1788. Atherton's motion to adjourn without a vote was a very real threat. Word of New Hampshire's approval reached Poughkeepsie on the 24th. Historically, New Hampshire ended up being the ninth state to ratify, thus, making the new constitution operative for the nation. News of this approval significantly affected the tone of the proceedings in New York, shifting Antifederalist efforts to limiting the power of a strong federal government through a demand for a bill of rights.

Historical deviation, the New York convention voted to approve the Constitution on July 26, 1788, on a vote of 30 to 27, this coming after news arrived that New Hampshire and Virginia had become the ninth and tenth state to ratify. After New York's approval, North Carolina's convention adjourned without voting on the Constitution on August 2, 1788, by a vote of 185 to 84. Rhode Island would hold out for almost two more years until it ratified the Constitution on May 29, 1790.

August—The events depicted in this time are mostly historical with some minor deviations. John Hancock was ill during the Massachusetts convention debates and did mostly remain silent. But he delivered a key closing speech in favor of ratification, and he was supported in public for the first time in years by Samuel Adams. The convention voted to ratify the Constitution on a vote of 187 to 168 with the understanding that a bill of rights would be added.

Samuel Adams supported Hancock's position on ratification, so his actions in the book represent a deviation.

John Collins became governor of Rhode Island on May 3, 1786, months before Shays' Rebellion in neighboring Massachusetts. His election was supported by poor farmers and workers who barely met the property requirement to vote.

The Penobscot Expedition, organized to dislodge a British force established on Penobscot Island in August 1779, resulted in the worst American naval defeat until Pearl Harbor.

George Washington's Patowmack Canal, proposed after the Mount Vernon Compact between Virginia and Maryland, was started in 1785, the same year as the Mount Vernon Conference, and took 17 years to complete and extended the navigability of the Potomac River inland by about 50 miles to Harper's Ferry. The Erie Canal, connecting the Great Lakes with the Hudson River, stretched for 363 miles. Governor DeWitt Clinton, George Clinton's nephew, gained approval from the New York legislature for $7 million for construction in 1817. When completed in 1825 it competed with the Patowmack Canal and led to the latter's bankruptcy.

Regarding the purchase of land owned by Massachusetts in the State of New York, Gorham and Phelps did buy the land from Massachusetts, but were unable to make the third yearly payment to Massachusetts and were forced to sell the land to Robert Morris.

Ideas to build what eventually became the Erie Canal had been kicked around since the 1780s before construction began in 1817.

1789
April—Historical deviation. George Clinton won his fifth election by beating Robert Yates 6,391 to 5,962 in 1789. It was during his sixth election in 1792 that the votes from three counties were thrown out by Burr and the Legislature, denying Federalist John Jay the victory by 108 votes. This, understandably, created hard feelings among the Federalists and Jay would end up winning election for governor in 1795, running against Robert Yates. Jay won while serving as the first Chief Justice of the United States.

The Federalists controlled both houses of the New York Legislature in April, 1789, as the Clinton political machine was losing its grip.

July 13—Jefferson's chief mission in France was to establish the new United States as an equal power to the established European states. The events described in the French revolution are historical. Thomas Jefferson was present and an active participant.

August 2—Historical deviation. Reverend Jacob Gruber's actual speech was on August 16, 1818. This chapter excerpts much of the speech. Some local slaveholders who heard his sermon sought an arrest warrant against Gruber for inciting a slave riot and he would be arrested two months later.

Gruber was successfully defended by Roger B. Taney, later the Chief Justice of the U.S. Supreme Court who authored the infamous Dred Scott Decision in 1857 that ruled that the Founders' words in the Declaration of Independence, "all men were created equal," were never intended to apply to blacks.

In his defense of Gruber in 1819, Taney told the court that freedom of expression was protected by the Maryland Constitution, even about slavery, adding, "No man can be prosecuted for preaching the articles of his religious creed, unless his doctrine is immoral, and calculated to disturb the peace and order of society." He continued, "Mr. Gruber did not go to the slaves; they came to him. They could not have come if their masters had chosen to prevent them." This, Taney said, countered the prosecution's claim against Gruber.

But Taney went further, saying, "A hard necessity, indeed, compels us to endure the evil of slavery for a time. It was imposed upon us by another nation, while we were yet in a state of colonial vassalage. It cannot be easily or suddenly removed. Yet, while it continues, it is *a blot on our national character*, and every real lover of freedom confidently hopes that it will be effectually, though it must be gradually, wiped away; and earnestly looks for the means by which this necessary object may be best attained. And until it shall be accomplished, until the time shall come when we can point without a blush to the language held in the Declaration of Independence, every friend of humanity will seek to lighten the galling chain of slavery, and better, to the utmost of his power, the wretched condition of the slave."

Yet four decades of increasing profits yielded from the shift from growing rice, tobacco, and indigo to a cotton monoculture, boosted by the efficiency of the cotton gin, made plantation owners very wealthy. This, combined with a growing fear of slave rebellion triggered by the bloody revolution in Haiti from 1791 to 1804, Gabriel Prosser's attempted Richmond slave rebellion in 1800, and Nat Turner's slave rebellion in 1831, as well as the increasingly harsh political clashes over slavery, caused the defenders of slavery to rationalize it and justify as a positive good. When they did, they not only abandoned the Declaration of Independence's natural rights claims, they rejected it.

August 12— Historical deviation. The use of a people viewed by the leaders of a nation as expendable as a buffer against hostile tribes isn't new—the Mexican government did so in the early 1820s when they invited Americans into what is now Texas (so long as they promised to convert to Catholicism— most didn't) to settle a dangerous region plagued by Comanche and Apache war parties. Ironically, the region was on its way to being settled when, in

1813, amid the chaotic wars for independence from Spain, a royalist force defeated republican rebels at the Battle of Medina south of San Antonio. More than 1,000 rebels were killed and entire families were wiped out soon after by a Mexican force that included a young lieutenant Antonio López de Santa Anna, the future dictator of Mexico.

1796
June 1—Historically, Vermont, a territory in dispute with New York and, at one point, a self-declared independent republic, became a state on March 4, 1791; followed by Kentucky on June 1, 1792, followed by Tennessee on June 1, 1796. This occurred under the new Constitution, ratified in 1788. The old Articles of Confederation also had a process by which new states could be admitted, only requiring the approval of nine states, thus, making the admissions process easier as more states were added.

1800
April—The Weeks murder trial happened in 1800. The well in question where the body was found in late 1799 was dug by the Manhattan Well Company, founded by Aaron Burr.

May 31—The Gnadenhütten Village massacre south of New Philadelphia in 1782 by American militiamen is a historical event.

Weyapiersenwah, or "Blue Jacket," was decisively defeated by the U.S. Army at the Battle of Fallen Timbers in 1794—but in this timeline, the formation of a new national government didn't happen so the alliance of British and Native tribes in the Old Northwest delayed the settlement of Ohio and lands to the west.

June 15—Historical, except that Paine moved in 1802 (not 1800 per this timeline) after leaving France. A bullet pierced Paine's house, entering his bedroom in an apparent assassination attempt on Christmas Eve, 1805. His sharp quill had accumulated many powerful enemies.

1801
October 12—By 1804, Santo Domingo (Haitian) General Dessalines proclaimed that all people would either be laborers or soldiers with all laborers being bound to a plantation in a system of serfdom. Craftsmen, artisans, and other skilled persons were exempt.

Toussaint Louverture was captured by the French in 1802 and died in France as a prisoner in 1803.

1802
January 2—Burr was involved in Tammany Hall's founding and its conversion from a social club to a powerful political machine.

February 15—Historical deviation, Eacker, an ally of Burr, was accused of claiming Hamilton would work to overturn Jefferson's 1800 election, leading to Hamilton's son's challenge.

July 2—Per Donald Ratcliffe in "The Right to Vote and the Rise of Democracy, 1787–1828" citing Robert Dinkin "...by the end of the 1780s the qualified electorate in the thirteen states probably fell in the range from about 60 to 90 percent of adult white males, with most states toward the upper end. When some of his figures for individual states have been slightly adjusted to conform to revised figures given above, his tabulation places six states at around 90 percent (New Hampshire, New Jersey, Pennsylvania, North Carolina, and Georgia), and three states above 80 percent (Massachusetts, Delaware, and South Carolina); Rhode Island, Connecticut, and Maryland stand between 65 and 70 percent, followed by Virginia and New York at about 60 percent, or just below."

1803
March—President Jefferson, and Democratic-Republicans in general, were opposed to a sea-going navy as navies were thought to have more royalist tendencies—best to keep the navy small and republican.

June—The chapter describing a sermon in New Rochelle is based on a Revolutionary War sermon by John Witherspoon, a Presbyterian minister, the president of Princeton college, a member of the Continental Congress, and a signer of the Declaration of Independence and the Articles of Confederation.

July—Morgan Lewis fought in the Revolutionary War and the War of 1812. In the New York gubernatorial election of 1804, he defeated fellow Democratic-Republican Aaron Burr, the sitting Vice President, dealing a major blow to Burr's career. He was the commander at the Battle of Fort George in the War of 1812 and was criticized for being too cautious.

Stephen Van Rensselaer was lieutenant governor of New York under John Jay from 1795 to 1801. In 1801 he was promoted to major general as commander of the New York state militia's cavalry division.

Andrew Jackson was elected by the officers of the Tennessee militia to be the commander in 1802. At the time he was also a member of the Tennessee supreme court. He was elected to the U.S. House of Representatives for one term and served from 1796 to 1797. He didn't serve in the U.S. Senate until 1823.

The ancient Greek writer Plutarch was well-known among educated Americans as were the details of Alexander the Great's victory over Darius III at Gaugamela.

October—Under the Articles of Confederation, there was no national patent law, so inventions could only be protected in a state where a patent was granted. Article I, Section 8 of the Constitution gave Congress the power "To promote the Progress of Science and useful Arts, by securing for limited Times to Authors and Inventors the exclusive Right to their respective Writings and Discoveries." Eli Whitney applied for his cotton gin patent in 1794, only six years after the Constitution was ratified. The cotton gin significantly increased the profit of the slave-based plantation economy and pushed the South towards a cotton-only agricultural base away from the mixed production of tobacco, rice, indigo, and cotton. This in turn stimulated increased demand for slave labor. In this alternative history, this process was delayed by almost a decade.

1804

July 12—Historically, Alexander Hamilton died of a gunshot wound the day after being shot by Aaron Burr in their infamous duel.

Jefferson's words critical of slavery and his accomplishments to curtail it are historical. Jefferson owned slaves and had children with a slave named Sally Hemings as well. Rarely do people and history follow neat narratives to suit modern tastes. Life was, and is, complicated.

August 19—Éleuthère Irénée DuPont did build a powder mill in Delaware which started to produce gunpowder in April 1804. DuPont's father, Pierre Samuel DuPont, was friends with Thomas Jefferson and is credited with the idea of purchasing Louisiana from Napoleon's France.

October 17— Jefferson's favorite Roman scholar was Marcus Tullius Cicero. Jefferson's key Ciceronian texts were derived from *Tusculan Disputations* a discourse on pain and death. Jefferson owned more than forty Cicero titles and is thought to have modeled his life on the classical era philosopher and statesman.

November 14—On New Year's Day in 1804, Jean-Jacques Dessalines, took power in Haiti, killing the last of the remaining white residents. Because the Haitian economy was so devastated, Dessalines instituted a system that was essentially the same as slavery—except whips were banned. Dessalines declared that every citizen would either be a laborer or a soldier with everyone under control of the state in a system of serfdom. Every laborer was bound by law to a specific plantation. Essentially, slavery, but with black masters, not white. This system was hard to perpetuate, and in about a decade, began to breakdown, with the government parceling out land, shifting the economy from one of the export of sugar based on the brutal exploitation of slaves or serfs, to a subsistence economy where coffee became the main cash crop.

Made in the USA
Columbia, SC
25 November 2022

72065998R00178